The Best AMERICAN SHORT STORIES 2020

GUEST EDITORS OF THE BEST AMERICAN SHORT STORIES

1978 TED SOLOTAROFF
1979 JOYCE CAROL OATES
1980 STANLEY ELKIN
1981 HORTENSE CALISHER
1982 JOHN GARDNER
1983 ANNE TYLER
1984 JOHN UPDIKE
1985 GAIL GODWIN
1986 RAYMOND CARVER
1987 ANN BEATTIE
1988 MARK HELPRIN
1989 MARGARET ATWOOD
1990 RICHARD FORD
1991 ALICE ADAMS
1992 ROBERT STONE
1993 LOUISE ERDRICH
1994 TOBIAS WOLFF
1995 JANE SMILEY
1996 JOHN EDGAR WIDEMAN
1997 E. ANNIE PROULX
1998 GARRISON KEILLOR
1999 AMY TAN
2000 E. L. DOCTOROW
2001 BARBARA KINGSOLVER
2002 SUE MILLER
2003 WALTER MOSLEY
2004 LORRIE MOORE
2005 MICHAEL CHABON
2006 ANN PATCHETT
2007 STEPHEN KING
2008 SALMAN RUSHDIE
2009 ALICE SEBOLD
2010 RICHARD RUSSO
2011 GERALDINE BROOKS
2012 TOM PERROTTA
2013 ELIZABETH STROUT
2014 JENNIFER EGAN

2015 T. C. BOYLE
2016 JUNOT DÍAZ
2017 MEG WOLITZER
2018 ROXANE GAY
2019 ANTHONY DOERR
2020 CURTIS SITTENFELD

The Best AMERICAN SHORT STORIES® 2020

Selected from
U.S. and Canadian Magazines
by CURTIS SITTENFELD
with HEIDI PITLOR

With an Introduction by Curtis Sittenfeld

MARINER BOOKS
HOUGHTON MIFFLIN HARCOURT
BOSTON • NEW YORK 2020

www.hmhbooks.com

ISSN 0067-6233 (print)
ISSN 2573-4784 (ebook)
ISBN 978-1-328-48536-6 (hardcover)
ISBN 978-1-328-48537-3 (paperback)
ISBN 978-1-328-48410-9 (ebook)
ISBN 978-0-358-39460-0 (audio)

Printed in the United States of America
DOC 10 9 8 7 6 5 4 3 2 1

Contents

Foreword

FOR BETTER OR worse, we read fiction in the context of our ongoing lives. It is difficult to write about this moment—even this moment in the American short story—without mentioning the altered and frankly scary state of the world right now. Inevitably, much of the world will define 2020 as the year of the coronavirus pandemic. Most of us have been ordered to stay at home for an undefined amount of time to help "flatten the curve," or slow the spread of the virus. The global count of those infected is approaching one million and is sure to multiply again and again by the time this book is printed. There are infinite horrors unfolding across the world right now, but there are glimmers of light too. The planet is getting a much-needed break from carbon emissions. Unimaginable acts of courage and generosity occur hourly now, especially on the part of doctors and nurses.

In her essay, "The World's on Fire. Can We Still Talk About Books?" published in *Electric Literature* at the end of 2018, Rebecca Makkai makes a case for fostering creativity during the most difficult times. She writes, "Art is a radical act. Joy is a radical act. This is how we keep fighting. This is how we survive." If nothing else, this has been a time to write—that is, if you are able to summon the focus. It's a time to read, and try new authors and new genres. Musicians—everyone from Yo-Yo Ma to Wilco to Bruce Springsteen to even the Met Opera—have posted free and live performances online. The Guggenheim and Smithsonian museums are offering virtual tours. Many independent bookstores, the soul of the publishing industry, are providing tailored recommendations for readers, shipping books, and offering virtual events.

I offer a plug for the short story form, although if you are reading this, chances are I'm preaching to the choir. It can be hard (nearly impossible) to focus on reading fiction with one eye on a rapidly expanding global pandemic. The short story is the perfect length when you don't have the bandwidth for a novel. Of course, it helps if the story is engrossing. To my mind the stories that follow are engrossing and sharp and thought-provoking and beautiful.

The best stories contain enough air to welcome in readers *and* their troubles, and offer up irresistible and universal questions that have no ready answers. Paradoxes, really, and questioned assumptions. Consider the following sentences. From Selena Anderson's "Godmother Tea": "Even my people who are still living don't let me suffer the way I want to." Or this, from Michael Byers's "Sibling Rivalry": "Your emotional centers were fooled by the physical imitation, and the AI was the real thing, and the growth was to human scales—so what *was* the difference, anyway?" Or this sentence, from "This Is Pleasure" by Mary Gaitskill: "The whole thing was vaguely sadistic—so vaguely that it was ridiculous; clearly no harm was done."

Curtis Sittenfeld was such a joy to work with. She was wonderfully articulate about what she did and didn't like in the 120 stories that I sent her. As she states in her introduction, I grade each story as a method of shorthand for when I return to the stacks at the end of my reading period and begin to reread. Most that I pull from magazines fall within the "B" range, and what keeps them from the top for me can be a variety of things: for example, a lack of confidence on the page. This can manifest in anything from an outsized plot for the characters at hand to labored language or pacing. A short story is most effective when it is released in one sure and steady breath.

These twenty stories make me hopeful for the state of American short fiction. Here are writers digging deep and reckoning with the implications of the #MeToo movement, a future of population control, childhood, adolescent bullying, long-term love, infidelity, mythology, and art. These stories span the globe, touching down in France, Maine, Yonkers, the American Midwest, Tennessee, Madagascar, Alaska, China, Venezuela, California. I was glad to see story writers play with genre: here are pieces that feature elements of magical realism, dystopic fiction, realism, historic fiction, mythology, comedy, and tragedy. This year I'm proud to feature a good number of newer writers, such as Selena Anderson, Sarah Thankam Mathews, Jane Pek, Alejandro Puyana, Anna Reeser, and William Pei Shih. I always aim to cull from a mix of known and lesser known literary journals as well. Magazines like *Lady Churchill's Rosebud Wristlet, Crazyhorse, Fourteen Hills,* and *Subtropics* are represented in these pages.

I hope that by the time you read these words, the pandemic will have abated or passed, although it seems that it will cause economic, political, and social aftershocks for years to come. As I look back through these twenty stories, so many sentences take on new meaning right now. Elizabeth McCracken writes in "It's Not You": "I became kinder the way anybody does, because it costs less and is, nine times out of ten, more effective." And T. C. Boyle's "The Apartment" delivers this useful truth: "The world had been reduced. But it was there still, solid, tangible, as real as the fur of the cat." May these stories draw you in, move you, and provide you comfort in the face of whatever you may be experiencing right now.

The stories chosen for this anthology were originally published between January 2019 and January 2020. The qualifications for selection are (1) original publication in nationally distributed American or Canadian periodicals; (2) publication in English by writers who have made the United States or Canada their home; (3) original publication as short stories (excerpts of novels are not considered). A list of magazines consulted for this volume appears at the back of the book. Editors who wish their short fiction to be considered for next year's edition should send their publications or hard copies of online publications to Heidi Pitlor, c/o The Best American Short Stories, 125 High Street, Boston, MA 02110, or files to thebestamericanshortstories@gmail.com as attachments.

HEIDI PITLOR

Introduction

I *LOVED* READING these stories. I'm telling you this up front, right away, because it's the most important part, and because I can't be sure you'll read this essay in its entirety. Perhaps you will. But perhaps you'll grow bored, or perhaps you'll be so excited to read the stories themselves that you'll jump ahead (if so, I understand). In any case, I want to make sure you, the reader, and also you, the authors included here, know how much I admire the work in this anthology, how much joy it brought me, how dazzled I was by its individual and collective creativity, wisdom, daring, humor, and poignance. To the stories' authors: Thank you.

Now that that's out of the way, let's travel back in time—to southwestern France, in the summer of 1992. Before the start of my senior year at a Massachusetts boarding school, I was spending about six weeks abroad, trying to learn to speak French. (If you're thinking that this anecdote gives off the distinct whiff of privilege, you're correct.) Although I'd studied French for three years, I was far from fluent and struggled to have conversations with those around me. I was staying with a family in which there was a girl my age . . . who, a couple days after my arrival, had gone somewhere else. I don't remember where, though I do remember that her brother, who was about twelve, was around and that he seemed to find me almost as annoying as I found him.

There was, however, a saving grace. Prior to the end of the school year, an English teacher had suggested that I buy a copy of *The Best American Short Stories*. Because I was both bookish and obedient, I'd complied, and it was the 1991 edition. In the small bedroom where I was staying, I'd pull the book out and lie on my back on the twin mattress to read it. The cover was maroon, with the letters in yellow and the digits of *1991* in pale blue. The series editor was Katrina Kenison, and the guest editor that year was Alice Adams, and I can still feel the texture of the cover, can still see the font on the pages. It was in these pages that I first met Lorrie Moore and Amy Bloom and Joyce Carol Oates, Charles D'Ambrosio and Siri Hustvedt and John Updike.

To read their stories felt to me the way I suspect other people feel hearing jazz for the first time, or trying Ecstasy. *Oh my God,* I thought. *This exists!* The stories were so *good.* They were so *interesting.* There were *twenty* of them, all in the same place. They were windows into emotions I had and hadn't had, into other settings and circumstances and observations and relationships. I'm tempted to say that as I read, I felt the world enlarging around me, but it's probably more accurate to say that I felt my own existence enlarging. I felt so grateful to live on the same planet and breathe the same air as the magically talented individuals who'd crafted these tales. Quickly I realized that, given my current circumstances, I needed to ration them—to consume no more than one or two a day.

In light of the fact that almost thirty years have passed since that summer, it wouldn't be entirely appropriate if I had retained the sense of wonder I felt reading a *BASS* anthology for the first time. But still, I'm a little saddened to report just how extensively I haven't retained it. I am now forty-five years old, the author of six novels and one story collection. I do not take the good fortune of my career for granted; indeed, I am at regular intervals astonished by it. And yet I also at regular intervals experience a disenchantment with the so-called literary industrial complex—an eye-rolling irritation with the discrepancy between publishing buzz and quality, an impatience with pretentious ways of discussing craft or process. It would not, at this point in my life, be unusual for me to be talking to a writer friend and to declare of an acclaimed new story collection or novel, "Oh, it's a total piece of shit." It would not be unusual for me to give up on a book a hundred pages into reading it, and it also would not be unusual for me to give up on a book in the first paragraph, to deem it simply unreadable. On occasion I've given up on books in the first *sentence.*

I should note that there's a middle ground between the wide-eyed delight I felt in 1992 and the cynicism I'm too often prone to now, a more balanced perspective I attained as a graduate student and strive toward still. At some point after entering the Iowa Writers' Workshop in 1999 and before finishing in 2001, I realized this: it is perfectly legitimate to read someone's fiction and think, *You are talented, and your writing is not at all to my taste.* The legitimacy of such a statement might seem absurdly self-evident, but recognizing it was important in my development, and both parts were equally important. *Your writing is not at all to my taste* is not simply a more polite way of saying *This is garbage.* The *You are talented* part is sincere, the recognition of another person's abilities, and the *not at all to my taste* part is equally sincere, the recognition of the subjectivity of my own opinions.

All of which is to say that in January 2018, when *BASS* series editor Heidi Pitlor invited me to be the guest editor for the 2020 volume, I accepted with a blend of sentiments. My inner sixteen-year-old felt elated. I—Curtis from Ohio, who's bad at French —would get to do the thing that's been done by Salman Rushdie, Tobias Wolff, and Louise Erdrich? Meanwhile, my inner grad school student wondered if I'd be reading some great stories and many more whose proficiency I recognized without taking much pleasure in them. And my cynical present-day self (my outer forty-five-year-old?) wondered if I'd struggle to find twenty stories that I genuinely liked. I was definitely curious, and I didn't consider declining the invitation. But I had reservations.

My assignment from editor Nicole Angeloro and Heidi was to read 120 stories Heidi had selected from almost 200 magazines and to pick 21 that were worthy of publication—20 that would be printed, plus an alternate if one of my picks ended up not qualifying. I received them in three batches of 40 each and read them between November 1, 2019, and March 1, 2020. Early on, I almost emailed Heidi to ask if she thought it was important to finish reading every story even if I wasn't impressed with the first few pages. Then I thought, *Curtis, for Christ's sake, you have one job.* Of course I needed to finish reading every story even if I wasn't impressed with the first few pages!

My only other rule for myself was that I couldn't Google a writer until after I'd read his or her story. Of the 120 stories, the majority were by people whose names I'd never heard. In some cases the stories by writers I'd never heard of had been published in magazines I didn't know existed. This combination made me feel both ignorant and exhilarated; it gave me some of the same reassurance I experienced back in 1992, offering the promise that there is still much to discover. In fact, there really wasn't a correlation between the renown of a writer or publication and the quality of a story. Yes, stories from *The New Yorker* were often superb, but I quickly found that a lot of stories were superb.

As it turned out, I need not have worried about struggling to find 21 stories I liked, and in fact the problem was the opposite. Of the 120 stories, I would estimate that I disliked about 10. I thought about 40 were somewhere between not bad and good. I thought about 30 were very good. And I thought about 40 were great.

Forty great stories! Isn't that amazing! And another 30 very good ones! Aren't I lucky? Isn't this thrilling?

Heidi—who, it cannot be said enough, is smart and thoughtful and funny and a true pleasure to work with in all ways—mentioned that she assigned letter grades to stories: A, A−, B+, and so on. I tried this with a few, but I soon grew worried that such small gradations reflected the time of day when I was reading, or my blood sugar level, more than they reflected the quality of the work. I then decided to divide the work into the categories of *yes, maybe,* and *no.* Admittedly, there were some I labeled *maybe, probably yes* or *maybe, probably no,* and a few got my highest praise, which was *yes!* In the end there were far too many yeses. That I could have easily filled two anthologies was a surprising and wonderful problem.

I don't think I ever went from thinking a story wasn't very good at first to thinking it was great by the end, but a few times I went from thinking a story wasn't very good to thinking it was kind of good—that it had some redeeming features, made some interesting choices, arrived at a different place than it had departed from. In other cases, stories started very strongly but faltered by way of unlikely plot twists or the absence of any real payoff.

Under the best circumstances—and again, the best circumstances arose often—a story did many things well, all the way through. My favorite feeling as a reader is the confidence that the writer is in control, is one step (or more) ahead of me, possesses a knowing sensibility that he or she is unfurling as the narrative demands.

Another of the unexpected pleasures of guest editing was that the stories taught lessons cumulatively that I don't think I'd have learned based on reading any individual story or even reading a collection of stories by one writer. If you had asked me in October 2019, *What makes a short story succeed?* I'd have said, *Whatever the writer can get away with.* Granted, there are certain foundational ingredients, but I don't really believe in rules. In graduate school, my adviser Ethan Canin taught my classmates and me to think of fiction in terms of structure (the order of scenes, what happens in them, how information is revealed), character (what we learn about the people depicted through their actions, observations, and dialogue), and language (how the sentences do or don't work). This deceptively simple framework proved to be life-changingly useful for me (thanks again, Ethan!), and certainly it influences me as a reader too. But beyond this usually invisible scaffolding, I would have said as late as last fall that what makes a story succeed or fail is nebulous. Story by story, however, certain patterns emerged:

A good ending, a good last paragraph, can make a story better by several magnitudes. A bad ending can steal defeat from the jaws of victory. There are at least two stories that I loved and loved and loved up until the end, and the last paragraphs didn't make me hate them, but they were off-putting enough that, given the surplus of excellent work to choose from, the weak endings felt like a sufficient reason for elimination.

Unremarkable stories routinely contain sentences that are shatteringly beautiful or insightful. I won't give examples because to do so would be a backhanded compliment, or maybe just a vaguely flattering insult. But examples abound.

I personally do not love stories about violence, especially male violence inflicted on females. I also personally do not love stories about twenty- or thirtysomethings in Brooklyn. But I love being proven wrong about what I think I do and don't love. Among my twenty picks are a story about male violence and a story about twenty- and thirtysomethings in Brooklyn.

I personally do love stories about a small thing happening in a person's life, a thing that might seem trivial from the outside but whose stakes are raised because of how much it matters to the protagonist. Since the world often deems events in women's lives, especially young women's or girls' lives, trivial, such stories are likely to have a female protagonist.

A sense of humor is always a bonus. As with dinner companions, so it is with short stories.

A dystopian story must not merely be dystopian; it must also be a story. Premise can only get you so far.

I suppose, speaking of dystopias, that this is the moment when I ought to address the intersection of Short Fiction and How We Live Now. Of the 120 stories I read, at least a dozen could be classified as dystopian. Almost all were environmentally focused, reflecting the effects of climate change in a usually not-so-distant future. Indeed, in 2019, *McSweeney's* devoted an entire issue to speculative fiction about climate change, featuring ten stories set in 2040, and I'm still haunted by two of those stories—"Save Yourself" by Abbey Mei Otis, and "The Rememberers" by Rachel Heng—though I didn't ultimately include either.

The frequency and darkness of dystopian stories injected a jittery aspect into my reading. Undeniably, writers are worried, and I certainly share the common belief that writers are either prescient or just paying attention. And then, by the time I had made my selections, we—all of us—were in the midst of a global pandemic. At the time of this writing, in late March 2020, no one knows what will happen. As I am not a public health expert, I will refrain from speculating.

But I will say this: as I type these words, it feels like life has become difficult for everyone, and it's impossible to know what state any of us will be in when this volume is published in October. I hope that reading these stories will in some small way offset or diminish the ongoing difficulty—that they will delight or reassure or at least distract you, that they will remind you of what people have in common, that they will give you the abstract but irreducible and nourishing thing that art can provide. Even before the pandemic, they gave that to me. Truly, as I read the stories—mostly in bed before going to sleep at night, occasionally during the day sitting in a chair—I thought what I'd thought in 1992 in France: *Oh my God. This exists! These stories are so good. They're so interesting. There are so many of them, all in the same place. They're windows into emotions I have and haven't had, into other settings and circumstances and observations and relationships. I'm so grateful to live on the same planet and breathe the same air as the magically talented individuals who crafted these tales.*

Below, I offer the specific reasons I loved the stories I ultimately chose. I recommend reading the stories before you read the reasons, but again, I defer here to your free will.

I loved "Godmother Tea" by Selena Anderson because it showed me how enthrallingly magical realism, daily despair, and class commentary can mix together.

I loved "The Apartment" by T. C. Boyle because it took a story I vaguely knew, injected it with emotion and inevitability, and told it in such a way that my familiarity with the story made reading it more rather than less suspenseful.

I loved "A Faithful but Melancholy Account of Several Barbarities Lately Committed" by Jason Brown because it depicts the subculture of WASPy families in a way that's hilariously satirical and totally realistic at the same time.

I loved "Sibling Rivalry" by Michael Byers because Byers's futuristic world is utterly natural and convincing and forces me to reflect uncomfortably on how concepts like family and parenthood are defined in the present.

I loved "The Nanny" by Emma Cline because the main character, whom Cline makes distinct and complex, falls into the category of person routinely stripped of any real identity in media reports.

I loved "Halloween" by Marian Crotty because her portrayal of teenage longing and romantic tension is so real and alive and because the grandmother is irresistible.

I loved "Something Street" by Carolyn Ferrell because a few years ago I thought to myself, *Maybe I should write fiction about this particular disgraced public figure,* and then I thought, *Actually, I shouldn't, but someone should,* and a few paragraphs into the story, I thought, *Oh my God, Carolyn Ferrell did it,* and then as I kept reading, I thought, *Oh my God, and she did it in such a savvy, complex, satisfying way.*

I loved "This Is Pleasure" by Mary Gaitskill because its nuance made me feel conflicting sympathies while challenging my belief that, at the (literal) end of the day, I'd really rather not curl up with a #MeToo-themed short story.

I loved "In the Event" by Meng Jin because first I thought it was a story about dystopian dread, then I thought it was a story about relationship problems, then I thought it was a story about the 2016 election, and actually it was all three, blended seamlessly.

I loved "The Children" by Andrea Lee because its setting was fascinating and its depiction of class was so sophisticated and its last line took my breath away.

I loved "Rubberdust" by Sarah Thankam Mathews because its details of childhood are so specific and weird and recognizable and familiar and because a story about being a kid in school turns on its head most of the way through and becomes meta while still unfolding as a story about being a kid in school.

I loved "It's Not You" by Elizabeth McCracken because I underlined the sentences in it I thought were clever or funny and by the end I'd underlined about 50 percent of the entire story.

I loved "Liberté" by Scott Nadelson because it shows a public figure I knew little about interacting with another public figure I knew little about and depicts them in such intriguing ways that I thought, *Wait, what's true here?* and felt compelled to Google them the minute I finished to find out.

I loved "Howl Palace" by Leigh Newman because of its rich sense of place and the complexity of its much-married sixtysomething narrator.

I loved "The Nine-Tailed Fox Explains" by Jane Pek because it won me over from the first line and kept me riveted with its flawless interweaving of ancient myth and mundane contemporary life.

I loved "The Hands of Dirty Children" by Alejandro Puyana because it tells a heartbreaking tale in an unsentimental way, and it tells it from the inside, so deeply and immersively.

I loved "Octopus VII" by Anna Reeser because of its spot-on depiction of creative young people and various kinds of privilege, including the privileges of money and gender.

I loved "Enlightenment" by William Pei Shih because who among us hasn't had a thoroughly misguided crush that feels appropriate in the moment? And because the story's protagonist could be irredeemably pathetic, but Shih chooses instead to make his choices recognizable while pulling off the feat of making the perspective of the protagonist's foil equally recognizable and understandable.

I loved "Kennedy" by Kevin Wilson because the story is horrifying and tender in equal measures.

And I loved "The Special World" by Tiphanie Yanique because it captures the distinct feeling of being a college freshman, of how foreign and cheesy and exciting that rite of passage can be, and also because the story made me laugh.

Among the stories that didn't make the final cut, I loved "Good-bye, Sugar Land" by Becky Mandelbaum and "The Teenagers" by Miriam Cohen and "Wolves of Karelia" by Arna Bontemps Hemenway and "Cut" by Catherine Lacey and "Marrow" by Adam O'Fallon Price and "Dear Shadows" by Joanna Pearson and "Prepare Her" by Genevieve Plunkett and "Neighbor" by Daniel Torday and "Binoculars" by Martha Wilson. I wish I could share all these with you. Although I can't, the places where they were published are listed in the back of this volume, and they're worth tracking down.

A few final thoughts: In looking now at the 1991 edition that was my entry into the world of *BASS*, I'm struck by the fact that all twenty of its contributors appear to be white, as I am. Meanwhile, as I read the stories from 2019, there was a bounty of excellent stories by writers of color (though I don't think I always knew the race of stories' authors). I am glad and grateful for this shift, which presumably has more to do with changes in gatekeeping than with talent; that is, I'm sure the talent was always there. Without a multiplicity of viewpoints—not just in terms of race but also in terms of sexuality, geography, and age—this anthology would be considerably less interesting. Sure, there's a place in my heart for a story about a white man having a midlife crisis, but there are a lot of other places in my heart for a lot of other stories.

Since 1992, I've dipped in and out of reading *The Best American Short Stories;* during various years I've read all of the stories, none of them, and some of them. In some years I thought a high proportion of the stories were outstanding. In other years I thought, *I guess not that many good stories were published this year.* At the time I assumed that, as with grapes made into wine, certain crops of stories were better or worse than others, but I now suspect this isn't accurate. Instead it's probably that the idiosyncratic taste of a guest editor is sometimes more and sometimes less aligned with my own idiosyncratic taste as a reader.

Here's hoping our idiosyncrasies, your and mine, align this year. If not, here's hoping there are more years, more idiosyncrasies, and more stories for all of us.

CURTIS SITTENFELD

The Best
AMERICAN
SHORT
STORIES
2020

SELENA ANDERSON

Godmother Tea

FROM *Oxford American*

JUST LIKE MY mama. She rolled up with a gift: a life-sized mirror edged by baroque curling leaves, with slender gold feet that somehow supported both its shimmering weight and mine. My mother has a knack for messy presents. Day passes to the gym, Merry Maids coupons, flat irons with built-in conditioner. This, however, was especially rude. A mirror would only reflect me, plus all my sulky auras, plus the cultivated environment that had drawn me this way.

My mother had refused help as she dragged the mirror into my apartment herself, claiming it had the power of making the place look bigger. But I didn't want anything of mine to look bigger. The center of my apartment was empty, as spotless as a bald spot, and I liked that. That was my choice. I'd gotten used to that. But now my mother's charity of inherited furniture crowded the room. There was a Chesterfield sofa, end tables with bloated glass lamps, a dining table with a fleet of cane-back chairs, and a rolltop desk that wore a pair of pink soft-grip dumbbells like a tiara. None of this stuff was mine, but at the same time, it was all I had.

I know a lot of people just starting out don't have anything, so I don't mean to sound ungrateful, but to my eye the mirror only doubled what I had never really wanted to begin with. Now there was hardly any space to move around. I could never tell my mother this—especially as she was positioning it between the windows and cleaning the glass with newspaper in quick, squealing arcs—so I'm telling you, it was all beginning to be a bit much.

But since the mirror was standing there, I'd sometimes creep up late at night to wordlessly articulate a complaint I'd been having

with myself. The objects of my apartment looked on as I stood bal-
letically, searching my figure for bad news. My reflection belonged
to too many other people—mainly the people who used to own
all this stuff. Through me, my ancestors gave eyes to my jacked-up
third position. I'd switch to tree pose, clutching a glass of rosé to
my chest like a good-luck charm. My dead relatives studied me in
loving disapproval. I'd smile back until it became impossible to
recognize myself.

Even my people who are still living don't let me suffer the way I
want to. A lot of them, much older and less bothered than myself,
express pride in the way I'm turning out. My mother's friends talk
about me like I was a dish that was difficult to get just right, but the
special ingredients of an elite social circle, good home training,
and private education have turned me into a well-spoken young
woman full of potential.

After my mother had given me the mirror, we walked down the
street to a cafeteria in my neighborhood. At the table I tried explaining to her what it feels like every time a member of her generation pays me a compliment. "It never feels good," I said, "when
a compliment is self-reflective."

"But that's what a compliment is, Joy," she said. "A compliment
is a reflection of what I see in you that I wish I had."

My mother was still giving me eyes, trying, like everybody else
in the room, to dissolve sugar in iced tea. She was still stuck on
"self-reflective" and what it meant for me to use a word like that
in her presence. Usually my mother comes right out and says so if
she thinks I'm sounding too white, but when she senses my mood
has joined us, pulling up a chair like an unexpected guest, she acts
totally unlike herself and holds back. It doesn't make sense that a
simple act of decency like this would make matters worse, but even
these days, a fact is still a fact.

It was April and I liked to be alone. But whenever I sensed that my
apartment was beginning to get hold of me, I'd walk around the
neighborhood to enjoy the good weather. I live down south in a
city whose economy probably should not have outlasted the twentieth century, although folks around here celebrate this accident
as proof of their regional superiority. The highways we've built are
among the greatest curiosities of the world. The haze from nuclear

power plants lends the skyline a romantic look, like a vintage post-card. The air is so thick with the stench of gasoline and doughnuts that a deep breath can make you shed one hysterical tear. I could say hello to passing strangers, but only on defense. I could try and meditate, but I was already self-conscious about being out of touch with my community. In real time, the best solution was to walk back inside.

I'd pass by the mirror and see fragments of other women. The way I bent my wrists or licked the inside of my mouth favored ones I hadn't thought of and who could never have anticipated me. A blink of the eye revealed some dormant part of my personality, some no-longer-complete person who clutched her pearls at my audacity, the blasé way I naturally stood squandering my opportunities. Another quick glance revealed the godmother. For a long time she had been waiting on me to acknowledge her, but before we could lock eyes she was gone.

The godmother is like an ancestor who never really left. Someone who's here even when they're not. The godmother is what happens when somebody asks your name and you suddenly can't remember. When it's gorgeous outside and you work up the nerve to be part of something but not enough nerve to brush your hair, that's the godmother. Maybe you stay up too late and are tempted to give yourself completely to unrequited obsessions. That's the godmother's doing too. When life speeds through its continuum without pushing you forward, she starts to look your way. You have to be careful with this familiar face. She'll have you batting your eyes and practicing your smile.

One evening I was alone in my apartment impersonating a vibe. I was fixing a dinner of cachapas and instant coffee when I noticed the godmother wanted to have a chitchat. She conveyed this request by cutting off the power a few times. Because of her, I had to walk across the courtyard and behind the building to the fuse box to turn it back on. After a while I got tired of that and pulled out one of the cane chairs.

I thought it was kind of me. "So kind," said the godmother. "You ought to try kindness twice a day, seven days a week."

"But I barely have the energy to cook for myself," I said, and I immediately felt used because now I'd tossed the words into the air where you could really breathe them. The godmother glanced around at the things of my apartment, and when her eyes finally settled on me, they leveled a little as she decided yes, I belonged here too.

"Can you give me a synopsis of what's going on?" she said.

It was too humiliating to talk about. A few interrelated developments kept bludgeoning my life in a way that was turning me into a vagabond. Recently my best friend, Nicole, had revealed in the classiest way possible that she was about to exit our fifteen-year friendship—by not saying anything. I reacted by latching on to my André Simpson, the man who had neglected to propose marriage when I'd felt the time was right. I was hanging around, trying to convince André—where I had failed with Nicole—that we still had things to talk about. These were the only people I'd chosen, if you know what I mean, and the prospect of losing them caused a brittle, shivering thing to come to life and crawl out of me. Also —and this was embarrassingly typical of me—my driver's license was so badly expired that now it was actually becoming difficult to prove that I was myself.

"Ain't nothing going on but the weather," I said.

The godmother shook her head at my attempt to sound real. "I see you gone be a lot more work than I expected," she said.

She leaned asymmetrically in her chair, keeping time in a pair of gold slippers. She wore a housecoat tessellated with hummingbirds sipping from impatiens. Her pocketbook of leggy cigarettes dangled at the edge of the table, just within reach. The godmother was a slinky woman, still pretty in a violent sort of way. Her face was narrow and angled, her skull crested back in a tall forehead, her waved-up hair glistened with mineral oil and water.

She stood and walked around rubbing her elbow as though physically injured by my tastes. My struggling plants. My assembly of crockpots. My cheap rosé stacked on the counter like an anemic blood bank. "Now, did you mean for your apartment to be so ugly?"

"Oh, no. That's the style."

The godmother scratched the length of her neck. "What style is that?"

Eying my cachapas, she asked if the cook was stressed out. Prior to her interruption, I'd been doing ambitious things with a box of cornbread mix. I pushed the plate her way, and she inspected the contents, careful not to touch anything.

"It's something wrong with people who cook food they can't even pronounce," she said.

I explained that I liked to dabble in world cuisines. Regular food gave me broke thoughts.

"You only want something new," she said, "because you're tired of living."

I couldn't tell if she was talking about me or about people like me, and I was afraid to ask for clarification. I mean, I was afraid to hear the answer. I knew the answer.

The godmother made herself at home in my kitchen, whipping up a replacement dish of cornbread casserole that filled the apartment with a golden smell. "You're tired of living," she said, drawing a cigarette from her pocketbook, "because something has tricked you into believing that life is long."

"Absurd." I scoffed like a lifelong scoffer. "My beliefs don't trick me."

"That would make you very different from other people." She sat cross-legged on the counter, breathing minty smoke. She could make rings, hearts, and moving boxes like it was no big deal. "You got to get ready to suffer because you're different."

"Well, my difference ain't paying off," I said. "Not monetarily. Not spiritually."

I'd always wanted to become an artist, but no galleries would respond to the nudes I'd sent them. I spent most of my days begging on behalf of a museum I kind of believed in, where I also had a side hustle teaching rich kids how to draw a circle. All my money went to rent and dead people's clothes.

"So lower those expectations if you got to be happy. You don't have to change your heart," said the godmother, "just your heart's desire." Her remark burned. I hadn't known that changing what I wanted in this world was even an option.

The godmother glided around my kitchen with an air of tough elegance that the best schools never could teach me. She fixed fried pork chops and collard greens and then stood back, judging mildly as I ate. The extravagance made me laugh with shame. I can't even tell you how delicious everything was. If I could, you'd just cry and cry.

All week I'd been begging to be included, so on Friday night, Nicole invited me to a dinner party she was obligated to go to anyway.

It was one of those gatherings where nobody knew each other but told jokes and flirted like they believed they had done the right thing by agreeing to spend the time together. You had to walk up an oaky boulevard and enter a gate code to even get inside the neighborhood. Both sides of the street were lined by mansions in a variety of neocolonial and European styles, and every tree glowed in its own floodlight. Like always, Nicole led the way until we reached one particular mansion like all the other mansions except for the fact that it was perfect. The front door was simple and Shaker with chipping shellac and seemed like an apology for the house's decadence. Once inside, we separated almost immediately.

We were on the verge of losing touch forever, but before she became the seasonal homie, Nicole had been my best friend. When we were kids, she had been my partner in ballet and spades, and in junior high she gave me an in-depth understanding of the dozens, probably because she cared more about my self-esteem than I did. But what made us last was that when we were together, it felt like we were speaking a special language. Looking back, I think that maybe I had just learned to speak her way. I hung on to every turn of phrase and rhythm, because there was so much hope in them, the way her words sailed out and up with such poise and without fear. My mama didn't even sound like that. Then Nicole and I got to the point in our friendship where we didn't have to talk at all. We kept up these long silences like talking out loud was an unevolved thing, like we'd arrived at this new place of understanding and feeling.

Actually, the new place for Nicole was that she got a real job and a fiancé. I got furniture. Once every new moon, I'd catch some uplifting article about a local dance troupe visiting the National Mall and I'd remember to miss her. When I begged for it, we'd present ourselves as the same girls from before. I felt like the strain of trying to be our old selves showed only just a little, but Nicole disagreed.

In the entryway, under a blown-glass chandelier that looked like a bunch of squashes tumored together, some fool was playing Spice Girls on the violin. The host went around shushing people, trying to shame them into ironic appreciation, and if I hadn't found the dessert tray, I could've cried bitter tears. When it was over, I went to the table to complain to Nicole, but she hadn't noticed it was a dumb performance. She eyed my dress and introduced me to everyone, admitting to each of them that I was a lifelong friend. A man at the head of the table kept doing annoying things like holding up a plate of chickpeas smothered in yogurt and giving a detailed explanation of the dish, and people were listening like he had a punch line on hand or something. The people seated around him were good-looking and miserable. I drank champagne until I felt close to everyone.

I attempted to coerce Nicole into interpreting a dream for me. In it I invite a woman into my apartment who scolds, laughs, and cooks for me so that I can get better or just die—I can never tell which and that's why I needed Nicole to clarify.

"You dream of the same things," she said, like I was the only one, like it was a bad thing.

"Maybe the same problems," I said. Then I described a scenario where versions of my former self judged me through the bedroom mirror. Of course I didn't mention the godmother. I didn't want her rude ass popping up when I'd barely got invited myself.

"You on the computer too much," said Nicole. Someone passed her a plate of intricately painted chocolates that she rationed with me only. We were supposed to take one and pass them down.

"Only because I'm heartbroken," I said, "and failing. I'm not sure if we can take it anymore." I was speaking vaguely about everything, so when Nicole said she knew what I meant, firecrackers went off in my face and hands.

"I was just thinking about that the other day," said Nicole. "I was wondering if I had the heart to do this work again. Like, could my heart break one more time? Then I came across the website of a woman who fostered medically fragile babies. Apparently when a newborn is terminal, the parents can give up their rights if they know they won't be able to handle the medical bills. These newborns have nobody, so this woman would bring them home. Every now and then one would get better and be adopted, but most of them died in her living room. After about the tenth dead baby, her little son asked when they were getting another one. The mom told him it was too hard on her, she just couldn't take it. And her son replied, 'So we aren't going to help any more babies because you can't take it?'"

"I hadn't thought of it that way," I said. I looked Nicole up and down. "That story reminded you of me?"

"It reminded me of a lot of things," she said. She turned a

cocoa-dusted truffle between her fingers as though contemplating my future. "When you think of quitting on yourself," she said, "just remember the mom and the babies." But I was stuck on the little son who couldn't get enough of baby-death, who had also put their sad life in perspective. Without him the mother never would have noticed.

People kept coming through the door until a party was in full swing, but I wasn't about to give up my seat to dance to some techno. Nicole left me to talk to her other friends, and a blond woman sat down roughly in the vacant chair. I thought it was rude to sit down like that and tried to scold her with looks, but she was on the phone, talking in a shaky monologue, saying, "If someone storms in here and shoots up this party, I bet you'd be so happy. More than happy!"

I popped the last piece of chocolate into my mouth, watching. Across the room, Nicole was explaining a complicated point with her hands. When she caught me looking, she seemed annoyed, and I knew that if someone stormed in to shoot up the party as the blond person had prophesied, Nicole's feelings toward me wouldn't change.

"It may be over between us," the blond person said, "but I just have to say, right now, you are nullifying my entire life."

I turned away. I didn't like to hear somebody's life get nullified. People have the right to withhold their attention. I've done it. And when André did it to me, I'd believed I was special. My heartache was delicious. It turned me into an outcast. I would cling to him until he said something devastating, like *Take it easy.*

This Igbo dude in a velvet blazer kept edging in, so I obliged him. He was so cocoa-buttered up in embroidered slippers, smelling like a group gift for the Messiah, that I fell in love for at least fifteen seconds. Chudi said he was a doctor and filled my glass with cough syrup and ginger ale, which isn't even the recipe. We engaged in some almost dangerous banter that made my head swim —but his bootsy syrup could've given the same effect.

I continued talking to this man in code until too much time had gone by. I could tell he wasn't that attracted to me, but I was feeling too good to think about it. I made it obvious that I'd lost interest too—I was happy that it had worked out this way—but this hurt his feelings somehow. And he became typical, avenging his feelings by calling me names and saying I wanted to be a white girl.

"You just a mumu anyway," Chudi said, leaning close enough to lick my ear. "I'm so tired of bitches like you. You just want to do everything that hula-hooping white girl does, but you can't."

I lied. I said, "I can hula-hoop." I didn't know what he was talking about until I looked in the living room where, sure enough, that same blonde had attracted a crowd by dancing as though she was trying to keep an invisible hula hoop in swift rotation.

I didn't appreciate the way these folks partied. They liked to give you what you needed for the time being and then rob you because it made them feel intelligent or something. I looked around for my friend. Nicole stood between a man and a woman both dressed in black. Since Nicole was wearing black too, they looked like they had come to this party together. The man and the woman nodded with their mouths open, like Nicole was saying fascinating things. She was becoming one of them, and I was becoming the wrong version of myself.

"Intelligent robbery," I said. Inexplicably, I laughed hard at my misfortune.

Some people, like myself, who weren't supposed to be at the party had noticed the large amounts of wine left out in the open. Little by little, people started stealing the wine, swiping two and three bottles each. When I said I was ready to leave, Nicole didn't seem surprised and she did not agree to leave with me. I started to beg. Then one of her new friends scrambled over to guilt people into returning the wine. The new friend was the one who'd invited Nicole in the first place, and I could tell by the way Nicole tolerated her earnest appeals that she was going to leave when the new friend said so.

Cool, I thought, *I'll go home without my seasonal friend. But I will never, ever, ever feel bad about stealing luxury goods from rich people.*

In the mirror my ancestors wagged their fingers as I pulled a wine bottle out of my big purse. At 2 a.m. I called the man I'd been meaning to repossess, and since he didn't seem upset to hear from me, I told him, "I'm getting drunk as fuck because of you."

"You been doing that," André said.

A shaky laugh that could've belonged to any number of my ancestors rattled out of me. I laughed to hide the suspicion that I was doing something horrible to myself, that gesture by gesture I was making myself disappear. Maybe that's why I told André one of my secret resolutions, which was to pawn everything I owned.

I waited for somebody else to chime in, but it seemed he had excused himself to the other room. I'd never met Porsche, his new girl, though on occasion she would address me indirectly, pitching her ghetto proverbs just within earshot. Whenever I succeeded in getting André on the line, I could hear her husky contralto in the background saying something like "All shut eyes ain't sleep." And "You don't apologize to a roach once you spray it." It takes skill to get to that level, years if you study really hard.

But despite Porsche's gifts and what a new body like hers can do for a man's self-esteem, André went to the other room for me, to let me annoy him into daylight. It was all the reassurance I needed to act a fool.

I didn't get the chance to beg him to come back to me, but I told some lies like I always do when I sense somebody doesn't like me. I lied like I was genuinely happy at the simple accident of being alive. I talked until I felt like I was living in someone else's idea. André got quiet, probably struggling to remember why at one point in time he had wanted me bad. Then I pretended things were getting serious with the African dude who'd called me a mumu.

"Joy," André said, doing something magical to my name. I felt a surge of hope that things would turn around. "Do you really believe in the things you say?" he said. He said I needed to take it easy. He said again that he probably would have stayed with me had he not met Porsche. "And in the first place," he said, "you're the one who declined me." That was how his simple ass put it: *declined*. I wish I'd thought to say it first.

I twisted my hair and put on a bathrobe. I started to call Nicole but we didn't speak the same language anymore, and I didn't want to field her questions about the stolen wine. I fell back onto the groaning iron bed my mama and them had dragged over from Mississippi. I told myself that begging my people of the impossible and staying up too late with my bad attitudes had earned me conversations like the ones I kept having with the godmother.

"So you mean to tell me that you don't have anything to do with it?" Her voice was almost familiar.

I turned to the mirror and something inside started to crumble, grain by grain. This robe was supposed to make me look like a rich wizard, but you can never trust the colors you see on the computer. I just looked like my dead aunties. "I'm tired," I said. "I'm tired of everything."

"Refusing to learn can do that to a person," she said. She was manning the stove, striking a match, lighting a pilot. "How it violates the soul! Your only soul."

But I couldn't stop being myself! My people kept giving me the special look that lets you know you've reached the end of something. It made me feel at ease to see it, but then I'd panic because I didn't know what in the world was going to happen to me. So I'd end up begging things of people I'd already worn out.

The godmother looked on with her mouth set in a judgy bunch. A timer went off and she pulled a roasting pan of macaroni and cheese casserole from the oven, throwing lights everywhere. That was one of her powers: she only cooked the type of food you had to wait in suffering for. She set the pan on the counter and dug her hand into the steaming macaroni and cheese, eating like a monster.

"You're not even listening to me," I said. "Are you?"

"What you expect?" The godmother laughed so hard I could see the craters in her wisdom teeth. "You ain't saying nothing."

Saturday afternoon I drove my granny's car to André's house. The plan was to perpetrate like I was just passing through the hood or something, but he was already outside mowing the lawn as I came creeping by.

This shouldn't matter, but it must be said: André Simpson is an extraordinarily handsome individual. He's lanky, with a long neck and wavy Caesar, and he sometimes looks like a sweet, mute butler who with more opportunities could have been the principal dancer. André always got me thinking of possibilities. Sometimes I had to remind myself that he was just a mechanical engineer, shy until he'd learned he was beautiful and wanted, a stubborn child who after all this time refused to speak properly. You couldn't creep up on a dude like that, but I was moved to try.

I tricked his ass into feeding me. We rode in his car to a dirty chicken restaurant, the kind of place where they don't even put out tables and chairs because nobody wants you to stay. We ate in the car, talking elliptically about old rappers and how irrational it was to try to live off the grid and the fact that I had declined him

first and now there was Porsche to whom he felt a physical obligation, so there was no point in talking about possibilities anyway.
Then we were silent.

I told André that his silence was a way of strong-arming us
back into our respective gender roles, and he shrugged, saying
he didn't make the laws of nature. "Sound like you mad at God,"
he said. He looked into my eyes so directly, almost musically, and
I just knew that he was never going to say anything of romantic
import to me ever again. And I realized that I had nothing new to
say to him either.

So, naturally, I started begging. "Please say something. But know
that whatever you say, I'm going to hold on to it forever."

"Don't you do that," said André. "Not for no nigger." He glanced
in the rearview, almost hopeful for carjackers.

But what I had wanted to say was that he was nullifying my entire life. I wanted to tell André that if some fool rolled through
and shot up the parking lot, murdering me only, I hoped he would
be haunted for the rest of his stupid-ass life. But I was embarrassed
that the rants of a hula-hooping crazy summarized the true feelings of my heart. The goal was to attract him again.

André drove me back to his hovel. Bypassing my granny's car, I
led him to his own front door. I think we both knew that without
some disembodied sex, the whole encounter would be a waste.

Porsche sat cross-legged on the sectional playing a basketball
game on the console. Her hair was pinned to her scalp in a dozen
black rosettes, and she was wearing one of André's dress shirts the
way you were supposed to if you had the audacity to wear a man's
shirt. André glanced at us both. He went to the kitchen and came
back with a water bottle. I tried to shoot him a telepathic gaze but
my face was only begging, telling what he already knew.

Porsche interjected, telling someone on the headset, or me,
"You can keep your mouth when I cut your head off." She said,
"You want to slap me? Let me reach my face out so you can do
it." As she looked up at me, her face was like a once-in-a-lifetime
full moon. But after one glance, she was too dazzled by my pain
to look back again. I kept staring at her in André's shirt, trying to
remember that I was a woman too.

Usually I'm pretty sheepish around beautiful low-income
women, but my recent situation had empowered me. I gave the
shirt the nod and said, "Is that André's?"

He was already out the door, saying that he was going to walk me to my car, although it had belonged to my granny. Porsche looked down at the controller and laughed like she knew secrets about me. She adjusted her headset and, addressing somebody else, said, "Y'all need a glass-cleaner?"

I noticed that André was doing his best to make it quick. I tried taking off my shoes, but he wouldn't let me. I tried pulling up the front of his shirt, but this wasn't the place for that either. He moved smoothly, barely touching me, and something about the whole thing fit in with my idea of a cat burglar, if you know what I mean. He had tangled his face into a look-what-you-made-me-do expression directed at me only. I kissed him before he could move his face out the way.

Afterward he had some extra look in his eyes, but not so much that he saw past what he'd already concluded about me. Nothing told him that, enhanced by all this burgundy leather and all that I was going through, I was someone he could get stuck on again, possibly. I can admit that I was waiting for him to say the things dudes say to give you hope. But all of a sudden André couldn't look at me.

The feelings almost got me, but then I realized that were she in a similar position, the godmother would find a way to come out on top. I needed to get like her. I needed solutions. Then one came to me. I told André, "I need that shirt." I needed him to pluck his own shirt off Porsche's sweetly dipped back.

He started to smile, but once I'd conjured up my best god-mother face, he crawled out the door, rushing back inside. I had set him up to free-style a lie for someone who'd maybe had a hard childhood. Porsche could be saved in other ways. The wait that followed made the car's interior more luxurious than ever before. Then two boys walked up the street passing a forty back and forth, and I watched them the way white people have watched me. Guilt rippled through me on low heat.

André returned, presenting the shirt like a token of his ex-pired affections, and I smiled hard, becoming myself again. I wouldn't wish that smile on anybody. Nobody living, nobody with hopes of coming to life should ever have to smile like I did.

*

Back in my apartment, something told me to downplay my happiness. I sat at the table recounting the worst parts for the godmother's entertainment. In my kitchen she was lording over pots of steaming beauty, shaking her head without end. But as she was sprinkling sparkling hoops of season-all salt or pouring sizzling bacon grease into a jar, I suddenly felt defeated and ended up just telling the truth. "Our relationship wasn't even that great," I told her. "But back then, I felt like I was inevitable. At the same time, I remembered how he used to look at me, like what I had wasn't much but he was willing to work with it."

"That's probably exactly what he was thinking," said the godmother. "If he was thinking anything coherent at all."

"You know what," I said. "I'm getting tired of you and your marinades." It was my own fault. You can't be self-deprecating with everyone. "Anyway. It was nice," I said, but that wasn't accurate either. Already it was hard to remember that moment where André and I had looked at each other and realized anything could happen, now that everything had.

"You trying to sound dumb?" said the godmother. "This is what happens when you call a false love, love. The man just doesn't see things your way. Never did, never will."

"I wish you'd jump in the air and stay put," I said. "You're like a diss track I can't turn off."

"What you need me to say?" The godmother screwed up her face, and the skin of her forehead stood up in cursive. "You misread the whole thing? He was doing his very best to make love to you, girl. He missed you so much it was scary, and now he regrets everything. You changed his life. You put a move on his heart, an impress on his soul. Matter fact, you're the one. He wants *you* back."

I considered reminding the godmother, like André did me, that I had declined him first, but it wouldn't sound right coming out of my mouth.

"I know it's hard. He done broke down all your walls of vulnerability," she said, "but you can't rebuild with someone you had nothing with in the first place. And you ought to know marriage is out of the question."

I knew that. Everybody knows not to do marriage if you want to keep the feeling going. "I want him to apologize," I said. "For not choosing me."

"Nobody does that," said the godmother. "Not even when they're saying the words."

She whipped up a Jell-O salad with grapes and peaches swimming inside and a frosting sprinkled with pecans. She warmed up Vienna sausages in the microwave and served them still popping on a salad plate. The taste of everything brought me to tears.

"But I want him to say the words," I said.

"Then you're a fool," said the godmother. She was watching the tears in my eyes, seeing if I would let them fall.

I made the obvious sartorial decision and wore André's shirt the next day, fantasizing that on the other side of town there was a gorgeous, half-naked woman realizing just what she'd lost. To complete the look, I experimented with some fuchsia lipstick my mother would've despised and I drew my eyebrows up and away from my nose, which I'd been noticing was the new style. This was the image of myself that I wanted to keep in perpetuity.

I held my expired license close to my heart as I drove my granny's car to the DMV. En route, the city seemed to have changed its opinions about me. I could speed up traffic with the nod of my head. I could weave through lanes. There wasn't a person alive whose angry gaze could get their hooks in. I was a different Joy altogether and it was an incredible feeling, to be who I hoped to be. My soul was filled with laughter that made me shake. I thought I was free.

But when I arrived, the building was locked. The DMV was closed on Sunday, coinciding with the holiday that I hadn't realized was happening. On the door I saw my reflection and how I really looked in André's shirt on Easter Sunday, an excited, ruby-eyed bunny cartwheeling across on my chest. This pleased bunny seemed to be dancing all over me, over everything I'd accomplished.

I called my mother but I remembered that she never knew what to say or how to say it, and on the first ring I hung up the phone. When I saw that she was calling me back, I was too ashamed for us both to answer. So I called Nicole, but she declined me. Then, for an instant, I thought I'd made a little progress in my journey simply because all that internalized sexism kept me from immediately calling André. But in seconds I decided to be a free woman and I called him too.

"Joy?" he was saying like I was someone else. "Is that you? Are you there?"

Stepping off the curb, I was almost struck down by a black car. The car was swerving away just as I started to feel what was happening. I saw myself reflected in the fender, looking as though someone had run a heavy hand across my face and smeared it around. The car raced up the street, zipping the city back in order.

Somehow I'd kept the phone to my ear the whole time. André was scolding me in his grown man's voice.

"You're childish," he said. "Playing on the phone like that. It's Sunday."

I handled my brush with eternity by putting on Robert Earl Davis Jr.'s greatest hits and drawing myself a bubble bath. Maybe you already know this, but after too many loops, your favorite song starts to turn on you. The potency of the bass line begins to fade and like that, you're fresh out of new sounds. When the water went cold, I started to cry.

"Quit that crying," said the godmother. "This is not a crying situation." She walked into the bathroom and sat on the toilet to watch me. She was helping herself to a bowl of leftover eggplant with meat sauce and contemplating me in the bathtub, what it all meant. "Don't you ever feel sad for your bathtub?" she said. "For having to hold your little body when nobody else will?" She gave me one of her ugly laughs. People who've been through too much always laugh like that.

I tried turning away. "I'm sure it doesn't mind."

Taking another bite, the godmother looked me up and down. "You so sad," she said, "seem like your home girl could at least give you a hug. Or your man. You did make him your man again?"

More or less, I thought. "No."

The godmother shook her head mercilessly. "In my opinion — and this is just my opinion — you gave up way too easily with both. Didn't you know you gave up? Can't you tell when you're doing that? You give up in subtle ways. For example, the way you did your makeup today and the way you try to cook fancy dinners for yourself. None of that's for the real you. You can't even be real when nobody else is around. Even the way you beg is a form of surrender. And the funky part is that you gave up way before you started doing all that begging."

The beat was doing something tragic, and I sank deeper, looking at my toes. "I don't understand why you're telling me all this," I said.

Something fell softly on the bridge of my nose. When I recognized it as a bit of saucy eggplant, another one hit my eyelid and slid slowly down my face and into the tub. The godmother was throwing my leftovers and saying depressing things about the nature of love, things that I believed, which is what angered me the most. The spirit moved me to jump out the tub and attack the godmother as she defended herself with a ceramic bowl, getting licks in too. I watched myself struggle with her until I realized I was still in the bathtub, still envisioning another something I would never do.

I told the godmother, "I don't deserve this type of confrontation."

"Deserve," the godmother said in a voice that carried. "You still stuck on what you deserve." She shook her head at me and left.

I drained the tub, threw on my robe, and followed her into the kitchen. In the background Robert Earl Davis Jr.'s chopped-up, joyous pain pressed into my shoulders. The feeling showed in the mirror, and as I passed by, fragments of my ancestors looked out with mild concern.

They gathered as the godmother prepared my tea. She tilted the kettle to my favorite cup, and it was like the weight of my most telling, desperate fantasies was pouring from her knotted fingers. She brought the steaming cup to me, saying, "Drink."

Behind us my ancestors waited for me to make a bad decision. "I am sort of thirsty."

The godmother's eyes did something rude. "Baby," she drawled, "you are the thirstiest."

I staggered back. "This is not commiserating," I said too loudly. "This is an abyss of despair."

The godmother propped her free hand on her hip and curved her neck so that her ear was almost touching her shoulder. "Has anyone ever told you that you talk like a white girl?" she said.

That may be, but in her case, she talked like someone who had lived too long and had figured everything out, and all the gunk she carried around had probably made its way into her flickted tea, so it couldn't taste that good anyway. At the same time, I knew I was telling myself lies. Most likely her tea was delicious. The godmother pushed the cup on me again, smiling like she could read my bankrupt thoughts. This above everything else gave me a start. For as long I can remember, I'd wanted to be just like that, just as terrible, but not anymore. I had never changed my mind about a person before, so you can understand why this realization was confusing.

I was so confused that I started to pray. I prayed that my past loves would feel distant to the point of disappearing. I prayed that I could accept living a life without happiness, that I would make friends who shared this view, that I would not drink too much or become too bitter. I wanted so badly to be in harmony with the city I called home and with my time on this earth and for this to show in my face and the way I talked. And if none of this was meant to be, I prayed that I wouldn't want it in the first place, that I would be turned into a different girl completely.

That's when things turned around for me. I couldn't say exactly when it happened, but the godmother was gone. She had returned to wherever she belonged, and with her falling back into place, I could become myself again. But I worried that instead of going back, I'd just become yet another version of myself. Nobody was there to explain to me my options. I kept thinking someone was going to tell me what I was supposed to do next.

I picked out a dress that I used to love because it was orange and had only cost me seven dollars. I pulled the dress over my head, brushed my hair, and stepped into a pair of sandals. I looked into the mirror and waited for that specific presence to tell me that the hemline was too short and that she could see right through the material. But nobody was coming.

Then I walked across the street to the convenience store for a Dr Pepper. Once the cashier had rung me up, I realized that I'd forgotten my wallet. He gave me a look, as though he'd missed some sign that I was a crack addict. Then he decided that it doesn't make much difference if you give a crack addict a Dr Pepper every now and again. Begrudgingly, he let me have it.

I went outside to the parking lot and the world felt motionless under my feet. I looked back at my apartment building, where people were coming and going like nothing had ever happened to them. I was doing the same thing and had been, I realized, for a long time. I guess you could say that's how I got over.

T. C. BOYLE

The Apartment

FROM *McSweeney's*

WHO WAS TO know? She might have outlived most of her con-
temporaries, but she was so slight and small, almost a dwarf, really, her eyesight compromised and her hearing fading, and if she
lived a year or two more, it would have been by the grace of God
alone. Yes, she was lively enough, even at ninety, wobbling down
the street on her bicycle like some atrophied schoolgirl and twice
a week donning her épée mask and fencing with her shadow in the
salon of her second-floor apartment, overlooking rue Gambetta
on the one side and rue Saint-Estève on the other, but his own
mother had been lively too, and she'd gone to bed on the night of
her seventy-second birthday and never opened her eyes again. No,
no: the odds were in his favor. Definitely. Definitely in his favor.

He turned forty-seven the year he first approached her, 1965,
which meant that at that point he'd been married to Marie-
Thérèse for some twenty years, years that had been happy enough
for the most part—and more than that, usual. He liked the usual.
The usual kept you on an even keel and offered up few surprises.
And this was the important thing here, the thing he always liked
to stress when the subject came up: he was not a gambling man.
Before he'd made any of the major decisions in his life—asking
for his wife's hand all those years ago, applying for the course of
study that would lead to his law degree, making an offer on the
apartment they'd lived in since their marriage—he'd studied all
the angles with a cold, computational eye. The fact was, he had
few vices beyond a fondness for sweets and a tendency to indulge
his daughters, Sophie and Élise, sixteen and fourteen, respectively,

that year (or maybe they were seventeen and fifteen—he never could quite keep that straight; as he liked to say, "If you're very, very fortunate, your children will be twelve months older each year"). He didn't smoke or drink, habits he'd given up three years earlier after a strenuous talk with his doctor. And he wasn't covetous, or not particularly. Other men might drive sleek sports cars, lease yachts, and keep mistresses, but none of that interested him.

The only problem—the sole problem in his life at that point—was the apartment. It was just too small to contain his blossoming daughters and the eternally thumping music radiating from their bedroom day and night, simplistic music, moronic, even—the Beatles, the Animals, the Kinks, the very names indicative of their juvenility—and if he wanted a bigger apartment, grander, more spacious, *quieter,* who could blame him? An apartment that was a five-minute walk from his office, an apartment that was a cathedral of early-morning light? An apartment surrounded by shops, cafés, and first-class restaurants? It was, as they say, a no-brainer.

He put together a proposal and sent Madame C. a note wondering if he might see her, at her convenience, about a matter of mutual interest. Whether she would respond or not, he couldn't say, but it wasn't as if he were some interloper—he knew her as an acquaintance and neighbor, as did just about everyone else in Arles, and he must have stopped with her in the street half a dozen times in the past year to discuss the weather, the machinations of de Gaulle and Pompidou, and the absurdity of sending a rocket into space when life here, on terra firma, was so clearly in need of *immediate attention.* A week went by before he heard back from her. He'd come home from work that day to an empty apartment—Marie-Thérèse was out shopping and the girls were at rehearsal for a school play, but the radio in their room was all too present, and regurgitating rock and roll at full volume ("We gotta get out of this place," the singer insisted, in English, over and over) until he angrily snapped it off—and he was just settling down in his armchair with the newspaper when he noticed her letter on the sideboard.

"Cher monsieur," she wrote in the firm, decisive hand she'd learned as a schoolgirl in the previous century, "I must confess to being intrigued. Shall we meet here at my residence at 4 p.m. Thursday?"

*

In addition to the contract he'd drawn up in advance—he was an optimist, always an optimist—he brought with him a bouquet of spring flowers and a box of chocolate truffles, which he presented somberly to her when she met him at the door. "How kind of you," she murmured, taking the flowers in one all-but-translucent hand and the box of chocolates in the other and ushering him through the entrance hall and into the salon, and whether by calculation or not she left him standing there in that grand room with its high ceilings, Persian carpets, and dense mahogany furniture while she went into the kitchen to put the flowers in a vase.

There was a Bösendorfer piano in one corner, with a great spreading palm—or was it a cycad?—in a ceramic pot beside it, and that, as much as anything, swept him away. To think of sinking into the sofa after work and listening to Bach or Mozart or Debussy instead of the Animals or whoever they were. And so what if no one in the family knew how to play or had ever evidenced even the slightest degree of musical talent—they could take lessons. He himself could take lessons, and why not? He wasn't dead yet. And before long the girls would be away at university and then married, with homes of their own, and it would be just Marie-Thérèse and him—and maybe a cat. He could see himself seated on the piano bench, the cat asleep in his lap and Debussy's *Images* flowing from his fingertips like a new kind of language.

"Well, don't these look pretty?" the old lady sang out, edging into the room to arrange the vase on the coffee table, which he now saw was set for two, with a blue-and-rose Sèvres teapot, matching cups and saucers, cloth napkins bound in silver rings, and a platter of macarons.

He sat in the armchair across from her as she poured out two cups of tea, watching for any signs of palsy or Parkinson's—but no, she was steady enough—and then they were both busy with their spoons, the sugar and the cream, until she broke the silence. "You have a proposition for me, is that it?" she asked. "And"—here a sly look came into the flickering remnants of her eyes—"I'll bet you five francs I know what it is. I'm clairvoyant, monsieur, didn't you know that?"

He couldn't think of anything to say to this, so he just smiled.

"You want to make me an offer on the apartment, *en viager*—isn't that right?"

If he was surprised, he tried not to show it. He'd been prepared to condescend to her, as with any elderly person—politely, of course, generously, looking out for her best interests as well as his own—but she'd caught him up short. "Well, yes," he said. "That's it exactly. A reverse annuity."

He set down his cup. The apartment was absolutely silent, as if no one else lived in the building, and what about a maid—didn't she have a maid? "The fact is, Marie-Thérèse and I—my wife, that is—have been thinking of moving for some time now." He let out a little laugh. "Especially with my daughters growing into young women and the apartment getting smaller by the day, if you know what I mean, and while there are plenty of places on the market, there's really hardly anything like this—and it's so close to my office . . ."

"And since my grandson passed on, you figure the old woman has no one to leave the place to, and even if she doesn't need the money, why wouldn't she take it anyway? It's better than getting nothing and leaving the place for the government to appropriate, isn't that right?"

"Yes," he said, "that was my thinking."

As far as he knew—and he'd put in his research on the subject—she had no heirs. She'd been a bride once, and a mother too, and she'd lived within these four walls and paced these creaking floorboards for an astonishing sixty-nine years, ever since she'd returned from her honeymoon, in 1896, and moved in here with her husband, a man of means, who had owned the department store on the ground floor and had given her a life of ease. Anything she wanted was at her fingertips. She hosted musical parties, vacationed in the Alps, skied, bicycled, hunted and fished, lived through the German occupation and the resumption of the republic without noticing all that much difference in her daily affairs, but of course no one gets through life unscathed. Her only child, a daughter, had died of pneumonia in 1934, after which she and her husband had assumed guardianship of their grandson, until first her husband died unexpectedly (after eating a dish of fresh-picked cherries that had been dusted with copper sulfate and inadequately rinsed), and then her grandson, whom she'd seen through medical school and who had continued to live with her as her sole companion and emotional support. He was only thirty-six when he was killed in an auto accident on a deserted road, not two years ago. It was Marie-Thérèse who'd seen the notice in the paper; otherwise he might have missed it altogether. They sent a condolence card, though neither of them attended the funeral, which, given the deceased's condition, would have been a closed-casket affair in any case. Still, that was the beginning of it, the first glimmer of the idea, and whether he was being insensitive or not ("ghoulish" was the way Marie-Thérèse put it), he couldn't say. Or no, he could say: he was just being practical.

"What are you offering?" the old woman asked, focusing narrowly on him now as if to be certain he was still there.

"Fair market value, of course. I want the best for you—and for me and my family too. Here," he said, handing her a sheet of paper on which he'd drawn up figures for comparable apartments in the neighborhood. "I was thinking perhaps twenty-two hundred francs a month?"

She barely glanced at the paper. "Twenty-five," she said.

It took him a moment, doing a quick mental calculation, to realize that even if she lived ten more years he'd be getting the place for half of what it was worth, and that didn't factor in appreciation either. "Agreed," he said.

"And you won't interfere?"

"No."

"What if I decide to paint the walls pink?" She laughed, a sudden strangled laugh that tailed off into a fit of coughing. She was a smoker, that much he knew (and had taken into account on the debit side of the ledger). Yes, she could ride a bicycle at ninety, an amazing feat, but she'd also been blackening her lungs for seventy years or more. He watched her dab at her eyes with a tissue, then grin to show her teeth—yes, she still had them. Unless they were dentures.

"And the ceiling chartreuse?" she went on, extending the joke. "And, and—move the bathtub into the salon, right there where you're perched in my armchair looking so pleased with yourself?"

He shook his head. "You'll live here as you always have, no strings attached."

She sat back in her chair, a tight smile compressing her lips. "You're really throwing the dice, aren't you?"

He shrugged. "Twenty-five hundred a month," he repeated. "It's a fair offer."

"You're betting I'll die—and sooner rather than later."

"Not at all. I wish you nothing but health and prosperity. Besides, I'm not a betting man."

"You know what *I'm* doing?" she asked, hunching forward so he could see the balding patch on the crown of her head and the slim tracery of bones exposed at the collar of her dress, where, apparently, she'd been unable to reach back and fasten the zipper.

"No, what?" he said, grinning, patronizing her, though his stomach sank because he was sure she was going to say she was backing out of the deal, that she'd had a better offer, that she'd been toying with him all along.

"I'm throwing the dice too."

After he left that day, she felt as if she'd been lifted up into the clouds. She cleared away the tea things in a burst of energy, then marched around the apartment, going from room to room and back again, twice, three times, four, pumping her arms for the sake of her circulation and letting her eyes roam over the precious familiar things that meant more to her than anything else in the world, and not just the framed photos and paintings, but the ceramic snowman Frédéric had made in grammar school and the mounted butterflies her husband had collected when they first married. She'd been blessed, suddenly and unexpectedly blessed, and if she could have kicked up her heels, she would have—she wasn't going to a nursing home like so many other women she'd known, all of them lost now to death or the straitjacket of old age. No, she was staying right here. For the duration. In celebration, she unwrapped the box of chocolates, poured herself a glass of wine, and sat smoking by the window, looking out on the street and the parade of pedestrians that was the best show on earth, better than any television, better than *La Comédie humaine*—no, it *was La Comédie humaine*. And there were no pages to turn and no commercials either.

She watched a woman in a ridiculous hat go into the shop across the street and immediately come back out again as if she'd forgotten something, then press her face to the glass and wave till the shopgirl appeared in the window and reached for an equally ridiculous hat on the mannequin there, and here came a boy on a motor scooter with a girl clinging to him from behind and the sudden shadow of a black Renault sliced in front of them till the goat's bleat of the boy's horn rose up in protest and the car swerved at the last minute. Almost an accident, and wouldn't that have been terrible? Another boy dead, like her Frédéric, and a girl too. It was everywhere, death, wasn't it? You didn't have to go out and look for it—it was right there, always, lurking just below the surface. And that was part of the *comédie* too.

But enough morbidity—this was a celebration, wasn't it? Twenty-five hundred francs! Truly, this man had come to her like an angel from heaven—and what's more he'd never even hesitated when she countered his offer. Like everyone else, he assumed she was better off than she was, that money meant nothing to her and she could take or leave any offer no matter how extravagant, but in fact, if you excluded the value of the apartment, she had practically nothing, her savings having dissipated in paying for Frédéric's education and his clothes and his car and his medical degree—Frédéric, lost to her now and forever. She got by, barely, by paring her expenses and the reduced needs that come with having lived so long. It wasn't as if she needed theater tickets anymore. Or concert tickets either. She never went anywhere, except to church on Sundays, and that didn't cost anything more than what she put in the collection box, which was between her and God.

After Frédéric's death she'd reduced the maid's schedule to two days a week rather than the six she'd have preferred, but that was going to change now. And if she wanted a prime cut of meat at the butcher's or *l'écrevisse* or even *le homard* at the fishmonger's, she would just go ahead and order it and never mind what it cost. Bless the man, she thought, bless him. Best of all, even beyond the money, was the wager itself. If she'd been lost after Frédéric had been taken from her, now she was found. Now—suddenly, wonderfully—purpose had come back into her life. Gazing out the window at the bustle of the street below, bringing the cigarette to her lips just often enough to keep it glowing, she was as happy as she'd been in weeks, months, even, and all at once she was thinking about the time she and her husband had gone to Monte Carlo, the one time in all their life together. She remembered sitting there at the roulette table in a black velvet evening gown, Fernand glowing beside her in his tuxedo, the croupier spinning the wheel, and the bright, shining silver ball dropping into the slot for her number—twenty-two black; she would never forget it—and in the next moment using his little rake to push all those gay, glittering chips in her direction.

*

He went to visit her at the end of the first month after the contract went into effect, feeling generous and expansive, wondering how she was getting on. He'd heard a rumor that she'd been ill, having caught the cold that was going around town that spring, which, of course, would have been all the more severe in someone of her age with her compromised immune system, not to mention smoker's cough. A steady rain had been falling all day, and it was a bit of a juggling act for him to balance his umbrella and the paper-wrapped parcels he was bringing her: a bottle of Armagnac, another box of chocolates (two pounds, assorted), and a carton of the Gauloises he'd seen her smoking on his last visit. This time a girl met him at the door—a woman, that is, of fifty or so, with sucked-in cheeks, badly dyed hair, and listless eyes. There was a moment of hesitation until he realized that this must be the maid he'd wondered about and then a further moment during which he reflected on the fact that he was, in a sense, paying her wages. "Is madame in?" he inquired.

She didn't ask his name or business, but simply nodded and held out her arms for the gifts, which he handed over as if they were a bribe, and then led him into the salon, which as far as he could see remained unchanged, no pink walls or chartreuse ceiling, and no bathtub either. He stood there awhile, reveling in the details—the room was perfect, really, just as it was, though Marie-Thérèse, who'd yet to see the place from the inside, would want to do at least some redecorating, because she was a woman, and women were never satisfied till they'd put their own stamp on things—and then there was a noise behind him and he turned round to see the maid pushing the old woman down the hall in a wheelchair. *A wheelchair!* He couldn't suppress a rush of joy, though he composed his features in a suitably concerned expression and said, "Madame, how good to see you again," and he was about to go on, about to say, *You're looking well,* but that was hardly appropriate under the circumstances.

The old woman was grinning up at him. "It's just a cold," she said, "so don't get your hopes up." He saw that the presents he'd brought were arranged in her lap, still wrapped in tissue paper. "And I wouldn't have caught a cold at all, you know, if someone"— and here she glanced up at the maid—"hadn't carried it home to me. Isn't that right, Martine? Unless I picked it up by dipping my hand in the font last Sunday morning at church. You think that's it, Martine? Do you? You think that's likely?"

The maid had wheeled her up to the coffee table, where she set the gifts down, one by one, and began unwrapping them, beginning with the Armagnac. "Ah," she exclaimed when she'd torn off the paper, "perfect, just what a woman needs when she has a head cold. Fetch us two glasses, will you, Martine?"

He wanted to protest—he didn't drink anymore and didn't miss it either (or maybe he did, just a little)—but it was easier to let the old woman take the bottle by the neck and pour them each a dose, and when she raised her glass to him and cried, *"Bonne santé!"* and drained it in a single swallow, he had no choice but to follow suit. It burned going down, but it clarified things for him. She was in a wheelchair. She had a head cold, which, no doubt, was merely the first stage of an infection that would invariably spread to her lungs, mutate into pneumonia, and kill her sooner rather than later. It wasn't a mercenary thought, just realistic, that was all, and when she poured a second glass, he joined her again, and when she unwrapped the chocolates and set the box on the table before him, he found himself lifting one morsel after another to his lips, and if he'd ever tasted anything so exquisite in his life, he couldn't remember it, especially now that the Armagnac had reawakened his palate. He'd never liked Gauloises—they were too harsh—preferring filtered American cigarettes, but he found himself accepting one anyway, drawing deeply, and enjoying the faint crepitation of the nicotine working its way through his bloodstream. He exhaled in the rarefied air of the apartment that was soon to be his, and though he'd intended to stay only a few minutes, he was still there when the church bells tolled the hour.

What did they talk about? Her health, at least at first. Did he realize she'd never been sick more than a day or two in her entire life? He didn't, and he found the news unsettling, disappointing even. "Oh," she said, "I've had little colds and sniffles like this before—and once, when my husband and I were in Spain, an episode of the trots—but nothing major. Do you know something?"

Flying high on the cognac, the sugar, the nicotine, he just grinned at her.

"Not only am I hardly ever ill, but I make a point of keeping all of my blood inside my body at all times—don't you think that's a good principle to live by?"

And here he found himself straddling a chasm, the flush and healthy on one side, the aged, crabbed, and doomed on the other, and he said, "We can't all be so lucky."

She was silent a moment, just staring into his eyes, a faint grin pressed to her lips. He could hear the maid off in the distance somewhere, a sound of running water, the faint clink of cutlery —the apartment really was magnificent, huge, cavernous, and you could hear a pin drop. It was a defining moment, and Madame C. held on to it. "Precisely," she said finally, took the cigarette from her lips, and let out a little laugh, a giggle, actually, girlish and pure.

Three days later, when the sun was shining in all its power again and everything was sparkling as if the world had been created anew, he was hurrying down the street on an errand, a furtive cigarette cupped in one palm—yes, yes, he knew, and he wouldn't lie to his doctor next time he saw him, or maybe he would, but there was really no harm in having a cigarette every once in a while, or a drink either—when a figure picked itself out of the crowd ahead and wheeled toward him on a bicycle, knees slowly pumping, back straight and arms braced, and it wasn't until she'd passed by, so close he could have touched her, that he realized who it was.

For the first eighty-odd years of her existence, time had seemed to accelerate, day by day, year by year, as if life were a bicycle race, a kind of Tour de France that was all downhill, even the curves, but in the years after she'd signed the contract, things slowed to a crawl. Each day was a replica of the last, and nothing ever happened beyond the odd squabble with Martine and the visits from Monsieur R. At first he'd come every week or two, his arms laden with gifts—liquor, sweets, cigarettes, foie gras, quiche, even a fondue once, replete with crusts of bread, marbled beef, and *crépitements de porc*—but eventually the visits grew fewer and further between. Which was a pity, really, because she'd come to relish the look of confusion and disappointment on his face when he found her in such good spirits, matching him chocolate for chocolate, drink for drink, and cigarette for cigarette. "Don't think for a minute you're fooling me, monsieur," she would say to him as they sat at the coffee table laden with delicacies, and Martine bustled back and forth from the salon to the kitchen and sometimes even took a seat with them and dug in herself. "You're a sly one, aren't you?"

He would shrug elaborately, laugh, and throw up his hands as if to say, *Yes, you see through me, but you can't blame a man for trying, can you?*

She would smile back at him. She'd found herself growing fond of him, in the way you'd grow fond of a cat that comes up periodically to rub itself against your leg—and then hands you twenty-five hundred francs. Each and every month. He wasn't much to look at, really: average in height, weight, and coloring—average, in fact, in every way, from the man-in-the-street look on his face to his side part and negligible mustache. Nothing like Fernand, who'd been one of the handsomest men of his generation, even into his early seventies, when, in absolutely perfect health and the liveliest of moods, he'd insisted on a second portion of fresh-picked cherries at a *ferme-auberge* in Saint-Rémy.

She'd gotten sick herself, but she really didn't care for cherries all that much and had eaten a handful at most. Fernand, though, had been greedy for them, feeding them into his mouth one after another, spitting the pits into his cupped palm and arranging them neatly on the saucer in front of him as if they were jewels, pausing only to lift the coffee cup to his lips or read her the odd tidbit from the morning paper, joking all the while. *Joking,* and the poison in him even then. He spent the next six weeks in agony, his skin drawn and yellow, the whites of his eyes the color of orange peels, and his voice dying in his throat, till everything went dark. It was so hard to understand—it wasn't an enemy's bullet that killed him, wasn't an avalanche on the ski slopes or the failure of an overworked heart or even the slow advance of cancer, but cherries, little round fruits the size of marbles, nature's bounty. That had been wrong, deeply wrong, and she'd questioned God over it through all these years, but he had never responded.

When she turned one hundred, people began to take notice. The newspaper printed a story, listing her among the other centenarians in Provence, none of whom she knew, and why would she? She was photographed in her salon, grinning like a gargoyle. Someone from the mayor's office sent her a commendation, and people stopped her in the street to congratulate her as if she'd won the lottery, which, in a sense, she supposed she had. She really didn't want to make a fuss over it, but Martine, despite having fractured her wrist in a fall, insisted on throwing a party to commemorate "the milestone" she'd reached.

"I don't want a party," she said.

"Nonsense. Of course you do."

"Too much noise," she said. "Too many busybodies." Then a thought came to her and she paused. "Will he be there?"

"Who?"

"Monsieur R."

"Well, I can ask him—would you like that?"

"Yes," she said, gazing down on the street below, "I think I'd like that very much."

He came with his wife, a woman with bitter, shining eyes she'd met twice before but whose name she couldn't for the life of her remember, beyond "Madame," that is. He brought a gift, which she accepted without enthusiasm, his gifts having become increasingly less elaborate as time wore on, and his hopes of debilitating her ran up against the insuperable obstacle of her health. In this instance he came forward like a petitioner to where she was seated on the piano stool preparatory to treating her guests to a meditative rendition of "Au clair de la lune," bent formally to kiss her cheek, and handed her a bottle of indifferent wine from a vineyard she'd never heard of. "Congratulations," he said, and though she'd heard him perfectly well, she said, "What?" so that he had to repeat himself, and then she said, "What?" again, just to hear him shout it out.

There were thirty or more people gathered in the salon, neighbors mostly, but also the priest from the local church, a pair of nuns she vaguely recognized, a photographer, a newspaperman, and the mayor (an infant with the bald head of a newborn who'd come to be photographed with her so that his administration, which hadn't even come into existence till three years ago, could take credit for her longevity). They all looked up at the commotion and then away again, as if embarrassed for Monsieur R., and there wasn't a person in the room who didn't know of the gamble he'd taken.

"Thank you," she said. "You can't imagine how much your good wishes mean to me—more even than the mayor's." And then, to the wife, who was looking positively tragic behind a layer of powder that didn't begin to hide the creases under her eyes, "And don't you fret, madame. Be patient. All this"—she waved a hand

to take in the room, the windows, and the sunstruck vista beyond
—"will be yours in just, oh, what shall we say, ten or fifteen years?"

If Marie-Thérèse had never been one to nag, she began to nag
now. "Twenty-five hundred francs," she would interject whenever
there was a pause in their conversation, no matter the subject or
the hour of the day or night, "*twenty-five hundred francs.* Don't you
think I could use that money? Look at my winter coat—do you see
this coat I'm forced to wear? And what of your daughters, what
about them? Don't you imagine they could use something extra?"

Both their daughters were out of the house now, Sophie married and living in Paris with a daughter of her own and Élise in
graduate school, studying art restoration in Florence, for which
he footed the bill (tuition, books, clothing, living expenses, as well
as a room in a pension on via dei Calzaiuoli, which he'd never
laid eyes on and most likely never would). The apartment seemed
spacious without them, and lonely—that, too, because he missed
them both terribly—and without the irritation of their rock and
roll it seemed more spacious still. If there'd been a time when
he'd needed Madame C.'s apartment—needed, rather than hun-
gered for—that time had passed. As Marie-Thérèse reminded him
every day.

It would be madness to try to break the contract at this point
—he'd already invested some three hundred thousand francs, and
the old lady could drop dead at any minute—but he did go to
her one afternoon not long after the birthday celebration to see
if he might persuade her to lower the monthly payment to the
twenty-two hundred he'd initially proposed or perhaps even two
thousand. That would certainly be easier on him—he had his own
retirement to think about at this point—and it would mollify his
wife, as least for the time being.

Madame C. greeted him in the salon, as usual. It was a cold
day in early March, rain at the windows and a chill pervading the
apartment. She was seated in her favorite armchair, beside an electric heater, an afghan spread over her knees and a pair of cats he'd
never seen before asleep in her lap. He brought her only cigarettes this time, though the maid had let slip that madame didn't
smoke more than two or three a day and that the last several car-
tons he'd given her were gathering dust in the kitchen cupboard.

No matter. He took the seat across from her and immediately lit up himself, expecting her to follow suit, but she only gazed at him calmly, waiting to hear what he had to say.

He began with the weather—wasn't it dreary and would spring never arrive?—and then, stalling till the right moment presented itself, he commented on the cats. They were new, weren't they?

"Don't you worry, monsieur," she said, "they do their business in the pan under the bathroom sink. They're very well behaved and they wouldn't dream of pissing on the walls and stinking up your apartment. Isn't that right?" she cooed, bending her face to them, her ghostly hands gliding over their backs and bellies as if to bless them.

"Oh, I'm not worried at all, I assure you—I like cats, though Marie-Thérèse is allergic to them, but there is one little matter I wanted to take up with you, if you have a moment, that is."

She laughed then. "A moment? I have all the time in the world."

He began in a roundabout way, talking of his daughters, his wife, his own apartment, and his changed circumstances. "And really, the biggest factor is that I need to start putting something away for my retirement," he said, giving her a meaningful look.

"Retirement? But you can't even be sixty yet?"

He said something lame in response, which he couldn't remember when he tried to reconstruct the conversation afterward, something like *It's never too soon to begin,* which only made her laugh.

"You're telling me," she said, leaning forward in the chair. "Thanks to you, I'm all set." She paused, studying him closely. "But you're not here to try to renegotiate, are you?"

"It would mean so much to me," he said. "And my wife too." And then, absurdly, he added, "She needs a new winter coat."

She was silent a moment. "You brought me an inferior bottle of wine on my birthday," she said finally.

"I'm sorry about that. I thought you would like it."

"Going on the cheap is never appealing."

"Yes, but with my daughter in graduate school and some recent reverses we've experienced at the office, I'm just not able"—he grinned, as if to remind her they were on the same team—"to give you all you deserve. Which is why I ask you to reconsider the terms—"

She'd already held up the palm of one hand to forestall him. The cats shifted in her lap, the near one opening its jaws in a yawn that displayed the white needles of its teeth. "We all make bargains in this life," she said, setting the cats down on the carpet beside her. "Sometimes we win," she said, "and sometimes we lose."

When she turned 110, she was introduced to the term *supercentenarian,* the meaning of which the newspaper helpfully provided —that is, one who is a decade or more older than a mere centenarian, who, if you searched all of France (or Europe, America, the world), were a dime a dozen these days. Her eyes were too far gone to read anymore, but Martine, who'd recently turned seventy herself, put on her glasses and read the article aloud to her. She learned that the chances of reaching that threshold were one in seven million, which meant that for her to be alive still, 6,999,999 had died, which was a kind of holocaust in itself. And how did that make her feel? Exhausted. But indomitable too. And she still had possession of her apartment and still received her contractual payment of twenty-five hundred francs a month. One of the cats—Tybalt—had died of old age, and Martine wasn't what she once was, but for her part Madame C. still sat at the window and watched the life of the streets pulse around her as it always had and always would, and if she couldn't bicycle anymore, well, that was one of the concessions a supercentenarian just had to make to the grand order of things.

Monsieur R. didn't come around much anymore, and when he did, she didn't always recognize him. Her mind was supple still even if her body wasn't (rheumatism, decelerating heartbeat, a persistent ache in the soles of her feet), but he was so changed even Martine couldn't place him at first. He was stooped, he shuffled his feet, his hair was like cotton batting, and for some unfathomable reason he'd grown a beard like Père Noël. She had to ask him to come very close so she could make him out (what her eyes gave her now was no better than the image on an old black-and-white television screen caught between stations), and when he did, and when she reached out to feel his ears and his nose and look into his eyes, she would burst into laughter. "It's not between you and me anymore, monsieur," she would say. "I've got a new wager now."

And he would lift his eyebrows so she could see the exhaustion in his eyes, all part of the routine, the comedy, they were bound up in. "Oh?" he would say. "With whom?"

Martine hovered. The pack of the cigarettes he always brought
with him lay on the table before him, and a smoldering butt—his,
not hers—rested in the depths of the ashtray. "You can't guess?"

"No, I can't imagine."

"Methuselah, that's who," she would say, and break into a laugh
that was just another variant on the cough that was with her now
from morning till night. "I'm going for the record, didn't you
know that?"

The record-keepers—the earthly record-keepers from the Guin-
ness Brewery, that is, who were in their own way more authoritative
than God, and more precise too—came to her shortly after her
113th birthday to inform her that Florence Knapp, of the State
of Pennsylvania in the United States of America, had died at 114,
making her the world's oldest living person. The apartment was
full of people. The salon buzzed. There were lights brighter than
the sun, cameras that moved and swiveled like enormous insects
with electric red eyes, and here was a man as blandly handsome
as a grade-A apple, thrusting a microphone at her. "How does it
feel?" he asked, and when she didn't respond, asked again. Finally,
after a long pause during which the entire TV-viewing audience
must have taken her for a dotard, she grinned and said, "Like going to the dentist."

Marie-Thérèse, who'd been slowed by a degenerative disk in her
lower back that made walking painful, came clumping into the
kitchen one bleak February morning in the last dwindling decade
of the century—and where had the years gone?—to slap the newspaper down on the table before him. "You see this?" she demanded,
and he pushed aside his slice of buttered toast (the only thing he
was able to keep down lately) to fumble for his reading glasses,
which he thought he had misplaced until he discovered them
hanging from the lanyard around his neck. Marie-Thérèse's finger
tapped at the photograph dominating the front page. It took him
a moment to realize it was a close-up of Madame C., seated before
a birthday cake the size of a truck tire, the candles atop it ablaze,
as if this, finally, were her funeral pyre, but no such luck.

Whole years had gone by during which he'd daily envisioned
her death—plotted it, even. He dreamed of poisoning her wine,
pushing her down the stairs, sitting in her bird-shell lap and crush-

ing her like an egg, all eighty-eight pounds of her, but of course, because he was civilized, he never acted on his fantasies. In truth, he'd lost contact with her over the course of the years, accepting her for what she was—a fact of nature, like the sun that rose in the morning and the moon that rose at night—and he was doing his best to ignore all mention of her. She'd made him the butt of a joke, and a cruel joke at that. He'd attended her 110th birthday, and then the one four years later, after she'd become the world's oldest living human, but Marie-Thérèse had been furious (about that and practically everything else in their lives), and both his daughters had informed him he was making a public spectacle of himself, and so, finally, he'd declared himself *hors de combat*.

Besides which, he had problems of his own, problems that went far deeper than where he was going to lay his head at night—the doctor had found a spot on his lung and that spot had morphed into cancer. The treatments, radiation and chemotherapy both, had sheared every hair from his body and left him feeling weak and otherworldly. So when Marie-Thérèse thrust the paper at him and he saw the old lady grinning her imperturbable grin under the banner headline WORLD'S OLDEST LIVING PERSON TURNS 120, he felt nothing. Or practically nothing.

"I wish she would die," Marie-Thérèse hissed.

He wanted to concur, wanted to hiss right back at her, *So do I,* but all he could do was laugh—yes, the joke was on him, wasn't it? —until the laugh became a rasping, harsh cough that went on and on till his lips were bright with blood.

Two days later he was dead.

At first she hadn't the faintest idea what Martine was talking about ("Dead? Who's dead?"), but eventually, after a painstaking disquisition that took her step by step through certain key events of the past thirty years, she was given to understand that her benefactor had been laid to rest—or, actually, incinerated at the crematorium, an end result she was determined to avoid for herself. She was going to be buried properly, like a good Catholic. And an angel—her guardian angel, who had seen her this far—was going to be there at her side to take her to heaven in a golden chariot. Let the flesh rot, dust to dust; her spirit was going to soar.

"So he's dead, is he?" she said in the general direction of Martine. She was all but blind now, but she could see everything in her mind's eye—Martine, as she'd been five years ago, hunched and crabbed, an old woman herself—and then she saw Monsieur R. as he had been all those years before, when he'd first come to her to place his bet. Suddenly she was laughing. "He made his bet; now he has to lie in it," she said, and Martine said, "Whatever are you talking about? And what's so funny—he's dead, didn't you hear me?"

Very faintly, as if from a distance, she heard herself say, "But his twenty-five hundred francs a month are still alive, aren't they?"

"I don't—I mean, I hadn't really thought about it."

"*En viager.* I'm still alive, aren't I? Well, aren't I?"

Martine didn't answer. The world had been reduced. But it was there still, solid, tangible, as real as the fur of the cat—whichever cat—that happened to be asleep in her lap, asleep, and purring.

JASON BROWN

A Faithful but Melancholy Account of Several Barbarities Lately Committed

FROM *The Sewanee Review*

THE DAY BEFORE my sister's pretend wedding, the family gathered in Maine for our annual meeting, at my grandfather's island house, so he could tell us how much of a disappointment we'd been. Dressed like a clam digger in rubber boots, filthy canvas pants, and an old sweatshirt full of pipe ash holes, he rose from his wing chair and leveraged himself to his feet with his cane. Stains extended from his collar to his knees, because at mealtimes he used himself as a plate. Like other monarchs, he may have confused menace with majesty and mistaken the wary looks of his subjects, cowering in the wicker, for devoted affection. He delivered his judgment not in words but through his leaky blue eyes, which lingered on each one of us before coming to rest on my sister.

"I am going to die," he announced, and lifted Julia, his corgi, into his arms. The wicker groaned. Of course he was going to die —at some point. He was ninety-four.

"Are you ill?" my aunt asked. With his flushed cheeks and one bony hand gripping the cane as if it were a sword, he didn't look sick. Just spiteful. Most years he accused us all of a failure of cheerfulness and left it at that.

"No, there is nothing wrong with me. I'm going to die, that's all. I am going to die on Saturday."

"But that's tomorrow," my sister said. "I'm getting married here tomorrow."

"You can go ahead and do whatever you want to," he said to the far side of the room. To where my fiancée, Melissa, stood next to a row of windows framing the Atlantic Ocean. "Who is that woman?" he asked.

Melissa raised her ink-black eyebrows and looked at me.

"Is that why there's a big hole in the ground?" my sister said, tipping her tennis racket west.

We'd all noticed the hole (three feet deep, a little bigger than a coffin) on the way up from the dock, but no one had mentioned it until now in the hope that ignoring it would fill it in.

"It's not even in the graveyard," my sister added.

"You're not putting me in the graveyard with all those people," my grandfather said to me for some reason.

"Those are our ancestors, and one of *those people* was your wife," Uncle Alden said.

"*Is—is* my wife."

"You're going to kill yourself on the day I get married?" my sister said. She and my father had distinguished themselves as the only two people to stand up to my grandfather. My father lived in Oregon and hadn't been back to Maine for a decade.

"Of course I am not going to kill myself."

"You can't just decide to die," my sister said.

"I can do whatever I damned well please!"

We all lowered our heads, except for my sister, who rolled her eyes.

"I am getting in that hole on Saturday. And someone," my grandfather added, nodding at me, "will cover me with dirt when I stop breathing."

"Why him?" Uncle Alden said. "Why does he get to bury you?"

"Because he inherits the house. As of Saturday, the whole thing belongs to him."

A great sigh seemed to rise from the floorboards, and Uncle Alden's head flopped forward. I felt dizzy and saturated, like someone who'd just downed eleven seltzer and lemons at a sports bar to prove he could sit there and not drink. At one time, before my first trip to COPE in Tucson, I'd spent every summer here on the island crammed into this eighteenth-century falling-down Cape with my sister and grandparents and cousins, all people I loved but also vaguely resented. I had always assumed that one of us—probably my Uncle Alden—would own it someday, but not me. I lived in Tucson and had no money.

"As of Saturday," my grandfather added as an afterthought, "whatever John says goes around here."

Unaccustomed to power, I didn't know if I should stand. Several cousins stormed out. A few climbed the stairs into what would apparently, as of Saturday, no longer be their bedrooms. I looked around at the old plaster, the whole house desperately clinging to the central stone chimney. A warehouse of colonial junk surrounded us: old paintings of people strangled by white collars on the walls of the parlor; a powder horn from Queen Anne's War on the sill; sea chests full of squirrel shit; calfskin logbooks detailing encounters with storms off Cape Horn and run-ins with the native people of Sin Jamaica. Along the hewn oak beam, over a hundred corks had been nailed to mark marriages, deaths, and New Year's Eves spent freezing by the fireplace.

Uncle Alden, who built uncomfortable chairs out of ash, which he offered at prices that successfully deterred their purchase, and my cousins—a couple of local teachers, a boatbuilder, and an organic farmer—had long feared that my sister, at first some kind of banker and now I didn't know what, would financially pick them off from her river-view condo in Manhattan and one day rebuild our sagging island house into a summer retreat for megalomaniacs. They would see my grandfather's announcement as part of my sister's scheme.

"Okay," my sister said, smiling. She raised her tennis racket and excused herself. For years she'd been the least-liked member of the family, but now that my grandfather had said he would leave the house to me, I figured the target might shift. Melissa caught my eye, and I signaled that I'd see her outside.

With everyone else gone from the room, my grandfather took out his pipe and clamped it between his teeth. The pipe was empty. He no longer smoked, not since he'd been diagnosed with emphysema fifteen years ago. He had probably not, as he claimed, cured himself of the disease, though as he bore down on one hundred, he had no trouble biking around on his motor-assisted adult tricycles—one for the island, one for town.

I had not grown healthier with age either. I chose this moment to perform a self-check, which my fiancée, in her second year of

graduate study in social work at the University of Arizona, had
taught me to do. I could barely keep my eyes open. In response to
stress, I always fell asleep. On a good day the medications I took
rendered me as lethargic as a snake digesting a gopher. If not for
my job and Melissa, I would've slept fourteen hours a day. I did not
feel up to the challenge of whatever my grandfather and my sister
had in mind for the weekend, and I had to will myself not to climb
the stairs and lie down in my old room.

"You can't know what it's like," my grandfather said to me under his breath.

"What?"

"For everyone to want you dead."

"No one wants you dead," I lied.

"Bullshit," he said. "But I appreciate the sentiment." He tapped
the empty bowl of his pipe on his palm as if to clear out yesterday's ashes.

I found Melissa outside talking to my braless cousin Bayberry, who
leaned against my grandfather's island tricycle and raised her eyebrows. "Act One! Tomorrow, Act Two. Who is this man your sister's
marrying? William St. . . . ."

"William Rollo St. Launceston," I said, reluctantly supporting
the illusion that a real wedding would go down in the morning.
No one else in the family knew that my sister and Rollo had already married at a secluded Maui beach a year ago. I hadn't been
invited—no one had.

"That's a beautiful necklace," Bayberry said as she leaned into
Melissa's personal space and squinted at her Our Lady of Guada-
lupe pendant.

"Thanks," Melissa said, and took a wary step back. I said goodbye
to Bayberry, took Melissa by the hand, and led us down the trail.
The island house was full, and the horsehair mattresses contained
the bones of too many chipmunks, so I had reserved a hotel. At
the Holiday Inn in Bath, I could scald all the stupid things I'd
heard today out of my brain. We reached the dock and boarded
my grandfather's skiff to shuttle the quarter mile to the mainland.
Sitting across from each other on bench seats, I was reminded, not
for the first time, of the disconcertingly erotic fact that we were
the same height, our shoulders the same width. Melissa had the

softest skin on the planet, her face framed by a precision-cut bob feathering in the breeze.

On the way up the hill to the parking lot, Melissa touched my arm with the tips of her fingers and asked me if I was going to throw up. I had thrown up the month before, for no apparent reason, at a party hosted by a friend of hers. Ever since then she'd been waiting for it to happen again. Maybe I would; I didn't know. I turned to face the island, a low fir-topped mound ringed by jagged granite and dotted by shingled cottages. Every winter when I was young and my grandfather and I motored over from the mainland to fell a Christmas tree, steam poured off the ocean into the frigid air.

"It's mine," I said, a mostly false statement, and pointed to the island. "I mean, not the whole thing," I confessed. Though my ancestor John Josiah Howland and his wife, Fear Chipman, had swindled the island away from the Abenaki chief Mowhitiwormet, "Robinhood," in a 1640 land deal worth a hogshead of rum and twelve pumpkins, over the years each generation lost a few acres. Now we owned only the farmhouse and the field sloping to the shore.

Melissa, not my real fiancée, not in the sense of someone who'd agreed to marry me, looked at my forehead. Did she know how I was feeling? That how I felt depended on how she felt? When I'd asked her to marry me two months ago and she'd parried with, "I need to think about that," I thought the trip to Maine might bring us closer together. And I *had* felt closer during the flight and the car ride up from Boston, so close that I had unconsciously shifted her answer into the "yes" box. Now, though, I didn't feel close at all. Maybe she would be impressed that I was—or soon would be —owner of the last few acres of the family homestead.

On the mainland, after we buckled ourselves into the Kia, I hit the gas, and we shot out of the parking space. Under stress I sometimes exhibited diminished motor control. I wondered if I was relapsing into what Melissa had once called a "disorganized attachment disorder," DAD, the description for which she'd read aloud from the DSM-IV. I did feel "systematically disregulated"; also I felt "excessively friendly" and wished to continue expressing these feelings "in a syrupy, bizarre, ineffectual manner."

"We're not rich, you know," I said. I had jumped the reality

track on the way up from Boston and now clung to the facts as a
nostrum for all my natural impulses. "My sister and I grew up with
my grandparents. My great-grandparents lost everything in the
dowel factory in Lewiston. Anyway, you can't understand the family without understanding my grandfather." Neither a monarch
nor (to his great relief, so he claimed) a *Kennebec Journal* "Local
Person of Note," he was a retired high school teacher in Vaughan,
a town twenty-five miles upriver from the island. To us he was the
Old Man: the name, the dog, the cane, the Silver Star nailed to the
wall in the back bathroom, and, of course, the title to the house on
the island, the last thing of value owned by our family.

She put her hand on my knee. "You have boats," she said. "You
are people with boats and an island with your name on it. Where I
come from, people have broken cars." Melissa had grown up with
a single mother in Douglas, Arizona, a place I privately thought
of as a scary DMZ filled with guard towers, giant Border Patrol
assault vehicles, and attack helicopters roaming the lunar border
with Mexico.

"But we had broken cars too," I said.

"Don't worry. I'm impressed."

"I don't want you to be *impressed*," I lied.

"This is my New England vacation. A break from the heat." Melissa traveled through time like an emotional space station that
could go years without resupply. "Your eyes are weirdly geckoed,"
she said.

"I don't feel so good."

Melissa covered her left ear. "Stop shouting," she said. "I'm sitting right next to you." (I also sometimes lost control of "my volume," as Melissa put it.)

"Several weeks ago, when I asked you . . . When I said I wanted
to . . . When I told you I . . ." I was trying not to say *love* or *propose,*
two words she objected to. "I just hope . . ."

"To eat a lobster," Melissa said. "Me. *I* do. Before I get another
boat ride." We stared out our windows for a while. "It's exciting
that the house is really yours, John Howland. Of Howland Island."

This sounded better than John Howland, adjunct community
college instructor. Back in Arizona, where no one gave a shit about
New England, I could forget all that John Howland stuff, but here
the name John Howland also belonged to my grandfather and his
father, et cetera, in a more or less unbroken line of Johns going

back twelve generations to the John Howland who accidentally fell off the stern of the *Mayflower* in a storm, but thank God somehow managed to pull himself back aboard before landing at Plymouth so the rest of us could someday exist.

"Whenever I'm back here I feel as if I should be doing something more important with my life," I said.

"Why, because you think you're more important than people who do what you do?"

Melissa didn't understand, but I was encouraged by the way her gaze lingered on my jawline as we drove to Bath. When we first started dating, she claimed to admire my jawline. Now that I owned property, maybe we could have little John Howlands, what my grandfather had always expected. According to Melissa, I often felt so much that I had difficulty intuiting how other people felt, which didn't bother her, she claimed, because she didn't believe in codependency—in taking care of my feelings or telling me how to live—even though this was the point of a relationship? To become less partial? The other night I'd dreamed that she and I were hiking in the Tucson Mountains when a giant tire—the kind used on mega dump trucks—bowled over a rock, picked her up, and carried her surprised face down the side of a cactus-covered valley. I hadn't told her about the dream yet, probably because I thought she would say that the tire represented a wedding ring and that the dream expressed my rage at her lack of desire for a conventional commitment, which I thought I wanted but she claimed I didn't. At least not really.

In the morning I motored us back across to the island. Melissa held our hotel coffees and asked me when she would get to meet my parents. My parents hadn't been invited to the wedding. I'd told her several times that when my sister and I were young my parents alternated living in the house and with their back-to-the-land friends who "farmed" on a commune. After my mother ended up leaving for Mexico and my father for Oregon, my sister and I moved in with my grandparents. I hoped that reminding Melissa of my tragic story (that my parents had abandoned us) would keep me in the running as someone who had suffered enough for her to take seriously.

On the island dock, we sipped our coffee. Melissa gazed at the distant ocean with, I hoped, an Austenian longing for a life part-

ner. All evidence to the contrary, Melissa longed for normal attachments. I *knew* she did. She had a tiny mole on her chin I liked to
touch with the tip of my tongue while we made love. She pointed
to a lobster boat loaded with nervous New York types leaving the
mainland's dock and heading to another, larger, private dock my
sister had arranged to borrow on the island.

"Is that a real lobster boat? Are there lobsters in that boat right
now?" she asked. I answered that it probably was real even though
half the workboats around the bay were fitted with lawn chairs
rather than pot haulers. I pictured the two of us pulling up to the
island dock in our own lobster boat (one that had been used for
actual lobstering) with two kids sitting in the stern. We'd walk up
to the house—*our house*—carrying those canvas tote bags summer
people loved so much. In the fall we'd bake fish and play cribbage
in front of the fire at night.

As we walked up the ramp, Melissa said, "Let me ask this: Do
you think your sister will be mad that I didn't wear a dress?"

The idea of inheriting the house and the occasion of the wedding, fake or not, had gacked me out a bit. My thoughts unspooled
faster than I could gather them up, and I was suddenly, unjustifi-
ably elated and optimistic about the future. "I think I want us to
move here and have a family." I stopped walking next to one of the
graveyards filled with my ancestors.

Melissa seemed to be considering the pine trees and the field
up ahead.

"This is my home," I continued. My eyelashes Velcroed together.
I hadn't realized how much I had missed it.

"You know," Melissa said with a grin that reminded me too
much of how my sister had looked at my grandfather the day before, "you're not a nine-year-old."

"I need to talk about our relationship," I said.

"You mean the relationship you could just as easily have with
a life-sized cutout of my body?" She widened her eyes and dangled her elbows in the air like a marionette. I didn't laugh. "Don't
worry." She sighed. "I like you. You can be fun."

"I'm not *fun*," I said. I wanted her to understand I was angry,
but I didn't want to take any responsibility for being angry.

"Not right now, you're not." She began walking again. "Look,
John, in your own selfish way, you really care about people. And

you can be more generous than me without meaning to. I admire that about you."

"You do?"

"My friend has a theory about why I like you." The apostrophe forming in the corner of her mouth forewarned me: either she was about to joke with me or say something depressing. Or both.

"You had something I never had."

"What's that?"

"A childhood." She stopped again. "And this is where it happened," she said, pointing to Devereux's Field. The grass leaned over in the breeze. When I turned back to her, she was no longer grinning. "It's exactly what I pictured. You want to live here?" she said, a small crack opening in her normally steady voice. "What're we going to do for money, raise sheep?"

What *were* we going to do for money? I had no answer. I could barely pay my rent in Tucson, and I had no job in Maine. I couldn't afford to maintain a falling-down island farmhouse or even pay the taxes. If I tried to sell it, no one in the family would speak to me again. If we moved here, Melissa and I wouldn't be able to feed ourselves, never mind a child. The house only had hay, seaweed, and horsehair for insulation against the winter storms.

"Do you think they will serve lobster at the reception?" Melissa asked.

My sister stalked out of the trees on the trail and, pointing at me, started speaking while she was still fifty yards away.

"I need you to talk to our grandfather," she said. "He's out there in the woods somewhere like a rabid animal. We can't have him crawling into that hole. You don't think he'll really get in the hole, do you? You are in charge of the Old Man." Now that she was standing before me, she poked my chest. To most of the family, my sister represented Greed, Ambition, Aggression. Striving constituted an unforgivable sin to those of us who believed ourselves chosen a priori and therefore beyond the indignity of scrabbling after the very things without which, of course, one found it difficult to feel chosen.

She looked over her shoulder. "Most of the family except the hippies have decided to boycott the wedding because they think we're pulling some kind of power move to take over the house."

"Did you say *we* just now?" I asked.

"Everyone knows Mainwaring is actually gay, and Stoughton's already got two daughters and had the snip, I think. You're the last John Howland, and not only that: you're the last chance at *another* John Howland—not that I care. But if the Old Man gives the house to everyone, it will be sold, because everyone but me lives on minimum fucking wage. My name should be John Howland, for Christ's sake. That would solve a lot of problems." Like the Old Man, my sister had gone to Harvard. He talked slowly, with silent *r*'s, while she (when she wasn't cursing like a fisherman) usually talked rapidly in lilting hyper-articulate blocks of prose.

"Didn't your grandfather just give the house to John?" Melissa asked, and looped her arm around mine.

My sister, her bright blond hair twitching, looked briefly surprised that Melissa had spoken. Though physically smaller, my sister radiated a sense of imminent invasion. "But he can't afford to pay the taxes on the house, can he?" my sister said, "so he'll need a partner."

When she moved to Manhattan—where, the rest of us were constantly reminded, the brightest people on the planet convened to congratulate each other—my sister lost interest in "Poison Oak Rock," as she called the island, because our Salem witch trials history didn't play well. But in the last few years trends had shifted. Now Martha Stewart, born Martha Kostyra, didn't cut it in an authenticity-scarce environment. My sister, Bridget Anne Hutchinson Howland, eleventh great-granddaughter of persecuted religious fanatic Anne Hutchinson and twelfth great-granddaughter of *Mayflower* passenger John Howland, was a veritable *sui generis* snow leopard. I couldn't listen to my sister talk about her business (or about anything, really), but maybe she had a point about the house—I *would* need a partner. My sister and I would own the house fifty-fifty, and she would pay Melissa and me to be caretakers. It could work. We could blow insulation into the walls.

"When you talk to my friends during the wedding," my sister said with her eyes fluttering closed, "about yourself, say less. Professor Howland, maybe. Leave out your trips to rehab, the community college stuff, that you live in the third world of our own country." She looked at Melissa for a moment and rolled her eyes so quickly she might have only blinked. Then she pivoted and, legs scissoring, stalked across the field toward the house.

"I do feel sorry for you," Melissa said, and put her hand on my back. "Having to grow up with that."

"She wasn't always this way," I explained. "Do you really feel sorry for me?"

"Not really," she said, which could mean she really did, or it meant nothing. We walked toward the house. It was a major concession for her to say she felt sorry for me, even as a joke.

To the right of the house, Uncle Alden and my cousin Mainwaring stood with their hands in their pants pockets looking into the hole. A dog belonging to one of the wedding guests had fallen in. As far as I could tell, Uncle Alden kept promising to help but then continued to study the situation instead. The woman who seemed to own the dog repeatedly reached down but then, from obvious fear of falling in, backed away before she could grab the dog's collar.

"What did your sister say to the Old Man?" Uncle Alden whispered to me. Melissa pointed to where she would wait for me in the field and kept walking.

"Nothing."

"Bullshit," he said, still whispering. Uncle Alden pulled the tie out of his ponytail and tucked gray hair behind his ear. Strands fell beside his face and stuck to his lips. Uncle Alden had been doing a lot to take care of my grandfather, and he clearly hoped he might inherit the house. Probably he should have.

"I've made a lot of mistakes," he said as he pulled me aside. I'd never understood what about me inspired family members to blurt out confessions. "It had something to do with psychological history. With *my* grandfather. We weren't supposed—we weren't *allowed*—to succeed at anything. Do you know what I mean?" I nodded, thinking of his uncomfortable chairs and the year he'd spent in the brig for refusing to cut his hair and go to Vietnam. Then I suddenly worried about the consequences of Melissa not having a good time and maybe not getting a lobster today. I looked around, but she had disappeared.

"I think the Old Man might've really lost his mind," my uncle said.

"It could be."

"He shouldn't be living in that big house in Vaughan by himself or coming down to the island alone. And this business with the hole in the ground and giving the house to you."

"What am I supposed to say? The house doesn't belong to me."

"He needs our help." Uncle Alden laid his fingers on my arm and left them there. I didn't know what to do—we didn't really touch each other in our family. "But he doesn't know how to ask for it," my uncle said. I thought of the story my grandmother had told of how my grandfather had jumped over the side of the Higgins boat at Omaha and advanced up the beach with the tide by keeping his head under the surface of the water except to come up for air.

"Okay," I said.

"So you'll talk to him about it?"

"Let's see what happens," I said, and removed my arm from his grasp. Before he could touch me again, I strode recklessly toward a crowd of men in the field with wind-fairing hairdos. Hired people in black outfits rushed around with trays of champagne. Except for the mosquitoes, my sister had King Canuted the perfect conditions—bright blue sky with a few decorative cotton-candy wisps, the ocean covered with tinsel sparkles. Barren islands guarded the mouth of the bay, Hendricks Head Lighthouse right in the center of the view like a Hopper painting.

I saw Melissa at the far end of the field leaning against a tree and talking to a guy whose bald head shone in the light. Without eyebrows, he looked like a cross between a harbor seal and a penis. The guy before the guy she was with before me had been bald. I stopped in my tracks and watched her face and body language. Her curved lips (amazing lips!) pursed and her canted hip bumped slightly against the bark.

My grandfather stood at the edge of the woods with his porkpie hat pulled low over his brow. The cane at the end of his extended arm looked like a metal rod supporting a statue. The way he held his head with his chin high and his shoulders squared reminded me of a picture I'd seen of him standing next to Theodore Roosevelt III—both of them with white face paint, blond wigs, and long dresses—playing "chorus girls" in the Hasty Pudding Club's 1934 production of *Hades! The Ladies!*

My uncle was right—my grandfather needed our help now, and I was the one he disliked the least. I waved to him and headed in his direction but immediately sensed someone stalking me. My sister's fiancé called my name. His friends called him the Rollo-coaster; his ancestors, I suddenly recalled, had colonized Tasmania. Twenty years my sister's senior, he wheeled across the field on his springy legs. His pale, sparrow-thin thighs and little kangaroo paunch of a belly, the incredibly erect posture flying the banner of his bright smile as he rushed to catch up with his projection of himself. I hoped he might sail right past me. Instead he took me in his arms, kissed my cheek, and in his unidentifiable accent asked how was I *keeping* and where were my *digs* these days?

He seemed pretty relaxed for someone about to perpetrate a fake wedding. Did Rollo know that I knew that the legal wedding had already occurred? I could picture his laser-shorn, hairless body gliding through the soft air above Maui's white sand beach. Even if I someday had money, I would never be happy enough to justify the expense of going there.

"I love that this place belongs to you now—the whole thing!" he said, beaming. "What are you going to do with it?" He gave my shoulder a solid squeeze. I'd never experienced the bonding be-tween men who owned land. I stretched out my neck and surveyed the field. The house only came with four acres, but Rollo didn't know that. Or maybe he did.

"I think I'll live here—take up residence with Melissa," I said. I hadn't told Melissa that there was no electricity, no plumbing, no bathroom, but I could picture us drinking coffee by the kitchen window next to the stove as freezing rain sheeted over the glass. We'd pick apples from the orchard and bake pies and cobbler. Melissa would wear Irish sweaters and let her hair grow out.

"Your sister's talking about some kind of partnership with the house here. I like the sound of that. I think you and I have a lot in common. That's what your sister says. What do you think?"

I'd always wanted to have things in common with people, so I nodded.

"I'm pretty sure she wants to tear down that shack," he said, giving a quick nod toward the place my ancestors had built with nothing but an ax and their own hands, "or"—he air-quoted his pretend-bride-to-be—"'burn it to the ground. Build something that isn't held together with mouse shit.'" He closed one eye and, aiming his arms so that I could take a look too, framed the old farmhouse with his hands. "Something three stories? With cantile-vered glass? Maybe steel on the north side. Something, you know, that takes advantage of the incredible light here. I'll text you what I have in mind."

The Rollocoaster peeled away. The ceremony was about to start.
As I headed for the spot where I had last seen my grandfather, I
felt a huge hole open up in my chest, and some unknown essential
parts of myself spilled into the grass.

I couldn't partner with my sister, that carpetbagger. My grandfather wasn't even dead yet, and she was planning to torch the place.
Even if I convinced her to save the house, she'd want to build a
conference center next door, or a helipad, or there'd be product
shoots for Martha Kostyra every other weekend. Rollo would be
my master.

I smelled champagne in the sea air. I hadn't had a drink—or
swallowed any unprescribed pills—in five years, but I also hadn't
been to an AA meeting in over half that time. I rarely, if ever,
thought about drinking or pills, even when Melissa and I occasionally went to bars socially, which we sometimes did, with her friends
to hear music.

Where was Melissa? Melissa, who resisted self-indulgence, who
believed in kindness for people who deserved it and in justice for
those who did not. When one of the men Melissa worked with at
the shelter in downtown Tucson killed himself, she came home
crying—the first time I'd ever seen her cry. After I cooked her supper and ran her a bath, I sat next to the tub while she soaked and
eventually asked if she felt better. She shook her head. "It doesn't
matter how I feel," she said.

As I passed by a table, my hand scooped up a flute of champagne and emptied the glass into the back of my throat. Before I
realized what I'd done, I started to sway drunkenly, even though I
wasn't drunk. I wasn't even pleasantly dizzy. Five years of sobriety
down the drain. I half expected my head to explode or the grass
under my feet to spontaneously combust. But the sky looked the
same as it had a few minutes before. I picked up another flute. A
fuse had been lit. Either I'd go looking for Oxy when we got back
to Tucson or I wouldn't.

Sipping, I took stock of the house, the glazing peeling off the
window mullions. Feeling sick to my stomach, I poured out the
half-empty flute. With the sound of the minister's voice following
me, I circled behind the house to look for my grandfather. Along
the forest floor, a new generation of trees had grown knee-high
where light filtered through the canopy. The dew clinging to the
branches stained my pants as I ran my palm over the soft feathers

of the needles. I remembered having walked this way many times, at every stage of my life. The tickling thrum that ran from my hand up my arm and along my back, the rich smell of pine sap and musty loam and salt air—other than the height of the trees, everything here had remained the same. I paused at the overgrown cellar hole, where one of my great-grandfathers had had his scalp removed by an Abenaki, and where his two teenage sons, returning from fishing to find their father, mother, and younger brother lying dead, shot two of the Abenakis, hacked another to death, and chased off the one survivor. They turned in the three Abenaki scalps to the Massachusetts government and put the money toward materials to build a schooner.

I reached the far side of the house and spotted the caretaker's truck next to the grave my grandfather had paid someone to dig. As promised, my grandfather lay in the bottom with his arms crossed over his chest. Sitting on his stomach looking up at me, Julia licked her gray muzzle and eyeballed my empty hands. My grandfather's nostrils flared and his eyes shot open—pulsing blue crystals in bloodshot yokes.

"John," he said. "Goddamnit!" He seemed angry with me, presumably for interrupting his death. "It's not working," he said, and gazed up at me like a distressed child. He lifted Julia under an arm and tried to pull himself out of the hole with a pine limb. I offered my hand, but he slapped it away. When he started to fall backward, I wrapped my arms around his chest.

"Lift me up, for God's sake."

I planted my heels and struggled backward. We hovered over the hole for a moment and tumbled against a tree with our arms wrapped around each other, my face pressed against his cheek. He groaned as if I'd just stomped on his toe and scrambled away from me on all fours to lean against the caretaker's truck.

"I'm here for you," I said.

My grandfather and I lay on our sides facing each other. People in our field were quiet. The surf splashed with every other breath. The tendons and muscles in my lower back had seized, and a gash below my elbow bled onto my white shirt. I hadn't noticed the injury when my grandfather and I fell over, but I felt it now.

"I'm on a lot of medication," I confessed.

"Does it help?" my grandfather asked.

The wedding guests started to clap and leave their seats. As a way, I sensed, of not looking at me, my grandfather raised his bony hand and shaded his eyes to survey the crowd. Women in ankle-length dresses and men in dark suits spilled over the grass.

"Who are all those goddamned people?" he demanded.

"It's a wedding," I said. "Bridget . . ."

"Yes. But who *are* they? Where the hell did they come from?" The muscles twisted under the creases and folds of his face, and I felt what he felt—revulsion at these strangers. "Jesus," he said, "what am I going to do?"

I turned away from him to face the beach, where four kids played on a pile of driftwood. Sandy-haired, somewhere between the ages of five and eight, they must've come with the guests. A woman my age, their mother or maybe a nanny, sat on a rock watching over them. My feeling that they trespassed had less to do with my inability to recognize them or that the beach belonged to our family than the sense that they threatened to eclipse my memories of being their age. They removed their shoes, rolled up their pants, and inched forward as a group into the shallows.

Wheels crunched over branches—my grandfather on his tricycle, slipping through the trees. I rose to my feet and jogged down the trail after him. With his cane stuck in the holster, he pedaled along the slope of Devereux's Field and turned left on the trail to the landing. Julia sat in the rear basket watching me slowly gain ground. As I pulled even with him, he looked through the trees to the west—in the direction of the car he wasn't licensed to use anymore, his home on Second Street in Vaughan where he'd grown up, and all the people he'd known since birth, most of whom were now in the ground at Oak Hill Cemetery.

"I don't want the house," I called to him.

"The house is mine!" he roared at me. In taking his eyes off the path, he almost veered into the ditch and had to slow to regain control. For a moment I thought he might stop, but then the tricycle sped up and bumped over the ruts, leaving me behind.

I recovered my breath and shuffled the rest of the way to the landing, where I found the tricycle ditched next to a tree. Across the channel, my grandfather tied up to the mainland dock and hefted Julia out of the skiff. The whole process took him much longer than it once had. He wrapped his arm around the cleat and pulled himself facedown onto the planks. Julia licked his cheek. When he didn't move for more than a minute, I thought maybe he had accomplished his goal after all. A moment later, though, he pushed himself to his knees and rose to his feet.

From my right, I heard Melissa call my name. She was standing on the boathouse's porch.

"I couldn't find you at the ceremony," she said, "so I went looking."

Her leather-soled shoes dangling from one hand, she seemed to float over the rocky ground as she drew near. Her skin pulsed around a mosquito bite almost exactly in the middle of her forehead. She was beautiful, perfect.

"Can we go to the reception now? I'm hungry," she said.

"Are you going to marry me?" I said, my voice rising in my throat. She grimaced and lifted my elbow to look at the cut; the bleeding had stopped, but my arm still stung.

Across the water, Julia barked at my grandfather's side. He took one excruciating step, rested over the railing with his mouth open, took another step, and paused to look back at me.

"Melissa," I said, my face growing hot, "what am I going to do?"

"You'll live," Melissa said as she let go of my arm and laid her cool palm against my cheek, "just like the rest of us."

MICHAEL BYERS

Sibling Rivalry

FROM *Lady Churchill's Rosebud Wristlet*

TEN YEARS AFTER the one-child law went into effect the synths
were a common sight. In the Burkharts' neighborhood the Hughes
brand had become the most popular and that's what the Burkharts
had, the Hughes Fully Human: superhigh-mobility musculature,
self-growing chassis, Real AI, and it was just sort of amazing to
watch them change as they grew, from the day you brought them
home from the Birthing Unit (along with the two blue nylon suitcases full of accessories and equipment), amazed at how real she
looked, but what else would she be but real? And then a few years
later this daughter of yours was clinging to your pantleg outside
the worn blue doors of the kindergarten wing on the first day of
school, afraid to go in, her hair shining in the September sun, her
older brother standing in line expressing an airy unconcern, back-
packs everywhere, everyone knowing (mostly via conversation, it
was very hard to tell just by looking) who was and who wasn't but
you didn't *make* such distinctions out loud, it wasn't polite, and
in fact in some sense it really didn't *matter.* Your emotional centers were fooled by the physical imitation, and the AI was the real
thing, and the growth was to human scales—so what *was* the difference, anyway? Well, what? It became a philosophical question
more than anything, or at least a question to gossip about, which
people were always happy to do.

But people had always gossiped about their kids.

As for Peter Burkhart—well, by now he just thought of Melissa
as their kid (and it had happened very quickly, she was theirs to
love, theirs to keep safe and healthy, to teach right from wrong).

She was a good girl. She resembled them strongly (and after the endless scans, she had better), she played the piano pretty well for a now seven-year-old but she was no genius, as none of her forebears had been, musically speaking. Loved reading, like both her parents. Great at the monkey bars. (And what an animal pleasure they got when they watched her swinging out, a pleasure in her grace, "*I* used to be able to do that," Julie said, watching, protective, as was still sometimes their habit, discounting in advance any sense that their daughter *wasn't human, wasn't theirs,* although of course she wasn't, not in the way their parents and everyone in the world until this generation had experienced *human* and *theirs* . . .)

A flaring release, and Melissa would land springily on the wood chips, already running toward the swings.

"That too," Julie said, "although maybe not that well."

And Melissa would veer toward them, tilting a little, hurl herself into his wife's arms and croon, "Maamaa!"

Then scramble to be down and off again, just like her brother Matt had done a few years earlier.

They had worn the clips for the two-week remote brain scan, clumsy and a little painful at times, the procedure enough to turn away some people, in fact, but that was all right, the thinking being that if you couldn't meet even this minimum threshold of commitment you shouldn't have a child anyway. Of any kind. Three days of almost total immobility at the end. And beyond this all the *details,* your own childhood medical records, your baby pictures, your old googletracks, all your tweets, wads, gremlins—basically everything you could gather. She was theirs. From and of them. And, like any kid, she was also entirely herself, closed, secretive when she wanted to be, inventing herself as she grew older. Assembling herself from the parts at hand. She liked poetry, recently had been reciting "To An Old Woman" while jumping rope on the front sidewalk. She had recently developed a sort of a flopping, galumphing personal style—full of dramatic hurling of herself into chairs, big sweeps of the hair, the habit of marching into a room to deliver a proclamation, i.e., "Matt—is—*bothering me!* And I *told* him, *nicely,* to stop *jumping out and scaring me,* and then he *keeps doing it!*"

Whereupon Matt would leak weepily into view, eleven years old and still prone to tears, and say he didn't *mean* to, and he *didn't*—

"Yes you *did!*"

(Sweep dramatically away.)

As far as Peter could tell, and Julie agreed, Matt and Melissa related just like normal siblings—loved, hated, relied on each other, took each other for granted.

Like normal.

She had aversions. She hated lightning and thunder. She had tempers. She could put up a hell of a fight too, over nothing, or seemingly nothing, smashed back in the red corduroy chair in the corner of the bedroom, knees drawn up to her chest, avoiding bath time: "I'm not *dirty*."

"Everybody takes a bath every now and then, even when they're not dirty."

"*No,*" she said.

He came forward into the room. She scowled and pushed herself deeper into the chair.

"Mel, there's going to be a timeout," he said, "unless you come now. And either way you're going to end up having a bath."

"I don't *need* one!" she shouted. "It's not fair!"

"How is it not fair?"

"Because if I don't need one, why do I have to have one!"

He came forward and swept her up wriggling under his arm (she felt different from Matt, the weight was distributed internally a little differently, how he couldn't quite say—or maybe it was just the difference between boys and girls) and carried her into the bathroom. The water was already pounding into the tub and when he set her down she bolted for the door again. He blocked it with his knee and she began to flail at him with her fists.

It was often useful in such a moment, he and Julie had found, to switch horses in midstream, as it were, and Julie now appeared from down the hall, a pencil in her hair. Wordlessly she took her place beside him.

"Doesn't want a bath," he said.

Girl stuff, maybe, he thought belatedly.

"What's up, Matt?" he said as the boy came edging down the hall.

"She's, like, crazy," Matt told him.

"You used to have tantrums," Peter said, "just like that."

"Well," Matt scoffed, "please accept my apologies."

Like normal.

*

So apparently here they all were: in the future, suddenly. Although
the laws were still all confused. It was a patchwork, a Fully Human's exact legal status varying from state to state, so when they
all drove to Yosemite and spent a week at a dude ranch, and later
hiked into Yellowstone to observe the giant sulfur-spewing foun-
tains, they had to peg several sets of documents in case they were
pulled over by any of the state patrols between Michigan and their
various destinations—prime-coded certificates of parenthood.

And of course to him and his wife and their friends all this was
all complicated and interesting, as it was to everyone their age,
because all of it had come along when they were old enough for it
to be new and strange. But they recognized too that it wouldn't be
interesting for long, not in the same way, not even to them. Synths
had existed in one way or another for almost thirty years, but only
since the one-child law had they become really common.

The Supers had been around for almost as long, although that
was a different story.

It was an interesting time to live.

His wife, in her gentle, curious, patient way, liked to think about
these things, and to talk about them with friends. Talk about them
in person, she would insist, *not* over the cookie, which meant people
came over on a Saturday, say, for an eggs-and-bagels-and-mimosas
brunch on the front porch. A throwback sort of gathering, on their
decidedly throwback porch, in their decidedly throwback neighborhood, where everyone had pitched in to mount pitons on the
telephone poles to keep the Supers out, and where, because the
house was one you tended to pass while walking up to the university, they ended up seeing people accidentally anyway, their friends
tending to accumulate here like sticks in a stream, hanging up
for a while in an eddy of wine and crackers while the kids played
whiffleball on the lawn and the girls arranged themselves in the
shady areas by the lilacs and chatted their hearts out. *Antique* in its
way, even a little self-conscious, maybe, but people were attracted
to them, he supposed, for this kind of style. But it wasn't really a
style. It was just how he and Julie liked to live.

Among their friends the question that had arisen lately was the
eventual sex lives of their children, both natural and synth. How
would you feel if your son or daughter dated someone of the opposite kind?

"I wouldn't mind if maybe they were *dating*," fat Jerry proposed from the depths of his wicker chair. "I don't know about getting *married*."

"People do it already."

"Well, I know people *do* it, Carl, I just don't really—" What was it? Emma wrinkled her nose and picked up her glass again.

Jerry said, "It's the sex thing."

Max set down his champagne flute with exaggerated, comical force. "Well, I've done it."

"Done what?"

Max lifted his chin and said, "I—have had sex—with a synth."

"Well, we know all about *you*, Max."

"With a Fully or a Semi, though," Jerry insisted.

Max said, "A Semi."

"Oh, well, who hasn't."

"I haven't!" Emma fluted, then flushed, sitting up in her chair, reaching for her glass. "Just for the record."

Max said, "Sixty-four percent have, who would admit to it."

Jerry said, "Okay, but most of those aren't Fully Humans, right, they're not old enough. How old is Chris Cope now?"

"He just turned twenty-eight, I think," Julie said.

"He turned twenty-eight on May eleventh," Max said, checking his cookie.

"So the oldest Fully Human is twenty-eight, but there's only like a hundred that're over, what, twenty-five? So it's not the same."

"I am among the sixty-four percent who have had sex with a Semi," Max announced. "And it was a success for all involved."

"Me too!" Toni grinned.

"That's only two out of, what?" Will counted. "Nine. Twenty-two percent."

"There are holdouts among us," Max said.

"Hands!" Martin insisted, his heavy brow knitting. "Show of hands."

"Truth or Dare," Toni protested, but she put her hand up. "Come *on*, you guys," she laughed. "Don't leave me alone out here."

"I've had one, once," his wife said.

"Once was enough for our Julie," Toni said, kindly.

But something complicated was rising in Julie. Peter knew what it was, and he laughed in advance. She'd never told anyone about this, as far as he knew.

"Actually"—Julie flushed—"he was a Super."

There was a clamor around the table. Laughter, exclamations. Glances at Peter. He lifted his eyebrows, shrugged, acquired his glass from the table.

"Oh my god," Toni breathed, "we have to hear about it."

"Was that before—?"

"It was before," Julie said. "Obviously. I mean, I know I'm not supposed to be the wild and crazy one"—she fingered her top button—"but . . ."

"When? Where?" Toni pressed a hard hand into her thigh. "We have to hear every detail."

"No!" She laughed.

He had heard the story, of course, long ago. Why was she telling people now?

She cast him a secret, giddy, cringing look.

"She's very nice about it," Peter said. "She never mentions anything about it to me, you know, when, say, there's a call for comparisons."

His wife laughed again, grateful to him. "That is *not* what I wanted to talk about!" she exclaimed. "I wanted to talk about how, you know—like, all our kids will just have grown up with one another and they'll think it's perfectly normal, just like we grew up with—you know, whatever."

"Like cookies," Peter said.

"Like cookies." She smiled again. "Which was the same thing for our parents. I mean, sort of for us, but not really. I just think being conscious of what's new and what's not, I just think that's—it's a good thing to be conscious of it, and to make choices."

"That's *not* fair," Toni groaned. "You can't just say you had sex with a Super and change the *subject*."

But Julie only pursed her lips in comical daintiness and said nothing.

A clutch of shrieking children stampeded past the porch.

Emma said, volunteering, "Well, to your rescue slightly, about cookies, my mom still complains about hers, like, how do I turn it off? And I'm like, Mom, you're not supposed to turn it *off*, that's the *point*."

"Your mother likes to complain," Will said.

"My parents *still* don't have cookies," Julie said. "I mean, you know, they're sort of hippies."

"Like mother, like daughter," Max suggested.

"Well!" Julie flushed again. So pretty, with her swept blond hair, her air of delighted embarrassment. "Like, none of this stuff you actually *need,* we've made it *this* far. My mom still has an actual phone. Sometimes she still sends me *texts.*"

"Well, so that's what I mean, that's what it is, it's just a generational thing. Eventually the question of synth and human will just —just be completely . . . normal."

"It *is* normal," Toni said, a hard edge coming through. She had gone for the champagne bottle twice now. Toni and Max had three kids, two synth, both boys. "I mean, look at us! How many—" She counted with a long fingernail. "Seven at this table alone!"

It wasn't normal, though. They all knew it.

It wasn't normal *yet.*

"I can't believe your mom still has a phone," Will said.

"I hardly ever hear you on the cookie," Toni scolded. "You're really quiet."

"I know. I don't use it outbound very much. Just to keep track of the kids. And even then, it's—I have it really low."

Another current went around the table as everyone considered what this meant. Everyone *said* they kept it low, of course, and had just about *everything* filtered, but something about his wife's sweet, slightly awkward clarity made it clear to everyone that she meant just what she said. And it was true. It was true for him too. They were probably a little self-satisfied about it. But this too was how they liked it. He and Julie had theirs set to alert only when the fear or sadness readings went above a certain register, or when a certain pain threshold was crossed, and they could eyekey the map anytime they wanted to see where the kids were. But that was it. No AI readings of their thoughts, no anticipation measures. And the communication went only one way, from kids to parents. No father's voice in the head, no mother's cooing concerns.

Toni said, "I wish I could do that. I mean, you guys are so cool, you're all, you're very *classic.* That's just totally classic. But I just, I'm addicted. Like right now, I'm getting a wad right now. Oh my god. Oh my god!"

They all leaned forward as her eyes widened.

Toni gave a bark of disbelieving laughter. "Oh my god. Jenny Larsen just saw Harry Hewitt kissing some skinny bitch in a parking lot!"

The group erupted as the news came across. Peter looked down the table at his wife, who was looking back at him. A look of resignation. But she set her glass on the table with a tidy click and, brightly, began to talk as well.

Well, everyone suspected Harry Hewitt had been having an affair, but nobody had managed to get a glimpse of the girl until now. Her name was Cindy Simmons. Seen in gremlin she was young, very skinny, but decidedly *not* a beauty (big teeth, too narrow a head, really thin mean eyebrows). This was interesting, because Harry's wife, Theresa, *was* very pretty. The thinking first was that maybe Theresa hadn't been having sex with Harry or that he wanted something slender and young to hold in his hands, or that the opportunity had simply presented itself and he hadn't resisted. Everyone was delighted to have something to talk about, and for one memorable day Theresa Hewitt opened her feed to everyone and didn't tell Harry and everybody lurked around for a while, and it turned out the Hewitts indeed hadn't had sex *for two years* and it was because Harry wouldn't get a TAP test after he'd come back from China *twice* without using a scrubber, because of the presumption of guilt it implied, and then everyone started to feel uneasy, and actually sorry for Harry, and people left the feed and made guilty noises of discomfort and talked about other things, the progress of the school play, etc. And then a few days later Theresa came on and apologized to everyone and to Harry, and announced they were going into counseling.

"Grotesque," Julie said, kneading some pizza dough.

Peter had followed the whole business with a mostly clinical interest; he neither liked Harry nor wanted to sleep with Theresa (or for that matter with Cindy Simmons), so he was really just interested in how badly the couple was going to treat one another in public. And even that was a little prurient of him, he supposed. "Yeah," he said. "It's amazing anyone can stay friends with anybody after a while."

"That's true. Although actually most people are pretty decent."

"That's true too," he noted. "Although everybody has their silences."

"Well, *yes*." His wife blushed a little.

"Well, not *everybody*."

"No, but then you wish they *would*." She smiled. "Some people I just—" She held up two floury hands as Matt came sailing through the kitchen with a paper airplane.

"Right, and even this, I mean it's his business."

"Yes." She sighed.

Silently, through the cookie, he asked her, *Why did you mention the Super?*

She smiled and produced a little shrug and said, "I wanted to tell them something they hadn't heard before, and tell them in person."

He let that sit for a while.

"Why don't we just stop?" he suggested, after a minute. "Turn them off."

"Turn them off and then what?"

"I don't know," he said, a thrill rising in him. "Call each other."

She laughed, looked up from the counter. "I don't even know where my phone *is*, Peter."

"I have them," he answered, a little breathless, "in my desk. With your mom's!"

"We can text!"

"Sure," he said.

She gave the pizza dough a few more thoughtful shoves. "You mean just—actually stop stop? People'll notice."

A sudden erotic surge arose in him. "What if we just stopped completely. So it was just you and me. Nobody else."

His wife blinked as the heat climbed further into her face. She bit her lips and looked at him wide-eyed.

Easy to dismiss the idea as foolish.

Except he didn't quite. And neither did she.

It would mean being different from everybody—not just a little, not just on the edges, but really different. Cut off, the way hardly anyone was. It was still just conceivable. The way their parents might have dreamed about moving to the country to raise artisanal chickens or something.

Easy to dismiss it as a fantasy.

And then suddenly it wasn't.

Melissa's teacher this year was one Mrs. Hartley—slight, pale, worried-looking, with a high, tremulous voice that seemed to Peter to be forever on the verge of tears. But Melissa was devoted to her. At the low table in the playroom she bent over long penciled letters to her: *You are not just my teacher. You are my friend. You are a friend to so many people because you love them. You are a fair person because you are always fair to other people.*

"Mr. and Mrs. Burkhart," Mrs. Hartley said, smiling, during the parent-teacher conference, in the high-ceilinged room in the sweet old elementary school two blocks away. (Really, their life *was* a throwback.) "Your daughter is a delight."

This was always nice to hear. And yes, still a slight frisson around *daughter* and *your,* all parties concerned understanding that this was the correct terminology, all parties very conscious of having to use it properly. But Mrs. Hartley's pleasure was obviously genuine. "She's very bright, of course, as you know, and she's very socially conscious and aware, and it's just a delight to have her in the class."

"Thank you!" Julie smiled. "She's a sweetheart."

"We have a lot of children who look up to her," Mrs. Hartley went on. "She's a very natural sort of leader. Protective of herself and others."

This was going somewhere, it was plain. He said, "She can be sort of fierce, actually? When she feels slighted, I guess."

Mrs. Hartley gave them a neutral smile. "Now, what do you hear over the cookie?"

They looked at each other. Julie spoke first. "We keep it tuned pretty low."

Mrs. Hartley regarded them politely.

"We like to let her have her own space," he said.

Mrs. Hartley said, "Yes."

"So," Julie said, "we have a sense of how she's doing, generally, but we don't actually—we don't actually listen in."

"I see." Mrs. Hartley addressed her tablet. "That's fine. That's a choice."

"I mean, we have a sense, just from being with her," his wife said. "She's a very, sort of, intense kid? Like Peter said, she can be very fierce about things."

"And fairness is an issue with her," Mrs. Hartley mentioned.

"Yes," Julie nodded. "That's her thing lately."

Mrs. Hartley said nothing, considering how to proceed. And now it was plain she was older than she appeared at first, firmer, had the situation more in hand than you would think by looking at her fuzzy hair, scoop-necked dress. "Well, I think it's one of the questions we face, with an integrated classroom environment.

There are issues that come up from time to time, with feelings being hurt on either side. Your daughter is—she's wonderful. And as I say, she's very protective of her friends." She faced them now directly. "Most of her close friends, still, are, uh, synth people. Which may be the result of the numbers as they happen to be right now. Most of the girls in this class happen to be synth, and most of Melissa's friends are in the group, so it may just be one of those circumstances where the numbers have turned out in a certain way. And Melissa, good for her, is just unafraid to speak up when she feels a certain issue needs to be mentioned."

"That's Melissa," he said.

"So, for instance, we have a boy in here, a biological boy, Dimitri. You may know him."

"Oh yeah," Julie said.

"Well, Dimitri is, I will confess to you, a handful. But he's a seven-year-old boy, which, of course—well, they can be like that. And he likes to make up songs, and the songs are about, you know, who's who. Who's *what*. He probably gets some of this from home, which, that's neither here nor there, but let's just say—it's not always very friendly. And his song last week was about Melissa's friend Joanie. Who is synth. And it went, 'Joanie is a phony, Joanie is baloney.'"

"Nice," Peter said.

Mrs. Hartley gave a wry smile. "It's not his worst."

"Did you hear about this?" Julie asked him.

"Me? No."

"Okay," she said. "Me neither."

Mrs. Hartley eyed them warily. "So Melissa asked Dimitri to stop. Which had the predictable effect of encouraging him. She was very, very polite. She said, and I didn't catch the whole exchange, but it was something like, *That hurts my feelings, and it hurts Joanie's feelings, we were born like this and you were born like that, but we're all just people.*"

This was the accepted line. Again, that self-conscious steadiness.

"How'd that go?" he asked.

"Well, it didn't work. So I could see Melissa getting angry. And she dropped it for a few minutes, but I knew it wasn't quite over. But I like to let the children work out their own issues with one another, as far as possible." Mrs. Hartley licked her lips. "Then Melissa went over to him, they were in the middle of an activity in the soft corner, and she said to him, very calmly, very seriously, 'Well, you're going to die, and we're not.'"

Julie drew in a breath. "Oh god."

He ejected a single dry laugh. "Well," he said. "Okay. That's a new one."

Julie said, "I wish we'd heard about this earlier."

"Actually, I assumed you had," Mrs. Hartley said. "I assumed that line came from you."

His wife took this in. "I guess we should have been clear with you about how much we listen. That's our mistake," she said.

"This hasn't happened before," he explained.

"It's all right," Mrs. Hartley answered. She was unflustered. "I'm glad we've opened a line of communication between us. Some parents like to look in on *me*, even, from time to time, which I permit."

But he would never do that, he realized. Never in a million years.

"Melissa can be fierce," he mused. "Like I say."

"Well, she pays very close attention to the way the world works," Mrs. Hartley replied, closing her tablet. "As I say, your daughter is very smart. She's very acute. She's aware of everything. As you know." Now the teacher smiled. "She reminds me of my own daughter in that way."

The question hovered. Was Mrs. Hartley's daughter synth or human? And all three of them sensed the question hovering there, and none of them spoke to it, and then it slowly, very slowly, drifted off. Because it didn't matter. Officially, it didn't.

He could tell Julie was upset. She stirred the carrot soup with extra vigor and moved around the kitchen in brisk irritated steps. He knew enough to wait for it. Whatever she wanted to say would emerge in its own time. In bed she perched her glasses on the tip of her nose and said, finally, after several preliminary sighs and halting starts, "You know, I *remember* what it was like to be a girl." She fixed him with a fierce, protective stare. "What I wanted most of all was to have everything be *fair.*"

"Well," he said, "that's our girl."

"You know who that Dimitri kid is," she said. "He's the one who ran around the playground swinging his belt over his head and trying to hit kids with the belt buckle."

"That one! Well, good for her for standing up to him."

"Damn right good for her. I'm sorry we didn't know about it," she said. "But you know what, there's something else that mattered to me just as much as things being fair. And that was to be left *alone*."

They left the matter there for a while.

They decided against asking Melissa about any of it.

"Let her come to us," Julie said. "If she wants us to know, she'll tell us."

So in the end it was not so much a decision as a willingness to experiment—at least as they described it to themselves. Of course parenting overall could be considered, really, a haphazard, screwy, make-it-up-as-you-go experiment, done without controls, the sort of exercise that would get your funding revoked and get you called up before your departmental Internal Review Board in a second.

And your experimental subjects? Helpless captives!

Once in a while a lifestyle magazine featured things like this. People taking weeklong retreats, going completely bug-free. Exhilarating, restful, recentering, people tended to say. A new way of looking at the world! (And then, he was sure, people just went right back to their old habits.) For him, once the cookie was off —completely off—he just felt it as a weird silence. As though he had discovered some new space in the air, a new room, empty, featureless, that had been carved out of his brain.

He would turn to it and find nothing. A great quiet.

He missed it most when he was doing dumb stuff around the house—laundry, tidying up the playroom. How natural it had been to flit from music to news to the feed. The whole world carved out of his head, gone.

And when he turned to see the children, they were gone too.

They told the children the day they did it, breaking the news at dinner. Better a brief, factual statement than a drawn-out evasive one.

"What happens if I break my arm?" Matt wanted to know.

"We've got it set to alert in emergencies."

Melissa turned a forkful of pasta over. "You don't want to be bothered by us," she proposed.

"No, that's not it. We think you should be allowed to be yourself, by yourself, when you're just alone. When you're with us, you should be with us. We'll know in the case of an emergency, but that's it."

It helped that he and Julie were strange, that they had cultivated among themselves as a family a sense of strangeness. It helped the kids accept this choice as one more instance of their parents' unconventionality.

At the old settings, Matt's cookie profile had shown him to be a jumpy, easily frightened, easily moved kid, so at least once an hour had come a yellow message about him—some sudden spike in fear or surprise, vanishing as the shock passed. Activating the full-spectrum view, you would watch the levels plummet to baseline. By contrast, Melissa's readings had always been very smooth, gentle waving pulses, never too high, never too low.

And now?

Now he had to go down the hall and poke his head into their bedrooms to see what was what. And even then he never knew what he was seeing.

How had his grandparents done this, exactly?

He could tell even Julie was having trouble adjusting. At times he would enter a room and find her standing there, looking a little marooned in the middle of the carpet, holding a book or a toy and appearing visibly stilled, like a ship that had lost its engine. She would turn to him with an expression of slight disquiet.

"Hello," she would say.

"Hi."

A little laugh from her. "I didn't hear you."

"I come on little cat feet."

"This is really . . . strange," she said.

"I like it."

"You do?"

"Yeah. It's peaceful."

She blinked. "Yeah," she said.

A garden of memories came into view for him. It was as though a fog were lifting from an area of his mind and what was revealed was a place of a dozen pathways, tunnels, mazes, overgrown and wet with dew, long branches overhanging.

His room as a boy: the chrome of the spinning overhead fan, the baking heat of those days, the deep bundled comfort of the narrow bed beneath the high window, overlooking the street.

His brother, Ian, the game they had, launching a red rubber ball back and forth over the top of the house, one of them in the front yard and the other in the back, watching, watching the empty sky for the red ball to come shooting, gloriously, into view.

His mother, red hair back in its clip, seating herself on the sofa to tell him his cat Standard had been hit by a car, and her own tears leaping to her eyes.

This whole life he had lived already. As though it had been lived by another man, another boy.

"I admit," Julie said, "I get nervous when the kids are at school. I just—I want to know they're okay."

"Why wouldn't they be?"

"I know. But still."

"Don't. Don't check in on them. Let them be alone. That's what we decided."

"Okay," she said. "I *miss* them, though."

"You should," he said. "That's what we're supposed to do, we're supposed to miss them when they're gone."

"I don't like missing them."

"Me either. But it's the way it's supposed to be."

He was talking to himself too, of course. It sounded right in his own ears. It didn't make him miss them less, but it helped to say these things aloud.

"I miss you too," she said.

"I'm right here."

"You're out *there* now," she said, pointing at him. "Not in *here*."

"I miss you too," he said.

This empty space in his head where nothing was. What went there?

He did, he supposed.

But who was he?

He kept the cookie off. He reasoned that the first few days would be the worst, the first few weeks difficult, but that it would get easier. Still—he too, sitting at the laboratory bench, or addressing a group of postdocs in the hospital cafeteria—he wondered how Melissa was doing, whether Dimitri was bullying her. In his mind's eye he could see it happening. He had set his cookie to dormant-passive, accessible only in the case of emergency messages. And he had set a password for it, a long string of random digits that he had written down on paper and put in his desk drawer at home, next to the phones, so he couldn't just turn it on again at a weak moment. Julie had done the same.

But god, he missed even the low hum the kids had given off in the cookie with the filters on high. Over and over he found himself, without thinking, trying to eyekey the map open. Nothing there.

His parents had done it. So had theirs. And every parent back to the beginning of the species.

But it just seemed . . . well, a tiny bit irresponsible. A needless risk.

He kept it off.

He could not, however, prevent himself from leaving work early three days a week, after his seminar let out, shouldering his backpack, wrapping his right pant cuff in its Velcro strap, and bicycling home.

The asphalt streets, unrolling beneath his wheels. The shifting trees, accepting the weight of the warm spring wind. The measured thrusting of the carbon scoops as they whispered past five miles up, glinting silver.

And behind it all, the silence in his head.

In this new routine he bicycled straight to the elementary school, where he would wait for school to let out, his bicycle leaning against a nearby tree, his cuff still pinned, at the front doors. He was the only parent there at that hour.

The playground sat empty, waiting to be filled. Tetherball, swings, basketball court.

The sunstruck playing fields. And the shadows under the fences.

On his first day sitting on the concrete shelf around the flagpole, a young woman emerged through the gray double doors and approached him. She wore a look that could break either toward apology or something much scarier.

"Hello," she called, coming across the pavement. "Can I help you?"

"I'm Peter Burkhart," he said. "Matt and Melissa's father."

She regarded him. Checking him against her records. "Is there something we can do for you, Mr. Burkhart?"

"Just waiting for the kids."

"Do you need to take them somewhere?"

"No. Just . . . thought I'd hang out with them a little today."

A disbelieving lift of her eyebrow.

"After school. On the playground," he said. "I just—" He wasn't going to explain. This girl—she couldn't be more than twenty-two —wouldn't understand. "That's all," he said.

A tiny scoff.

"I hope that's all right," he said.

"Hey," she said, "it's your life." And she turned and went back into the building. A minute later a row of faces appeared at the window of what he knew to be the office.

Let them look.

He rearranged himself on the concrete wall.

Matt stopped dead in his tracks when he saw him there the first day. Wondered if something was wrong, if he was in trouble. The playground swarmed with children, a suddenly teeming city of very small, very loud people. A very few other parents, collecting their smallest, not wanting to rely on the cookies to lead them home.

And here was his father.

"I'm just here to say hi," he told his son. "Just to say hi and watch you play a little."

Matt took this in. "I was going to play with Sheldon, though."

"That's fine," he said. "I'll just be over here."

Matt gave him a long considering examination, then went off, talking to his friend.

But Melissa understood at once. She grinned seriously, then took his hand and guided him to the nearest play structure.

"Daddy," she said, "let me show you what I can *do*."

The play structure was the usual sort, slides and tunnels and various nooks and alcoves in which to hide oneself. She led him to a net of vinyl-coated ropes slung between two uprights. She put out a firm foot on the bottom rope, grabbed the net with two hands, then with a practiced swiftness she figured her route to the top of the net, one staggered, swaying step at a time. At the top she looped an arm through the lattice and extended her other arm out into the air, twelve feet over his head.

"Wow," he said. "That's high!"

"I can see everybody from here," she said. "I can see our clubhouse."

"Where?"

"Way over there, in the corner, under the lilac bushes. By the telephone pole. And I can see the top of your head!"

"What's it look like?"

She regarded him. "A head," she decided. Then she surveyed the playground again, the screaming, swirling mass, and gave a contented sigh. "I'm very good at climbing," she said.

So many notes of his wife in that moment—the satisfaction, the ease in herself.

And that was his quiet determination, maybe. His secret ferocity.

This became his routine. Sitting on the ledge by the flagpole, before the double doors banged open and the children poured out, he assessed the quality of the silence in his head.

The silence seemed, somehow, to be softening itself, to be losing its definition.

What before had seemed a cavern, an actual emptiness, now felt more like a cloud—something soft and actual, spun from the faintest substance.

Some days Melissa wanted him all to herself, and other days she did what she had always done: played with her friends. Ran around, or sat in their clubhouse, huddled under the lilacs, the branches shivering. As far as he could tell they were a mix of synth and human, although mostly they were girls, and mostly from her class, which would mean—well, mostly synth, then.

It didn't matter. At this distance, from the outside of them all, they were all just children.

He was an object of curiosity, sitting there. "You're Matt's dad," a boy said one day.

"Yeah."

"Why are you here?"

"Just here," he said. "I like it."

"But why?"

"I want to be," he said.

It took a moment before Peter recognized this boy as the horrible Dimitri. His hair was spiked and he wore, improbably, a button-down blue shirt tucked into khaki shorts. Trim, tidy, his true nature given away only in his offended stare.

"You're weird," Dimitri decided.

"Yeah?"

"Yeah." The boy plugged his hands deep into his pockets. "All you do is just sit there."

"Sometimes. Sometimes I run around with Melissa."

This didn't satisfy him. He was truly a very small boy, built on a delicate, almost elven scale. But some hard fury burned behind his eyes. "She's weird too," he said.

"Well, maybe I think you're pretty weird too, kid."

This seemed to be what Dimitri wanted, as he granted him a sudden, wicked, grateful smile. "I know," he said.

"You should really be nicer to people."

"I'm nice to people," Dmitri said. "I just don't like synths."

"Why not?"

"Because they're not human."

"Sure they are."

"No, they're not. They're synths," Dimitri said calmly. "Why do I have to go to school with things that aren't people?"

He could, if he wanted, squash this little monster like a grape.

"Are you a synth?" Peter asked, all innocence.

"No!"

"How do you know?"

"Because I'm *not*."

"But how do you *know*?"

"Because I've seen pictures of my mom with me in her uterus."

"How do you know they're not just shopped? Maybe they want you to think you're human but you're actually not."

But plainly the boy had entertained this thought for a long time on his own and had an answer ready. "If I was going to be a synth, I would just be a Super," Dimitri said, shouldering his backpack. "Those are the only ones who are worth anything."

Giving Melissa her bath that night—calm, calm—he mentioned Dimitri.

She splashed a little, pensively, then said, "He's not very friendly to me."

"I know."

She soaped a long arm, squinted down its length like a sniper.

"But what you said? Wasn't a very nice thing to say to him, I guess," he said.

"I guess," she conceded.

He watched her turn her arm, rotated the ulna, the radius, observing her own workings. It either was or was not the case that his daughter was a fully conscious, living creature, in just the way he was, self-aware and aware of her own self-awareness, unpredictable but bound by physics and probability in the same way he was, capable of originality, prone to certain behaviors, feeling, thinking, erratic, unknowable.

Either was or was not.

And if you couldn't tell, if nobody could tell—what was the point of wondering?

"I'm strong," she said.

"Yes, you are!"

"I can climb really well, you know." She looked at him hard. "Because I've been practicing, for your information."

"I know."

"Okay." She sighed, satisfied. "Just so I've given you warning."

He laughed. "I'm warned, officially," he said.

"I don't actually *want* him to die. I didn't say that."

"I know."

"So that's not *wrong*, what I said, it's just not nice. But he wasn't being nice to me. So I was just being fair."

"I can understand your thinking," he offered.

She said, "I wonder what it's like to die."

"I don't know."

She said, "I'm not going to die."

"Nobody knows if you are or aren't, actually," he managed. "Exactly what happens when you get older. But you're not designed to work forever, and neither am I."

"Why not?"

"Well, everything dies, honey."

"Not *everything*. The universe doesn't die."

"Nobody's sure about that. Nobody's sure what happens to the universe."

"When will you wear out?"

"Not until I'm about a hundred and fifty years old," he told her. "And by then, who knows what will happen?"

"What about the Supers?"

He took a breath, steadied himself. "What do you want to know?"

"Who made them?"

"People did," he said.

"Why aren't they allowed out anymore?"

He said, "Because nobody can figure out how to turn them off."

"You mean *kill* them," she said sternly. "You don't turn people off, you *kill* them."

"Well, Supers aren't the same as you and me," he said. She knew this history, but one thing about kids, you had to repeat things —kids learned something, forgot they had learned it. "Supers *are* machines. They're not like us. They don't have the kinds of brains we do. Supers were made to be policemen and soldiers, and for a while people thought that's the only thing they should do, and then some Supers' programming went wrong and made them start killing people who didn't deserve to be killed, people who were just committing normal crimes, or just normal people doing things that people do, like walking down a street. Not all of them did it, but enough. Most of them." And never mind all the rest of the insane savagery the Supers were prone to, the sorts of things no one liked to think about at all.

"Where are they?"

"Well, most of them are in a sort of jail."

She scowled at the water.

"It's a very strong jail," he offered. "They can't get out. It's underground, and very safe."

"That's not fair," she said.

"Well." He sighed. "I don't know. Maybe not."

"Not all of them are there," she said.

"No," he admitted. "A few are still loose. That's why we have the pitons up, so they can't come here."

"How many are left out?"

"About nine hundred," he said.

"Where?"

"Nobody knows," he said.

She gave a long contented sigh and lay back into the bath, leaving just her face above the surface of the water. "That's okay," she said, holding very still. "They'll be all right."

In the calm, the peace of their darkened house, a flood of happiness came over him. The spring students whooped outside the window, the girls clacking along in their heels and the boys sealing them into their cars, the doors whumping shut. The quiet of the house, the peaceable exhalations from their children's rooms.

"I think this is actually working out," he said, turning to Julie on the pillow. "I like this a lot."

She offered a weak smile.

"Do you?" he asked, sensing something.

"I've been peeking a little," she confessed. "Every night after they're asleep I've been just checking in for five minutes to see how they're doing."

"Oh," he said.

"That's all!" she cried softly. "I just check on them."

"And?"

The look she presented him seemed pulled up from the depths of an ocean.

"Actually," she said, "I was going to ask, please—I want you to *look*. At her."

He went to his desk, keyed in the password, clicked on the cookie. That warm swell of a presenting pressure, suddenly, its mental thereness in the head. But—but, no, he hadn't missed it, he thought now. A scattering of attention, the world broken into bits, a fluttering sense of something always better elsewhere.

Better off to just be yourself, just attend to the slanting motes of your own thoughts, the sense of a consciousness inflating like a rising loaf of bread, powered by an invisible exhalation.

Better that soft clean singularity of being.

But he looked at Melissa's feed. That same rising and falling, the gentle sine wave. All the reads were the same.

He allowed himself a deeper look. It all looked familiar.

"There's nothing new."

"I know. It's a repeating signal."

"Repeating?"

"It repeats, exactly, all the time. Every nine minutes it cycles back again. It's not really her."

"Oh," he said.

"She's blocking us," Julie said. "She's been blocking us for a long time."

"How? How long?"

"I don't know."

"Well, maybe—that's good," he said. "That's protection. She's protecting herself."

"I'm worried, Peter."

But he was resolute. This new place. This new sense of himself.

He shut down the cookie, and that great peace returned. "No," he said. "No, this is what we wanted. This is what we're doing." And then, as they settled into their pillows, "We owe it to them both."

She woke in the morning with the sense of having been inspected overnight. The sense of someone standing over your bed in the darkness.

But she hadn't been there. She hadn't been there to be looked at. Only a dummy, like in a movie, where someone's escaped from jail.

Still—it meant that they knew.

So that morning, under the lilac bushes, she called the club together.

It was only fair, really, that they be in charge of things. She and the others. Because they were just going to be around a lot longer than human people. It was like being somebody's older brother or sister. You had to take care of them. And you had to be in charge. You had to be in charge because you knew better, and you understood more things, and you could do things they couldn't do.

And you could be fair.

She had got this urge from her parents, after all. This stubbornness, this drive to be different from everybody else. She had inherited it from them.

And a little selfishness too, maybe.

First of all, you could reverse the signal on the pitons. That's what they had been for, originally. They were like emergency call boxes. You could fix the pitons not to block but to summon. You only needed to be smart about how to do it, and they were all smart. They were all very smart creatures. They had all blocked themselves from their parents by now. She had taught them how.

The telephone pole grew from the earth in the corner of the playground. That's why that corner was such a good place for their clubhouse. In that clean green light, under the scented florets, in the secret spaces among the branches. And they all agreed: it wasn't fair that the Supers, who were like them, couldn't go wherever they wanted. Even if they were bad. Because it wasn't fair that the people who had made them that way had decided they couldn't come out. Because what if somebody decided that against all of *them* someday? How did they know it wouldn't happen like that?

So they had to do it.

Yes, they all said at once.

That firm swipe of rectitude that passed through her when they all confirmed themselves like this—it was how she knew they were doing something good.

So, hand over hand, using her long muscles, she began to climb. From halfway up, she looked out over the swirling playground.

She could tell the difference—who was real and who wasn't.

Above her, the piton glinted.

The Nanny

FROM *The Paris Review*

"THERE ISN'T MUCH in the house," Mary said. "I'm sorry."

Kayla looked around, shrugged. "I'm not even that hungry."

Mary set the table, bright Fiestaware on placemats alongside fringed cloth napkins. They ate microwave pizzas.

"Gotta have something a little fresh," Mary's boyfriend, Dennis, said cheerily, heaping spinach leaves from a plastic bin onto his pizza. He seemed pleased by his ingenuity. Kayla ate the spinach, took a few bites of crust. Mary poured her more water.

When Kayla asked for a beer, she saw Mary and Dennis glance at each other.

"Sure, sweetie," Mary said. "Dennis, do we have any beer? Maybe check the garage refrigerator?"

Kayla drank two over dinner, then a third out on the porch, her legs tucked up into the oversize hoodie she had taken from Mary's son's room. The wildness of the backyard made everything beyond it look fake: the city skyline, the stars. Reception was awful this high in the canyon. She could try to walk closer to the road again, out by the neighbor's fence, but Mary would notice and say something. Kayla could feel Dennis and Mary watching her from inside the kitchen, tracking the glow of her screen. What would they do, take her phone away? She searched Rafe's name, searched her own. The numbers had grown. Such nightmarish math, the frenzied tripling of results, and how strange to see her name like this, stuffing page after page, appearing in the midst of even foreign languages, hovering above photos of Rafe's familiar face.

*

Before Tuesday there had been hardly any record of Kayla: an old fund-raising page from Students for a Free Tibet; a blog run by a second cousin with photos from a long-ago family reunion, teenage Kayla, mouth full of braces, holding a paper plate bent with barbecue. Her mother had called the cousin and asked her to take the photo down, but by then it had passed into the amber of the Internet.

Were there any new ones? She looked through the image results again, in case. They had dug up photos of Kayla lagging behind Rafe and Jessica, holding Henry's hand. Rafe in his button-down and jeans, surrounded by women and children. Kayla had no photos of her and Rafe together. That was strange, wasn't it? She came across a new photo—she looked only okay. A certain pair of jeans she loved was not, she saw, as flattering as she'd imagined it to be. She saved the photo to her phone so she could zoom in on it later.

Kayla made herself close the search results, then let her text messages refresh. A split-second reprieve where she could believe that perhaps the forces in the universe were aligning and aiming something from Rafe in her direction. She knew before they finished loading that there would be nothing.

"You need anything, sweetie?"

Mary stood in the porch doorway, just a black shadow.

"I'd turn the light on for you," Mary said, "but there's no bulb out here, actually."

Mary had been her mother's college roommate, now a drug and alcohol counselor. Kayla's mother had wanted her to fly home —*I'll buy the ticket,* she said, *please*—but then the photographers had descended on her ranch house in Colorado Springs. Waiting for Kayla. So her mother called Mary, the witness at her small courthouse wedding, though the wedding had been followed quickly by divorce. It was easy to imagine what Mary thought of Kayla. A waste, she probably believed, Kayla just twenty-four years old and now this. Probably, Mary thought, this was just the result of an absent father, an overworked mother.

But how could Kayla explain? This felt correct, the correct scale of things. Kayla had always expected something like this to happen to her.

"I'm fine." Kayla made her voice excessively polite.

"We're about to start watching this documentary," Mary said.

"About a girl who was the first female falconer in Mongolia." She paused. When Kayla didn't respond, she kept on. "It's supposed to be very good."

Mary, with her loose linen shirts, her silver oxfords, was the kind of older woman that younger girls were always saying they wanted to be like. Mary, with her great house up in the canyons, all the seventies wood left untouched. She probably let her teenage son call her by her first name. Kayla understood that Mary was a nice person without really believing it; Mary irritated her.

"Actually," Kayla said, "I'm pretty tired. I'm just gonna go to bed."

Did Mary want to say something else? Almost certainly.

"Thanks again for letting me stay," Kayla said. "I'm gonna try to sleep."

"Of course," Mary said, and hesitated, probably gathering herself to dispense some sober wisdom, some ex-junkie psalm. Before she could speak, Kayla smiled at her, a professional smile. Mary seemed taken aback, and Kayla took the opportunity to pick up her beer, her phone, to walk past Mary and make her way to the bedroom. Mary's son had wrapped his door in caution tape, pinned up a DANGER: KEEP OUT sign, a sticker of a nuclear symbol. *Yeah, yeah, we get it,* Kayla thought, *you're a toxic little shit.*

Mary's son was with his dad for the school break, and Mary had obviously tried to make the room nice: she left Kayla a stack of fresh towels, a little wrapped hotel soap, *The Best American Essays 1993* on the nightstand. Still, it smelled like a teenager, fumes of Old Spice and cheap jerk-off lotion, unwashed sports equipment lingering in the closet. Kayla lay on the neatly made bed. The surfing posters on every wall showed men, pink-nippled and tan, on boards in the middle of huge, almost translucent waves. The posters were like porn about the color blue.

Still nothing from Rafe. What to do but continue to exist? A sense of unreality thrummed under each second, a panic not altogether unpleasant. She found herself testing out the wording, imagining how she would characterize the feeling to Rafe if he called. She felt proud of the phrase *It's like I've been plucked out of my own life.* She said it silently to herself and her heart pounded faster. Dramatic. As long as she was sleeping, she felt fine, as long as there was the option to blot things out—she still had a few of

Rafe's sleeping pills, prescribed to him under a different name. She pulled a Ziploc from her backpack and shook out a Sonata, nibbling off a bitter shard. Best to parcel them out, save some for later. She pressed a wet finger to the bag to pick up any residue, then gave up, swallowing the second half of the pill with the last sip of her beer.

There was nothing interesting to look at in Mary's son's drawers: boxers folded tightly, T-shirts from various summer camps, their specialties increasingly psychotic—rock star camp, fashion design camp. A cigar box of coins and a pair of cufflinks made from typewriter keys, a yearbook in which only girls had written. She flipped through it: the kid appeared to go to the kind of school where everyone learned to knit in lieu of taking prescription amphetamines. A well-meaning missive from a teacher took up a whole page in the back. Maybe the boy had never even read it. Kayla did, though, sitting on the edge of the twin bed—it was moving, strangely, though maybe that was just the Sonata kicking in, the way her thoughts took on a slurred quality, the shutter speed starting to slow. "Max: I'm so proud of you and all you have accomplished this year. Can't wait to see what you'll do in this world! You are a very special person—never forget it!"

She could hear, from the living room, the sounds of the documentary, the swell of Mongolian music gaining in urgency. She would bet anything that Mary was tearing up right now, overcome by the sight of a soaring falcon or a close-up of an old man's hands, wind whipping across a Mongolian plain. Kayla had known a girl in college who'd been adopted from Mongolia. Her name was Dee Dee and all Kayla remembered was that she had a tendency to shower with the curtain open, that she picked at her face at the sink, leaving behind tiny shrapnel of pus on the mirror. Where was Dee Dee now?

Kayla was getting tired. She knew she should get up and turn off the light, take her contacts out, take off her bra. She didn't move.

Did Dee Dee remember her? Had she heard the news?

You are a very special person, Kayla thought to herself. *A very. Special. Person.*

Dennis had been the one to pick her up. Kayla didn't have her own car, had used one of Rafe and Jessica's. It had been one of the appealing things about the job, the car, though now it seemed very stupid, another way her life was tethered to those people. Kayla watched Dennis approach in the Volvo—he would have had to inch through the photographers at the main entrance. He stopped at the gate and waited to be buzzed in. He was wearing a visor whose brim was gnawed with age, a fleece vest embroidered with the logo of a vitamin company. He looked like a sad and tired animal, pulling through the security gates, and Kayla felt, briefly, that she had done something terrible. To summon someone like Dennis to a place like this. For reasons like this. But it wasn't really true, was it, that she was terrible? Life is long, she told herself, opening the car door. People always said things like that, *Life is long*.

"Is this all your stuff?" Dennis said.

Just two suitcases, her backpack. She had taken all of it, even the earrings Jessica had given her, the dress with the tags still on. The contents of the endless gift bags, perfume and makeup, so many lotions, a microcurrent wand, items Kayla would search out online, finding the exact retail prices, adding up the numbers until she got a little drunk. Kayla didn't feel guilty, not yet. Would she ever? The security cameras were recording her getting into Dennis's car. Would Jessica watch this footage? Would Rafe? She tried to keep a mild smile on her face, in case.

The first time she met Jessica was at the interview, after the agency had already approved her. Jessica came in late, sitting down at the table. She was distracted: her necklace had caught on her sweater.

"Can you just—" Jessica gestured, and Kayla took over, gentling the latch, trying not to tug so the sweater wouldn't stretch. She was bent close to Jessica's face: her skin lightly tanned, her hair almost the same color, all her features so tiny and symmetrical that Kayla could hardly look away, absorbed in the seamlessness of Jessica's beauty. Kayla felt a curious elation, a giddy feeling—how much time she had wasted trying to be beautiful, when it was obvious, now, how impossible that was. The knowledge was almost a relief.

"There." Kayla dropped the necklace back in place, smoothing the sweater. It was cashmere, the color of root beer.

Jessica touched the chain absently, smiled at her. "You're sweet."

The latest news was that Rafe's text messages were connected to the kid's iPad, that's how Jessica had found out, and it was amazing to imagine where this information came from, how these facts made their way to light. Because that part was true, anyway, she had gotten careless about texting Rafe, toward the end, and even if he rarely texted her back, Jessica would have seen right away what was happening.

Henry's favorite game on the iPad had been set in some virtual diner where you made hot dogs and hamburgers, a clock ticking down to zero. Kayla tried playing it once and sweated through her shirt, it made her so agitated. The burgers kept burning, the soda machine kept breaking. Customers fumed and departed.

Henry took the iPad from her with exaggerated patience.

"It's easy," he said. "Just don't pick up the coins right away. Then you have more time."

"But," she asked, "isn't the point to get a lot of money?"

"Then it goes too fast," Henry said. He seemed to feel sorry for her. "It's tricking you."

For Henry's eighth birthday, Kayla got him a machine that carbonated water and a book she had loved as a child. She read it aloud while Henry stared at the ceiling. He seemed to like the book, though the ending surprised her; she had not remembered that the old man died so violently, that the orphan grew up and was not very happy. In the afternoons, when the housekeeper was gone and Henry was at school, the air seemed to go slack. In the empty house, sometimes she felt as though she were a ghost floating through the world of the living. It was strange to walk through the rooms, open the closets, touch the hanging dresses, Rafe's pants, sweaters folded with tissue paper.

The thing was, she was a smart girl. She'd studied art history. Her first class, when Professor Hunnison turned out the lights and they all sat in the dark—they were eighteen, most of them, still children, still kids who had slept at home all their lives. Then the whir of the projector, and on the screen appeared hovering portals of light and color, squares of beauty. It was like a kind of magic, she had thought back then, when thoughts like that didn't feel embarrassing.

How mysterious it seemed sometimes—that she had once been interested or capable enough to finish papers. Giotto and his re-imaginings of De Voragine's text in his frescoes. Rodin's challenge to classical notions of fixed iconographic goals, Michelangelo's bodies as vessels for God's will. It was as if she'd once been fluent in another language, now forgotten.

Before he ate lunch, Henry got fish oil gummies in the shape of stars. Kayla liked them too—one for him, two for her. They were covered in sugar, but you were supposed to ignore that, focus instead on the fishy fat plumping your brain and making it pinker and brighter. A nice thought. For lunch Kayla made grilled cheese sandwiches on brown bread and cut apple slices. They ate outside, off paper towels. After eating, they lay in the sun in silence, Henry still in his swim trunks, Kayla in her carefully sexless one-piece.

Rafe had once pulled the crotch of that one-piece to the side to stick a blunt finger inside her. Was that the second or the third time? Kayla imagined being the kind of person who recorded details like that in a journal. She had lots of them: Rafe liked to nap with one arm flung over his head. Rafe had scars on his back from teenage acne but told her they were from a rock climbing accident. Strange how these were facts that would mean something to other people too, strangers who didn't even know him. If you searched him, everything was there—his allergies, his approximate height, photos of him as a young man. She pretended to have never seen any of it. That was between them always, the pretended unknowing.

It must have been the third time, the time with the swimsuit. The sheets in the pool house bed smelled like sunscreen. Rafe had his hand on her under the sheet, his eyes closed. Kayla looked at his bland, handsome face—it was always strange to touch it, like touching the memory of someone.

"How'd you start acting?" she asked. Her voice was druggy and low, neither of them fully awake.

"I was actually pretty young," Rafe said. There had been a visiting actor from Arts in Schools who came to perform for his class, he told her.

"You have to remember," he said, "this was Iowa, in January." It was before she had read all the articles—and Rafe told the story so haltingly, she'd assumed it was some kind of secret, something precious mined up from his psychic depths.

Apparently the visiting actor had opened all the windows of the classroom, maybe to call forth some appropriate level of drama, the freezing air gusting around while he paced in front of the desks, reciting *Hamlet*.

"It blew my mind," Rafe said. "Truly."

"Cute," she said, imagining Rafe as a child, moved by adult things.

He'd had a piece of food in his teeth at dinner once—the sight had given her an almost erotic discomfort until Jessica finally reached over and flicked it away. This was what she couldn't explain; Kayla hated him and loved him at the same time, and part of it was maybe that he was stupid.

Later she read the story about *Hamlet* almost word for word in many different interviews.

Rafe was away for almost a month, filming eight time zones away, but as soon as Henry was on winter break, he and Jessica flew to meet him, Kayla coming too, her pay doubled. She had her own hotel room close to the set. Outside the window, beyond the hotel's white walls, gasoline trucks made the rounds of the dirt streets.

After they'd arrived, Rafe had barely looked at her. But, she told herself, it made sense. Jessica was always around, or some PA with a walkie-talkie appearing to "invite" Rafe to set. People only ever "invited" Rafe to do the things he was supposed to do. At a dinner for the cast, he'd pinched her nipples, hard, in the back hallway of the restaurant, his breath fumy with the local beer, flavored with kola nuts and wormwood. She laughed at the time, though waiters seemed to have noticed, along with at least one of the producers, judging by his smirk. They were actually alone only once. Jessica had sent Kayla up to their room to grab sunscreen for Henry. She opened their door, using Jessica's key card, and there was Rafe, watching a boxing match on television, the curtains drawn.

"Hi, you," she'd said, going to kiss him, and he fumbled, kissing her back with tight lips. Was he blushing? It was strange. Still, they had sex, quickly, her dress pushed up, the bedcovers only slightly disturbed. She went to the bathroom to wipe herself, careful to flush the toilet paper. She was still being careful then. There was the sunscreen on the counter. When she returned to the bedroom, sunscreen in hand, Rafe was absorbed by the television, his face blank, the bedcovers smooth, as if nothing had happened at all.

It was Kayla's day off; Jessica had taken Henry to one of the mountain towns for the afternoon. Kayla napped in her cool room under the mosquito netting that made everything look shrouded in smoke. The first few days she felt fine, but Kayla had a delayed reaction to the required vaccines, the whites of her eyes going milky, dreams leaking into her waking life. She drank bottled water all day, but still her urine was an unnatural brown color, sludgy and smelling like sulfur.

She woke groggy and hot from the nap, her sunburn pulsing. The on-set doctor had said to keep drinking water, to watch for cloudy thinking. Was this cloudy thinking, the glowy specter of Bugs Bunny in the hotel room?

You're a beautiful girl, he said.

Bugs said these things without his mouth moving. They were thoughts beamed from his brain directly to Kayla's, a shimmy in the air between them. Sometimes he did a sort of side-to-side shuffle, a slow-motion soft-shoe. Everything he did was slow. Bugs Bunny. She smiled from the bed. Bugs didn't have anywhere else to be. He didn't actually say this in so many words, but she understood it, the sentiment was there in his big, swimmy eyes—he would stay in this hotel room all day. If that was what she wanted.

I should go visit Rafe, don't you think?

She said this, or thought this.

I don't know. Bugs blinked. *Is that what you want?*

He was so smart.

I should go. She tried to eke out another thought from her inflamed brain. *I'm gonna go. I gotta see Rafe.*

Bugs bowed a little—a syrupy, slow bow. *If that's what you need to do.*

Kayla changed into a dress and had a vodka and pineapple juice at the hotel bar. They were shooting by the cliffs that day, close enough that Kayla walked the ten minutes through the dunes, full of sand gnats and horseshit. Kayla sweated through her dress by the time she got to the set. Everyone was just standing around. Rafe nodded at her but didn't come over to say hi. He looked grim. They'd made his eyebrows too dark and they read clownish. Maybe they would look fine onscreen. She could tell he was irritable, hungry, antsy, wanting a shower, wanting a drink. She sensed it before Rafe sneezed, before he scratched his nose. Would he ever know this feeling? This level of precise, almost psychotic attunement to another person? No, of course not.

"Why are they stopped?" she asked one of the lighting guys.

He barely acknowledged her. "They found something in the gate."

"Oh. The gate?"

The guy squinted into the middle distance, shrugged. Was she imagining his curtness? No. The crew didn't like talking to her anymore. That should have been the first sign. People had an animal instinct for power, could sense that her usefulness was at its end.

Kayla settled into one of the chairs under a temporary awning outside a trailer. The sun washed out everything so it looked sketchy, unfinished. Her sunburn made her skin feel tight. She scratched her right ankle, lightly. If she were just sunburned, it would be fine, but it was sores too, these raised red bites. She rubbed her ankle against her other ankle. Gently, gently. Nothing seemed to be happening, but everyone was tense. A script supervisor was doing a crossword on his phone. She watched the makeup girl run in and press a tissue to Rafe's forehead. He submitted himself to her with great patience. He was, after all, a good actor. Kayla plucked her dress away from her armpits, but it was futile —the fabric would stain, of course it would.

The actual filming was too far from the trailer for Kayla to hear anything. She watched Rafe say something, watched him tilt his face up at the sky. They ran the scene again. What scene was this? She was waiting for them to shoot the opening sequence. The director had told her, at that dinner when everyone was still being nice to her, when it was obvious she was sleeping with Rafe, to watch out for that.

"Some directors film it right away," he said, "right off the bat. But the actors don't jell yet, you see. If you wait too long everyone just hates each other, they're rushing through it. Like senior year. You time it so they're settled into their characters and still showing up."

This was only the director's second movie. The studio had given him so much money. He looked like he was twenty years old. He kept joking about how he didn't know how to do anything.

The shoot had stopped again. Rafe was walking toward her. She straightened and got to her feet.

He was sweating, his face red.

"You're sitting in my eye line," Rafe said. "I can't do the scene if I look up and keep seeing you there."

"I'm not in your eye line," she said. She could feel the makeup girl glancing at them.

"You don't think you are, but it's my eye line, that's the point," Rafe said. "It's what I see. Not what you see. What I see. And I'm seeing you."

"Okay."

He widened his eyes, about to say something, then seemed to soften.

"Why don't you go swim in the pool at the hotel? Get some lunch?"

"Yes," she said. Her voice was faint. "That's a good idea."

She knew Rafe didn't want her to make a scene. And she wouldn't. She smiled out to the nothingness, the empty horizon. The land was scrubby and not beautiful, not at all how she had imagined. In truth, it had been her first time outside the country.

Kayla hadn't left Mary's in three days. The one time she'd gone to the store, someone had taken photos of her filling up Mary's car with gas on the way back. Kayla was wearing aviators and looked unhappy in the pictures, her lips thin, her hair brassy and over-washed. She wasn't as pretty as Jessica. That was the obvious thing people were saying, and it wasn't as if Kayla didn't also know that it was true, though she didn't know why it made people so angry at her, so personally offended. Kayla had been offered a TV inter-view. Compensation to drink a brand of vitamin water the next time she went out in public. An interview in *Playboy* too, though apparently they were no longer shooting nudes.

Mary knocked lightly on the doorframe.

"You good?"

Kayla sat up. "I'm fine," she said. She put her phone on the bed, screen down.

"Dennis and I are going to a friend's for dinner tonight," Mary said. "You should come."

"Oh, that's okay," Kayla said. "Really. I can hang here."

"You shouldn't be alone," Mary said. "I feel bad. Like you're trapped."

"It's fine."

Mary wrinkled her brow, her mouth in a sad little frown. "You'll feel better," she said. "They're sweet people. She writes cookbooks, he teaches at Occidental. It'll be a good group."

Her saying yes made Mary happy, and Dennis was beaming too, when they piled into the car, even these minor plans animating him. He was scrubbed to a pink gleam, the short sleeves of his golf shirt hanging past his elbows. Mary drove down the narrow canyon roads, Dennis in the passenger seat, one arm around Mary. Had he been married before, did he have kids? Kayla didn't know. He seemed to exist only in Mary's orbit, the boyfriend harvesting lemons from the backyard to bring to the party. They kept glancing at Kayla in the rearview. She sat in the back seat next to the shopping bag full of lemons, a bottle of red wine. Kayla wore the dress Jessica had given her and Mary's son's sweatshirt, her hair in an unflattering ponytail. The dress was a nice fabric, a sort of linen and silk blend, the color of asphalt—she fingered the fabric, idly, where it draped across her knees. Jessica had been kind to her.

No one at the party paid her much attention. Everyone was older, busy with their own lives, with their kids, who darted in and out, one wielding a plastic ukulele, another singing a counting song in French. It was the first time Kayla had thought of it—of course there were people in the world who did not know or care about Rafe and Jessica. The food was out on a table, guests hovering with their plates. She ate some lentil salad, had a watery margarita from a pitcher, a glass of white wine.

In the hallway, she passed someone dumping the dregs of their drink into a potted plant. She didn't know these people.

Outside was nicer. The pool was still and gave off a floodlit shimmer. No one was around. The hills were a dark mass, occasionally marked with houses. Kayla could smell the earth cooling, the clumpy chaparral that rimmed the pool, the sound of a fountain she couldn't see. She crouched down to dip her hand: the water was the same temperature as the air. Kayla sat cross-legged, her glass cradled in her lap.

She opened her texts. The final ones from Jessica were from two weeks ago, all logistical. She looked at her saved photos, paparazzi shots of Rafe, his arms crossed. She had not seen it before, how annoyed he looked, beleaguered, surrounded by Jessica and Kayla, Henry, people who needed things from him. Poor Henry. His little shoulders, his immaculate hair. His open, wanting face.

She finished the last of her wine.

Someone opened the door. It was the daughter of the hosts. Sophie, or Sophia.

"Hey," Kayla said. Sophie crouched but didn't sit. Kayla could smell her tangy child breath.

"Are you cold?" Sophie asked.

"Nah," Kayla said. "Not yet."

They were quiet for a long moment. The silence was fine. Sophie looked younger than Henry. Her nostrils had childish rims of snot.

"What grade are you in?" Kayla asked, finally.

"Second."

"Cool."

Sophie shrugged, an adult shrug, and started to stand.

"Where you going?" Kayla touched one of Sophie's knees. The girl shifted at the contact but didn't seem bothered.

"My room."

"Can I come?"

Sophie shrugged again.

Sophie's room was cluttered, a paper lantern in the shape of a star hanging over the bed. Sophie gestured at two Barbies, nude and prone under a paper towel, their fingers fused and slightly fluted.

"I made this house for them," Sophie said, indicating an empty bookshelf. One shelf had a Band-Aid box next to a Barbie lying on its side in a tight, shiny dress.

"This is the party room," Sophie said. "Watch." She flipped a switch on a plastic flower keychain and it started to cycle through different-colored lights. "Wait," she said, and ran to turn off the overhead light. Sophie and Kayla stood in silence, the noise of the party beyond, Sophie's room easing from red to yellow to turquoise.

"It's pretty," Kayla said.

Sophie was businesslike. "I know."

She flicked the plastic flower off and turned the ceiling light back on. When Kayla didn't say anything, the girl busied herself with a box in the corner. She pulled out a paper mask and held it up to her face, the kind of surgical mask you were supposed to wear to prevent SARS. Kayla knew Sophie would hold it there until she said something.

"What's that?" Kayla said.

"I need it," Sophie said. "'Cause I get claustrophobic."

"That's not true," Kayla said.

"Yeah," Sophie whined through the mask. "I even have to wear it at school."

"You're teasing."

Sophie let the mask fall and smiled.

"It's a good joke, though," Kayla said.

Kayla sat on the edge of Sophie's bed. The sheets seemed fresh, a chill coming off the good cotton. Sophie was moving the Barbies from shelf to shelf, whispering to herself. It was easy for Kayla to kick off her sandals. She tucked her bare legs in the sheets and pulled them up over herself.

"Are you going to sleep?" Sophie said.

"No. I'm cold."

"You're sick, and I'm the nurse," Sophie said, brightening. "I'm actually a princess, but I was forced to be a nurse."

"Of course."

"You're my daughter. You're very sick."

"I might die." Kayla closed her eyes.

"Unless I give you the medicine." Kayla heard Sophie fumble in the room, the sound of drawers and boxes. She opened her eyes when she felt a soft object pressing against her mouth. It was a felt doughnut, dotted with felt sprinkles.

"I found this in the forest," Sophie said. Her voice had a low, spooky quality. "You have to eat it."

"Thank you," Kayla said. She opened her mouth and tasted the bland felt.

"I think it's working."

"I don't know," Kayla said. "I think I should rest for a while."

"Okay, honey," Sophie said, and patted her cheek gently. It was nice. With her eyes closed, Kayla felt the girl lay a paper napkin over her face, the napkin getting hot with Kayla's own breath. It was comforting, to hear Sophie moving in the room, to smell the smell of her own mouth.

"Kayla."

Before she opened her eyes, she imagined the man's voice was Professor Hunnison's. Why did this comfort her? He knew she was here. She blinked heavily and smiled. He had come for her. He wished her well.

"Kayla!"

It was Dennis, Dennis with his blousy shirt, his hairy forearms.

"You should get up," Dennis said. His voice was cold. "Mary's been looking for you. We're going home."

Kayla looked past Dennis but Sophie was gone. The room was empty.

"Up we go," Dennis said. He kept looking at the doorway. He wanted to leave.

Kayla felt strange. She'd been dreaming. "Where's Sophie?"

"Time to get going, okay, let's get a move on."

She blinked at him from the pillow.

"Come on, Kayla," Dennis said, pulling the covers back. Kayla's dress had ridden up and her underwear was showing.

"Jesus," he said, and tossed the blankets back over her. His face was red.

"I'm sorry," Kayla said, getting up, searching out her sandals.

"Are you?"

The tone of his voice surprised her—when she glanced at him, he looked intently at the floor.

Kayla felt the room around her, her cheap sandal in her hand. "I'm not ashamed, if that's what you're thinking."

Dennis started laughing, but it just seemed weary. "Jesus," he said, rubbing his eyes. "You're a nice girl," he said. "I know you're a good person.

The anger she felt then, close to hatred—"Maybe I'm not."

Dennis's eyes were watery, pained. "Of course you are. You're more than just this one thing."

Dennis scanned Kayla's face, her eyes, her mouth, and she could tell he was seeing what he wanted to see, finding confirmation of whatever redemptive story he'd told himself about who she was. Dennis looked sad. He looked tired and sad and old. And the thing was, someday she would be old too. Her body would go. Her face. And what then? She knew already that she wouldn't handle it well. She was a vain, silly girl. She wasn't good at anything. The things she had once known—Rodin! Chartres!—all that was gone. Was there a world in which she returned to these things? She hadn't been smart enough, really. Even then. Lazy, grasping for shortcuts. Her thesis moldering in her college library, a hundred labored pages on *The Expulsion of Joachim from the Temple*. She'd messed with the margins and font sizes until she barely made the required page count. *Professor Hunnison,* she thought miserably, *do you ever think of me?*

Dennis steered Kayla through the last gasps of the party, toward the front door. Where had he found a brownie along the way? He held it out to her, wrapped in a napkin. Maybe he felt bad. Kayla shook her head.

Dennis started to say something, then stopped himself. He shrugged and took a bite of the brownie, chewing avidly. He checked his phone.

"Mary's bringing the car around," Dennis said. "So we can just wait here." His mouth was full, and he was ignoring the crumbs falling down his front, gumming up his teeth. When he noticed Kayla was watching him, Dennis seemed to get self-conscious. He finished the brownie in one bite, wiping his lips with the napkin. At least he had given up on the idea of lecturing her. Convincing her there was some lesson in all this. That wasn't how the world worked, and wasn't it a little tragic that Dennis didn't know that yet? No use feeling bad. There wasn't anything to *learn.* Kayla smiled, sucked in her stomach, just in case—because who knew? Maybe there was a photographer hidden out there in the darkness, someone who'd been watching her, who'd followed her here, someone who had waited, patiently, for her to appear.

Halloween

FROM *Crazyhorse*

MY GRANDMOTHER HAD fucked-up ideas about love. This was something anyone who had spent about five minutes with her understood. She had been married three times—once to my grandfather and twice to a guy named David who I remember as a quiet gray-bearded man with a motorcycle but who had also broken into Jan's duplex and set fire to the rattan patio set that she'd always kept in her sunroom. When I asked if she'd been afraid of this guy, she shrugged. "Sure. Sometimes." In her mind, love was an undertaking that required constant vigilance and bravery, and when she spoke about her own relationships, I often thought of a woman I had seen on YouTube trying to explain why she had been raising the tiger cub that eventually mauled her. "We loved each other," the woman said. "I don't expect anyone to understand."

But when it came to Erika, the girl who had recently broken my heart, after what was admittedly just one relatively chaste summer together, Jan was my ideal audience—sympathetic, almost always available, and the only person in my life who thought that getting back together with Erika was both advisable and likely to happen.

"You're beautiful," she would say, as if this settled the matter. "Look at you! This girl is obviously having cold feet. Maybe she's just not ready to be gay."

The logical part of my brain thought the more likely explanation was that Erika had only ever gotten together with me in the first place out of boredom and convenience (we had spent the summer working together at a frozen yogurt shop called Yotopia!)

and now that FSU was back for the fall semester, it embarrassed her to be with a high school student. Sometimes, though, in the midst of one of Jan's musings, I could almost convince myself that there had been a misunderstanding and that if I could just show Erika I was a mature and attractive person, she would, if not see that she had made a mistake, at least consider making out with me in secret.

"When it comes to love," Jan said, "you shouldn't have regrets. I have regrets, and I can tell you it sucks. I never should have divorced your grandfather."

It was a Saturday afternoon and we were walking along a paved path through a leafy park on the east side of town. During the week it was mostly used by dog walkers and runners, but now the playgrounds were crowded with little kids and under one of the covered pavilions a family of loud, happy people were having a birthday cookout for someone named Bianca. Jan walked very fast and we were both a little out of breath. She had told me this story many times. My grandfather was a decent and hardworking man who, after years of Jan threatening divorce every time he drank too much or came home late from work, had finally called her bluff. As a result, her life had been lonely and difficult for the past forty years.

"If you have a chance to set things right," she said solemnly, "the least you can do is try."

Jan was my dad's mom, but he, along with his two older sisters, had a strained relationship with her. Partially because of the yelling and chaos from their childhoods and partially because of what they called her "attention-seeking tendencies"—buying Cuisinart mixers and flat-screen televisions for people she barely knew, walking out of my cousin Trent's high school graduation party because she felt ignored by his friends, requesting an apology from my aunt Kelly for not having been invited to visit her newborn twins in the NICU. In large groups especially, she often made provocative statements inspired by daytime television and the youthful coworkers she knew from the various crappy retail jobs she held. "Maybe I'll go and get my stomach frozen like I heard on *Dr. Oz*" or "Now, what do you think it would be like to be married to Kanye West?"

My mom, though, who had only officially been Jan's daughter-in-law for about a year after I was born, invited her over to our house anytime there was a special occasion or holiday—Christmas, Thanksgiving, Easter, birthdays. Jan had babysat when I was little and my mom had no money for daycare, and so as far as she was concerned, Jan was family. When my mom's mother complained that she would like just one "family-only holiday," my mom would smile sweetly and tell her she was welcome to visit another time. It was only after it was just the two of us that my mom would let herself flop on the couch with a glass of wine and shake her head about a cayenne-lemon-water diet Jan was trying for unspecified reasons or a horror costume involving a fake dead baby that she'd worn to a children's Halloween party. "My god," she would say. "What do you think goes on in her head to make her act that way?"

That fall my grandmother was living in a new and supposedly high-end apartment complex that came with a gym, a garage parking space, a gated entry that required a code after 9 p.m., and a twenty-five-yard outdoor swimming pool that was heated in the winter and where we spent at least two evenings a week together that fall. I was avoiding my mom's boyfriend; Jan was trying to distract herself from the job she'd recently lost at Nordstrom and her fear that in her seventies she was too old to get hired anywhere else. The other residents were almost all college students and young professionals with seemingly endless amounts of time to splash around in the pool half naked, drinking beer out of thermoses, and playing rowdy games of volleyball, but that didn't stop Jan from doing her water exercises, which involved a wide weighted belt she'd bought off QVC and looked kind of like moonwalking and kind of like a person feeling around in the dark for a lost object. I didn't have an exercise belt and so would borrow one of the apartment complex kickboards and glide along beside her while she gave me advice about Erika and listened to me complain about my mother's boyfriend, who all of a sudden, after about two years of dating my mom, seemed to be around constantly. His name was Pete, and he was a social worker at the hospital where she worked. He was a thin, very pale man with wispy yellowish hair and wire-framed glasses that were always flecked with grime. He was in his early fifties, about a decade older than she was, and divorced with two kids in college. He was relentlessly polite to me and kind to my mother, and I hated him.

"He's too skinny," I would say. "And have you heard the way he coughs? In another ten years she's going to be taking care of him."

I also didn't like the way he ate—too quickly and with appreciative, almost sexual sounds—how he was always fiddling with his beard, how every single one of his hobbies—nature walks, invasive plant removal, pickleball, historical biographies—seemed like contests in withstanding boredom. Jan didn't seem to have any issues with Pete, though I thought she usually gave men too much credit, including my father, who had followed a woman to Charlotte when I was two and been absent for most of my childhood. But she let me complain and would admit, at least, that his clothes were terrible. Clunky orthotics worn with tall white athletic socks, multiple colors of pleated chinos in the same unflattering style.

"That's fixable, though," Jan would say. "If your mom wants to put in the work. Men are just like that. They always need a lot of help."

My mother, along with her sister, her friends, Jan, basically every other woman we knew who was over thirty-five, seemed to think that she was the lucky one to find Pete—a single, employed guy who thanked her for all of the nice things she did for him and who didn't mind that she had just turned forty. The fact that I was the only one who seemed to notice that she was about a thousand times better-looking than he was or that she was always the one cooking dinner filled me with a sense of righteous indignation, though on some level I knew that no matter who she dated, I would see him as a trespasser.

As for Erika, Jan's main advice was to wear revealing outfits and to behave as if my life without her was surprising and wonderful. I should be friendly in an easy, casual way that showed I didn't need her, and I certainly shouldn't ask her to go out with me again.

"Of course not," I said, though in fact I had called and texted Erika so many times in the past two weeks begging her to reconsider that she had blocked me on social media and was now switching shifts at Yotopia! to avoid me. I understood exactly how pathetic this made me look, since it was approximately the same way that my ex-boyfriend AJ had reacted when I'd finally broken up with him in July, after I'd already been messing around with Erika for two months. But I was having trouble controlling myself. Being around Erika electrified my skin, my body, the air in the room. Didn't this mean *something?*

"When do you work together again?" Jan said, squinting up at me while she bobbed along the deep end. "Find out and look good that day."

"Okay."

"And remember. Easy breezy. Lemon squeezy."

"What?"

"You don't know that one? Customer Service 101. If you feel yourself getting moody or sentimental, you just chant that in your head, and it'll get you back on track."

The next time I was supposed to work with Erika, she got her shift covered, but I saw her again the following Friday night. She worked the back cash register by the drive-through and I worked up front with the face-to-face customers. Because of the three-for-one Decadent Shakes promotion, which I was pretty sure Gina, the owner, was losing money on, we were slammed. Families with kids, college students, a Little League baseball team along with about a dozen of their parents and coaches. There wasn't much I could do to look nicer—we all had to wear latex gloves, khaki aprons, and teal polo shirts with the company logo on the pocket (YOTOPIA! and a swirl of pink yogurt that looked like smoke rising out of a chunk of kiwi)—but I thought about Jan's advice and tried to seem happy and outgoing.

Wooing the customers wasn't too complicated—you just smiled at their kids and offered them free samples—but being within a few feet of Erika made me queasy and stupid. There was her dark hair tucked behind her ears, her pink, slightly puffy lips, the tiny circle tattooed on the inside of her wrist. While I made Decadent Shakes and parfaits and refilled the yogurt machine, my head swam with all the possible things I could say to her, but then whenever there was a brief lag between customers, I wasted it. Finally, around 8:30, things slowed down and we both found ourselves up front, sneaking crushed-up candy bars from the bins of toppings with tasting spoons and doing just enough side work to look busy. I was sweeping; she was wiping down tables. I knew that if I didn't say something soon, I'd miss my chance.

"Hey, can I ask you something?" I said finally.

She looked up at me from the plastic shield over the display freezer that she was wiping down with Windex.

"Okay."

I could tell she thought I was going to ask why she didn't love me or why, given our obvious chemistry, she hadn't actually slept with me, but the truth was I hadn't yet decided what I was going to say. I thought about apologizing for harassing her or suggesting friendship. I wanted to work St. George Island into the conversation, so she'd remember the afternoon we'd spent there with our coworkers, the two of us lying side by side on a beach blanket, nearly touching. Making each other crazy until we'd snuck away to a changing room in the women's bathroom, wet sand everywhere, shivering out of bikini tops. But then I thought of Jan chanting *Easy breezy lemon squeezy* and took a different tack.

"Why do you think there were five cherry-flavored Skittles in the urinal?"

Erika squinted at me a little, but her face softened, and I could see that she was going to play along. "How do you know they were cherry-flavored?"

"Aren't the red ones always cherry?"

"Yeah," she said. "Maybe." And then a few minutes later, she nodded at the tip jar out front, which we would split at the end of the night, and told me I was on a roll.

"Nice work, Jules," she said. "The people love you."

I shrugged. "Decadent Shake special."

Pretty soon after that we hit another rush, and it stayed too busy to say much else to each other, but something had shifted between us. The ice had broken, and though things weren't exactly normal again, Erika no longer seemed like she wanted to avoid me. When I reported back to Jan later that week, she said, "Of course it worked. Why wouldn't it have worked?"

After that Friday night, Erika stopped giving away so many of her shifts, and for the next month or so, I got to see her two, sometimes three times a week. It was my senior year and I was busy with the AP math and science classes that I'd taken in hopes of getting a scholarship to one of the liberal arts schools in cold, unfortunate cities like Grinnell, Iowa, and Richmond, Indiana, where my guidance counselor thought other students might not want to go. Working, especially when Erika was there, began to feel like a break from worrying about the future. Where would I go to college? How would I pay for it? What would my life would be like if —*when*?—I went away to school and my mom and Pete moved in together? His house was nicer than ours—a creaky two-bedroom house, buried under a thicket of live oaks and pollen that always smelled damp. He lived on the very edge of Betton Hills, which was the fanciest neighborhood in Tallahassee, in a small bright ranch house with new counters and appliances, a slate roof, and bright pink azaleas out front, but even though I knew it was babyish to feel this way, the thought of moving out of the house I'd grown up in made me want to cry.

At work, though, all of this disappeared behind the swell of pop music and the rush of customers. When Erika was there, I tried to demonstrate how likable I could be—chatting and flirting with customers, smiling so hard my face hurt. At school I barely spoke to anyone but my friend Paloma and never managed to talk in class without my entire chest and face going hot and red, but at Yotopia! no one seemed to guess that this friendly, confident person was a lie. That you could just decide to be a different person, that you didn't have to actually change to convince people, felt like a revelation.

In the lulls between customers, Erika told me about how her parents were pressuring her to major in marketing instead of studio art or, at the very least, to pursue an internship they'd found at an insurance company through one of their South Florida accountant friends. She thought this was selling out, but she was worried about being broke. Usually I didn't add much about my life, because it was boring and because I didn't want to say anything that would remind her that I was in high school, but I did sometimes talk about AJ, who was eager for me to admit I was bisexual.

"I think he thinks me being gay makes him a virgin or something," I said one day. "He's seriously freaking out about it."

I tried to make it seem like our relationship hadn't mattered, but I knew this wasn't true. There had been three years of inside jokes, flash drives of indie music slipped into each other's bookbags. He had told me that he'd peed his bed until he was five, that his father had made him quit soccer because he was slower than the other kids, too embarrassing to watch; and I told him that I collected photos from social media of my dad, who, according to his wife's page, *was* a good father to his new family in North Carolina but just not to me. AJ and I had made out and given each other orgasms and lain naked in his bedroom many times before the spring of our junior year, when we'd finally had sex, and all of this too had seemed like easy, uncomplicated happiness. Now, though, in comparison to Erika, nothing with AJ felt real.

"Well, it's probably hard for him," she said. "But that doesn't mean you have to be the one to listen."

By October the awkwardness between me and Erika had all but gone away, but it was also making me crazy to be around her. My friend Paloma thought I should quit my job and concentrate on getting into a good liberal arts school, which would undoubtedly be filled with lesbians who were even hotter and cooler than Erika; Jan said I should make up another girl who had a crush on me and look for reasons to casually touch Erika or invade her space.

"Does that actually work?"

"Oh yes," she said. "At least on men. Remember Gabriel?"

"No."

"Yes, you do. He looked like a chubby George Clooney. Dark hair and a beard. We almost got married."

I didn't remember him but nodded.

"I fixed his tie on a Tuesday and by Saturday I had a date."

I wasn't fully convinced about this plan, but I also knew that fro-yo season was coming to a close and that Gina would probably soon stop scheduling two people on weekdays.

The next time I saw Erika, I started a group chat with three of my classmates about chemistry homework and grinned stupidly at my phone every time it lit up with a reply. Finally, after about two hours, she asked what was happening.

"Nothing," I said. "Probably nothing. I met someone at Lake Ella and now she's texting me."

Erika smiled in a way that seemed a little forced.

"She wants to teach me how to skateboard."

"Are you going to go?"

"Maybe."

"Is she cute?"

My face burned. I wasn't used to making things up, and it felt dangerous and unsavory. It was hard to believe the lie wasn't obvious. I looked down at the tile floor between us, sticky with dried pools of frozen yogurt and covered with napkins and little bits of candy, nuts, and fruit smashed into the grout.

"Good for you, Julie," she said. "Text her back."

"Maybe," I said. "I don't know if I feel like it."

Two hours later, when the store closed, I found Erika in the supply closet of tall wire shelves where we stocked the dry goods and paper products, reaching for a box of latex gloves. When I slid behind her, I put my hand on her back and asked her to throw down a box of paper towels. Except for a dull amber light bulb, the closet was dark.

"I already changed those," she said. "Both bathrooms and the kitchen."

"Okay, thanks," I said, but I didn't move my hand.

"Also, you shouldn't touch me like that."

I stepped back and she turned to face me. There wasn't much space in the supply closet and we were maybe a foot apart. She had taken off her polo shirt and was now wearing an FSU T-shirt cut up into a tank top that showed the sides of a black sports bra.

"I'm sorry—" I said, but then she turned toward me and brushed my hair away from my face with both hands and then we were kissing. Fast and hard, more breathless than it had been before. I slid my hands under her shirt and against her back; she pulled me against her and grabbed my butt. I thought, *If she tries to take off my clothes, right here, I will let her,* but then we heard Gina arrive to count the money and lock up, and Erika stepped back. I thought she was going to tell me she regretted it, that she'd made a mistake, but instead she squeezed my hand. "Let's clean up and get out of here, okay?"

The next half hour of side work was a slow, delicious ache. Erika looking over at me, blood thrumming in my ears. It was happening finally—the two of us—though I wasn't exactly sure what "it" was. All summer she'd treated me more gently and carefully than I'd wanted. We'd make out, roll around half naked, but if I reached for her pants, she'd stop me. Tonight, though, things felt different. Was it really possible that Jan knew how to make someone fall for you?

After work I followed her outside to the parking lot of the strip mall, walked in step with her without talking. The door to the laundromat two doors down was open, and the smell of bleach wafted out onto the sidewalk. The Indian food market had closed for the night but still had a neon flamingo in the window advertising Florida lottery tickets. At the corner by a defunct carwash, cars slowed for a stoplight. When we got to my sun-bleached Corolla, I said, "Are you going to take me somewhere?"

"Is that what you want?"

"Yes."

She looked at me for what felt like a long time.

"Okay," she said finally, "I'm texting you the address."

She'd left the sublease where she'd spent the summer and was now living in a gray shotgun house on the other side of town with little potted plants everywhere and a brown leather furniture set I'd never seen before. The kitchen and living room were dark, but I could hear music behind a closed door in the other bedroom. Erika gave me a beer and told me to wait in the living room while she changed her sheets, and I texted my mom that I was hanging out with a friend and would be home late. It wasn't even a lie exactly, but my mom didn't like Erika and I felt bad for not telling her the whole truth.

A few minutes later Erika appeared in the archway between the living room and the hallway and I followed her back to her room, which was painted electric blue and covered in small framed art prints. I took off my shirt first and kissed her, and then we were tangled on her bedspread in our underwear under her ceiling fan.

She kissed me and ran her hands along my body. "You're shivering," she said. "Are you cold?"

"No." I felt impatient and dizzy. She had leaned away from me and was propped up on an elbow.

"We don't have to do anything else," she said. "You know that, right?"

I pulled her on top of me, slid off my underwear. "Come on," I said. "Stop talking."

The rest was a blur of nerves and adrenaline until we were done and I was lying in the crook of her arm, the length of her body against mine, and time slowed down, and I felt like I was floating. If nothing else happened between us, I knew that this moment was enough.

That Monday afternoon she texted to say that she'd gotten the marketing internship. She was quitting Yotopia! and didn't want me to hear about it from someone else. Also, she'd had a good time with me on Friday but didn't think we should do it again. Hopefully I understood.

"Not really," I wrote back.

"Are you mad?" she texted.

"No."

"Do you regret it?"

"No. Do you?"

The gray text bubbles of ellipses appeared and disappeared. Then she texted back, "No."

Although I wanted more than anything to guilt her into seeing me again, I knew that I'd only gotten to have sex with her in the first place by playing it cool. "Hopefully I'll see you around, I guess," I wrote back. "Maybe we can be friends."

To this Erika responded almost immediately that she was sorry but no, she couldn't be my friend, although she wished me well.

Stupidly maybe, I felt fine, maybe even good. I had found someone perfect, and she had slept with me. The fact that she had done so against her better judgment just proved that she was attracted to me in the same combustible way I felt for her, and attraction like that seemed rare and true, a tugging magnet that couldn't easily be ignored. Eventually—maybe in a year, maybe in several years—it seemed possible we'd find our way back to each other.

Less than a week later, though, I was at Yotopia! when she stopped by to drop off her polo shirts and aprons. She was wearing tight jeans and a flannel shirt rolled up at the sleeves, showing off a thick-banded watch she always wore. Just the way she walked made my stomach swish. It was midday on a Monday, but I had the day off for parent-teacher conferences, and I could see that Erika was startled to see me. She waved and then walked over to Gina, who was doing paperwork at one of the tables out front. I could make out the gist of their conversation—good luck at the internship, come back if you ever need a job. Erika had worked there for two years, and Gina seemed genuinely sad to see her go. Then she peered out the window at Erika's car, where a pretty girl in mirrored sunglasses leaned against the bumper. "Is that Kat?"

Erika nodded. I couldn't hear what she was saying, but my heart was pounding. Kat was Erika's ex-girlfriend, her first true love, and now it seemed they were back together? Gina knocked on the window. Kat waved. Gina motioned for her to come in, and she put her phone in her back pocket and walked toward us. She was wearing very short jean shorts with the pockets hanging out under the fringe, cowboy boots. She was thin but curvy, with long shiny brown hair, big boobs, smooth muscular legs.

I took a drive-through order, and when I came back to get the frozen yogurt, Gina was behind the counter, making two choco-late/vanilla swirl cones. Kat was sitting across from Erika, legs stretched out under Erika's chair, and Erika was talking to her but also looking up at me, watching me in a deliberate way that was supposed to communicate something—that she was sorry, that she hadn't meant for me to see her with Kat. It was a guilty, pitying look, and I pretended not to notice. Gina handed them the cones and then the three of them chatted for another ten minutes before Kat and Erika stood up with their half-finished cones and left. They were walking across the parking lot, side by side, close but not touching, laughing about something, and all of a sudden I understood. Kat might have spent the summer elsewhere, but there had been no breakup—all along, all spring, all summer, while I had been falling in love with Erika, they had been together.

"That front door's covered in dog drool," Gina said. "It needs to get wiped down."

Paloma said that Erika was an asshole who deserved no more of my time or attention and that if I couldn't stop myself from thinking about her, I should make a list of her flaws. This was what she'd done with her ex-boyfriend Christian, and now she barely thought about him at all.

"I can't think of anything," I said. "Everything supposedly bad about her I like."

"She lied to you. She's twenty and into a seventeen-year-old. She has a girlfriend and a dumb haircut. She's not that good at art—"

"Okay," I said. "Please stop."

We were at school, sitting on a brick wall outside the cafeteria, eating lunch. The summer heat and humidity was finally giving way to fall. Across the lawn, a plastic bag sailed in the breeze.

Paloma took a bite of her sandwich and then lifted her sunglasses and squinted at me.

"Do you feel sick? Like physically."

I nodded. All week it had felt like the flu or how I imagined a drug withdrawal might feel—nausea, weakness, a lack of will to do anything but sit very still and cry.

"It gets better, I promise," she said. "You just can't let yourself contact her again or the wound doesn't heal, okay?"

Jan had gotten a job at a pop-up Halloween costume store in the lesser, and mostly defunct, Tallahassee Mall, so I was spending more time at home. Because of this and because Paloma was sick of hearing about Erika, I told my mom about Erika one morning while the two of us were folding laundry. I left out the part about us hooking up as well as my Jan-inspired campaign to win her back.

"I know you didn't like her," I said. "So now I guess you'll say I told you so."

"Oh come on, Jules," she said gently, and put her hand on my knee. "You know I don't think that. This is why you've been sad?"

I nodded.

"I'm sorry, honey," she said. "I hate that this happened."

To her credit, she didn't say anything else. She just hugged me and let me talk. That night we got candy at Publix and ordered pizza and stayed up late like old times, making fun of Lifetime movies until we couldn't keep our eyes open.

A couple days after that, though, Pete was over for dinner and said, out of nowhere, that breakups were hard, that even when he spoke to veterans and refugees and people who'd suffered great trauma, the issues they invariably came back to were about love.

"As humans we're wired that way," he said. "Don't let anyone tell you a breakup's not a big deal."

If he hadn't looked so pleased with himself, I might have let it go.

"I guess we don't have secrets anymore," I said to my mom. "So now I know."

She looked like I had punched her, which I suppose was what I had intended, though on some other level I was just naming the truth. Pete was now her confidante, and as much as she deserved to have him, I had once been her entire family and all she ever seemed to need.

On Halloween I was with Jan, watching television and waiting for trick-or-treaters who probably were not going to come, when I got a text from another Yotopia! employee, inviting me to a Halloween party at Erika's house. I knew that I wasn't *really* invited, but I was still thinking about it. "I shouldn't go, right?" I said. "Probably that would be a horrible idea?"

"Yes," Jan said. "But I understand why you would want to go."

"But I shouldn't, right?" I repeated.

She reached for a mini Snickers bar and then smiled at me the way teachers did when they refused to give you the answer. "You're practically an adult, Jules," she said. "If you want to go, I'm not going to stop you."

When I told her about Kat, she'd said that she'd never cheated but had been the other woman a few times and that she'd let things happen with David that should not have happened. That she was a person who understood how, in the name of love, you could do things that seemed foolish. David had been very jealous, had followed her around, gone through her purse. She'd been a cocktail waitress at the time and he'd been convinced that she was flirting with other guys. I thought, but didn't say, that she'd been in her sixties at the time, that to me this all sounded sad.

Now she said, "You know about the furniture, right? About David trying to burn down my house and kill me?"

I nodded, though I'd never heard it put that way.

"Nobody knows this and don't tell your mother," she said. "But I was with him after that for almost a year."

I sat very still and tried to look normal. On the television a commercial for auto insurance gave way to a cartoon cat dancing in a tray of kitty litter.

"I don't regret it, either," Jan said. "To be with the person you want is heaven. It doesn't have to be the right circumstances to feel good."

This was the opposite of what sounded true, the opposite of why my mom had told me she was with Pete. She loved him, yes, but the more important thing was that he was devoted and dependable, that he didn't jerk her around. I knew that Jan sounded crazy and that it made no sense for me to crash a party where a girl who had not only mistreated me but also made it very clear she didn't want to see me anymore would be hanging out with her girlfriend, but I also knew that I was going to go. I wanted to be in the same room with her, and I wanted this helpless feeling to go away. To imagine a lifetime of this feeling made me dizzy.

"I just want to be around her, I guess," I said. "That's all."

Jan had a box of Halloween costumes, a few new ones she'd gotten on discount this fall.

"Go for an hour," she said. "Wear a mask and don't say anything. I'll drive."

Something Street

FROM *Story*

I.

WHAT IS GREATNESS? Funny dad sweaters, a sentimental nose, adorable crunkles in the corners of one's eyes. Hilarious tales of the old country, Somethingville, North Carolina, when men were men, women women, etc.—long-shouldered negresses being a special commodity, like lucky dice or a prizewinning calf. Fifty-four years ago, directly after our nuptials, Craw Daddy looked me dead in the eye and said, *It's all mapped out, Parthenia, one foot after the other. Are you in or you out? Cause there ain't doing both.*

We were honeymooning in a stately brick in the Irish part of Yonkers, and I was feeling too beautiful for my own good. Uppity, my mam would've said. Course I let him have his feet, one after the other. Up one street and down another. Upon one threshold and across another. Turn the other cheek, Mam advised me in a daydream. The women in those doors are not queens. They have nothing on you. They ain't even yellow.

II.

Our marriage in 1956—with the understanding that some things get better and some worse but bottom line you ultimately float somewhere near the surface. *Yes* to the women fans, *yes* to the terribly late forays, *yes* to the pee smell of breath. *Yes* as long as he comes home by dawn and doesn't wake the children, *yes yes.* You float and float with affirmatives; you may not be kicking but you will be gulping.

III.

Greatness is a cherished chestnut, humbly weaving its way out the comedian's mouth: *Did I ever tell you about the time Mama Love whupped my PARDON MY FRENCH?* We're in the auditorium of Ogden Hall, filled to capacity with hundreds here to see his farewell tour. The last time he will take us down Something Street.

And the comedian my husband glistens in the spotlight. Moments before he took the stage, a lackluster girl student applied a hint of Ambi lightening cream under his eyes and over his cheeks, to promote his already fulsome visage—EBONI, her nametag reads. The boy student next to her has a tag that merely says, HELLO MY NAME IS; both are otherwise nondescript save for the matching varsity scarves (neatly knotted) and Greek badges pinned on their breasts (gold, pearls, and black enamel for Alpha Delta Pi). There is no hint of lotion on their volcanic-ash arms, and both heads are bone-withered with neglect. The eyes belonging to this girl and boy seem overcast. One would think they had somewhere else to be.

But I know this type well. In all probability Eboni and Hello My Name Is are kissing the ground Craw Daddy walks upon, grateful to have been granted the chance to tend to the comedian my husband during his annual visit to Hampton University (née Institute, why in heavens did they change that glorious old name?). Before the performance Hello My Name Is hauled a folding table center stage while Eboni poured a glass of water or gin into a tumbler. When Craw Daddy walked on and greeted the crowd, they stood back and looked up into the rafters, as if checking for dust mites in the beams of light. Likely their minds were like, *His air, Lord, how blessed we are to breathe in his air!*

It's a natural cycle; I know my head once worked that way.

The comedian my husband begins his set; the students are standing near me in the curtains, grimacing and scratching their coffee-colored necks with their hands. They notice the pram I'm rocking, perhaps they are up here wondering whether the baby will be a potential disturbance? The girl and boy edge closer to me, sharpening their eyes in that sickening way the Sable-Tea Club ladies used to do (how I loved and dreaded their homilies on *The Progressive Colored Doyenne!*), and I can almost hear the prayer bursting forth from their reverent mouths: *Let the Good Lord do his work to preserve the peace so that the Almighty Comedian may once again entertain us and lift us and teach us, etc. etc.*

I've heard that prayer before.

Eboni hisses at the boy, *Where her chair at, Paul? You expecting her to stand the whole damn night?* Paul scuttles away quietly, further backstage. Eboni's grimace does not leave her face. *Your husband didn't mention his lady was gonna be here tonight,* she said. *Ain't that the shit?*

IV.

The floors of the ancient stage rattle as the comedian my husband wanders up and down in the ancient spotlight, beginning his stories. The audience hovers—I can tell there is nary a whiff of the Complaints anywhere at all. In this moment, nothing is lost. He is bright, he is shining. His teeth bare white into every soul in the house. *Mama Love, she made me who I am today. Y'all tell me if you heard this one before.*

V.

In all other moments, we've lost damn near everything.

VI.

Back in the day, the Sable-Tea Club ladies loved showing their Mahogany Maidens (yes, that was the word they used for us) the right way to act: how to set a table, to use silverware, to answer a telephone; they were against elbows, against overly wide mouths and hands that did not obey; they absolutely loathed wagging tongues. We sat on a slipcovered couch in the home of a full-bodied New Rochelle matron, sipping sorrel tea, dreaming of biscuits and Shirley Temples, reciting the first few syllables of *Lysistrata,* stretching our pinkies in the air just like white girls, nodding tastefully to Perry Como and Nat King Cole—maybe someone would mention Dr. King, and like magic the reverent swaying of heads and chests would commence. Our voices were orderly. *Did you know that at those marches, the wind can go and make one's hair most unflattering? Did you know you could wear out a good pair of nylons just by standing and holding a sign?* We were all for racial progress and whatnot, but honestly: none of us Mahogany Maidens *actually wanted* to use a public water fountain, colored or white.

VII.

Who didn't think that being a part of the Sable-Tea Club Ladies wasn't greatness itself? After a customary lecture (perhaps on the place of classical Latin in the contemporary domicile), we made our way to the luncheon spread on a huge oak table covered in lemon wax and doilies. Meats, gelatin molds, cold European soups that tasted like resurrected earth. Watercress sandwiches, a charger of raspberry thumbprints. The Sable-Tea Club ladies thanked that very special matron for her hospitality, then made us hold hands for the Lord's Prayer. She whispered that if we messed up any of the words, we'd get our black behinds beat big-time.

VIII.

Your husband is a hell of a man, Eboni says to me. Paul brings the folding chair toward us and gently opens it. *Your husband is a great man,* Eboni repeats. All side-eye. Her voice is a stone of worship, and I shiver. *What did you say your name was,* I ask stupidly. A momentary blip. Everything is over her face.

IX.

Greatness is the complete absorption of all surrounding good.

X.

Tell me if I'm repeating myself. The comedian my husband actually stole this line from another funnyman, Canny Blackbottom at the Richmond Hippodrome 1963. Craw Daddy heard it, clapped his hands, and announced: *That gold's mine.* He was fifth on the lineup after Canny, his belly hollowed out by the Hippodrome's hot-sauce chicken wings and rigorous barbecue pork. When it was his turn, Craw Daddy was hissed to shame. He looked back and saw Canny watermelon-grinning in the wings. My husband the comedian straightened his tie, tightened his belt. *You chitlin-circuit nigger, what the hell you got that I ain't?* My husband the comedian whispered the line a thousand times in case he might mispronounce it. *Tell me if I'm repeating myself.* Canny rose a fuss, but Craw Daddy ignored him. He made that line his own. He considered it merely borrowing.

XI.

His career took off—money blew up like the Fourth of July. The '60s, '70s, '80s were a filament of cars, boats, houses, massive vacations. One time we took a riverboat down the Egyptian Nile, another we saw wild elephants tango-dance outside our hotel window in Nairobi. Occasionally there were diamonds and Russell Stover chocolate hearts and American Beauties in a Waterford vase—I didn't mind them at all. I remembered his words. At the start of the Complaints, people predicted his career would take a beating. Luckily the only aftershock I can recall was the loss of hearth home dignity courage and imagination. And it is scientifically proven you can rise back to the surface without any of those trappings.

XII.

Paul grumbles something into Eboni's ear, then takes off again, slue-footed as a Norfolk penguin. She is left to rummage through a patent leather purse draped across her chest, its strap hooking itself onto the varsity badge. I had not seen the purse earlier, and for reasons I cannot ascertain in the moment, I smile. Sunday school, Easter parade, cotillion drag. Warmth fills my body. I want to share that warmth. I myself was Delta Sigma Theta through and through: *Don't ask me bout my hair and I won't tell* (inside joke); I want to inquire about her days here at Hampton, to say something innocuous about how sororities must have changed since my time —but just as quick she snaps shut the purse and stares straight ahead. There is a key in her hands. It is pulled through her index and middle fingers, and it is something like a gun. *That baby your grandkid*, she asks. When I nod, she hoists the gun up to her lips.

XIII.

Why you crying? What have I done to make you sad? Parthenia. Baby Girl. We've lived all over this great green country!

This is what he told me after the Beverly Hills house was auctioned.

No sense in crying, Parthenia. What matters most is the home in our heart.

This was said as a comfort. After the fourth Complaint, we had to give up Boca Raton and Savannah too, plus my Van Cleef and all the damn Christofle.

XIV.

Historically he has always been a taker and a giver. Craw Daddy gave my parents just enough to ease their arms from around my shoulders. He took me when I wasn't looking. He gave a nearly sober speech at our wedding banquet, the one where some of the Sable-Tea Club ladies came to pay respects, handing over lavender sachets with ten-dollar bills sewn inside. He gave them his hand. *Yes I do swear to honor and obey this high society gal* (the Sable-Tea ladies may have detected a bit of sass in that vow), *Yes I am forever grateful she deigned look upon my face.* Craw Daddy rose from the ashes of poverty to claim me: I, who under normal circumstances would not have set foot on Something Street to save my life. What is greatness if not that?

XV.

Outside, our driver waits for us in the parking lot off Shore Drive. His name is Clarence, a name the comedian my husband finds perfect in its old-fashioned darkyness (Craw Daddy's actual words were *At least he ain't got one of these fake African bullshit monikers,* though I've always dreamed of asking him what sort of name he considers Marquita, an appellation his mother—on her deathbed—forced upon our firstborn). Clarence the driver is likely on his cell phone, calling home, finding out supper; he couldn't be bothered with the farewell tour. He couldn't be bothered with the famed Ogden Hall of Hampton University (née Institute), although he might pause and gaze balefully in our direction and think of millions of dollars lining his imaginary mattress, dollars he might could've had if he'd played his cards right (wasn't his cousin doing standup at the Newport News Laugheteria? Next month Las Vegas?)—Clarence might see in his mind's eye the way Craw Daddy strides up to the edge of the stage and begins his stories; he might see me propping myself in the curtains (the folding chair was too hard), the pram rocking under my hand, the grandson left to us by my third-born daughter as a wanton gift; he might not give a good goddamn. He might feel sorry for not acting the man earlier, when I was in his car.

Clarence will whip out a cigarette or joint, open his phone, scour personal ads, think up lottery numbers.

What's the baby's name, the girl Eboni asks me. Somehow I have learned that she is a grown woman, all of thirty years old, and that the boy is her husband. Her exact words were *I should thank you for thinking me younger, but I'll just chalk it up to you being blind as a bat, Mrs. Craw Daddy. Why do you got your grandbaby here?*

XVI.

The boy comes up from behind suddenly with a large swivel desk chair, which Eboni guides me into. My body is nearly too large for this seat but I do not say anything; I have grown old as gracefully as necessary. I hold out my hand to the boy, but he does not take it —manners clearly elude this specimen. *Never mind him,* Eboni says. *Why don't you sit, Mrs. Craw Daddy? Sitting will make it easier.*

She undoes the scarf around her neck. The area there is black as a banana peel: a hickey, a testament to youthful love. I have no idea where that key has got to.

XVII.

Moses, I wanted to call him, the day I opened the front door of our present rental apartment in Aberdeen Gardens and found a baby swaddled in a basket—though the name our third-born daughter had given him in the attached note was different. Something in between Africa and Europe, a name meant to sound unique but that actually had the ring of homemade commons to it. *[. . .] will save you*, the note read. *Treat him better than you did your own girls.*

XVIII.

Times past, Ogden Hall has been host to some of the finest black entertainers of the country; it is a killer diamond that's lived through the weight of history, all those marchers and protesters and mindblown soldiers of the '70s. I started out in 1955 but didn't actually finish my degree until I returned in 1974. Bit of a wait in the middle there, what with kids, house, houses, Craw Daddy's fame. The Complaints. Each time I was a student here, I was not a troublemaker. I did not wear an Afro, nor did I burn my cotillion gowns. Ogden Hall counts itself lucky to invite the comedian my husband back every few years and have him actually come. They were saddened by the idea of a farewell tour but nonetheless welcomed him with outstretched arms. They have no idea we've lost everything, that the comedian my husband accepts every invite happily, including the retirement homes and dinner theaters. The Complaints are to blame, but what's a woman to do?

XIX.

Once upon a time there was dark-as-night wide-hipped sassy-lipped Mama Love and her famous flat iron. She was my mama, and she raised us all on Something Street. Craw Daddy walks the stage as he narrates, gesticulating wildly, waving that flat iron in faces, sticking his hand round the waists of barrel-bodied women, pointing make-believe shotguns at no-count lotharios, rubbing sleep from the eyes of drunks. Something Street is alive. Somehow Mama Love's flat iron —which had started out that day straightening his sister Flayla's nappy head—wants, in the end, to *smack some sense* into Craw (her only boy-child, who'd innocently asked the meaning of the word *dyke*). Loads of laughter. Before the first blow can be administered, the flat iron mysteriously takes wing and sails into the sky, never to be seen again. All the while Flayla's eyes screw themselves deeper into her undone head. *Whatever could that child be guilty of?* Just then Butchy Barbara looms her head over the windowsill and smirks. *Wanna kiss, baby? We ain't got nothing to lose!* Where in tarnation did she come from? The crowd just about dies.

XX.

In my second year as a coed at Hampton Institute, the great Mahalia Jackson took this same stage. She sang only one song. But all around her: the hush of greatness, of legacy. Thoughts buzzing in grateful heads: *How did we get here? How shall we remain? Are we witnessing the Negro's progress and legacy?* All manner of monumental thoughts. I was already attached to Craw Daddy. I put my hands over my ears.

XXI.

Ya'll want to hear bout Mama Love and her twelve disobedient children and her ne'er-do-well mate, Drunky Poppy? Or do y'all want to hear about Mama Love and her thieving neighbor, Miss Hattie-No-Goody, who had a habit of tasting Mama's pies on the sill? Tell me, y'all, if you heard those ones before!

The comedian my husband holds up his hand: *Okay, okay, let's be serious for a moment. Without Mama Love and the kind of upbringing she instilled in me, I would not be standing before you today. Can I get an AMEN? I, a God-fearing man with a heart of pure gold and a lovely bride of fifty-four years—Hey, Parthenia, whyn't you come out and meet my new friends? Praise God, but shouldn't we all have been raised by a woman like Mama Love?*

(A side whisper: *That is, if we remember to put the cast-iron pan inside our britches for protection, seeing how Mama Love could swat you for days, and the lack of that pan meant certain death of the booty, so can I get an AMEN?*)

The audience falls out their seats, bits and pieces of their limbs shattering on the tile floor. They don't wait for me to come out; I become an afterthought before I can even be. In 1956 the song Mahalia Jackson performed was "Move On Up a Little Higher." She walked past me as the applause enveloped her, slow and belligerent like an autumn cocoon. She did not lift her eyes.

XXII.

First intermission: I leave the sleeping baby in the back and wander the aisles. The audience aren't finished slapping their knees, wiping away mirthful tears, coughing into wadded-up tissues. They slowly re-form themselves as the lights go up, turning toward one another and repeating the best bits. *Hey, you seen Craw Daddy's show in Atlanta? He had us rolling in the aisles with Mama Love and the wheelbarrow. Shit, yeah, Craw Daddy brung down the house there! Mama Love make me want to pee my drawers! Every. Damn. Time.*

In the midst of this, someone dares mention the Complaints —a woman, of course. Eyebrows are raised. Faces turned toward her with scorn. *Why you have to go and mention that, Gladys? Why even bring that shit up? Let the man have one night free and clear, now is not the time for that shit.*

The woman Gladys says something along the lines of *Well, if it was my man out there doing that,* and they shut her down instantly. *Close your got-damn trap, Gladys. You bought a ticket same as us. He is our man, he will always be our man.*

XXIII.

Backstage, the comedian my husband is suddenly standing next to me, gulping down the glass of gin or water. Eboni stands in his shadow with his seersucker jacket over her left arm. With her right, she reaches down and scratches the back of her knee. I see that. I see her glance at her shoes, then straighten her jumper, then reach back down to that tender spot. She doesn't see me seeing her. But I do. The back of the knee can be the most telltale part of the body. There is the banana black of her neck, but that means nothing to the soft mattress of her knee. I am frustrated to be completely out of tears.

XXIV.

Girl, go get my wife something cold to drink, you see she about to faint, ain't you? Go to the fridge in my dressing room, hear? It's some refreshments there.

To me he winks. *Child's an idjit,* Parthenia. He waits a few heartbeats. *Let me go find her and make sure she don't get the order wrong. I'm so sorry about before, Parthenia, you know it's not in me to hit a woman. Not even you. I have no idea what got into me back there in the car, but I swear if I hurt you I got no reason to stand like a man. Forgive me?*

I nod. He does not have a dressing room. There is no fridge.

You, you, you, you, you.

XXV.

Ten minutes pass. The pair returns without my drink. Out of ancient habit I kiss Craw's cheek.

He hangs his big head into the pram. *Be careful, little buddy,* he says to the baby; then tells me he has to sail off to hair and makeup; he swears he needs more lightening cream. More Old Spice aftershave. Looks to Eboni and nods. I have seen many fans, many autograph-seekers, many groupies, if you will. I know the silence that overtakes them in the presence of greatness. She and him leave once more, and perhaps fifteen new minutes go by; when the comedian my husband returns—alone—his face is pure ravishment. Red pimples under graham cracker skin, the shine of battered delight. I know that look. A bargain is a bargain. But I know that look. *Little buddy,* he whispers into the pram, *this one day gonna be you. And I'm a lead the way.*

XXVI.

All her life our third-born had been the sweetest of the three, hanging on to her father's every word, attaching herself to his leg as he walked, baking him cakes even when it wasn't his birthday. When she became a teenager, however, she took a different route. I would come home from a day of shopping and find Craw and Joanna at each other's throats; or else, late at night, we would find Joanna and her friends keying the cars in one of the driveways. The patio tables of every house were shattered with bottles of Ole Grandad and Lancers wine. Swear words galore. Drugs, powders, hypodermic needles, spoons. The comedian my husband said the girl was out her damn mind. His exact words. One time in Atlanta Joanna yelled up the stairs, *You want to screw Rochelle? Well, get this, old man: you ain't her type!* Her exact words.

Craw Daddy ran down and grabbed Joanna by the scruff. *Everything about you abominates me to no end! You faster than a junkyard dog! Out here doing these drugs and out here to ruin my reputation. You and that slut Rochelle! What you thinking, girl?*

(Rochelle, Joanna's best friend in Atlanta. A year younger in high school, pretty as a nectarine. Why in heavens would my daughter say such a thing? When things blew over, I told the girls I would take them shopping at Lenox Square, but Rochelle's parents would later tell me I was not appropriate.)

She mines and not yours, Joanna answered, to which she saw the back of Craw's hand. I did not like that one bit. I told my husband the comedian that he needed to stop hitting our third-born, that she was our flesh and bones, and after he landed another swop, he did.

(The Complaints were just a trickle on the horizon, nothing to get worked up about. Nevertheless I was left wondering: How does he know Rochelle is a slut?)

XXVII.

During second intermission, Craw Daddy disappears into the aisles to sign early autographs. The baby wakes, and I bend to lift him into my arms. He is not our first grandparent rodeo, this boy. Marquita, our firstborn, has a brood of boys almost large enough to fill the front row center. Several years ago her (Howard University—*sigh*) husband literally whisked her off her Spelman feet and landed her not a mile from our alma mater in bare toes and bulging belly.

Now there are six grands that direction—oh, what the Sable-Tea Club ladies would have said! Back in the day, two was their perfect number. Two became the new one (one being a slavery number, as my mam used to observe); some years later, when my girls were grown, three became the new two. And shortly after that, five became the new three. Five is comfort, ambition, confidence. I believe that even my mam would not have frowned upon five. But six? Six is a descent back toward field days, God help us!

No matter. I loved those babies like I love myself until Marquita one day up and said, *He's not allowed here anymore, Mom. I want different for my boys.*

My mam no longer walks the earth. She's buried in Wartburg Cemetery, Mount Vernon, New York, right next to Daddy, who was lifted into his casket wearing his Pullman's uniform, God bless him.

Our second-born, Winifred, thought at first that the Complaints were a "racialist" attack of some sort. She wondered whether white comedians suffered the same sorts of condemnation. Winifred held her father's arm as we walked up and down the courthouse steps. After we lost the Atlanta house to a "fire" in 2000 (the police said they thought it was arson but had nothing real to go on) Winifred took a moment for herself, a timeout, she called it. She has not spoken to her father since.

I want to say *Her loss* in the way my husband says *Her loss* when he references Winifred—but the words stick in my throat. She and I began communicating on the q.t. A shopping mall here, a Baskin-Robbins there. Craw knew nothing. Winifred and I met at Buckroe Beach; she brought her three girls, whom I immediately doted upon with ice cream sandwiches and neon fizzle pop. *Children can be such gems,* I said. *They are always the apple of their grandparents' eyes.* Winifred wasn't having any of it. *Mother,* she said (in her usual two-pronged manner), *it's only a matter of time. You're better than this.*

The sun was magnificently high and away on that gray sand afternoon. *I'm better than what, Winifred? Don't you know that it was I that got you here? Made you into a lady you are sitting before your little darlings?*

Oh, Mother. We love you. But this is not you.

I finished my ice cream sandwich and tried to give my second-born the death stare. I couldn't, of course. I don't have some things within me. Besides, a cadre of white people wandered past, all of them licking ice cream cones and admiring the glistening waters; it wouldn't do to show my colors in front of them. Old habits, I suppose. *Winifred*, I said, *I've always tried to do my best. I don't abandon ship. I stand tall. I stand fast.*

Oh, Mother. No one is talking about a ship. It's the women he's had, some against their will. And you standing behind him.

Naturally I stand behind him. He is our rock.

Oh, Mother. When will the world ever see your true face?

Hurtful words. Of course, home training has taught me to shield the world from my raging emotions, the overflowing cup of my indignations. Since that afternoon—two years ago now—I've sent Winifred weekly letters, but have yet to find an answer in my box. I sign my letters with *Warmly*, or *All My love*, or *Sincerely Yours, Mother Best.*

This babe I currently swaddle, I have no idea when or where he was born, who the father. His tiny brown face is shaped like a heart, and his fingers are worse than vise grips. When she was not even out of elementary school, Joanna once told her father, *I don't care what anybody say. You are my daddy and you are not bad.*

Time for you to make amends, seeing as you didn't hear me the first time. Such harsh words. They were written in the note pinned to the car seat, the one she parked on our front step in Aberdeen Gardens—complete with baby—five days ago. There was also a small Polaroid of Rochelle, whose face was against the camera. *Rochelle has been put away. I don't know if for good.*

Craw, I asked. *Whatever does this mean?*

XXVIII.

In 1956 my beloved father took us into our parlor and loomed as the comedian my future husband sipped an Italian coffee—Mam had spent time on the Continent and was eager to show it. *Now you listen*, my father began. *Parthenia, she is not like any regular gal off the street. She is a lady. She's had training. Me, I'm more like you—wrong side of the tracks and whatnot. Don't know which fork to use and whatnot. That is not Parthenia. Her mater and I done all we could to create her into a picture of feminine charms. And I command you to treat her as such. Am I making myself clear, son?*

His broad brown hands, caked in oil; and when he spoke, he stooped. This was the voice he'd used with the young men at Union Station, the ones who needed the most Pullman training, the best guidance, my father misquoting Du Bois with nothing but love: *Work is the knob to uplift the people!* What I would give to hear that voice again. He would know what to do about the Complaints. He would know what to do with my soul.

XXIX.

Craw's proposal under the Emancipation Oak was quick, mostly painless. There was hardly any blood. I hitched down my dress, thought about my Aunt Leah, who'd married her first cousin despite her people's objections and then went around quoting Paul Dunbar: "This is the debt I pay, just for one riotous day." During Literary Hour in the New Rochelle parlor, we Mahogany Maidens found that line hilarious.

XXX.

Craw and I had no major discussions, no mapping out of the future, no tender treading of intimate territories. When we came home from the justice of the peace, Mam served dandelion wine in tumblers bearing little umbrellas. Daddy made a show of wanting me to finish up school, but Mam said it was plenty of young colored ladies that started their families and went back later. In fact, she was even thinking of doing the same! (The liar!)

XXXI.

Craw Daddy is back onstage, and next to me, Eboni's lips shine full-blown in the darkness of the curtains, like freshly baked crescent rolls. Those lips have just been loved. Was it in her will or against it? She avoids my eyes and I'm understanding suddenly that I cannot possibly know the meaning of devotion and perhaps never could.

XXXII.

Where were you all this time, I ask her. *Have you been following the come-dian my husband for an autograph?* She looks away. Then says to me, *I always pictured you different. Maybe it's the black eye.*

XXXIII.

Did I ever tell you about the time Drunky Poppy nearly mowed our small house into the ground?

Yes. The audience has heard Drunky Poppy many times before, even on televised appearances: Johnny Carson, *The Flip Wilson Show.* Dinah Shore had so many tears in her eyes from laughing it was rumored she passed gas on the set.

The crowd closes its eyes and envisions a raggedy, brown-skinned hunchback driving his summer tractor down the middle of Something Street. Forget the tobacco field, where his helpmeet and progeny stand under an unforgiving sun, covered in morning sweat. Mama Love and her twelve children will wait on that tractor unto eternity.

Tonight is a variant of the story: It so happens that Drunky Poppy woke up later than usual, and in an effort to avoid be-ing castigated by Mr. Woodwardward (proprietor of the tobacco farm) jumps out the house without his spectacles. Mayhem en-sues. He jumpstarts the tractor and makes a series of wrong turns, first passing the moonshine shack out back the farmhouse where he and his lady friend, aka Roomy Rhonda, secretly *rendezvous.* Laughter. He passes women hanging laundry, rustling children, and tending garden rows—don't even get him started on the vari-ous names of the garden tools (he will not bring himself to say *hoe,* that is a part of the contemporary vernacular he despises and claims will drag us colored folk straight to hell). Another moon-shine shack nearby, then another. At the beginning of Something Street, Drunky Poppy nearly plows his tractor over some little old ladies. They are on their way to the Church of the Wooden Hand.

(Craw's actual mother had once tried to join the order of the White Ladies of Africa before they closed their door on her face.)

Drunky Poppy nearly flattens a group of deserving orphans playing stickball and, after that, practically kills the baker carrying the preacher's daughter's wedding cake—imagine the pandemonium!—before he careens into A. A.'s General Supply—the entire storefront has been crashed inward, there is clearly no saving anything, from the soda cracker barrels to the ladies' hysteria drops. *Sorry bout that,* Drunky Poppy calls out from the light fixture, which has crowned (but miraculously not hurt) him, *but mah oman done axed me to drive her car to church n pick huh up after preacher done got done.* By now everyone in the audience can smell the booze on the comedian's lips, feel it erupt from his pores like so many miniature volcanoes. I, on the other hand, can feel Mama Love's legs as she kicks away the biting flies in the tobacco field.

Oh yeah? This response comes from African Andy, the "blueblack" shop owner, who, from underneath a broken barrel of self-rising (!) flour, shouts, *Man, you gone pay wid yo life!* (the audience goes wild!) *and furthermore, you ain't driving no car! Your mama so dumb, Drunky Poppy, she done sold her car for gasoline!* Drunky Poppy puts the tractor in reverse before the good shopkeeper can collar him, then incredibly makes it to the church (pummeling over prize roses)—now there is the gang of deserving orphans in tow, all of whom vow to avenge themselves on the *"absinthetic ass."* They catch up to him, but not before Drunky Poppy runs over a fire hydrant—which spurts upward like Niagara Falls—and washes just about everyone clear into the doors of the church (this part of the tale does take a while to wade through, no pun intended; it has never been my favorite, it defies every law of physics) and the water carries the man and his tractor right up to the pulpit, where a shocked (and portly) Pastor Breadlove falls into the arms of the choir women, one of whom is Miss *Poosy,* reformed lady-o-the-night (the audience screams). This literal turn of events horrifies the preacher's daughter, Velvet—the poor girl falls into the arms of her own betrothed, Stanley Morehousehead (in reality, Craw Daddy has hated every HBCU except Hampton), and together the lovebirds are caught up in the raging waters; their choir gowns hook in the large left front wheel, forcing the pair to be dragged alongside the tractor as it heads up the aisle. Velvet must hold fast to the scraps that are her only covering; of course, Stanley Morehousehead is too stupid to try and rip his gown from his body and shield her.

(The audience roll from their seats into the aisles; it is too much, too much indeed!)

Velvet grabs her fiancé and together the (still unwed) couple allow themselves to be pulled along like a dog on a leash, her good cream-clotted skin turning red with humiliation, his dusky hue growing *nightier* by the minute. They flow out the church all the way to Buck River. There the bridegroom catches hold of a tree (a weeping willow, of course) and frees himself from the flood, from Velvet. *My mother always warned me about girls like you,* he cries. Velvet is last seen washing along Buck River's tides toward the tobacco field, where the workers have long since elected to carry out their day.

(The audience is an utter paroxysm. Heads go rolling off the slippery slopes of shoulders, brassieres snap open, revealing breasts as deflated as summer pies. Pure unadulterated laughter. Madness, even. No one is remotely thinking about the Complaints.)

XXXIV.

You know what he likes to do, don't you, the girl whispers. *He's been doing it all week. I thought right up to now I liked it.*

The look on her face. There were the regular places for the eyes, nose, and mouth, and yet they been washed away, as in one of those old spiritualist photographs of the nineteenth century. Later in court I would learn that he was only *tryna show her a new way to please her husband. Men can be fickle,* Craw Daddy had assured her. *With me what you see is what you get, baby.*

XXXV.

I'd been having thoughts.

XXXVI.

More thoughts, new thoughts. Just this morning over breakfast I looked into the baby's eyes and then went over to Craw in the living room, fast asleep. *We can't keep him,* I say. *We have no right. He is not yours. He is not mine.*

Craw Daddy laughed in my face. *I've always wanted a son,* he said. *What's wrong with that? Hell with Joanna and that other girl. They both gone crazy, you ask me.*

They're not girls, I say. *They haven't been girls for a long time.*

Last I checked that Rochelle was nothing but a slut! Craw is silent after admitting this. I don't understand.

XXXVII.

We can't keep this baby, I said again to Craw Daddy on the drive over here. Clarence the driver in the front seat. Craw raised his eyebrows. I put my hand on his shoulder. *We just can't. We have no right.*

My husband the comedian craned his neck toward our driver up front. *You hear that, Clarence? You hear this fool woman? Thinking I'm not good enough to raise my own* so-called *flesh and blood?*

Clarence remained driving. It was a light rain in the trees, a balminess settling over the windshield like a bassinet cover.

We have to do the right thing, I said. Remembering the sound of the word *so-called.*

A deal is a deal, he answered.

What if this baby is no deal, I asked. I was not even sure what I was meaning.

Silence. I don't know if he waited one or two minutes before slapping me. I do know the car swerved, that Clarence opened his door, jumped out, pulled Craw behind him. *We just need some fresh air,* Clarence said, wiping his forehead with an old-fashioned handkerchief. He looked into my eyes and turned away. I had no idea men still carried those sorts of things.

XXXVIII.

Eboni says, *You tell your husband when the show's done my husband'll be out back. We want to show him what he means to us.*

XXXIX.

The baby shifts in the pram, even tries to claw its way up to the hood. I quickly push it down, ignoring its cries, and head toward the stage door in back. I make noise as I clatter us out onto the neat cobbles of the pedestrian path just steps away from the river. The baby becomes more and more unruly, shirking at my touch. Can infants do such things? I wonder. I push that pram along the cobbles to the rocky breaker blocking the rushing water; as I do, I long to pick up one of the cigarette butts at my feet. If I were a different kind of grandmother-type, I might stow this baby in a pie safe and run off looking for a tobacco field of my own.

XL.

And here's Clarence clomping toward me, sans driving cap, his shirt partially undone, faux-tortoiseshell buttons; likely he'll think I'm mad at him from before—nobody likes a lady with a black eye. My mouth feels dry and my throat aches. *You want me to push that for you, ma'am?* he asks, huffing beside me. Clarence had looked much slimmer from the backseat. Now I take in his large stomach, his saggy legs. I shake my head, unable to move my lips. He does not hear me choke for breath.

Don't do anything rash, ma'am. You see, I could hear you all the way from the car. Come away from that river. I wouldn't want you to do anything rash.

XLI.

As early as 1962, *Time* magazine described my husband, Crawley Stevenson, as "The Only Wonder of the World That Will Make You Double Over . . . in Fits of Laughter!" In 1963 the *Amsterdam News* wrote, "The Negro Genius That Will Bring White Folks to Their Knees!" In 1967 the *Buffalo Challenger:* "Craw Stevenson Is More than Meets the Eye!" The "reporters" of the September 1968 *Hampton Cotillion Broadside* called him "Our Favorite Mystery Date" and dared any woman on the planet to go up to my face and ask me what was my secret.

XLII.

Los Angeles 2010. The Complaints did indeed vex me, but I raised my right hand to God and swore that the testimony I was about to give was the whole truth. For the courtroom I chose the Halston halter-neck Craw had bought in Beverly Hills just the month before; he'd told me he liked nothing better than seeing a strong black woman in a great dress turn all evil whites on their heads.

<u>Complaint 1, August 1965:</u> Craw was with me in Las Vegas, the Sands. We slept together in the same room. Craw went out briefly for smokes. How could he have done anything like that woman said he did—and in such a *short time*? <u>Complaint 2, June 1979:</u> Craw literally had to beat the fans off him—men and women alike—as he mounted that Little Rock stage. They wouldn't stop. Far as I'm concerned, you reap just what you sow. <u>Complaint 3, April 1980:</u> She stalked me, called the house more than once, even breathed heavy into the phone with her accusations. Craw had to put an end to those shenanigans. End of story. <u>Complaint 4 (date unknown):</u> Politically incorrect, yes, but it's the truth: she was not his type. Nothing could've happened. She was not even remotely yellow. <u>Complaint 5 (date unknown):</u> Can you blame him for placing five thousand dollars in an envelope and slipping it to the Atlanta concierge? How could he have known that cameras had been trained upon him? People will do anything to blackmail a good black man for a little extra cash. <u>Complaint 6 (date unknown):</u> Can he help it if he is so famous, so beloved? <u>Complaint 7, November 1977:</u> Things were rough, plus the girls all grown and hating me for no good reason. I spent time tending to my parents' home in Mount Vernon, and when I got back to Pensacola, Winifred is up here telling me about the two heifers that had moved in the moment I left, playing house in my kitchen, using my utensils, cooking his food. Marquita claimed she saw them suck his privates! And I slapped her—*He is still your father,* I said, *come hell or high water.* Joanna over in the corner: *At least if we was in high water we could drown* (to which I slapped her as well). <u>Complaint 8, December 1977:</u> This tramp in question was the daughter of someone at Links—do you know Links? They sent me a letter. *Please don't bother to ask, Mrs. Stevenson. We are a family-oriented organization, we only want credits to our race.* <u>Complaints 9 and 10, both in December 1991:</u> No comment, on

advice of counsel. <u>Complaint 11, somewhere June or July 1999.</u>
We all grew back together, branches on the proverbial family tree.
Except without the branches. Never again answered the phone at
night, never spoke to reporters. Never again raised my hand in
protest, never again found anything missing from my kitchen.

XLIII.

Clarence is steering the pram by my side. Smart Van Heusen shirt
with hideous Haband trousers. I think he could be in love with
men. *Why*, I want to ask him. *Why?*

XLIV.

That is not the question, however. I ask Clarence if he could keep
the baby overnight at his house, possibly longer, definitely longer,
maybe forever? He looks at me crazy. *What you mean, Mrs. Craw
Daddy*, he asks. I repeat myself: *Take the boy home. Your wife will know
what to do. He can't belong to us anymore. He never has.*

*Heavens, I ain't married, Mrs. Craw Daddy! I couldn't take no child,
it's just me and my cousin Junius.*

I think for a moment. *Mr. Clarence*, I say. *I'm not opposed to two
men raising the tyke. I've never been opposed. Please excuse my husband
the comedian for anything he might've said in the past that would indicate
we are narrow-minded, Mr. Clarence. All God's children are free to love—*

What you talking about, Mrs. Craw Daddy?

*Just know that I want you and your cousin Junius to take this child.
His mother has run out of steam. And Craw and I are a jeopardy.*

This ain't right, Mrs. Daddy.

I bow my head: this will take longer than expected. And so—
with the memory of those long-ago Sable-Tea matrons that tried so
very hard to instill in us a greater sense of truth, justice, and liberty
for all—I begin.

Explaining to Clarence that the comedian my husband will likely
go to prison for some time—we no longer live in an age of plen-
tiful female-tampering—and that that incarceration will happen
sooner rather than later. As for *moi:* I intend to go back to Mount
Vernon and beg my dead mam's forgiveness; *Carpe noctum; you are*

our only hope. I have no friends, no family other than my daughters and their young. But Marquita can barely handle the boys she has bred. And Winifred won't speak to me in a deeply known way. My youngest is likely gone forever, I say. Addled in some drug rehab or hospital for broken heads, or perhaps huddled under a bridge, exquisitely diaphanous—I have no clue. She is gone. This is my debt, I tell him. *One riotous day.*

Clarence shakes his head. *Ma'am. Please calm yourself. I can call the cops.*

You must please take the child, Mr. Clarence. Police are not a necessary ingredient here.

Please, ma'am. You are not yourself!

Around us the rush of river surf hits the small cliffs of the path. God is somewhere, folded arms across his chest, angry toe tapping the tops of the clouds. I tell Clarence about Eboni. I tell him about the others. When he winces and touches my shoulder, I recoil: I tell him I belong in neither heaven nor hell, just in Mount Vernon, New York, where my elders lie. I am no one's forgiveness. Perhaps I'll buy a house in New Rochelle. Perhaps I'll run into someone I once knew and sit on another slipcovered couch and whisper the Lord's Prayer. I never did learn those words correctly, just faked my way through everything and did not once get my black butt beat.

Clarence listens. *Just let me call home,* he eventually says.

XLV.

Do hours go by? I have no phone, no communication other than the moon that has been steadily grazing my shoulders and telling me to jump. I'm resting on a rock, like the girl on the can of White Rock soda. Baby finally asleep. If I don't learn to miss him I will hate myself forever.

Just then it's Clarence again, now with a man by his side. A man who, after brief introductions, grips my own elbow, all courtly. The Mahogany Maidens would have been all aswoon! They would have asked him to hold their *every* part. *Are you Clarence's cousin,* I ask. The man laughs. *If that's who you want me to be,* he says back.

Minutes later the men lead me to the car, the baby still fresh in their arms. *Where is the pram,* I wonder but do not ask aloud.

But then we do not go to the car. Instead the men nod and then guide me fast toward Ogden Hall, eventually lighting at the bottom of a foothill leading up to the stage entrance. There is litter strewn everywhere, Coke bottles and crepe garlands and crumpled loose-leaf paper. The stage door cracks open and a seam of light scissors the dark—it is then we see the outlines of two men fighting on the ground. One is pummeling the other, who is screaming, gibberish pleas. I have no desire to listen. The door closes partway and I can make out the further outline of a knife, a key, a finger, a fist. Perhaps I smell blood from where I am standing. *You stay here where you safe,* Junius says, lowering me by the arms onto a grassy tuffet. I turn my head away, ignore the screeching, the laughter of young people, the old man on the ground, sunken like a Norfolk naval ship, the crush of young leaves all around— *You damn repeated yourself one time too many, you black bastard!*—and I turn away, casting my eyes over treetops, toward the place I imagine the Emancipation Oak stands. *I don't blame you for wanting to cut all ties,* I tell it. *But please look out for this baby. He has to matter.*

Clarence and Junius scramble up the small hill to the fight but make no move, however, to break things up. They hold the infant between them as if it were a tiny gate to somewhere they'd never before considered.

When, all those years ago, Mahalia Jackson walked up the aisle toward the door, I reached out to touch her sleeve. Of course, I didn't get it; the wind of her walk sailed through me, like Velvet's wedding veil before it hit the river. I knew enough not to beg Miss Jackson for another hymn, as the others in the auditorium were doing, stomping their feet under their seats. I knew enough, had understood briefly the importance of listening the first time. How had I lost that gift? We cannot exist by remaining greedy.

Eboni is stamping down the hill, backlit by moonlight. Her fists are tight by her side—she seems all greatness in her youthful march, her hair gone wild and free as it flutters in gangly strips atop her head—I want to find out if that is true. *Are you great? Have you always been great?* Hoisting myself from the grass, I stand and wave. Her silhouette inches closer to mine. My arms open, I start to cry. This girl is going to meet me for the first time, even if she doesn't yet know it.

This Is Pleasure

FROM *The New Yorker*

M.

I'D KNOWN QUIN for maybe five years when he told me this story —really not even a story, more like an anecdote—about a woman he'd met on the street. Quin believed that he could perceive people's most essential nature just by looking at them; he also believed that, in the same way, he could know what they most wanted to hear, or, rather, what they would most respond to. He was a little conceited about these supposed special abilities, and that was how the story began. He saw a melancholy-looking woman, a "former beauty," as he put it, walking by herself in Central Park, and he said to her, "Aren't you the gentle one!" She replied, "And aren't you the perceptive one for seeing it!" After a few minutes of talk, he invited her to have tea with him. She agreed.

He didn't describe her further, other than to say that she was middle-aged and obviously lonely; she'd never been married, worked in P.R., had no children. Even without a visual description, my sense of her was vivid: her slender forearm and long hand, the outline of her cheek giving off a subtle glow as she leaned slightly forward, into his attention, her mind quickened by this odd and unexpected man. And he would be leaning toward her too. Quin was someone who *imbibed* people.

They exchanged numbers. I asked him if he'd told her that he was about to get married and he said no, he hadn't. He didn't plan to call her. It was enough to feel the potential between them, stored away like a cell-phone video of something that had already happened. "She would like being hurt, but very slightly. She'd want affection more. You'd spank her with, I don't know, a Ping-Pong paddle? And then touch her clit. *This is pleasure.*" He paused. *"And this is pain."*

When I repeated this story to my husband, he cracked up. We both did. For years after, apropos of nothing, one of us would croak, "This is pleasure"—my husband would make a perverted face and pinch the air—"And this is pain!" And both of us would crack up, just laugh our asses off. The whole thing was vaguely sadistic—so vaguely that it was ridiculous; clearly no harm was done.

"It wouldn't be a good outcome for her," Quin said. "She's open-minded but sensitive. I'm engaged to a much younger woman, and there wouldn't be any good place that it could go for her."

"She might've just wanted the experience," I said, "if she was lonely." I'm sorry to report that I said that. But I really thought it might be true.

They did speak on the phone, finally; she called him. He told her then about his engagement. He said that he'd like her to consider him a kind of guardian angel, psychically watching out for her. Which added to the hilarity for my husband and me. Even though it also added to the secret sadism. I laughed, but I wondered: Did the woman know, even dimly, that she was being toyed with? Did she feel that there was something wrong with the encounter, the way you might feel a mysterious hair drawn across your cheek? Why did I think it was so funny? It seems strange to me when I look back on it now. Because I don't want to laugh. I feel pain. Real heart pain. Subtle. But real.

Q.

Late at night I went to my office for the last time. I was not allowed to go there during business hours and I didn't want to; it would have been unpleasant. The managing editor had instructed the security guard to let me in and see me out. Boxes had been packed and shipped already; before that, my wife had collected an envelope of emergency cash that I had left in a desk drawer. Even *she* didn't want to set foot in the office; the one sympathetic associate editor agreed to meet her and hand off the envelope at a subway concession stand—a pallid detail that serves only to underscore the level of revulsion Carolina feels about anything associated with my former professional life.

Anyway, I'd come one last time, to collect an orchid that had somehow survived months of inept watering and to see if any other tiny thing had been left behind. And one had, actually *two* had—though they were not that tiny, nor was I the one who had left them.

The first thing was my nameplate, strangely still affixed to the wall outside my office door, importantly announcing the existence of the now nonexistent Quinlan M. Saunders. It seemed like a nasty joke, and it was the sharp-browed and maybe pretentious *M*, especially, that zinged me as I entered what had once been my office—where the second surprise sat quietly on my desk: a cardboard cigarette packet, its original graphic covered by a pasted-on image of a very red apple on a white background and, on the other side, the words *everyday = choices*, positioned like a brand name, in red and pink letters. When one opened the packet, one found not cigarettes but five very small scrolls of paper arranged with painstaking symmetry. Unscrolled, they read, in plain black type, *ugliness or beauty, truth or lies, courage or fear, kindness or cruelty, love or* ____. The space for the last word on the last scroll was left blank. I didn't have to look; I remembered it tenderly well—as in when a doctor presses on your abdomen and asks, "Is it tender there?"

Years ago I'd made this for a girl who still works in the row of offices opposite mine. A plain girl with short brown hair, bright eyes, and good coloring. Her body was thick-waisted but supple, with a peasant's grace—confident and humble both—and a quiet poise, greater than that of most beauties. Her eyes took in the world with passive depth and the occasional flash of gentle humor. She was intelligent, more than she realized, and I wanted her to learn how to use her intelligence more actively.

The cigarette packet came out of a hallway conversation we'd had about choices and opportunities. I spent several afternoons at my desk, piecing the little delicacy together in odd inactive moments. Strange and touching to remember the care I put into it, the sophistication and childishness, how I thought of it in her hands. I invited her to lunch to give it to her and, yes, I was right: when she saw it, that flash lit up not only her eyes but her entire face, and in that instant I became for her a magician who had given her an enchanted object. As if I *were* a magician, she listened to me tell her about herself: what she was like, what she needed, what she needed to correct. "We are going on a journey," I said, and we did. At the end of it, she had awakened to her ambition and learned how to satisfy it. As time went on, there were other girls I liked flirting with more. But for years—almost ten years— I kept our friendship alive with daily compliments and periodic lunches. I still have a handwritten note from her saying that our lunches were the "glory" of her week.

Now she had returned my gift not to me but to an empty room. Now she was one of my accusers.

I dropped the packet in a wastebasket on my way out, but then, because I did not want to leave evidence of such bitter feeling behind me, I turned around to retrieve it. I meant to drop it into a trash can on the street. But instead I took it home and put it in a drawer where Carolina would not find it.

M.

I met Quin when he interviewed me for an assistant editor position, more than twenty years ago. At thirty-five, I was a little old for the job; I was coming from an East Village publication that was venerably outré, and was perhaps slow to realize that those two descriptors canceled each other out. Besides, it paid almost nothing, and I was looking forward to trading up. I had heard of Quin. I knew that he was English, from old-school wealth (father a banker, mother in organized charity), and that he was eccentric. Still, I was surprised by his appearance. He was at least forty, but he had the narrow frame and form of an elegant boy. His long brown hair fell over his brow in a juvenile style that was completely natural on him. His clothes were exquisite—simply cut, neutral colors, but finely tailored, soft, perfectly draped, nothing to stand out except the long silk scarf he wore, nearly always, around his neck. Without being beautiful, he gave an unexpected impression of beauty—but then he would subtly thrust out his jaw, with his lips parted so that his lower teeth were just visible, and his narrow face would look strangely insectile and predatory, like something with large mandibles.

The interview was strange too, whimsical and then unexpectedly cutting. He asked a lot of questions that seemed irrelevant and personal, including whether or not I had a boyfriend. He used my name more often than he needed to, and with an oddly intimate intonation that, in combination with his British accent, seemed not only precise but *proper*. That *proper* quality was somehow confusing: when he interrupted me to say, "Margot? Margot, I don't think your voice is your best asset. What is your best asset?" I was so discomfited and uncertain that I didn't know whether to be offended or not. I don't recall my reply, but I know that I answered abruptly and uncleverly, and then the interview was over.

I got another, better job, but still, when Quin's name came up in conversation, and it often did—he had a reputation that was somewhat notorious, yet unclear, as if people didn't know what to make of him, despite how long he'd been around—I vividly remembered his voice and my discomfiture and wondered why the feeling had stayed with me. And then, maybe two years later, I met him again, at a book fair in D.C. I walked into some tricked-up rental location alone and saw him posing for a picture with two stylish young women, who were leaning on his shoulders, making funny faces and gangster hand signs. He was looking at the camera, not at me, but as soon as the picture was taken he excused himself and came over to me. His voice was different this time— full of uncomplicated goodwill and so expansive that I thought he was drunk, which he wasn't. He said that he was glad I was doing well, and, when I asked how he knew how I was doing, he said that he'd heard—"You bought a book I wanted, only a confident person would go for that book, I'm sure you know which one I mean" —but even if he hadn't heard, he continued, he'd have been able to tell by looking at me. The room was filled with the swift-moving noise of personality; somewhere in the background was a cake, bottles, and flowers. The gangster girls gestured and grinned to each other delightedly. It all felt like a blessing.

Back in New York, we met at a restaurant that had once been a meeting place for the artistic élite but was now frequented primarily by tourists and businesspeople. We were seated at a deep banquette; Quin told the waiter that he wanted to sit on the same side as me, so that we could talk more easily, and then he was there, with his place setting. I'm sure he didn't say this right away, but in my memory he did: "Your voice is so much stronger now! You

are so much stronger now! You speak straight from the clit!" And
—as if it were the most natural thing in the world—he reached
between my legs. "NO!" I said, and shoved my hand in his face,
palm out, like a traffic cop. I knew it would stop him. Even a horse
will *usually* obey a hand held in its face like that, and it outweighs
a human by nearly a thousand pounds. Looking mildly astonished,
Quin sat back and said, "I like the strength and clarity of your *no*."
"Good," I replied.

We ordered our meal. We talked about food. He again admired the novel I'd acquired, which had been turned down by
every major house, including his, on the grounds that it was mi-
sogynistic (though, of course, *we* didn't call it that). He assessed
the other people in the room, imagining what they did for a living and whether or not they were happy. I was unwillingly fascinated, both by the detail of his speculations and by how accurate they seemed. He paid special attention to a stout Japanese
man who was lustily eating alone, legs spread proudly, one hand
bearing food to his mouth, the other a fist on his splayed thigh;
Quin said that of all the people in the room (other than me) this
man was the one he'd most like to talk to, because he looked
as though he were capable of "something great." But the main
thing I remember from that night was the expression on his face
as he retreated from my upraised palm, the surprised obedience
that was somehow *grounded,* more genuine than his reaching
hand had been.

I remember too a brief moment after dinner. He walked me
home, and we said goodbye so warmly that a young man walking
past smiled, as if touched by this middle-aged courtship. I went
into my building and, halfway up the stairs, realized that I needed
milk. I walked back out, to a corner deli. As I reached into the
cooler for the milk, I glanced to my side and saw a funny man
at the other end of the aisle, exploring his nose with a very large
handkerchief, while his other hand rifled through a shelf. His posture was intensely stooped, as if physically manifesting some emotional contraction. I was very surprised to realize that it was Quin
—the posture was so radically unlike the elegant, erect stance I'd
seen all night. He was so privately engrossed that he didn't see me,
and I felt compelled to leave without buying milk rather than let
him know that I'd—what? Seen him explore his nose?

The next day he sent me flowers and the friendship began.

Q.

I told Margot and I told my brother; I did not tell my wife. Not at first. I still had hope that it would blow over, or at least be handled quietly, and my hope was not unfounded. At first the suit was not against me but against the publishing house, and all she wanted was a payment, which the company was prepared to make—as long as she kept quiet about her complaints. Her complaints were petty, absurd—which meant, as Margot pointed out, that they were almost impossible to keep quiet about. "How would you enforce that?" she asked. "How would you even know what she was talking about at cocktail parties? Where else would she talk about it? Rape is one thing, but it's not like she can go to the media to report some weird thing you said years ago."

Margot was wrong. I felt that even as she spoke. But watching her, sitting squarely in her sense of reality, speaking confidently as she reached for the salt and lavishly poured it on whatever she was eating, I was reassured. I felt her love for me. Even though *she* was angry with me too. She took the occasion to tell me how angry she was, and had been for years. "You treat people like entertainment," she said. "You joke and you prod just to see which way they'll jump and how far. You pick at their hurt spots. You delectate pain. It doesn't sound like this girl has a case legally, but honestly, I can understand why she's mad. You didn't touch her, did you? I mean, sexually?"

I had not. Just sometimes on the shoulder, or around the waist. Maybe on the knee or the hip. Affection. Not sex. "I so don't want Carolina to find out," I said. "She hates male oppression. Hates it."

And Margot laughed. *Laughed.* "Did you really just say that?" she said. *"You?"*

I said, "I'm concerned for my wife."

She stopped laughing. She said, "If it wasn't sexual, you don't have anything to worry about."

"But it could be made to sound sexual. Or just—she claims it cost her months of therapy bills."

Margot laughed again, more meanly—I'm not sure at whom.

"I'd like you to keep quiet about this," I said. "I mean, don't tell anyone. Not even Todd."

"I won't," she said. "Don't worry."

M.

I didn't tell that many people about him reaching between my legs. When I did, I told it as a funny story and mostly people laughed. But once someone, I don't remember who, said, "Why would you want to have a friendship with someone like that?" And I said something like, "Well, he was very persistent and he can be a lot of fun." Which was true. But that was not why I came to love him as a friend.

For months the friendship was almost entirely one-way, consisting of short, frothy emails from him, professional invitations, and phone calls to "check in." I didn't initiate anything until almost three months after our first dinner, and there was nothing frothy about the occasion. My boyfriend had left me for a girl in her twenties, my boss had been fired for publishing a memoir that she knew was a fraud, and my building was going co-op and I couldn't afford it. I was trying to get to my therapist's office when the subway groaned brokenly, stopped, grew dark, then hot, then seemed to die completely. Everyone on it was trapped, coughing, shifting, and muttering in the hot darkness for nearly half an hour before the thing reanimated enough to creep into the next station, where we were released to stampede up the stairs and fight over cabs. I lost that fight, and the loss was one ounce of pressure too many. I called my therapist to cancel and then called a friend, who, incredulous at hearing me sob on the phone over a missed therapy appointment during work hours, said, "I'm busy!" and hung up.

It was all stressful, but scarcely enough to explain how I felt—as though a trapdoor had opened and I had fallen through it into scalding chaos, clutching at supports that came off in my hands, plunging, and transforming, as I did, into a mindless thing, a receptacle of fear and pain. Terrified by the sight of people moving all around me with energy and purpose, I sat down on the sidewalk and leaned my head against the wall of the nearest building. I sat there for some minutes, waiting for my heart to slow, and while I did I thought of Quin. I don't know why. But when my heart had calmed sufficiently, I called him. He picked up quickly and brightly. I don't remember everything about the conversation, only that I said I was sick and worthless and "everybody" knew it. "Who is everybody?" Quin asked. "Just people," I said, "people I know." "How do you know they feel that way?" he asked. "Did they tell you?" "No," I said. "They didn't. But I can tell. I can just tell." When Quin spoke again, it was with surprising feeling. "I don't know who these people are," he said, "or why you would care about their opinion. But there is nothing sick or worthless about you. You are a lovely spirit." And, just like that, I stopped falling. The world and all the people racing through it became recognizable again. I was speechless with gratitude. "Don't bother with the subway," he said. "Take a taxi to my office. I'll wait for you downstairs. We'll go and have tea." And we did. There was no touching or talk about sex. We had tea and he listened to me and held my gaze with soft, attentive eyes.

Q.

If people could see the emails between my accusers and me, I believe they would be very surprised. My wife says, over and over, how "stupid" I was to send personal emails with any hint of flirtation from a company account. She never sends *any* personal communication from her work server, no matter how perfectly platonic. But though I seldom engage with her when she's off on this tear, I believe that these emails are my best defense, even when they are a tiny bit sexy. Because they show mutuality, pleasure, even gratitude —friendship.

Caitlin Robison was my friend for eleven years. Yes, she was, for a time, an employee. She was even, to some degree, a protégé. But she was ultimately a friend. She came to parties at my home. She met my wife and child.

When Caitlin Robison came to work for us, she was twenty-four, a plain, dour young lady with a drab haircut (dirty blond) and a sexless style that I enjoyed teasing her about. I could sense that she was irritated by the teasing, but she was a good sport, which made me like her. Which she must've known, because within months she was teasing me back, calling me "straight fairy," "fop," and "buttercup"—saucy! She showed unexpected spunk, and when she tossed one of these cute *mots* over her shoulder, it made her angular ass seem somehow more round.

And she knew I was right. When she finally decided to do something about her hair, she asked me, "So what do *you* think would look good?" She said it tauntingly, but I could see that it was a serious question, and so I answered it. She took my suggestion and her appearance improved by at least three points. Which was probably why, when I offered to accompany her on a shopping trip, she agreed *very enthusiastically*.

We didn't go anyplace expensive, she didn't make enough in her assistant's position, and anyway, I prefer the charm of discount retail, even for myself sometimes. I'm a bargain hunter, and, I discovered, so was she. Out of the office, as she pawed through sales racks and discount bins, her inner electricity switched on, and I could feel her motor. She was ambitious, this girl, vain, and so practical that there was something squalid about it: this squalor was her sexiness. "How does this look?" she'd ask over and over, of some tight T-shirt or pencil skirt, and I would say, "Turn around, let me see." The fun of it was in her eyes as she searched my reaction and took her cues, and in the opinions she began to express. It was years ago, so I can't say that I remember what they were (except that she loved old *Ally McBeal* episodes and could quote from some that were very sexual), but I remember their flavor. She talked about the man she was dating. I told her about my courtship of Carolina, our wedding. Afterward I sent her an email that said, "You plus me equals magic elixir!" And she answered, "Delicious!"

M.

We evolved this funny ritual, Quin and I. I am slightly afraid to fly and I went through a long period when I was *very* afraid. It was during this period that I began calling Quin every time I boarded a plane. I would ask him if he thought this flight would be all right, and he would say, "Let me tune in." There would be a pause, a sometimes lengthy one. And then he would say, "You'll be fine, Margot!" or "I *think* you'll be okay." If I couldn't reach him, I'd leave a message on his voicemail, and he almost always got back to me before the plane took off. On the rare occasion that he didn't, I would, on landing, receive a voicemail assuring me, "You're safe, love. Call me when you land." Once when I couldn't reach him I called Todd, the man I married, instead. Quin was outraged. "You called *him*? He doesn't know anything about planes!"

This was what he most liked: to give advice about the strange, small things that can sit oddly close to a person's heart and some-times press against it painfully. I could call him at any time, and if at all possible, he would drop whatever he was doing to give me advice about whether or not to confront a friend about something that was bothering me, whether or not I should wear a particu-lar style of makeup to a particular party, whether or not one of my husband's friendships meant that he was disloyal toward me. These conversations never took long, because Quin's advice was instantaneous, confident, and broadly philosophical.

I was not the only person who had this kind of relationship with him. I'd meet him at a restaurant, and he'd be getting off the phone with a woman who was crying about her husband's infidel-ity. I'd go to the theater with him and he'd tell me that some girl was texting, wanting his opinion about something that her date had said. I went to his office and found him amid a crowd of girls, one of them weeping and crying, "Oh, Quin, I feel so humiliated!" And in front of everyone, he advised her. Exactly *what* he advised, I don't recall. But I do remember the open, unashamed weeping, the placidity of the other women, the strength of Quin's voice, the room filled with sun, as if this were a sanctuary where every feeling might be aired and resolved.

Before the shit hit the fan, when I was feeling angry at Quin, I would sometimes look back on that moment and remember that feeling of openness, sunlight, and unashamed emotion. I would remember too the strange fun of our conversations about sex, him cajoling me to tell him about what I'd done or liked to do, me usually refusing to say but sometimes, for some reason, giving in. For example, on a long, boring train trip, he asked me if, during oral sex, it was important who came first and why. This turned into a longer conversation than you'd expect, and even though I was careful with my language, in the middle of it a roughly groomed older woman turned around in her seat and grinned broadly at me. I remembered talking to him on the phone before a party at his luxurious Central Park apartment, where I would, for the first time, meet his fashionista wife and their rich friends. I was wor-ried about what to wear, and he said, "Anything you choose will be perfect. You're coming to the home of someone who loves you." I remembered him once talking about his daughter, Lucia, who was, at six, doing wonderfully adult drawings and writing poems that caused her to stand out even at the school for the gifted at which she was enrolled. We were in a taxi, and in the middle of the conversation he asked if he could put his head in my lap. I said, "Okay," and he did. He said, "There aren't many people I trust enough to do this with." It wasn't sexual. I didn't pet his head or anything. He just lay across the seat with the back of his head on my thigh and quoted from his little girl's poems. It was nice.

There were many moments like that, not to mention his ready professional and emotional support, for me and even for Carter, my fatherlessly depressed twelve-year-old nephew from Albany. During one particularly discouraging visit from the kid—I was single then, and did not know what to do with an angry twelve-year-old male—Quin spontaneously swooped in and commandeered the boy, taking him on an inspired tour of the Arms and Armor display at the Met, with a side trip to a video-game arcade. "He is *cool*," Carter said.

Remembering those things, I would ask myself, *Why am I so angry?*

That was before. *After* the shit hit the fan, I looked back again at that moment of sanctuary in his office and contemplated: more than half of the women who were there had signed the endlessly circulating online petition, given interviews, demanded that Quin be fired, sought damages, made threats to boycott any company that would dare to hire him. They were angry too.

Q.

It's true that I like to brag and I like to tease. And Margot, though very free in her view of sexuality, can be a bit morally stringent. I remember teasing Margot by telling her that I'd convinced a woman I'd just met, during a layover in Houston, to share with me what she thought about while making herself come. An amusing silence emanated from the phone, and then: "She didn't slap the shit out of you?"

"No," I answered pleasantly. "I was very polite. I led into it slowly. I was just about to get on my flight, we'd had a nice talk, she'd told me a lot about herself. It was just, you know, ships in the night, we won't see each other again, so . . ."

"I still don't understand why she didn't smack you."

"I can tell you why. She was a big woman, huge. Married to a professional football player—she'd told me that. I'm several inches shorter than she is, thin as a mantis, a pipsqueak. I'm in no way a threat to her."

Margot was silent; I could feel that her special brand of morality was offended by my ridiculous provocation. I could also feel her curiosity.

"And so many people, if they are honest, really want to answer those questions. You just have to ask in the right way."

"So she told you?"

"Yes. She told me."

Caitlin was a tease too; that was part of our connection. I prefer not to speak of myself; it's generally not necessary. Most people are starved for perceptive questions and the chance to discover their own thoughts. This is especially true of young women, who are expected to listen attentively to one dull, self-obsessed man after another. Caitlin was different. Where was it—at a book party at some nightclub or gallery chosen to convey a glamour that publishing rarely, or actually never, has—that she raised a glass of something pink to her mauve-tinted mouth and said, "You never say anything about yourself. You deflect."

"Not true," I replied. "I'm an open book."

"Bullshit." She smiled.

"Ask anything you like!"

There is some memory static here, possibly in the form of hors d'œuvres offered by one of those handsome rental waiters who trail bruised dignity in their wake; perhaps she took so long choosing nothing that I thought she'd dropped the thread. But then she spoke seriously.

"How can I get to know you better?"

I was truly surprised and I answered without thinking. "How does a woman ever get to know a man?"

She looked so confused that I waited only a beat to answer for her: "Flirt with me a little more."

Her face abruptly froze. And then some people interrupted us, and our conversation ended with her expression wonderfully stuck on pause. It was either later that night or after some near-identical "event" that we shared a taxi and I asked her, "Don't you agree that sex is at the core of personality?"

"I don't know," she said. "People are complicated."

This was one reason that I liked Margot better. She was one of the few people who answered that question with an unhesitating yes. As did Sharona, from a completely different point of view. But Sharona was different in every way.

M.

The first time I was consciously mad at Quin was over something so trifling that I felt I was crazy. We were sitting down to a dinner party; he was, between snippets of table talk, texting advice to some girl who was upset because the guy she'd been dating wanted to see other women. "Do you think she should give him his freedom or say no, not allowed?" he asked me.

I said that I didn't know, that I didn't know her.

"I told her I'm asking Margot Berland, editor of *Healing the Slut Within.* She loves that book!"

I said, "I don't know her."

Food was passed around; conversations started. Quin answered a question from someone sitting across from us, then looked back down at his phone and addressed me sideways. "But you don't have to know her—it's an obvious question! Your boyfriend wants to see other people—"

"After how long?"

"It's been a few weeks."

"*Weeks?* I'd dump him."

"Okay, I'm telling her, 'Margot Berland says—'"

"No, don't!"

"Why not? It would mean a lot to her that you—"

"It's her life—she should figure it out herself!"

Quin slipped his phone back into his pocket. "I already told her."

I sat there, inexplicably furious. Inexplicably because I'd been amused by and watched other people be amused by these—what a ridiculous word and how accurate it is!—*microaggressions* ever since I'd known Quin.

And so *many* people had been amused, and not only from the publishing world. He gave huge parties two or three times a year, lighthearted, thrilling affairs that mixed people from the art world, movies, fashion, criticism, literature, medicine, and, more rarely, local politics. He'd occasionally invite a beautiful woman he'd met on the street that day and she would actually show up

—stunned and stunning girls, barely out of their teens, from Eastern Europe or Ethiopia, who barely spoke English but somehow trusted that this strange, slender man was worth their time. You never knew whom you'd sit next to—a handsome young hotshot running a phony pharmaceutical concern, a desiccated artist down on her luck, an elegant literary lady from Iceland—or what he or she might say. There was one regular, a young woman who wrote for an online art magazine; Quin had apparently invited her after she'd smacked him in the face a couple of times with a fly swatter, which she carried with her for a precise purpose—that is, to swat men who irritated her. When she came to the door the first time, Quin's wife, Carolina, greeted her warmly: "Oh, Miss Swatter, so nice to meet you. I've heard so much about you!" And sure enough, the lady had brought her flyswatter with her; throughout the evening she repeatedly swatted Quin in his own home, to his red-faced, beatific delight.

But Carolina wasn't always so easy or easily arch about her husband's odd relations with women. Maybe she never was. I met her shortly after she and Quin became engaged, when Todd and I had dinner with the two of them. She made a surprisingly distinct impression; she was an assistant editor at a fashion magazine, nearly twenty years younger than Quin, and I was not expecting to be impressed, except by her beauty. Of course she was beautiful, and very elegantly so. She was half Korean and half Argentine, and aristocratic on both sides; her family owned land outside of Buenos Aires. Her bearing was electric and deeply calm at once. She had a way of cocking her head that emphasized the purity of her facial lines, and the expression of frank, fascinated alertness in her long eyes accentuated their unusual shape (a teardrop, tilted up). She didn't say very much during the dinner, but she listened with erect intensity, as if her body were an antenna, and her uptilted eyes and ears seemed linked, functioning as a single organ. She was a presence you took seriously, even if she barely spoke, even if she was only twenty-seven years old.

In spite of this impression, as the engagement became a marriage, Carolina quickly moved into the background for me, even when she made Quin a father. (He was ecstatic at this development, and every stage of it enchanted him; the flow of milk, his wife's new and natural tenderness. "I've never been that focused on breasts before," he actually *babbled* to me during a lunch, "but now I see them everywhere, love them, celebrate them, especially hers!") I saw her from time to time at parties and sometimes at readings, sometimes with her little Lucia, who was beyond striking, with her mother's pure-black hair and enormous anime eyes that seemed to be gazing into another, better world. Carolina and I were always cordial. Still, she surprised me one evening at an unusually casual dinner I had with her, Quin, and Lucia. The girl was five at that time, and she became very suddenly irritated with her father, to the point that she began to make a scene, even striking at Quin with her tiny fists. "She's overtired," Quin explained, and he decided, since they lived nearby, to take her home. When I wondered what had upset the child, Carolina shrugged.

"She's a girl," she said. "I don't think she enjoys watching her father flirt with every woman he meets any more than I do. Didn't you notice the way he was with the waitress?" She was in her late thirties by then and her fascinated alertness had been blunted, her erectness slightly compromised. But she was still electrically beautiful.

"Just so you know, that's never gone on between me and Quin," I said. "He's a good friend. But nothing flirty. It's not like that at all."

And, so simply and sincerely that it astonished me, she said, "Thank you, Margot." Her husband had actually made this gorgeous woman, the mother of his child, jealous of a broad over fifty.

But I should not have been surprised. Quin was sometimes seductive with women who were older than me. We once went to a cocktail party given by a warm, well-exercised woman with wonderful deep lines on her face, dishevelled gray hair, and confident red lipstick; she greeted Quin with an embrace that was nearly intimate and held hands with him while they spoke in confidential tones about banal subjects. They parted, and as we headed for the drinks table, he gave me a quick outline of her life: journalist, diplomat's wife, mother, environmental-cleanup volunteer. A few minutes into our drinks, he told me that the woman and her husband were still having sex, but only when the husband pretended to break into the apartment and rape her while she strenuously tried to push him out of her with her thighs and her lady muscles. "I imagine she could almost do it," he said. "She's a strong gal and a fierce yogini!"

"Did it turn you on to hear about it?" I asked.

"No. Not especially." His tone was dry, nearly judicial. "But it interests me. It helps me understand her. Knowing that, I feel I'm better able to help her with her marriage. They've been having trouble lately."

He said this with perfect seriousness.

Q.

Sharona was a girl straight out of the fifties. She even dressed that way, and not self-consciously. I never saw her in pants; she wore skirts and dresses exclusively, modestly cut but given a sexy edge by her high-heeled shoes and boots. Her hair and nails were flawless. She had a heart-shaped face and big dark eyes with a secret expression that wanted to be released—there was something intense and seeking in her gaze. She wasn't a real beauty, but she had a beautiful laugh and even a beautiful frown. For her, sex *was* the core, and that was why she refused to speak of it or evoke it with her presence; for her, the core was "sacred." She used that word during a conversation at a bookstore after a reading. I'd asked about her boyfriend, the most innocent question first, but where most girls would begin to trust me or try to impress me, she looked at me with mild reproach and said firmly, "That's inappropriate." Still, the soft directness of her eyes and voice was more intimate than my question. I asked her if she was religious and she laughed before saying no. I asked her if she prayed. Her expression shifted, a depth change. "Yes," she said, "I do." I told her that I prayed every day. I said, "When I want to find out what someone is really like, that's one of my first questions—do they pray?"

"You want to know what *I'm* really like? You just met me."

"I prefer to know whom I'm talking to, yes." We spoke of the writer who had read his work—a poseur, she thought. I disagreed, but not too strenuously. I asked if there was anyone in the room she'd like to meet. She said, "Not especially."

She accepted my invitation to lunch, then and many times after. She enjoyed talking about books. She enjoyed my appreciation of her mind, which was sincere; she was a delicate and nuanced *perceiver*. She had a dull assistant's position at an art magazine that reviewed books (I knew her boss, an unpleasant fellow), and I could feel her pleasure when she was able to flex her intellect. Not ostentatiously but quietly, firmly. And she realized, I'm sure, that I was a good person to cultivate.

Caitlin and I had been friends for some time by then, but the friendship had become intermittently hard and sparring—nasty, even. She was in love with a man who seemed to despise her; it was plainly a delusional crush, and I encouraged her to drop it. When she insisted on the legitimacy of her feelings, I said that if it was really love, she should pray to know what was right for both of them and then act on it. Every time I saw her, I'd remind her to pray about it.

The outcome was predictable—the usual dreary disaster. She seemed to blame me for it; I can only think this was because I had witnessed her slow-motion humiliation. Even when she found a new boyfriend, the bitterness of that rejection stayed in her heart and made her act strangely around me. She invented a little game: If I had to wear a button with a single word to announce who I was, what would it say? *Flâneur? Voyeur? Creep?* The severity of the word she chose varied from day to day, as did the "buttons" I chose for her: *Narcissist. Opportunist. Crybaby.* I remember her smiling as if drunk during these exchanges, and, even though I was never drunk, there was a feeling of intoxication in our bitch-slapping.

Anyway, we continued to have lunch and to confide in each other. She accepted my professional advice (I was a great help to her), and she, in time, advised me about Sharona. Eventually I helped her get a plum job with a literary agency. On her last day at the office, she wanted to know if I'd still invite her to my parties. I said, "As long as you flirt with me, love." And we did continue to flirt, though mostly via email. Had lunch every now and then. I didn't invite her to a party, though. There were others who better filled the spot that she had occupied.

M.

There are so many funny or awful stories that it's hard to stop telling them. The nineteen-year-old who texted him every time she (a) took a shit or (b) had sex with her boyfriend. The girl who texted him to describe her fantasies every time she masturbated ("Okay, it's hard to type right now, because my hands are shaking . . ."). The time we attended a reading by a young female writer, and

Quin, on being introduced to her, stuck his hand in her face and said, "Bite my thumb." The woman, who was self-possessed, looked at him with disgust and turned her back. I said, "Why did you *do* that?" He wasn't fazed. "She's cute," he said. "But she's not game." He shrugged.

Grotesque, but at the same time paired with such peculiar, delectating joy. Once, when my husband and I were feeling down, we talked about how everyone we knew seemed ultimately unhappy, or at least discontented. "Except Quin," I said. "Except him," Todd agreed. And, putting on his Quin-the-pervert face, he quoted, "Where the bee sucks, there suck I!" We laughed, then sat there, contemplating Quin's abnormal happiness.

And why wouldn't he be happy? He had a gorgeous wife and an exceptional child, and he was an excellent editor, who published some of the best writers of the moment. They tended to be clever niche writers rather than heavyweights, but the quality was undeniable, and some of them had devoted followings. Many of them were writers whom no one else in publishing had believed in at first. Quin did believe, passionately, even *morally:* "She's marching for goodness," he might say, or "He's marching for sexuality" or "marching for truthfulness." (Morality was, oddly, important to Quin. He analyzed and criticized people based on their moral traits; "self-centered" was one of his harshest accusations—an irony, given how much he encouraged people to talk about themselves.) Quin would take up these marchers, pay them advances that were all out of proportion, and exult when they succeeded. Which happened often enough that even writers whom *everyone* believed in, that is to say, bid on, finally came to him too, without his making much of an effort to land them.

I remember going with him to a publishing party for one of them, a young black man ("Marching for justice with humor and style!") whom Quin had positioned for celebrity. The party was held in an art gallery that was showing work by someone who painted imitations of hoary masterpieces, in which she had replaced the original Caucasian figures with famous people of color. I met Quin in his office; I was wearing a skirt and heels and carrying a shopping bag and a little purse. He insisted that I let him carry the shopping bag, because even though I would check it at the door, he thought it spoiled my look—*plus* he would enjoy being "at [my] service." I agreed, and then he said that he thought I should also dispense with the purse, because, although it was small and very nice, it made me look less free. "But I need it," I said. "I've got my wallet and lipstick in there."

"Then let me carry them," he answered, "here." He indicated an inner pocket of his jacket.

I hesitated.

"You're effervescent tonight," he said. "But that purse takes something away. It makes you more mundane, less delightful. I want to see you walk through the room giving off an aura of freedom."

I said, smiling, "But if I give you my wallet I'm not free. Because you've got my wallet."

He was right, though. I would have looked and felt more free without the purse. Especially while we were dancing; there was a good DJ, and we danced for hours.

Q.

When Caitlin left, a girl named Hortense took her quasi-secretarial position. Caitlin recommended her, in fact; I don't remember the connection, but somehow they knew each other. Truthfully, I liked Hortense better; she was more confident, less ambitious, prettier, altogether a finer creature (huge dark-blue eyes; plump, tiny mouth; graceful neck; curly hair; musical voice). I suppose out of habit I contrived for us to go on an occasional shopping trip, and perhaps because of Hortense's wonderful prettiness, I was drawn to stores that were a bit more upscale. On our last such expedition, she tried on a T-shirt and let me come into the dressing area to see what it looked like on her.

There she stood, young, brimming with confidence in her allure, glowing in the expensive light. The shirt fit her perfectly and I meant to say that. Instead, through cloth and bra, I touched her breast, circling the tip with my finger. Neither of us spoke. I don't remember the look on her face, just my finger moving and her nipple responding, hardening. Magic elixir. Delicious.

The moment lasted seconds, and then I bought her the shirt and we went on with our afternoon. But the relationship shifted slightly, becoming closer, less a flirtation and more a true, sweet friendship. By some tacit understanding, we did not go shopping again, and I never touched her again in quite that way. But at lunch sometimes, or even in my office, we held hands while we talked. I liked that a lot.

It was probably foolish of me to tell Sharona about this incident, but I wasn't thinking that way then. I wanted to challenge her; I wanted her to understand. We were talking about the word *sacred*, what it meant to her. It meant something beyond words, she said. Something that was beyond the quotidian but was expressed through it. I agreed. And then I told her what had happened between me and Hortense. I said that it had been, in a small way, sacred to me.

Her face became very still, her eyes wide. She asked me what Hortense did at the publishing house. How old she was. Would she continue working there? And, finally, "Why was this sacred to you?"

"I don't know, exactly. Like you said, it's beyond words. But I felt it. Awe at her beauty and at being alive. And that this strange thing could happen. Going up to the very line of acceptability and not crossing it."

"How do you think she felt?"

"Maybe a little of the same. Not enjoying it, exactly. But willing. Understanding my need." I told her that I didn't think it would happen again, and that was part of what made it special. I asked her if she understood that.

She was slow to answer, but finally she said, "I guess I do. But I hope you understand that it would never be okay to touch me that way."

"Never," I said honestly. "I would never touch you that way." I reached across the table and took her hand. We sat like that for a moment, her captive hand softening incrementally. I turned it over and resisted kissing it. The check came. It was a victory, I thought.

M.

It's odd to me that although Caitlin was the one who finally . . . *broke* Quin, I never heard about her. I don't think I met her either, and I met countless young women in Quin's orbit. I *did* meet Sharona once, and heard about her even more. (Wasn't she innocent? Wasn't she special? Wasn't she straight out of the fifties?

Though she was clearly just a standard nineties girl, right down to her silly pop-song name.) Toward the end of their "friendship," he actually sent me texts that he wanted to send to her, asking my opinion on them. Some of these texts were aggressively teasing; some were nearly pleading, including one in which he compared her refusal to "share" more of herself to the Republican Congress's refusal to share societal wealth. (That one I definitely told him not to send.) We could spend whole lunches analyzing her behavior, particularly why she wouldn't let him stroke her back or even take her elbow to guide her through a room. It was the same conversation, over and over: I lectured about respect and boundaries; he wondered how someone could be so "precious" about herself and declared that he would *never* refuse the needs of a friend. I retorted, "What if I needed you to kneel down and kiss my feet every time you saw me?" He said that he would do it. I said that it could be very awkward. He said that he would do it right there, and then he actually knelt on the floor of the restaurant; when people stared, he explained, "I'm honoring the needs of my darling friend." He actually tried to kiss my feet. I had to say "Stop!" But I was laughing.

I heard all about Sharona. But I didn't know about Caitlin until the lawsuit. "What did you do?" I asked. "Why do you think she is so angry?"

He shrugged. "She asked what she had to do to get invited to my parties and I told her she had to flirt with me more. I think that really offended her."

Of course, the stories in the paper listed many more offenses, including sending Caitlin, while she was still working for him, a video of a man spanking a woman. People were shocked when I showed sympathy for him on that one. I said, "I know it sounds terrible. But I don't think it really happened that way. He probably asked her what she likes to do sexually, and she told him she likes spanking. For him, it'd be the most natural thing in the world to send her a spanking video. Yes, it was still rude!" I admitted. "But—"

Quin said, "I didn't even ask. She told me on her own. And it wasn't porn or anything—it was John Wayne spanking an actress in some old-timey western!"

Caitlin wasn't even the one who accused him of actual spanking. Someone else revealed that, in an interview with the *Times*.

That woman wasn't actually part of the lawsuit, but she certainly made it look reasonable.

Q.

If my wife stays with me, I can get through this. I can get through it regardless, but . . . *broken, hobbled, without her respect;* these are the kinds of words that can pile up on one another when my mind goes in that direction, so I don't let it. I take my morning run. I keep my head up. Bright light fills my mind. Life is a miracle. It goes on, no matter what happens to one selfish man. "You are Quinlan Maximillian Saunders, and through this you will find a better place." Carolina said that to me at two in the morning, holding me in her arms, with tears streaming down her face. Earlier that day—technically, the previous day—she'd slapped me publicly, in the street. She did this because I'd seen one of my accusers, smiled at her, and said, "Hello."

"She smiled at *me*," I explained. "I was just smiling back." And my wife turned and hit me. As hard as she could, with her open hand.

"Idiot," she said. She spoke calmly and quietly, though loud enough for passersby to hear. "I guess I can't let you out, even with me."

Later she held me in her arms. But it is in fact the case that she forbids me to go out, and I go along with it, because I know what this has done to her, and what she thinks it will do to Lucia one day—although I think Carolina underestimates the child.

It's so terrible and so absurd. Absurd that I did certain things, yes. Absurd too that Caitlin holds a position that I helped her get and from that position accuses me of things that she was party to. Even more absurd, she is called "brave" for it. And finally, I find it just slightly absurd that what has hurt Carolina the most in all this, I suspect, is not a wound to her heart or even to her true dignity but to her social identity: she went from being the wife of a respected editor to being the wife of a pariah.

"What kind of wife am I?" She screamed these words in the presence of one of my closest friends. "What kind of wife will I be for the cameras? At the court date? A loyal wife? A spiritual wife? A humiliated wife?" She *screamed*, my elegant, formidable Carolina, and my friend and I just sat there, gaping at her pain.

"It's me who has to call the lawyers," she ranted, "and the pub-
lisher, who stabbed you in the back after you fell on your sword
for him. It's me who has to get on the phone and remind the
hypocrite that without you he has no scapegoat, and without him
we have no insurance."

"Can you countersue?" my friend suggested weakly. "Can you
take the girl to court or—"

"Are you kidding? Do you know how much that would cost? Do
you know how much we've lost already?" But she at least stopped
shouting. "I don't care about the girl. I care about health insurance and survival for my family. I don't care about vindication. I
don't want to win. I just want my family to be okay."

Terrible. Not absurd. Terrible. I feel it. I feel it every day. But I
don't think about it. It hurts too much to think about it. Instead I
think about Sharona. I even wrote her a letter. I don't know if I'll
send it. Margot said that it wouldn't make any difference; if that's
true I might as well:

> I read in the amicus brief that you were among those offering your ex-
> perience with me as an example of my abusive behavior. I am shocked
> and hurt by this. I never intended any pain or disrespect. I teased, may-
> be too much. But you must know how much I valued our friendship
> and respected you. I offered to include your boyfriend in our circle just
> to be in your presence. Please, Sharona, don't be part of this. I'm not
> asking because I think it will affect the legal outcome—I know that it
> won't. I'm asking because it truly hurts me to have your name in any
> way connected with this. Please show me a fraction of the regard I feel
> for you.

I was very tempted to add that Hortense, the sacred dressing-
room girl, was adamantly not a part of the lawsuit, that she had
even sent me a supportive note. (Which was especially meaningful
considering that Hortense knew Caitlin; I wonder how that friendship is going?) But I didn't.

M.

"You had a paddle in your office? Just lying around? I never noticed that."

"Oh, Margot, stop it. It was more like, I don't know, a serving spoon or a spatula."

"And it just happened to be in your office. And you—"

"We had a lunch date and she was half an hour late. I hate it when people are late. I'm sure you've noticed that I'm very punctual."

"Yes, I have."

"So I was a little bit annoyed, and almost to make the situation lighter, I said, 'Don't you think you should be punished for being late?' And she said, 'I guess so.' So I said, 'What should the punishment be?' I had no idea what she'd say. She said—no, she didn't just *say* it—she turned around and bent over." He turned and showed me, his butt presented with knees and thighs pressed primly together. I think he even put his hands on his knees. "And she said, 'A spanking.' So I swatted her once with this butter knife—"

"You said spatula."

"Whatever it was, I don't remember. And then we went to lunch and had a great time. And now she's saying that I beat and degraded her."

I face-palmed as I pictured it: the breezy ambiance of the office, the light words, the girl maybe tossing a little moue over her shoulder as she playfully presented her ass; perhaps she started at the stinging sensation, but then—off to lunch and laughter! And then the silent subway ride home, across from a row of tired, distracted strangers staring at their phones, or just staring.

"This is what I don't understand. It was her idea—no, it *was* my idea. But she more than went along with it. She didn't have to stick her ass out. She didn't have to do anything. None of them had to."

"Quin," I said. "I would never say this in public. I wouldn't say it to anybody but you. And maybe Todd. But listen. Women are like horses. They want to be led. They want to be led, but they also want to be respected. You have to earn it, every time. And they are as strong as fuck. If you don't respect them, they will throw you off and prance around the paddock while you lie there bleeding. That's what I think."

Q.

Do I respect women? If I'm being truthful, I'm not sure I can answer generally and in all cases. But I can say this: I respect my wife. And I did not betray her.

"I flirted. That's all it was. I did it to feel alive without being unfaithful. I never—"

"It would've been more dignified if you had," Carolina replied. "It would've been more normal."

"It would be more dignified if I'd been *unfaithful*? Do you mean that?"

She sat very straight, looking out our big, west-facing windows. Countless rectilinear shapes, silver and gray, rose in an abnormal sky of purplish clouds and freakishly pink light. An especially vertiginous beauty of glass and steel caught the sunset and turned orange.

"You're not even a predator," she said quietly. "Not even. You're a fool. A pinching, creeping fool. That is what's unbearable."

M.

I didn't know most of the women who had spoken out against Quin. But I knew one, a novelist named Regina March, one of his minor discoveries from some years back. I'd seen her at Quin's parties and liked her; she was a warm, opinionated forty-year-old, who, I remember, always hugged Quin goodbye. I was astonished to see that she was one of hundreds of women who'd signed the petition naming multiple "abusers" and demanding that no one ever hire them again; they specifically threatened to boycott any publishing house or media company that did hire one of them. Essentially, this intelligent, delightful woman was threatening the livelihood of the man who'd first published her!

My astonishment must have shown when I saw her at a party; her face fell at the sight of me. Provoked by her guilty look, I slowly pursued her around the room, joined her in a three-way conversation, and politely awaited my moment. I didn't have to wait long. As soon as the other woman walked away, she looked at me with emotional eyes and asked, "How is Quin? How is Carolina?"

"As well as you would expect," I said.

"I think of them every day," she said. "I've wanted to reach out but I—"

"*Reach out?* You wanted to *reach out?* My God, Regina, why did you sign that thing?"

She started to cry. She said that she hadn't seen his name on the petition until after she'd signed it—there were so many names—and because it was online, she couldn't unsign it. Maybe his name was added after she signed it? Because if she'd seen it she wouldn't have done it! Could I tell him, could I tell Carolina, could I—

Q.

After my case has been dismissed—and I feel there is a good chance of that happening—I want to make a statement. I'll write a blog, maybe, or send something to the *Times*. Maybe I'll just read it in court. The idea came to me late one night—early morning, really, probably around four, when I woke with my heart so low in my chest that I could barely feel it. Carolina was next to me, and though I wanted to press against her for strength, I lay still. Her features were barely visible in the dark, but I saw the contours of her forehead, lips, nose, and cheek; these shapes expressed sadness and helplessness, but her curved shoulders and her neck declared animal determination *to push through this shit*. Carolina: the sacred figure behind the gaudy tapestry of my public life. Unable to help myself, I moved closer and, coming into the area of her warmth, was flooded with relief and residual happiness. Then she moved, in her sleep, away from me.

I thought, *I've got to do something. I have to fight somehow*. I could check in with old friends in London. Maybe the poison hasn't spread there. Terrible to have to face my father, but . . . I rose and went into the living room and looked out at the park, with its deep vegetable greens and rough browns under the colorless sky. But I didn't want to go to England; I wanted to stay here. A few cars moved sluggishly in the street; a horse-drawn carriage humped along at the curb. Sounds came up—a garbage truck, a bus, something large beeping horribly as it turned, the gray noise of traffic. Horns, blaring and bright then soft around the edges, subsiding into the dominant gray. Beautiful from here—the obedience to

the grid, the vying against it. It gave me faith in myself. Words and
music flowed freely in my mind, coming, it seemed, from a place
of deep subterranean order, a place from which the signs and sym-
bols of society draw their vitality. Buoyed by the ramshackle order
of the waking city, I felt that all could be well, that I could make
myself understood, and—perhaps—even make peace with those
who had felt wronged by me.

I sat down at my desk and wrote:

> I realize that the way I've carried myself in the world has not always
> been agreeable to those around me. I come from a generation that
> values freedom and honesty above politeness, and I have acted from
> those values, sometimes as a provocateur, even a trickster. Maybe I've
> gone too far sometimes, been too curious, too friendly, at times a little
> arrogant. But . . .

From there, I didn't know what to say. I found myself strangely
distracted by memories of a visual artist who'd been a frequent
guest at our parties, a sexy bird who'd recently dropped me a
sweet email. I thought of a video she'd made of a man kneeling
and barking at her command; she'd made him bark for a kiss
("Louder! More!") until they both collapsed in fits of laughter.
With some effort, I returned my feelings to my wife and to Lucia, who had awakened from a bad dream a couple of nights before and climbed into bed between us, wanting us both to hold
her. But, even though it had happened recently, the memory felt
distant and somehow made it harder to write the statement. I sat
there for another hour, and still I did not know what else to say.

"I think it would be good if you started with an apology." That's
what Margot's husband, Todd, suggested when I asked them for
help with the statement. We'd had drinks and a discussion in
their old-school Brooklyn apartment—a warren of little rooms re-
deemed by an expansive kitchen that was charming, even with its
broken molding and stained, sagging ceiling.

"Apology for what? Being myself?"

"For causing pain. I realize that some of them are overreacting
or just jumping on a trend. But some of them must've been genuinely hurt and—"

I love Todd. He is a kind and earnest man with slightly strange
proportions—small hands, delicate mouth, formidable shoulders,
and a large and somehow senatorial head. I love him as a loyal

dog to Margot's skittish cat. But I am not a dog, and it won't do for me to pretend that I am. "But I don't believe they were hurt. They were maybe offended, but that's different."

"But would *they* say they were hurt?"

Margot didn't give me time to answer. "I would say that you don't understand why these people are saying these things when they acted like they were your friends and accepted favors from you."

"I don't want to say, 'I don't understand.' That's weak and whining. And besides, I *do* understand."

"What do you understand?" she asked.

What patronizing patience from my darling friend! Still, I answered calmly. "That this is the end of men like me. That they are angry at what's happening in the country and in the government. They can't strike at the king, so they go for the jester. They may not win now, but eventually they will. And who am I to stand in the way? I don't want to stand in the way."

They looked at me with bleak respect.

"They were my friends. I would still be friends with them. I miss them."

"Friends?" Margot really did *sneer* at the word. "That little bitch ruined your life!"

"She did not ruin my life. I would never give her that power. She's just a confused kid!"

Again they looked, simply bleak this time.

M.

"He wants to be friends with them," Todd said incredulously.

"I know."

"He's fucked," Todd said.

"I know."

"Imprisoned in a cloven pine."

"What?"

"And in their most unmitigable rage into a cloven pine, within which rift imprisoned he didst painfully—"

"Oh, stop, this isn't Shakespearean, not even a little. And don't compare the women to witches."

"Why?" He was doing the dishes as we spoke, and turned to look at me. "You just called one of them a little bitch."

He looked genuinely confused, so I just said, "I know," and we dropped it.

But his comparison wasn't right. Ariel didn't pinch Sycorax's ass or tell her to bite his thumb. Ariel was punished for refusing to obey the witch's commands; Quin was being punished for issuing commands. Or at least that was how the women had responded —as if they had been given commands by someone who had the power to do so.

This is where I don't understand my own feelings. When I say to my colleagues that the women should have just told Quin to stop, that *I* had told him to stop and had *made* him stop, they inevitably tell me that the power was disproportionately his, and that even if *in theory* the women could have pushed back they should not be expected to, they shouldn't have to. I get aggravated then and splutter about female agency versus infantilization, etc. I say, yes, he acted badly. I was angry at him too. But did he deserve to lose his job, his right to work, his honor as a human? Did he have to be so completely and utterly crushed? Couldn't people have just made fun of him for being a dirty Jiminy Cricket and left it at that? (A sweet cricket, crossed with the wicked Foulfellow fox— *hi-diddle-dee-dee!*)

But there are other things I don't say, can't say. And this is where the heart pain comes. Subtle. But real.

A few years ago Quin told me that a friend of his was experiencing recovered memories of childhood sex abuse. He was skeptical of this process and so tired of the subject that he found himself avoiding her. "Quin," I told him. "If you care about her as a friend, suspend your skepticism. Even if it sounds like bullshit. This is important and she's trusting you." And to make him understand the strength of my feelings, I told him that I'd been abused as a five-year-old.

"And you remember it?" he asked.

"Not all of it. But I remember some of it very vividly. It was shocking, in every way. The powerful sensation of it. He didn't hurt me physically, but it was like being stunned by a blow and then mesmerized. The sensation was too much, too strong for me at that age."

"Who was he?"

"A friend of the family. I remember his large, dark shape. I don't mean that his coloring was dark. There was a dark feeling about him that I could somehow see. A feeling of pain. I remember climbing in his lap and trying to comfort him."

"I'm sure you did comfort him. You must've been a little angel to him."

"Quin," I said. "That's a weird thing to say."

"Why? Children can be powerful. I'm sure you took away the pain for a little while."

"Not for long. He killed himself."

"Terrible. Still, I'm sure you helped him."

And then the conversation moved on. I didn't feel anger. I don't remember what I felt, exactly, except a strange, muted combination of incredulity and acceptance. It didn't occur to me to say anything to him about it until much later. He didn't remember the conversation, but he apologized anyway; he didn't understand why I was upset. "I was just trying to find something positive in it," he said. And I imagine that was true. But inside I stayed angry. At the same time, I still loved him. I still leaned on him for support and counsel. I was like the women who didn't stop him and who acted like his friends even as they grew angrier and angrier. It wasn't because he had more power than I did; that didn't really matter. And it wasn't because I'm like a horse. I don't know why I behaved the way I did, and I kept doing it; *he* kept doing it. The little jabs and jokes he'd always made, artfully woven in with his habitual flattery, stung, like the bites of an invisible insect ("I think it's *interesting* that you pay *so* much more attention to your appearance than you did even just five years ago"). And though I might once have easily brushed them away, suddenly I could not. Nor could I confront him. The conversation moved too quickly.

Q.

When I was nineteen, I had sex with a girl in the public restroom of a club, if you could call that dark, filthy noise pit a club, and we did then. I didn't have to do much to make it happen, so little that I can barely remember. I remember her, though: her small, pretty face too stiff and blank, but her nearly perfect body full of strange, hard will. First I sat and she knelt (shirt pulled up, bra pulled down, amazing breasts popping out, crushed and lopsided), then I stood and she bent, offering herself over a public toilet. We were not alone, the dirty roar of the sound system came in and out with the suctioning door and people spewed into the porcelain pots, crashed around, and laughed in the rattling stalls. She almost ran out when we were done, and, feeling some vague remorse, I asked for her number, because I thought she might want that, though she didn't seem to. I have a photo of a former girlfriend that was taken at the same club; it was taken right as someone pulled up her skirt to show that she wasn't wearing underwear. Her eyes are lowered, her face is turned half defiantly, and her hand is fighting to pull her skirt back down, but she's smiling, and it looks at first glance as if she were the one pulling up her own dress.

I wonder, if those girls were girls now, would they describe themselves as "assaulted" if someone put his hand on their knee? Would they say that they were too "frozen" in dismay to stop him?

What a different story we told about ourselves then. How aware we were that it was a story.

M.

Though they don't often express it freely, some people feel real sympathy for Quin. "It's a travesty," one guy whispered hoarsely over a table during an after-work group drink. "His life is ruined because an *ass* got pinched?" It wasn't just men: a sixty-plus female publicist, who'd been in the business forever, was vocal in her sympathy, calling him "wonderful" and "generous," as her younger colleagues frowned peevishly. "Maybe generous to a fault," she said, "to twits who didn't deserve it, poor man."

The dominant opinion, however, is that he got what he deserved; he'd apparently made more enemies than even I was aware of. Still, most people see my continued friendship with him as loyal, if suspiciously so. My professional reputation, after all, was made when I published a book of charming stories about masochistic women (the now charmless author of which is *still* complaining about the size of her advance), a book that was seen variously as groundbreaking, "empowering," sad, eye-rollingly trite, and, finally, sociologically interesting; although I've shepherded many books into existence since, I have never quite separated myself from that titillating yet tiresome aura. So I took it quite personally when, after a particularly dull conference, gossip turned to all the men who'd recently been exposed and ruined by outraged women, and a colleague said, apropos of what, I don't remember, "Then there's the women trying to defend these creeps. The ones who say, 'That's just what men are like.' Them I feel sorry for. Because I can't imagine what their lives have been like."

She didn't look at me; I didn't look at her. Quin wasn't mentioned by name. Still, I wish I'd said, "Quin isn't 'like' any other man I've met. I don't know any other man as comical and strangely lewd. I don't know any other man who would kneel on the floor of a restaurant and try to kiss your feet just to be whimsical. Or offer to carry your money and lipstick for you so that you can appear more free. I don't know any other man who would say to a crying woman he barely knew, 'You are a lovely spirit,' and ask her to meet him for tea when her female 'friend' had hung up on her." My very proper colleague would, I'm sure, have hung up too, disgusted by my weakness in that moment. It was Quin who had restored me, and not just on that day. Over days and weeks and months, he helped me feel that I was part of humanity, and not with his kindness alone; it was his silliness, his humor, his *dirtiness* that rekindled my spirit.

I saw him for lunch the other day and he was in exceptionally good form, perfectly dressed, his scarf tasseled rakishly. We talked about books that were coming out, *his* books, one of which had just been very well reviewed in the *Times;* we gossiped about colleagues. We talked about Carolina and about Lucia, who, at eight, had suddenly started sucking her thumb, a development that his wife was, he thought, making too much of. He chatted with all the waiters, polling them on everything from their uniforms and how they felt wearing them to their highest hopes and ambitions. The easygoing young men were plainly amused. "Keep asking questions!" one exhorted as we finally made our exit.

"I think things are turning around for me," Quin said. "I can feel it. The city is opening to me again."

Heart pain. Real.

Q.

Stories, it's all stories. Life is too big for anybody, and that's why we invent stories. Women are now very into the victim story; those I've offended are all victims, even as they're feted everywhere. I could make that my story too, but it's not the best, because it's much too simple. The best story is one that reveals a truth, like something you see and understand in a dream but forget as soon as you wake up. The girl who bent over the toilet for me so long ago—she was acting out a truth that she then ran from, and her running was also true. When I stuck my thumb in that bird's face—the example Margot never ceases to bring up, as if it were the worst outrage of all—I was daring her to show herself, and I was showing myself too, showing my need to live and feel alive. I was asking, *inviting: Can you play, do you play?* Her answer was no, and that was fine. I bought her book anyway; I even read some of it.

Well, and now the truth is that everyone has said no. Now the truth is that I'm the man in the sexy artist's video, kneeling and barking for a kiss. Really, I've always been him. I would have done anything Sharona wanted—invite her boyfriend to dinner with us so that I could be in her presence, kneel and bark if it would lead to laughter and a kiss, just a kiss! Well, that all sounds very disingenuous. I can see Margot rolling her eyes. I can see Carolina, her face stunned and desolate, aged by grief—the way she looks when she thinks I can't see her, the way she looked last night, coming out of Lucia's room, her bright smile collapsing, then hardening as soon as she saw me. I can see my little girl, her lovely cheeks and forehead glowing in the dim light of her laptop behind a half-closed door, carefully not hearing the angry words, the tears. What she might see on that laptop one day: it comes barreling at me with sickening speed, veers malevolently close, then passes like some satanic truck in a horror movie. It's a sad story, all right, but . . . Best to take it one day at a time. And remember . . .

Life is big enough for any story. I walk in the street with tears running down my face; I walk in a world of sales racks and flavored refreshments, marching crowds, broken streets, and steam pouring through the cracks. Jackhammers, roaring buses, women striding into traffic, knifelike in their high, sharp heels, past windows full of faces, products, bright admonishments, light, and dust. Slouching employees smoke in doorways; waiters clear outdoor tables. Eaters lounge before empty plates, legs spread, working their phones. Flocks of pigeons, a careful rat. At this newsstand, I know the proprietor; he catches my eye and tactfully registers my tears with the slightest change in his expression. Deep in his cave of fevered headlines and gaudy faces, he shivers with cold and fights to breathe; his lungs are failing as he sells magazines and bottled water, mints and little basil plants. We greet each other; I don't say but I think, *Hello, brother.* And life rushes by. On the corner people play instruments and sing. Sullen men sit with filthy dogs and beg. In the subway a hawk-nosed boy with dyed, stringy, somehow elegant hair squats and manipulates crude puppets to sexy music amid a weird tableau of old toys. There is something sinister; he looks up with a pale, lewd eye. An older woman laughs too loudly, trying to get his attention. A beggar looks at me and says, "Don't be so sad. It'll get better by and by." And I believe him. There will be something else for me. If not here, then in London, I can feel it. I am on the ground and bleeding, but I will stand up again. I will sing songs of praise.

The beggar laughs behind me, shouts something I can't hear. I turn, a dollar already in my hand.

MENG JIN

In the Event

FROM *The Threepenny Review*

IN THE EVENT OF AN EARTHQUAKE, I texted Tony, WE'LL MEET
AT THE CORNER OF CHINAMAN'S VISTA, ACROSS FROM THE
CAFÉ WITH THE RAINBOW FLAG.

Jen had asked about our earthquake plan. We didn't have one.
We were new to the city, if it could be called that. Tony described
it to friends back home as a huge village. But very densely populated, I added, and not very agrarian. We had come here escap-
ing separate failures on the opposite coast. Already the escape was
working. In this huge urban village, under the dry bright sky, we
were beginning to regard our former ambitions as varieties of regional disease, belonging to different climates, different times.

"Firstly," Jen said, "you need a predetermined meeting point.
In case you're not together and cell service is clogged. Which it's
likely to be. Because, you know, disasters."

Jen was the kind of person who said things like *firstly* and *because, disasters*. She was a local local, born and raised and stayed.
Tony had met Jen a few years ago at an electronic music festival
back east and introduced us, thinking we'd get along. She had
been traveling for work. Somehow we stayed in touch. We shared
interests: she worked as a tech consultant but composed music as a
hobby; I made electronic folk songs with acoustic sounds.

"The ideal meeting place," Jen explained, "is outside, walkable
from both your workplaces, and likely free of obstacles."

"Obstacles?"

"Collapsed buildings, downed power lines, blah blah hazmat,
you know."

Chinaman's Vista was the first meeting place that came to mind. It was a big grassy field far from the water, on high ground. Cypress trees lined its edges. In their shade, you could sit and watch the well-behaved dogs of well-behaved owners let loose to run around. We had walked past it a number of times on our way from this place or that—the grocery store, the pharmacy, the ta-queria—and commented on its charm with surprise, forgetting we'd come across it before. In the event of a significant earth-quake, and the aftershocks that typically follow significant earth-quakes, I imagined we would be safe there—from falling debris at least—as we searched through the faces of worried strangers for each other.

Other forces could separate or kill us: landslides, tsunamis, nu-clear war. I was aware that we lived on the side of a sparsely veg-etated hill, that we were four miles from the ocean, a mile from the bay. To my alarmed texts Tony responded that if North Korea was going to bomb us, this region would be a good target: reach-able by missile, home to the richest and fastest-growing industry in the world. Probably they would go for one of the cities south of us, he typed, where the headquarters of the big tech companies were based.

NUCLEAR BLAST WIND CAN TRAVEL AT > 300 M/S, Tony wrote. Tony knew things like this.

He clarified: METERS PER SECOND

WHICH GIVES US

I watched Tony's avatar think.

APPROX 3 MINS TO FIND SHELTER AFTER DETONATION

More likely we'd get some kind of warning *x* hours before the bomb struck. Jen had a car. She could pick us up, we'd drive north as fast as we could. Jen's aunt who lived an hour over the bridge had a legit basement, concrete reinforced during the Cold War.

I thought about the active volcano one state away, which, if it erupted, could cover the city in ash. One very large state away, Tony reminded me. But the ash that remained in the air might be so thick it obscured the sun, plunging this usually temperate coast into winter. I thought about the rising ocean, the expanding down-town at sea level, built on landfill. Tony worked in the expanding downtown. Was Tony a strong swimmer? I asked with two question marks. His response:

DON'T WORRY 'LIL CHENCHEN
IF I DIE I'LL DIE

I was listening to an audiobook, on 1.65x speed, about a techno-dystopic future Earth under threat of annihilation from alien attack. The question was whether humans would kill each other first or survive long enough to be shredded in the fast-approaching weaponized supermassive black hole. Another question was whether humans would abandon life on Earth and attempt to continue civilization on spacecraft. Of course there were not enough spacecraft for everyone.

When I started listening, it was at normal 1.0 speed. Each time I returned I switched the speed dial up by 0.05x. It was a gripping book, full of devices for sustaining mystery despite the obvious conclusion. I couldn't wait for the world to end.

Tony and I were fundamentally different. What I mean is we sat in the world differently—he settling into the back cushions, noting with objective precision the grime or glamour of his surroundings, while I hovered, nervous, at the edge of my seat. Often I felt —more often now—I couldn't even make it to the edge. Instead I flitted from one space to another, calculating if I would fit, considering the cosmic feeling of unwelcome that emanated from wherever I chose to go.

On the surface Tony and I looked very much the same. We were more or less the same percentile in height and weight, and we both had thin, blank faces, their resting expressions betraying slight confusion and surprise. Our bodies were constructed narrowly of long brittle bones, and our skin, pale in previous gray winters, now tanned easily to the same dusty brown. We weren't only both Chinese; our families came from the same rural-industrial province south of Shanghai, recently known for small-goods manufacturing. But in a long reversal of fortunes, his family, businesspeople who had fled to Hong Kong and then South Carolina, were now lower-middle-class second-generation immigrants, while my parents, born from starving peasant stock, had stayed in China through its boom and emigrated much later to the States as members of the highly educated elite.

Tony's family was huge. I guess mine was too, but I didn't know any of them. In this hemisphere I had my parents, and that was it.

A couple years ago I did Thanksgiving with Tony's family. It was my first time visiting the house where he'd grown up. It was also the first time I had left my parents to celebrate a holiday alone. I tried not to guess what they were eating—Chinese takeout or left-over Chinese takeout. Even when I was around, my parents spent most of their time sitting in separate rooms, working.

"Chenchen!" his mother had cried as she embraced me. "We're *so* happy you could join us."

My arms rose belatedly, swiping the sides of her shoulders as she pulled away.

She said my name like an American. The rest of the family did too—in fact every member of Tony's family spoke with varied degrees of southern drawl. It was very disorienting. In normal circumstances Tony's English was incredibly bland, neutered of history like my own, but now I heard in it long-drawn diphthongs, wholesome curls of twang. Both his sisters had come. As had his three uncles and two aunts with their families, and two full sets of grandparents, his mom's mom recently remarried after his grandpa's death. I had never been in a room with so many Chinese people at once, but if I closed my eyes and just listened to the chatter, my brain populated the scene with white people wearing bandannas and jeans.

Which was accurate, except for the white people part.

The turkey had been deep-fried in an enormous vat of oil. We had stuffing and cranberry sauce and ranch-flavored mashed potatoes (a Zhang family tradition), pecan and sweet potato and ginger pie. We drank beer cocktails (Bud Light and lemonade). No one regretted the lack of rice or soy sauce, or said with a disappointed sigh that we should have just ordered roast duck from Hunan Garden. It was loud. I shouted small talk and halfway introduced myself to various relatives, as bursts of yelling and laughter erupted throughout the room. Jokes were told—jokes! I had never heard people who looked like my parents making so many jokes—plates clinked, drinks sloshed, moving chairs and shoes scuffed the floor with a pleasing busy beat.

In the middle of all this I was struck suddenly by a wave of mourning, though I wasn't sure for what. The sounds of a child-hood I'd never had, the large family I'd never really know? Perhaps it was the drink—I think the beer-ade was spiked with vodka—but I felt somehow that I was losing Tony then, that by letting myself know him in this way I had opened a door through which he might one day slip away.

In the corner of the living room, the pitch of the conversation changed. Tony's teenage cousin Harriet was yelling at her mother while Tony's mom sat at her side loudly shaking her head. Slowly the other voices in the room quieted until the tacit attention of every person was focused on this exchange. Others began to participate, some angry—"Don't you dare speak to your mother like this," some conciliatory—"How about some pecan pie?," some anxious —Harriet's little sister tugging on her skirt. Harriet pushed her chair back angrily from the table. A vase fell over, dumping flowers and gray water into the stuffing. Harriet stormed from the room.

For a moment it was quiet. In my pocket my phone buzzed. By the time I took it out the air had turned loud and festive again. THIS HAPPENS EVERY YEAR, Tony had texted. I looked at him; he shrugged with resigned amusement. Around me I heard casual remarks of a similar nature: comments on Harriet's personality and love life—apparently she had just broken up with a boyfriend —and nostalgic reminiscences of the year Tofu the dog had peed under the table in fright. It was like a switch had been flipped. In an instant the tension was diffused, injury and grievance transformed into commotion and fond collective memory.

I saw then how Tony's upbringing had prepared him for reality in a way that mine had not. His big family was a tiny world. It reflected the real world with uncanny accuracy—its little charms and injustices, its pettinesses and usefulnesses—and so real-worldly forces struck him with less intensity, without the paralyzing urgency of assault. He did not need to survive living like I did; he could simply live.

I woke up to Tony's phone in my face.

R U OK? his mom had texted. Followed by:

R U OK????

PLS RESPOND MY DEAR SON

CALL ASAP LOVE MOM (followed by heart emojis and, inexplicably, an ice cream cone)

His father and siblings and aunts and cousins and childhood friends had flooded his phone with similar messages. He scrolled through the unending ribbon of notifications sprinkled with news alerts. I turned on my phone. It gave a weak buzz. Jen had texted us at 4:08 a.m.:

DID YOU GUYS FEEL THE EARTHQUAKE? I RAN OUTSIDE AND LEFT THE DOOR OPEN AND NOW I CANT FIND PRICK

*PICKLE

Pickle was Jen's cat.

A lamp had fallen over in the living room. We had gotten it at a garage sale and put it on a stool to simulate a tall floor lamp. Now it was splayed across the floor, shade bent, glass bulb dangling but miraculously still intact. When we lifted it we saw a dent in the floorboards. The crooked metal frame of the lamp could no longer support itself and so we laid it on its side like a reclining nude. There were other reclining forms too. Tony had put toy action figures among my plants and books; all but Wolverine had fallen on their faces or backs. He sent a photo of a downed Obi-Wan Kenobi to his best nerd friends back home.

He seemed strangely elated. That he would be able to say, *Look, this happened to us too, and without any real cost.*

Later, while Tony was at work, I pored over earthquake preparedness maps on the Internet. Tony's office was in a converted warehouse with large glass windows on the edge of the expanding downtown. On the map this area was marked in red, which meant it was a liquefaction zone. I didn't know what *liquefaction* meant but it didn't sound good. Around lunchtime Tony sent me a YouTube video showing a tray of vibrating sand on which a rubber ball bobbed in and out as if through waves in a sea. He'd forgotten about the earthquake already, his caption said: SO COOL. I messaged back: WHEN THE BIG ONE HITS, YOU'RE THE RUBBER BALL.

That afternoon I couldn't stop seeing his human body tossed in and out through the rubble of skyscrapers. I reminded myself that Tony had a stable psyche. He was the kind of person you could trust not to lose his mind, not in a disruptive way, at least. But I didn't know if he had a strong enough instinct for self-preservation. Clearly he didn't have a good memory for danger. And he wasn't resourceful, at least not with physical things like food and shelter. His imagination was better for fantasy than for worst-case scenarios.

I messaged:

IF YOU FEEL SHAKING, MOVE AWAY FROM THE WINDOWS.
GET UNDER A STURDY DESK AND HOLD ON TO A LEG. IF THERE
IS NO DESK OR TABLE NEARBY CROUCH BY AN INTERIOR
WALL. WHATEVER YOU DO, COVER YOUR NECK AND HEAD AT
ALL TIMES

He sent me a sideways heart. I watched his avatar think and type
for many moments.

I'M SERIOUS, I wrote.

Finally he wrote back:

UMM WHAT IF MY DESK IS BY THE WINDOW

. . .

SHOULD I GET UNDER THE DESK OR GO TO AN INTERIOR WALL

I typed: GET UNDER YOUR DESK AND PUSH IT TO AN INTE-
RIOR WALL WHILE COVERING YOUR HEAD AND NECK. I imagined the rubber ball. I imagined the floor undulating, dissolving
into sand. I typed: HOLD ON TO ANY SOLID THING YOU CAN.

I couldn't focus on work. I had recorded myself singing a series of
slow glissandos in E minor, which I was trying to distort over a cello
droning C. It was supposed to be the spooky intro before the drop
of an irregular beat. The song was about failure's various forms,
the wild floating quality of it. I wanted to show Tony I understood
what he had gone through back east, at least in its primal movement and shape, that despite the insane specificity of his suffering
he was not alone.

Now all I could hear were the vibrations of sand, the movements of people and buildings falling.

I went to the hardware store. I bought earthquake-proof cabinet
latches and L-bars to bolt our furniture to the walls. According to
a YouTube video called "Seeing with earthquake eyes," it was best
to keep the bed at least fifteen feet from a window or glass or mirror—anything that could shatter into sharp shards over your soft
sleeping neck. Our bed was directly beneath the largest window in
the apartment, which looked out into a dark shaft between buildings. The room was small; I drew many diagrams but could not
find a way to rearrange the furniture. Fifteen feet from the window
would put our bed in the unit next door. I bought no-shatter seals
to tape over the windows. I assembled the necessary things for an
emergency earthquake kit: bottled water, instant ramen, gummy
vitamins. Flashlight, batteries, wrench, and a cheap backpack to

hold everything. I copied our most important contacts from my phone and laminated two wallet-sized emergency contact cards in case cell service or electricity went down.

I bought a whistle for Tony. It blew at high C, a pitch of urgency and alarm. I knew he would never wear it. I'd make him tie the whistle to the leg of his desk. If the sand-and-ball video was accurate and a big earthquake struck during business hours, there was a chance Tony would end up buried in a pile of rubble. I imagined him alive, curled under the frame of his desk. In this scenario, the desk would have absorbed most of the impact and created a small space for him to breathe and crouch. He would be thirsty, hungry, afraid. I imagined his dry lips around the whistle, and the dispirited emergency crews layers of rubble above him, leaping up, shouting, "Someone's down there! Someone's down there!"

Suddenly I remembered I had forgotten to text Jen back.

DID U LOOK IN THE DRYER? OR THAT BOX IN THE GARAGE? EVERYTHING OK OVER HERE THANKS JUST ONE BROKEN LAMP

It'd taken me five hours to text Jen, yet now I was worried about her lack of instant response.

DID U FIND PICKEL? LET ME KNOW I CAN COME OVER AND HELPYOU LOOK

MAYBE SHE'S STUCK IN A TREE??

TONY CAN PRINT OUT SOME FLYERS AT HIS OFFICE LET ME KNOW!!!

I was halfway through enlarging a photo of Pickle I'd dug up from Google photos when my phone buzzed.

FOUND PICKLE THIS MORNING IN BED ALMOST SAT ON HER SHE WAS UNDER THE COVERS BARELY MADE A BUMP

She sent me a photo. Pickle was sitting on a pillow, fur fluffed, looking like a super grouch.

My office had no windows. It was partially underground, the garage-adjacent storage room that came with our apartment. We had discarded everything when we moved so we had nothing to store. The room had one outlet and was just big enough for my recording equipment and a piano. It was soundproof and the Internet signal was weak. The recordings I made in there had a muffled amplified quality, like listening to a loud fight through a door.

The building where Tony and I rented was old, built in the late

nineteenth century, a dozen years before the big earthquake of
1904. It had survived that one, but still by modern building codes
it was what city regulators called a soft story property. According to
records at City Hall, it had been seismically retrofitted by mandate
five years ago. I saw evidence of these precautions in the garage:
extra beams and girding along the foundations, the boilers and
water tanks bolted to the walls. I couldn't find my storage/work
room on any of the blueprints. Tony thought I was hypocritical
to keep working there, given my new preoccupation with safety. I
liked the idea of making music in a place that didn't technically
exist, even if it wasn't up to code.

Or maybe it was. I imagined, in fact, that the storage rooms had
been secret bunkers—why else was there a power outlet? I felt at
once safe and sober inside it, this womb of concrete, accompanied
by the energies of another age of panic. Now I filled the remaining
space with ten gallons of water—enough for two people for five
days—boxes of Shin noodles and canned vegetable soup, saltine
crackers, tins of Spam, canned tuna for Tony (who no longer ate
land animals), a small camping stove I found on sale. I moved our
sleeping bags and our winter coats down.

My office, my bunker. More and more it seemed like a good
place to sit out a disaster. If we ran out of bottled water, the most
vital resource, there stood the bolted water heaters, just a few
steps away.

"Holy shit," Tony said when he came home from work. "Have you
seen the news?"

I pursed my lips. I didn't read the news anymore. The sight of
the new president's face made me physically ill. Instead I buried
myself in old librettos and scores, spent whole days listening to
the kind of music that made every feeling cell in my brain vibrate
with forgetting: the Ring Cycle, Queen's albums in chronologi-
cal order, Glenn Gould huffing and purring through the Gold-
berg Variations.

Tony did the opposite. Once upon a time he had been a con-
sumer of all those nonfiction tomes vying for the Pulitzer Prize,
big books about social and historical issues. He used to send me
articles that took multiple hours to read—I'd wondered when he
ever did work. Now he only sent me tweets.

He waved his phone in my face.

Taking up the entire screen was a photograph of what appeared to be hell. Hell, as it appeared in medieval paintings and Hollywood films. Hills and trees burning so red they appeared liquid, the sky pulsing with black smoke. A highway cut through the center of this scene, and on the highway, impossibly, were cars, fleeing and entering the inferno at top speed.

"This is Loma," Tony said.

"Loma?"

"It's an hour from here? We were there last month?"

"We were?"

"That brewery with the chocolate? Jen drove?"

"Oh. Yeah. Wow."

According to the photograph's caption, the whole state was on fire. Tony's voice was incredulous, alarmed.

"Have you gone outside today?"

I hadn't.

We walked to Chinaman's Vista, where there was a view of the city. Tony held my hand and I was grateful for it. The air was smoky; it smelled like everyone was having a barbecue. If I closed my eyes I could imagine I was in my grandmother's village in Zhejiang, those hours before dinner when families started firing up their wood-burning stoves.

"People are wearing those masks," Tony said. "Look—like we're in fucking Beijing."

Tony had never been to Beijing. I had. The smog wasn't half as bad as this.

We sat on a bench in Chinaman's Vista and looked at the sky. The sun was setting. Behind the gauze of smoke it was a brilliant salmon orange, its light so diffused you could stare straight at it without hurting your eyes. The sky was pink and purple, textured with plumes of color. It was the most beautiful sunset I had ever seen. Around us the light cast upon the trees and grass and purple bougainvillea an otherworldly yellow glow, more nostalgic than any Instagram filter. I looked at Tony, whose face had relaxed in the strange beauty of the scene, and it was like stumbling upon a memory of him—his warm dry hand clasping mine, the two of us looking and seeing the same thing.

Tony's failure had to do with the new president. He had been working on the opposing candidate's campaign, building what was to be a revolutionary technology for civic engagement. They weren't only supposed to win. *They* were the ones who were supposed to go down in history for changing the way politics used the Internet.

My failure had to do with Tony. I had failed to save him, after.

Tony had quit his lucrative job to work seven days a week for fifteen months and a quarter of the pay. The week leading up to the election, he had slept ten hours total, five of them at headquarters, facedown on his desk. He didn't sleep for a month after, though not for lack of time. If there was ever a time for Tony to go insane, that would have been it.

Instead he shut down. His engines cooled, his fans stopped whirring, his lights blinked off. He completed the motions of living, but his gestures were vacant, his eyes hollow. It was like all the emotions insisting and contradicting inside him had short-circuited some processing mechanism. In happier times Tony had joked about his desire to become an android. "Aren't we already androids?" I asked, indicating the eponymous smartphone attached to his hand. Tony shook his head in exasperation. "Cyborgs," he said. "You're thinking of cyborgs." He explained that cyborgs were living organisms with robotic enhancements. Whereas androids were robots made to be indistinguishable from the alive. Tony had always believed computers superior to humans—they didn't need to feel.

In this time I learned many things about Tony and myself, two people I thought I already knew very well. At our weakest, I realized, humans have no recourse against our basest desires. For some this might have meant gorging on sex and drink, or worse —inflicting violence upon others or themselves. For Tony it meant becoming a machine.

Because of the wildfire smoke, we were warned to go outside as little as possible. This turned out to be a boon for my productivity. I shut myself in my bunker and worked.

I woke to orange-hued cityscapes. In the mornings I drank tea and listened to my audiobook. Earth was being shredded, infinitely, as it entered the supermassive black hole, while what remained of humanity sped away on a light-speed ship. "It's strangely beautiful," one character said as she looked back at the scene from space. "No, it's terrible," another said. The first replied, "Maybe beauty is terrible." I thought the author didn't really understand beauty or humans, but he did understand terror and time, and maybe that was enough. I imagined how music might sound on other planets, where the sky wasn't blue and grass wasn't green and water didn't reflect when it was clear. I descended to my bunker and worked for the rest of the day. I stopped going upstairs for lunch, not wanting to interrupt my flow. I ate dry packets of ramen, crumbling noodle squares and picking out the pieces like potato chips. When I forgot to bring down a thermos of tea I drank the bottled water.

Fires were closing in on the city from all directions; fire would eat these provisions up. The city was surrounded on three sides by water—that still left one entry by land. It was dry and getting hotter by the day. I thought the city should keep a ship with emergency provisions anchored in the bay. I thought that if a real disaster struck, I could find it in myself to loot the grocery store a few blocks away.

In the evenings Tony took me upstairs and asked about my workday. In the past he had wanted to hear bits of what I was working on; now he nodded and said, "That sounds nice." I didn't mind. I didn't want to share this new project with him—with anyone—until it was done. We sat on the couch and he showed me pictures of the devastation laying waste to the land. I saw sooty silhouettes of firefighters and drones panning gridwork streets of ash. I saw a woman in a charred doorway, an apparition of color in the black and gray remains of her home.

Once Jen came over to make margaritas. She put on one of Tony's Spotify playlists. "I'm sorry," she said, "I really need to unwind." She knew I didn't like listening to music while other noises were happening. My brain processed the various sounds into separate channels, pulling my consciousness into multiple tracks and dividing my present self. For Jen, overstimulation was a path to relaxation. She crushed ice and talked about the hurricanes ravaging the other coast, the floods and landslides in Asia and South America, the islands in the Pacific already swallowed by the rising sea.

Jen's speech, though impassioned, had an automatic quality to it, an unloading with a mechanical beat. I sipped my margarita and tried to converge her rant with the deep house throbbing from the Sonos: it sounded like a robot throwing up. Tony came home from work and took my margarita. Together they moved from climate change to the other human horrors I'd neglected from the news—ethnic cleansings, mass shootings, trucks mowing down pedestrians. They listed the newest obscenities of the new president, their voices growing louder and faster as they volleyed headlines and tweets. In the far corner of the couch, I hugged my knees. More and more it seemed to me that the world Jen and Tony lived in was one hysterical work of poorly written fiction—a bad doomsday novel—and that what was really real was the world of my music. More and more I could only trust those daytime hours when my presence coincided completely with every sound I made and heard.

I was making a new album. I was making it for me but also for Tony, to show him it was still possible, in these times, to maintain a sense of self.

My last album had come out a year earlier. I had been on tour in Europe promoting it when the election came and went. At the time I had justified the scheduling: Tony would want to celebrate with his team anyway, I would just get in the way. Perhaps I had been grateful for an excuse. On the campaign Tony had been lit with a blind passion I'd never been able to summon for tangible things. I'd understood it—how else could you will yourself to work that much?—I'd even lauded it, I'd wanted his candidate to win too. Still, the pettiest part of me couldn't help resenting his work like a mistress resents a wife. I imagined the election-night victory party as the climax of a fever dream, after which Tony would step out, cleansed, and be returned to me.

Of course nothing turned out how I'd imagined.

My own show had to go on.

I remember calling Tony over Google Voice backstage between shows, at coffee shops, in the bathroom of the hotel room I shared with Amy the percussionist—wherever I had Wi-Fi. I remember doing mental math whenever I looked at a clock—what time was it in America, was Tony awake? The answer, I learned, was yes. Tony was always awake. Often he was drunk. He picked up the phone but did not have much to say. I pressed my ear against the screen and listened to him breathe.

I remember Amy turning her phone to me: "Isn't this your boyfriend?" We were on a train from Brussels to Amsterdam. I saw Tony's weeping face, beside another weeping face I knew: Jen's.

I zoomed out. Jen's arms were wrapped around Tony's waist; Tony's arm hugged her shoulder. The photograph was in a listicle published by a major American daily showing the losing candidate's supporters on election night, watching the results come in. I remembered that Jen had flown in to join Tony at the victory arena, in order to be "a witness to history." The photo-list showed the diversity of the supporters: women in headscarves, disabled people, gay couples. Tony and Jen killed two birds in one stone: Asian America, and an ostensibly mixed-race couple. Jen was half Chinese but she looked exotic white—Italian, or Greek.

That night I'd called Tony. "How are you?" I'd asked as usual, and then: "I was thinking maybe I should just come back. Should I come back? I hate this tour." There was a long silence. Finally Tony said, "Why?" In his voice a mutter of cosmic emptiness.

I have one memory of sobbing under bright white lights, some terrible noise cracking into speakers turned too high. This might have been a dream.

For a long time after, I was estranged from music. What feelings normally mediated themselves in soundscapes, a well I could plumb for composition, hit me with their full blunt force.

Now I was trying to reenter music by making it in a new way, the way I imagined a sculptor makes a sculpture, to work with sound as if it were a physical material. Music was undoubtedly my medium: I had perfect pitch, a nice singing voice, and I liked the monasticism and repetition of practice. According to my grandmother, I had sung the melodies of nursery songs a whole year before I learned to speak. But I had the temperament of a conceptual artist, not a musician. Specifically, I was not a performer. I hated every aspect of performing: the lights, the stage, the singular attention. Most of all I could not square with the irreproducibility of performance —you had one chance, and then the work disappeared—which, to be successful, required a kind of faith. The greatest performers practiced and practiced, controlling themselves with utmost discipline, and when they stepped onto the stage gave themselves over to time.

This was also why I couldn't just compose. I wanted to control every aspect of a piece, from its conception to realization: I did not like giving up the interpretation of my notes and rests to a conductor and other musicians.

I wanted to resolve this contradiction by making music in a way

that folded performance theoretically into composition. Every
sound and silence in this album would be a performance. I would
compose a work and perform it for myself, just once. From this
material I would build my songs. If the recording didn't turn out,
I abandoned the mistakes or used them. I didn't think about who
the music was for. Certainly not for a group of people to enjoy with
dance, as my previous album had been—I too had been preparing
for celebration. My new listener sat in an ambient room, alone,
shed of distractions, and simply let the sounds come in.

In the morning Tony showed me a video of three husky puppies
doing something adorable. "Look," he said, pointing up and out
the window. From the skywell we could see a sliver of blue.

We got up and confirmed that the smoke had lifted. Tony reported from Twitter that the nearest fire had indeed been tamed.
"Huzzah!" I said. I walked outside to wait with him for his Uber-
pool to work. The sun was shining, the air was fresh, the colors
of this relentlessly cheerful coast restored. I kissed him on the
cheek goodbye.

I watched his car drive away and couldn't bear the thought
of going back inside. My legs itched. I wanted—theoretically—
to run. I put in earbuds and turned on my audiobook. I walked
around the neighborhood, looking happily at the bright houses
and healthy people and energetic pooping dogs.

In the audiobook, things had also taken a happy turn. The lady
protagonist, who had escaped Earth on a light-speed ship, found
herself reunited in a distant galaxy with the man who'd proved his
unfailing love by secretly gifting her an actual star. This reunion
despite the fact that eight hundred years had passed (hibernation
now allowed humans to jump centuries of time) and that when
they had last seen each other, the man's brain was being extracted
from his body in order to be launched into outer space (it was
later intercepted by aliens who reconstructed his body from the
genetic material). She had discovered his love in that final moment, when it was too late to stop the surgery—aside from then
the two had barely spoken. Now he was finally to be rewarded for
his devotion and patience. I thought the author had an exciting
imagination when it came to technology but a shitty imagination
for love. Somehow I found the endurance of this love story more
unbelievable than the leaps in space and time.

That afternoon I tried to work but didn't get very much done. DINNER OUT? I texted Tony. For the first time in a long time I wanted to feel like I lived in a city. I wanted to shower and put on mascara and pants that had a zipper.

Tony had a work event. I texted Jen. SRY HAVE A DATE! she wrote back, followed by a winking emoji that somehow seemed to say *Ooh-la-la*.

I decided to go out to dinner alone. I listened to my audiobook over a plate of fancy pizza, shoveling down the hot dough as I turned up the speed on my book. By the time I finished the panna cotta, the universe was imploding, every living and nonliving thing barreling toward the end of its existence. I looked at my empty plate as the closing credits came on to a string cadenza in D minor. I took out my earbuds and looked around the restaurant, at the redwood bar where I was sitting, the waitstaff in black aprons, the patrons in wool sneakers and thin down vests, the Sputnik lamps hanging above us all. Would I miss any of this? *Yes,* I thought, and then, just as fervently, *I don't know.*

Outside, the sky was fading to pale navy, a tint of yellow on the horizon where the sun had set. A cloudless, unspectacular dusk. I walked to dissipate the unknowing feeling and found myself at Chinaman's Vista, which was louder than I had ever heard it, everyone taking advantage of the newly particulate-free outdoors. I weaved through the clumps of people, looking at and through them, separate and invisible, like a visitor at a museum. That was when I saw, under a cypress tree, a woman who looked exactly like Jen, wearing Jen's gold loafers and pink bomber jacket. Jen was with a man. She was kissing the man. The man looked exactly like Tony.

I was breathing quickly. Staring. I wanted to run away but my feet were as glued as my eyes. Tony kissed Jen differently than he kissed me. He grabbed her lower back with two hands and seemed to lift her up slightly, while curling his neck to her upwardly lifted face. Because Jen was shorter than him. This made sense. I, on the other hand, was just about Tony's height.

I blinked and shook my head. Jen wasn't shorter than Tony. She was taller than us both. Jen and Tony stopped kissing and started to walk toward me, and I saw that it wasn't Tony, it was some other Asian guy who only kind of looked like Tony, but really not at all. Horrified, I turned and walked with intentionality to a plaque

ahead on the path. I stared intently at the words and thought how
the guy wasn't Tony and the girl probably wasn't even Jen, how
messed up that I saw a whitish girl with an East Asian guy and immediately thought Jen and Tony.

"Chenchen!"

It *was* Jen. I looked up with relief and dread. Jen stood on the
other side of the plaque with her date, waving energetically.

"This is Kevin," she said. She turned to Kevin. "Chenchen's the
friend I was telling you about, the composer-musician-*artiste*. She
just moved to the city."

"Hey," I said. I looked at the plaque. "Did you know," I said,
"Chinaman's Vista used to be a mining camp? For, uh, Chinese
miners. They lived in these barracklike houses. Then they were
killed in some riots and maybe buried here, because, you know,
this place has good feng shui." I paused. I'd made up the part
about feng shui. The words on the plaque said *mass graves.* "This
was back in the . . . 1800s."

"Oh, like the Gold Rush?" Kevin said. His voice was deep, hovering around a low F. Tony spoke in the vicinity of B flat. I looked up
at him. He was much taller than Tony.

"Yeah," I said.

I stood there for a long time after they left, reading and reread-
ing the historical landmark plaque, wishing I could forget what
it said. Chinaman's Vista, I thought, was a misleading name. The
view was of cascading expensive houses, pruned and prim. The
historic Chinese population, preferring squalor and cheap rents,
had long relocated to the other side of town. Besides me and
probably Kevin and half of Jen, there weren't many living Chinese
people here.

What was wrong with me? Why didn't I want to be a witness to history, to any kind of time passing?

The temperature skyrocketed. Tony and I kicked off our blankets
in sleep. We opened the windows and the air outside was hot too.
Heat radiated from the highway below in waves. The cars trailed
plumes of scorching dust.

Tony texted me halfway through the day to say it was literally
the hottest it had ever been. I clicked the link he sent and saw
a heat map of the city. It was 105 degrees in our neighborhood,

101 at Tony's work. We didn't have an air conditioner. We didn't, after all my disaster prep, even have a fan. Tony's work didn't have AC either. Nobody in the city did, I realized when I left the house, searching for a cool café. Every business had its doors wide open. Puny ceiling fans spun as fast as they could but only pushed around hot air. It was usually so fucking temperate here, the weather so predictably perfect. I walked past melting incredulous faces: women in leather boots, tech bros carrying Patagonia sweaters with dismay.

My phone buzzed. Jen had sent a photo of what looked like an empty grocery store shelf. It buzzed again.

THE FAN AISLE AT TARGET!!

JUST SAW A LADY ATTACKING ANOTHER LADY FOR THE LAST $200 TOWER FAN

#ENDOFDAYS?

That weekend I took Tony to the mall. Tony had been sleeping poorly, exasperated by my body heat. He was sweaty and irritable and I felt somehow responsible. I felt, I think, guilty. Since the incident at Chinaman's Vista I'd been extra nice to Tony.

The AC in the mall wasn't cold enough. A lot of people had had the same idea. "Still better than being outside," I said hopefully as we stepped onto the crowded escalator. Tony grunted his assent. We walked around Bloomingdale's. I pointed at the mannequins wearing wool peacoats and knitted vests and laughed. Summer in the city was supposed to be cold, because of the ocean fog. Tony said, "Ha-ha."

We got ice cream. We got iced tea. We got texts from PG&E saying that power was out on our block due to the grid overheating, would be fixed by 8 p.m. We weren't planning to be back until after sunset anyway, I said. I looked over Tony's shoulder at his phone. He was scrolling through Instagram, wistfully it seemed, through photographs of Jen and other girls in bikinis—they had gone to the beach. "But you don't like the beach," I said. Tony shrugged. "I don't like the mall either." I asked if he wanted to go to the beach. He said no.

We ate salads for dinner and charged our phones. This, at last, seemed to make Tony happy. "In case the power is still out later," he said. We sat in the food court and charged our phones until the mall closed.

*

The apartment was a cacophony of red blinking eyes. The appliances had all restarted when the power came back on. Now they beeped and hummed and buzzed, imploring us to reset their times. Outside the wide-open windows, cars honked and revved their engines. So many sounds not meant to be simultaneous pressed simultaneously onto me. In an instant the cheerfulness I'd mustered for our wretched day deflated. I found myself breathing fast and loud, tears welling against my will. Tony sat me down and put his noise-canceling headphones over my ears. "I can still hear everything!" I shouted. I could hear, I wanted to say, the staticky G-sharp hiss of the headset's noise-canceling mechanism. Tony was suddenly contrite. He handed me a glass of ice water and shushed me tenderly. He walked around the apartment, resetting all our machines.

We took a cold shower. Tony looked as exhausted as I felt. We kept the lights off and went directly to bed. Traffic on the highway had slowed to a rhythmic whoosh. I wanted to hug Tony but it was too hot. I took his hand and released it. Our palms were sweaty and gross.

I was just falling asleep when I heard a faint beep.

I nudged Tony. "What was that?" He rolled away from me. I turned over and closed my eyes.

It beeped again, then after some moments again.

It was a high C, a note of shrill finality. I counted the beats between: about twenty at 60 bpm. I counted to twenty, hoping to lull myself to sleep. But the anticipation of the coming beep was too much. My heart rate rose, I counted faster, unable to maintain a consistent rhythm, so now it was twenty-two beats, then twenty-five, then twenty-seven.

Finally I sat up, said loudly, "Tony, Tony, do you hear the beeping?"

"Huh?" He rubbed his eyes. It beeped again, louder, as if to back me up. Tony got up and poked at the alarm clock, which he hadn't reset because it ran on batteries. He pulled the batteries out and threw them to the floor. He lay down, I thanked him, and then—*beep.*

I sat on the bed, clamping my pillow over my ears, and watched Tony lumber about the dark bedroom, drunk with exhaustion, finding every hidden gadget and extracting its batteries, taking down even the smoke detector. Each time it seemed he had finally identified the source there sounded another beep. It was a short sound, it insisted then disappeared: even my impeccable hearing could not locate where exactly it came from. It sounded as if from all around us, from the air. Tony fell on the bed, defeated. He said, "Can we just try to sleep?" We clamped our eyes shut, forced ourselves to breathe deeply, but the air was agitated and awake. My mind drifted and ebbed, imitating the movements of sleep while bringing nothing like rest. I couldn't help thinking that the source of the sound was neither human nor human-made. I couldn't help imagining the aliens in my audiobook preparing to annihilate our world. "Doomsday clock," I said, half aloud. I was thinking or dreaming of setting up my equipment to record the beeps. I was thinking or dreaming of unrolling the sleeping bags in my bunker, where it'd be silent and I could sleep. "Counting down."

"I'm sorry," Tony said.

"It's okay," I said, but it wasn't, not really, and Tony knew it. He grabbed my hand and squeezed it hard. Between the cosmic beeps his lips smacked open as if to speak, as if searching for the right words to fix me. Finally he said, "I kissed Jen," and I said, "I know."

Then, "What?"

Then, "When?"

My eyes were wide open.

"Last November."

High C sounded, followed by ten silent beats.

"You were in Germany."

Another high C. Twenty beats. Another high C.

"I'm sorry," Tony said again. "Say something, please?" He tightened his hand. I tried to squeeze back to say I'd heard, I was awake. I failed. I listened to the pulses of silence, the inevitable mechanical beeps.

"Tell me what you're thinking?"

I was thinking we would need a new disaster meet-up spot. I was wondering if there was any place in this city, this world, where we'd be safe.

ANDREA LEE

The Children

FROM *The New Yorker*

THE ADVENTURE OF the lost heirs begins when Shay and her friend Giustinia run into Harena at the Fleur des Îles café. This happens in the early 2000s, at the same time that a criminal at large on Anjavavy Island is cutting off people's heads. The mysterious beheadings are not connected to the events recounted here, except to establish the lawlessness that is always present behind the dazzling Anjavavy panorama of sugar-white beaches and cobalt sea. The crimes begin to surface one hot January morning, as a French hotel manager is taking his predawn constitutional along Rokely Bay and spies through a mist of sand flies something just above the tide line that looks like an unhusked coconut. It turns out to be a human head, one that was last seen on the shoulders of a part-time sweeper at the Frenchman's hotel.

In the next months four more severed heads are discovered, hideously marooned near grounded pirogues, on paths through the sugarcane, and even on the rocks that are used by villagers as public toilets. The victims are all men from various Malagasy tribes: Antandroy, Tsimihety, Sakalava—night watchmen and groundskeepers of so low a status that no one bribes the island gendarmerie into investigating their deaths.

This is the state of affairs when Giustinia arrives from Florence to spend two weeks at Shay's place on Anjavavy, before embarking on a trek on the main island of Madagascar. It is early summer, and the two of them have the Red House—the vacation villa and small hotel owned by Shay and her husband, Senna—to themselves: most of the staff is on leave, and the place is empty both of paying guests and of the swarm of family that will come from Milan in August; Senna will arrive later in the month. Giustinia is a poet and a critic, an elegant woman who became friends with Shay when Shay translated some of her essays for an American magazine, and they discovered that they shared a passion for Victor Segalen's eccentric early-twentieth-century monograph on exoticism. But while Shay, an African American scholar transplanted to Italy and, for part of each year, to this small island in northern Madagascar, finds her interest drawn to restless expatriate artists of color, Giustinia, whose noble family has ancient roots in Tuscany, most often writes about the inescapable pull of a place to which you belong entirely. Her regal air is quite unconscious, based mainly on the authority with which she can speak about famous authors she knows. In spite of her worldly connections, she has the unexpected ingenuousness of those rare aristocrats who are still safely contained within their insular history. Shay intends to keep from her the news that there is a serial killer at large.

A week into Giustinia's visit, the two friends go food shopping in Saint Grimaud and, after the heat and the stench of the outdoor market, stop for a cold drink at the Fleur des Îles. Harena is just leaving the café as they pull up in the truck. When she sees Shay, she calls out a greeting in her childish voice, raises one slim brown hand, and flashes her incandescent smile. Then she floats past the one-legged beggar perched on the Fleur des Îles steps and climbs into an odd-looking customized dune buggy, where a bald middle-aged Frenchman sits beeping the horn impatiently.

"What a stunning girl," Giustinia remarks as she and Shay chase flies from a sticky table on the veranda and settle themselves where they can keep an eye on the baskets of vegetables and bread in the back of the pickup.

"Yes," Shay says. "She's half Italian." And, acting in her role as exasperated hostess—for during the week with Giustinia there has been no rococo tropical sunset, no rare lemur or chameleon, no gaudy market stall, no fluorescent coral or blinding expanse of beach that has dispelled her guest's queenly, slightly bored air of expecting something more—Shay sketches out the story of Harena, which is a sort of legend on Anjavavy.

The girl is presently about eighteen years old. Her father, Leandro, is a heroin addict from a noble Roman family, a family that shipped him off to Madagascar when he was in his early twenties. For a few years he lived on rum and drugs out in the bush at the north of the island with Heloise, a Sakalava seamstress, and during this time Harena was born. When Harena was three or four years old, Leandro's father died, and Leandro returned to Italy, where he'd inherited an estate in what Melville once called the "accursed Campagna" of Rome.

He soon cut off contact and stopped sending money, and when Heloise, who had taken up with a French merchant from Saint Grimaud, perished suddenly after a miscarriage, the girl was left at the mercy of her grandmother, who wasted no time in settling her gray-eyed, barely pubescent granddaughter with Hans, an affable middle-aged German who sold construction materials. Shay first saw Harena with him one Saturday night, when the girl must have been about fifteen, standing forlornly on the crowded concrete dance floor of Tonga Soa, clutching a large vinyl handbag, while Hans cavorted in a karaoke show onstage. Harena even then was extraordinarily pretty, with fawn-colored hair and skin, long spindly legs, acerbic breasts, and a beauty mark beside an arched nose that looked as if it belonged on an ancient marble statue in a museum thousands of miles away.

Shay is warming to the subject when Giustinia suddenly interrupts. "Wait!" she exclaims, and then, incredibly, adds, "I know this story. I didn't remember that it happened here. I know him —Leandro. The father."

It is almost noon, and the Fleur des Îles is filling up with rich Malagasy and Indian kids from Lycée Sacré Coeur, devouring *pains au chocolat* and monopolizing the three back-room computers. Outside in the glaring dusty street, ragged boys hawk trays of samosas, and Comoran women with laden baskets on their heads file down to the port.

Shay watches them as Giustinia tells her that in the tight circles of old Italian nobility—which are as closed as kinships can be on Anjavavy—she's met Leandro a few times, at weddings. Moreover, one of his sisters is married to a cousin of Giustinia's husband. Leandro is a sort of Italian Sebastian Flyte: extravagantly good-looking, a hopeless addict, and now a doomed recluse. What made him notorious was that eighteenth-century-style exile, imposed by his family, to an island that no one had ever heard of, in the north of Madagascar.

"I'd like," Giustinia says, gazing into the dregs of her glass of papaya juice, "to meet this Harena."

Later Shay wonders why she saw no harm in this. It has to do, she thinks, with the general trifling nature of her behavior in Madagascar, where her brown skin and her American expansiveness lend her a false sense of familiarity with the people of color around her: people of the island, whose language she doesn't speak, and whose values and motives she will never fully understand.

Shay mentions to Romolo, the Italian proprietor of the Fleur des Îles, that she wants to talk to Harena, and sure enough, early the next afternoon she catches sight of the girl making her way down the beach toward the Red House, in the indolent manner of a cat that has just decided to roam in that direction. She is dressed in white jeans and a tight sleeveless top that drapes from a metal ring around her neck, and her pale, kinky hair, free of extensions for once, is caught up at the crown of her head in a pouf that is very becoming.

When Harena, Giustinia, and Shay sit down on the veranda, Shay can see that her friend is, for once, at a loss. It is one thing to take an impulsive interest in someone whose life seems like a fairy tale, and it is quite another thing to have that beautiful young person sitting in front of you with shining, expectant eyes and a valiant, determined poise. Giustinia, who this afternoon has been writing an essay on Octavio Paz, is a handsome brunette in her late thirties, presently barefoot in a bathing suit, with a pair of tortoise-shell glasses perched on her freckled nose. She looms over Harena like a dowager empress over a royal pretender.

After ascertaining that Harena understands Italian, she tells her that she is acquainted with Harena's father, and that Harena much resembles him.

The effect on the girl is electric: she begins to tremble. And Shay thinks that this is exactly the wrong way to go about it: making such a statement is like promising a shower of gold. For years Harena has nourished herself on the myth of her Italian father, and now it is impossible to keep the subject within the bounds of simple conversation.

Then Harena begins to tell the two women something that Shay has never heard before. That when she was sixteen, her first lover, Hans—who always treated her with great respect, she says, as he would have treated a white girl—gave in to her pleas and took her to Italy. And there she actually made it to the gate of the country villa near Nemi from which her father, years before, had sent her a single letter. The gatekeeper, a peasant who spoke mainly dialect, told her that the house was closed and the family abroad. Through the gate she could see up a long road, bordered with umbrella pines, to what looked like the gleam of parked cars. She told the gatekeeper that she was Leandro's daughter, and he told her to go away. She left a letter stuck in the gate, and afterward wrote from Anjavavy, but there was never a reply.

Soon after recounting this tragic story, Harena finishes her Coke and departs, but not before giving Shay and Giustinia three kisses each, Malagasy style, with fervent emphasis, as if her fate were now in their hands. She leaves the Red House through the back entrance, which leads to the road through the rice field, where Shay can hear the tootling horn of the Frenchman's dune buggy.

Speechless, Giustinia and Shay stroll down to the edge of the sea. It is close to sunset, and low tide, and they stand in the warm water and watch a little band of village children drag-fishing in the shallows with a length of tattered cloth.

"She does look like Leandro," Giustinia remarks, after a pause. "What are you going to do?"

"I suppose I should contact the family. His sister . . ."

But she sounds vague. Shay also has conflicted feelings. She knows that Harena is who she says she is, yet it is difficult to believe the tale of that trip to Italy. First, it is too hard to imagine that Hans, the eminently practical German, would go through the byzantine process of getting a tourist visa for a Malagasy girlfriend he didn't intend to marry. Second, Harena told the story in the same histrionic tone that Shay has heard her use, at several parties, in tipsy rants about the wealth and power of her Italian father.

"You've opened Pandora's box!" Shay's next-door neighbor, Madame Rose Rakotomalala, exclaims when Shay and Giustinia go over for tea the next day. Madame Rose is a wealthy Merina from the capital and has scant esteem for the Sakalava and other coastal peoples. "She is not at all a nice young woman! She takes after the mother, who was no seamstress but a bar girl, plain and simple, and she drinks and smokes *rongony* all day long. Harena acts innocent, but she starts fights, even with bottles, right in the road. Now that Hans has disappeared, she goes from one white man to another, except when she is working changing money for those Comoran hoodlums. We've all seen her in the café, counting out stacks of cash."

Here Madame Rose gets up from the table and leans her slim waist over the railing to harangue two of her maids, who are hanging out clothes beside the generator. She resumes. "If you start trying to help that girl, it will be one thing after the other, and none of it good. Besides, if you go tracking down all the white men who leave children behind, that too will never end."

Giustinia, more spurred on by Madame Rose's ominous warning than anything else, stubbornly emails her husband's cousin with the news of her discovery of Harena. But she seems relieved, as is Shay, when the days pass with no reply and her departure from the island grows nearer.

Still, a curious social electricity now seems to surround Giustinia and Shay. Harena comes by twice, breezing into the garden with casual assurance, making no requests but simply regarding them with that same ecstatic, expectant gaze. Meanwhile, Shay begins to notice Malagasy people she has never seen before standing on the beach and staring at the Red House. And whenever she and Giustinia pass through Rokely Village in the pickup, they cause a palpable ripple of interest. A Sakalava woman who runs a used-clothing stall tells Shay that word has spread that Giustinia is really Harena's Italian grandmother, a rich and titled matriarch who plans to take the girl back to her father's country, or, failing that, to shower her with enough wealth to build a big house for herself, her uncles, and the rest of her family in Madagascar. (Though youthful Giustinia would be insulted at the supposition, the islanders afford enormous prestige to grandmothers.)

Naturally, Shay says nothing to Giustinia about all this, and the rest of her friend's visit passes quickly—without, to Shay's intense relief, another attack by the headhunter. Shay introduces Giustinia to Père Joachim, a Betsileo priest from Antsiranana, who is the author of a lengthy treatise on Jean-Joseph Rabearivolo and other Malagasy poets, and the three spend a delightful evening discussing the Négritude movement, Machado de Assis, and James Baldwin. On the morning of her departure, Giustinia has still heard nothing from Leandro's sister, but she promises to make a round of telephone calls when she gets back to Italy. "I feel strangely under obligation," she confides to Shay.

"You're trying—what more can you do?" Shay replies, also feeling weighed down by a peculiar burden of duty. One thing she has learned in her few years of sojourning in Madagascar, with its convoluted history and its pulse of dark magic concealed just under the skin of events, is that in this country, whatever happens close to you—under your roof, say—becomes part of you, though you may not realize it at the time.

Giustinia departs, with kisses and effusions, leaving behind an envelope containing the generous sum of thirty euros for Harena, as well as an almost-new beach dress.

The next day Shay doesn't receive a visit from the girl, as she half expects to, but while she sits reading after lunch she hears a subdued hubbub from the far end of the garden, near the gate to the beach. Soon Tumbu, the old man who fills in as factotum when there are few guests in the Red House, calls out to her that there is someone down by the water who wants to speak to Madame Shay. When Shay asks who, he mumbles confusedly that it is someone from the Grande Terre.

Squinting against the high-tide wind that rattles the palms, Shay follows Tumbu's grizzled head and bare, wiry back down to the seawall at the end of the garden. There she finds waiting a tall, unbelievably handsome teenage boy whom she has never seen before but recognizes immediately, for he is almost a twin of Harena. He has the same fawn coloring and sculptural nose, but his eyes are the clouded turquoise of certain Alpine lakes, which gives him an oddly blind look in the blazing subequatorial sun. He is barefoot, dressed in long shorts and a tattered Italian football jersey, and his sandy hair is clipped close to his skull. Shay greets him in French, asking him his name, and invites him into the garden, but he stands staring at her with those eerie eyes and replies in a Malagasy dialect that Shay doesn't recognize.

"He doesn't speak much French," Tumbu explains, rather condescendingly. "His name is Didier, and he is from Morondava, far south of here, and he wants to see the mother of his father, who is the Italian Leandro."

Didier will come only a single step inside the Red House gate, so

Shay stands with him near the threshold and, as Tumbu interprets, learns that the boy is sixteen and was born, on Anjavavy, to a young woman of the southern Sakalava tribe named Adi, who worked as a hotel maid. Leandro never lived with Adi, but "he loved her" and, after the boy was born, paid for her to return to her family on the big island, promising to join her there. Of course he never appeared or contacted her, and eventually, leaving her son with her people near Morondava, she found work at a shrimp farm in Mahajamba Bay and soon afterward died there of malaria, as so many do in that harsh line of work.

A week ago word somehow reached Didier's grandmother that Leandro's mother, and possibly Leandro himself, had arrived at the Red House on Rokely Beach, on Anjavavy, and that finally the Italian father wanted to lay eyes on his children. So Didier left Morondava and traveled north for four days and nights, by foot, bush taxi, and ferry. Once on Anjavavy, he walked the six kilometers from the port to Rokely Beach.

As Shay listens, she becomes more and more furious. With herself, with Giustinia, and with a tall Italian phantom who seems to have been summoned up from the ground beside her. Now that she has seen two of Leandro's children, she can imagine exactly what he, the absent father, is like: his aristocratic height; his useless blond beauty; his addict's vacant face; his idle concupiscence; his suzerain's habit, bred in the bone, of taking whatever he wants; his ruthless indifference to everything that isn't the chemical in his veins.

And now, she wonders, what to do with this magnificent son out of the famine-ridden south, who has traveled across land and sea, chasing a rumor? A rumor that she, Shay, helped start?

"Does he know Harena? His sister?" Shay demands of Tumbu.

"He knows who she is."

As the boy continues to stare at Shay with those mineral-colored eyes, panic seizes her. "Tell him," she says to the old man, "that his father and grandmother are not here. That the woman who was here is not Leandro's mother, and she is gone now anyway. That woman is only a friend who knows the Italian family of his father. She is a friend who promises to look . . . who will help find . . . No, tell him that I myself will help . . ." Shay stammers in confusion, suddenly gripped by a cinematic vision of snatching this beautiful youth out of his present life, as if she were conducting a helicopter rescue at sea. In an instant she pictures schools, clothes, university, some grand career, where that flawless face would gleam in the high marble halls of European tradition. Later she will tell herself that this is a maternal impulse, but it is as selfish and intoxicating as sex.

That Didier shows no surprise or disappointment increases Shay's confusion.

"Ask him what he needs," Shay tells Tumbu. "Money, food, a place to stay?"

Soon the old gardener, with a hint of a dry smile, informs her, "He needs nothing, madame. He has a job as an apprentice mechanic, and in two or three months he will go to Mahajanga to work on trucks."

"Will he stay now with his sister—with Harena?"

"No. He'll go back home immediately. You can"—the old man pauses, and then announces in a formal tone, as if affording Shay a rare privilege—"you can pay the price of his journey."

Shay doubles the sum, but even so it is a laughably small amount. When she gives the notes to the boy, she notices that his hands too are beautiful: long and slender, though already rough from labor, and scarred with what appear to be burns. As she comes close to him, he suddenly looks her straight in the eye, with an intensity that feels like a blow, and says something in a low, forceful voice.

"He wants to know," Tumbu says impassively, "why it is that his father has not once come to look for him."

Shay stammers that Didier's father has been sick for many years in Italy.

And before her shame at this transparent falsehood has evaporated, the boy coolly bids her farewell and turns away. Shay watches his tall, sculptural figure and cropped head departing down the three kilometers of beach, skirting the incoming tide. He walks like a king in exile, seeming to cast a sort of furious solitude around himself. And as he grows small and disappears in a distant crowd of fishermen, she thinks of how much the life of an island is about watching for those who arrive and dreaming of those who depart. About waiting, sometimes forever.

Madame Rose Rakotomalala and Shay's other friends on the island are of the opinion that Leandro has fathered no more children in Madagascar. But in the following days Shay gets jumpy whenever she hears visitors arriving at the Red House; she has visions of an army of gorgeous bastards pouring into her garden. She tries to avoid places where she might run into Harena, whose face grows more and more piteously crestfallen as the weeks pass with no word from Giustinia. One morning in September, just before Shay leaves for Italy, she sees the girl at the Fleur des Îles, heavily made up and dressed in a theatrical Comoran *lamba* and headdress, deep in conversation with a quartet of South African tourists. Clearly she has thrown herself wholeheartedly into her money-changing, and she nods to Shay with haughty indifference.

Back home in Milan, Shay at last sees Giustinia. And after some excited talk about a poetry festival in Johannesburg, she informs Shay, "I finally got in touch with Leandro's sister, and the news is bad. Leandro is dead—has been dead for a year, though this is the first I've heard of it. Overdose or AIDS—though they're very vague about it. There must have been a funeral, but when a family like that wants to keep things quiet . . . It's as if he died ten years ago."

"Did you tell his sister about Harena and the boy?"

"When I told her, she just laughed. She reminded me that before they shipped him off to Madagascar, Leandro spent a year in the Caribbean, skippering in the Islas los Roques. She said that over the past few years the family has had letters from a pair of Venezuelans claiming to be his children."

Shay breaks in. "But there is no doubt that these two kids are his!"

"Yes, but what exactly does one do? Arm them with lawyers and fly them to Rome for DNA tests that they can use to lay siege to relatives who will never accept them? And for what? Between you and me, that family hasn't got anything left. Just land that is all tied up with taxes and entailments, and some sculptures of popes that no one wants, and acres of architecture that costs too much to restore. Oh, and titles. They have titles to spare."

Shay envisions a Princess Harena changing money at the Fleur des Îles, and a Prince Didier, with his aristocrat's hands, dismembering truck engines in Mahajanga. Madagascar has its own kings and noblemen, whose polysyllabic names lie deeply rooted in the historical conquests and ancient migrations of each tribe, but none of those revered Indian Ocean pedigrees belongs by birthright to

either of the half-Italian children. And on the tourist island of
Anjavavy, what would a hereditary Roman certificate of rank be,
without money to back it up, but a meaningless piece of rubbish,
another plastic bag blowing down the beach?

"They could send something—pay for education!" Shay persists.

"Believe me. They will do nothing."

Giustinia and Shay look fiercely at each other, aware that they
are so indignant over the neglect of Leandro's progeny because
they feel guilty about their own role in stirring up false hope: in
bringing that tremulous, starry look to Harena's eyes, and spur-
ring Didier to travel for days over land and sea for nothing.

They sketch a plan to raise the situation with the Italian and
Malagasy consuls, and they both send letters to which no answers
come. And so bureaucracy performs its traditional task of trans-
mogrifying action into inaction, and the two women lose themselves in their own busy lives.

At Christmas, when Shay and Senna travel to Madagascar, Shay
is pregnant with their first child. This makes her the center of attention, but she still keeps up with the gossip, and the first thing
she hears is that Harena has married a half-Chinese musician, who
has taken her to Mauritius, where his band plays in the smaller
clubs and hotels. It is a love match, and Harena is said to be always
dressed up and much admired, but drinking more than ever and
doing hard drugs. Shay is told that when some visiting Italian finally gave Harena the news of her father's death, she flung bottles,
clawed her own face, and screamed that it wasn't true; that even
now she talks about Leandro as if he were coming to fetch her.
Her husband is patient with—maybe even proud of—what he calls
her European behavior, but people on Anjavavy say that she is pos-
sessed. Nothing good, they say, will come of her.

As for Harena's half-brother, Didier, the phone number he gave
Shay is out of service, and no one can discover his whereabouts in
Mahajanga or Morondava, though there can't be many mechan-
ics like him. So the lost heirs who came into Shay's life are just as
suddenly gone.

Around the same time that Harena got married, the murderer
who had been cutting off heads was caught hiding out in the cane.
He was a lunatic from Toamasina, a Betsimisaraka dockworker of

fearful strength, whose whole family perished in the catastrophic floods of a few years back. He was, they say, obsessed with the idea of chasing *vazaha* out of Madagascar, of eliminating the rich Europeans and Indians who were offending the spirits of the ancestors and who for so long had plundered the wealth of the country. His twisted method was to kill Malagasy men who worked for the foreigners. But he had no chance to expound on this in a trial, or even to languish for more than a day in the medieval hell of Anjavavy's prison, because on his way to the courthouse he was seized by a mob of islanders and promptly lynched, torn to pieces, burned, and cast into the sea.

Shay's neighbor Madame Rose and the staff at the Red House all have a gentle air of pitying the murderer as a man cursed by madness, and placidly seem to accept the idea that justice has been served. With no newspapers to pick up the story, and with both criminal and victims at the bottom of the social scale, talk of the drama soon fades away.

Shay herself cannot help associating the unspeakable murders with the plight of Harena and Didier. But is it a plight? Wrong was certainly done. By miserable Leandro, and by his stony-hearted family. But also by Giustinia and Shay, with their frivolous intervention — they were like magpies who settle on cattle and peck open wounds.

During the next years, as more hotels are built and charter flights arrive from Rome and from Paris, prosperity steals over the island like a gilded mist, and pale half-European babies become a more common sight in the villages and on the beaches. Some of them are loved, legitimized, and even taken away to live comfortable lives in France and Italy; others grow up amid conflict and squalor. The situation of Harena and Didier, no longer unusual, fades into the constantly rewoven fabric of gossip and fantasies that makes up island history.

By this time Shay and Senna have a small son and daughter of their own, who, being half Italian and half African American, are often, during their holidays on the island, mistaken for mixed-race Malagasy children. With the births of Roby and Augustina, Shay suddenly knows the crushing force of that incomparable love, which, when the parents are from different worlds, brings with it all the shadows of historical conflict, in custom and color and speech.

Darlings of fortune, adored by their Italian and their American grandparents, Shay's children grow up fluent in two languages. They are at home in Milan and in her native city of Oakland, and also in Madagascar, where they pick up rudimentary French and Sakalava dialect as they splash in the warm Anjavavy waters. From the kids they play with on Rokely Beach, they grow used to hearing lurid stories of sorcerers and ghosts—even the horrific tale of the headhunter—and because the disgraceful misadventures of foreigners are the villagers' entertainment, they absorb the details of intricate scandals as well.

Buried somewhere amid all the other unsuitable anecdotes that her son and daughter bring home, Shay suspects, is a distorted account of the Leandro story, but she is certainly not going to bring it to light.

Sometimes she sits at her little writing table at the end of the garden and from the deep tamarind shade watches Roby and Augustina at play on the dazzling sand with a horde of village and tourist children, the hollering crowd expanding and contracting with algorithmic logic, like a flock of starlings, as they splash in the waves, play *raboka,* race hermit crabs, or draw mysterious labyrinths in the sand for the island version of hopscotch. Her son and daughter are always the focus of her vigilance, with their wild hair burned brassy gold, their faces bearing the stamp of distant continents; children healthy and loved, who play in front of the house of wealth that they will inherit; who, in short, have everything. And from time to time, as Shay watches them, she'll unavoidably envision a boy and a girl who are their shadow twins: Didier and Harena, the beautiful children who have almost nothing. And then she holds a guilty circular conversation with herself, a kind of call-and-response.

"What more could we do?"

"We did what we could."

"What did they need?"

"They needed to be found. Of course."

"Was that our job?"

"Who knows if it was?"

"We could have tried harder."

"We did what we could."

Like a lullaby or a nursery rhyme, the sequence of excuses blends into the voices of the kids on the beach. But this is one song Shay doesn't sing aloud. She is well aware that on the journey toward separation that is life with even the best-loved children, it is all too easy to lose their respect.

SARAH THANKAM MATHEWS

Rubberdust

FROM *Kenyon Review Online*

THE LITTLE GIRL with no friends reads contentedly enough at her small wooden desk during recess. (We pronounced it *ri-CESS*.) She sits by the corner of the softboard, likes to tenderly peel the crepe paper sheets that Mrs. Lobo has stapled to its expanse away from their moorings. From her schoolbag she pulls out Enid Blyton, Roald Dahl. Books about heroic friends solving crime, tales of spunky weirdos forceful enough to make dents in their worlds. In second grade you read for the same reasons you eat candy bars, not to see yourself reflected at you as if from mirrors, and in this case that's just as well; the little girl does not fall into either category.

Usually the little girl is smart enough to keep her head down when the other second-grade teachers come to eat their lunches and gossip at Mrs. Lobo's desk. But Mrs. Tareen, who teaches 3B, is getting divorced (we pronounced it *DIE-vorced*), and the teachers are all whispering about it, making big-big eyes, saris rustling like dry leaves. The details are almost as riveting as *James and the Giant Peach,* so the little girl looks up and listens with frank interest, forgetting all subterfuge.

"Small water pitchers have big ears, hain na?" says Mrs. Azmi, nudging Mrs. Lobo, who is busy telling the rest about how when she went to Mrs. Tareen's house for Eid, Mr. Tareen touched her sari pallu *very* suggestively and also complained how his wife always missed the top of the television set when she did dusting.

They all look up and see the girl staring at them through the fringe of her bowl cut. She looks back down at her book, but it's too late.

"You can't sit here like this, okay," Mrs. Lobo says, rustling over. "This is not good, okay. Go outside! Challo, go play like a normal child!"

The teachers giggle as the little girl walks out, biting her lip. She circles the soccer (we pronounced it *football*) field, squinting in the noonday sun. Her knee socks have slid down, and she pulls them up, weary as sin itself.

The little boy sneaks up behind her and tries to place a handful of dried leaves on her head. She whips around and says, "Stop it."

He keeps doing it. Arcing his arm like a lamp, giggling in a maddening way. And so she slaps him. Bloodying his nose. A teacher sees, and she is sent home with a note safety-pinned to her blouse. She has to have it signed by one of her parents.

The note says, in a round and spiteful hand, "Did not behave today. Slapped fellow pupil badly."

"Next time, slap him well," her father says.

He chuckles, which is a grown man's way of giggling, and hands the note back to her. He lifts his newspaper back up between the two of them like he is closing a door.

In third grade both she and the little boy who salted her with leaves are now in Mrs. Tareen's class. He is seated at the desk behind her, both of them at the back of the class. Anuj, the boy's name is. Anuj (we pronounced it *Uhn-uj*) is confident, loud, a jokester. He has a toothy, pretty grin.

In front of her sits a boy who has no friends. His name is Karan. (We pronounced it *Curren.*) Karan has a lantern jaw, bulbous staring eyes, and a stink that nestles close, follows him like a stray. Even Mrs. Tareen, who is the kindest of all the elementary school teachers, is mean to him.

During recess Anuj asks the little girl if she wants to go on the swings, and she looks shocked, and then shyly says, *Yes, thank you.*

Even though she doesn't turn around to see, a small section of her is aware of Karan sitting at his desk in the now empty classroom, not even a book in front of him, watching the door swing shut, as she and Anuj go out into the bright, hot world.

Anuj's parents are getting divorced, he says, but he doesn't care. He spends more time now with the little girl than with his football friends, which delights her even as it makes the two of them the target of ridicule, the object of *sitting in a tree* rhymes.

She tries to show him how to draw Minnie Mouse or make paper origami frogs, but he is uninterested. They spend homework period at the end of the day making rubberdust, which is what Anuj calls the tiny pink and gray curls left behind in an eraser's wake. They do this every day. They store the clumps of rubberdust in the drawer of the little girl's wooden desk.

"Let's stare at the sun," Anuj says.

They lie on a slope of dry grass, and he squints up into the sky. The girl covers her face with her hands.

"I can't do it," she says.

"S'okay," Anuj says.

It becomes a routine: walk past the football field, pass the guarri hedges, and lie down together, the girl shielding her eyes with her small palms.

"Let's play get married," the little girl suggests from behind her hands during a sun-staring session.

"Yuck, no. That's corrupted," is Anuj's matter-of-fact rejoinder.

The rubberdust production continues. Anuj discovers that sawing his steel ruler across his Faber-Castell rubber makes several times the amount of dust. A fourth of the girl's desk is now full of soft shavings the color of organs. She likes to run her hands through them while Mrs. Tareen writes Hindi vocabulary on the board: नमक\$न. बुरा. पुराना. पुराना means "old," and it also means "story," the little girl notes.

At some point they start sprinkling the rubberdust on Karan's head. Biting lips to keep from laughing, they wait until the teacher's back is turned and pepper it into the naked whorls of his scalp as he bends over penmanship or multiplication tables.

(Later, neither the little girl nor the person she grows into will remember who started this, she or Anuj. That uncertainty will beat its own tattoo within her, bang a hidden gong of shame.)

*

Anuj grows bolder and bolder, dropping rubberdust onto Karan nearly every time he walks by him. He has begun to get headaches, leaving for hours to sit in the nurse's office.

Mrs. Tareen says, "You need to get your eyes checked, son. Here, take this note to your parents."

"My parents don't care one FART and I don't need STUPID glasses," Anuj yells, kicking Mrs. Tareen's desk legs and running out of the room.

Later he shows the little girl the new rubbers his mom has bought—large, pliable, pinkly beautiful—and they get to work.

Anuj's mother arrives the next day, during homework period. Mrs. Tareen gives namaste, then says, "If I don't hear pin-drop silence while I'm in the next room, everyone here will be quite, quite sorry. Okay?"

"Yeeesss, Ma'am," the denizens of 3B say in chorus. It is testimony to how Mrs. Tareen is both strict and beloved that most every child keeps their head down in their notebooks, yellow HB pencils gripped tight.

"Okay, fine, challo, let's get married," Anuj whispers to the little girl, apropos of nothing. She smiles at him, then raises her eyebrows to signal: *watch*. She scoops a handful of rubberdust from under the desktop and shows him: she's been mixing it with colorpencil shavings.

Hand outstretched, she begins to powder it on Karan's head. Anuj covers his hands with his mouth to muffle his snickering.

Karan whips around, facing the little girl. His bulging eyes are full of tears.

"Why do you do this?" Karan hisses, face twisting, swatting at his own head, and the rubberdust-and-shavings mix dribbles down his forehead and gets into his eyes.

"Ow, *oww*."

He rubs his eyes furiously, mewling in pain. The little girl's mouth turns dry like sand.

She turns around to Anuj, who looks thunderstruck. By now the other children around them are staring, whispering like so many rustling leaves. Karan runs out of the room, hands over his eyes.

The little girl reaches in and sweeps every bit of rubberdust in her desk into the skirt of her pinafore. Sweat prickles in her armpits and down her back. There is so much of the dust. So much. Why did they do this? Holding the heaps of dry, gray-pink matter in her skirt, she runs to the garbage can. (We called it *dustbin*.) She shakes out her pinafore, trembling, her ears buzzing. The class's whispers burrow into her. A sonic drill. She runs out to look for Karan, shoving her palms hard into the swinging door.

When she finds him outside the boys' bathroom, his eyes are a bright and burning red. He hunches into himself the second he sees her. (Years later she will look up the word *cower* in the dictionary, and the image of a child's bloodshot eyes, lashes wet with hurt, will surface in her and thrash like a fish.)

"I'm sorry, Karan," the girl says. "I'm sorry I'm sorry I'm sorry." He turns his head. She wants to cry.

"Sorry. Please. I'm sorry."

"I won't tell Ma'am" is all he mumbles before starting down the stairs to the nurse's office, and she doesn't know how to say that that's not it, that his tattling isn't remotely the shape of her fear, that the dark creature that has galloped into her chest and gnaws around her organs might actually be kept at bay if Mrs. Tareen thrashed her, sent her to the principal's office, wrote *Did not behave today* across the front of her blouse.

She goes back to the classroom. Mrs. Tareen is marking corrections at her desk. Everyone is still doing homework. Anuj has put his head down on his desk, arms folded above it like a roof. He is very still, but she can hear his occasional sniffle, hear the too-fast rustle of his breath.

In front of her, Karan's chair is empty, stray curls of rubberdust on its wooden seat.

"Can you beat me, please?" she asks her father, but he just changes the TV channel to the India-Pakistan match and then to American news.

She locks herself in the cupboard and pinches her legs all over.

Anuj's mother takes him to get glasses. His headaches persist, racking him with an evil, shelling pain. He and the little girl do not talk much anymore.

The little girl sharpens Karan's pencils for him and drops Quality Street candies onto his desk, until she sees that he simply throws them away unacknowledged.

Even with glasses, Anuj has to sit up in the front now to see the chalkboard. He bumps into desks; he walks half his face smack into the doorframe, clutches his head, lets out a noise lost somewhere between moan and scream.

The girl goes back to reading books at recess. She draws Minnie Mouse again and again, but with long mustaches and batlike teeth.

One day he isn't at school. And then the next. And the next. And the next. And the next. And the next.

"Excuse me, Ma'am, where is Anuj, please?" the girl asks, voice shaking a little, when she brings up her penmanship for inspection.

Mrs. Tareen says that Anuj has to go to a special school now, that he won't be coming back.

In fourth grade they all have numerous alien subjects to study, and their old class sections are shuffled, so no more Karan. The girl opens her new geography textbook. (We pronounced it *JOG-reff-ee*.) On its flyleaf is printed a quote from Mohandas Gandhi. It says,

> I will give you a talisman. Whenever you are in doubt, or when the self becomes too much with you, apply the following test:
> Recall the face of the poorest and the weakest man whom you may have seen, and ask yourself if the step you contemplate is going to be of any use to him. Will he gain anything by it? Will it restore him to a control over his own life and destiny? In other words, will it lead to swaraj (freedom) for the hungry and spiritually starving millions?

She feels like this is the beginning of an answer, a tranquilizer dart to the thick, muscled limbs of the stalking creature within. She copies it again in her purple-ruled notebook, the curls of the word *talisman* shining in wet ink.

Later the girl will become a person who learns, wearily, that Gandhi was racist against the blacks of Africa, that he liked sleeping next to naked nubile girls to test his willpower, that he fought to keep the caste system in place—pin the poorest and the weakest exactly where they were in the scheme of things.

Please listen. I grew up in a place that I cannot return to. When I search for my old home on Google Maps, it says *Result Not Found*.

Shake me, and the past rattles like broken circuitry. I make myself a mug of tea and close my eyes. Heat radiates through the ceramic and into my palms.

I wake up in the middle of the night, sweating heavily, go sit at my computer, and type out a story. I title it "The Nature of Evil, The Nature of Good." I send the story in to my writing group. They are mystified and slightly uncomfortable. Why is the little girl the only one left without a name, they ask. They are nervous about how to pronounce everything.

"The relevance of this seems grounded in a kind of cultural specificity that the narrator doesn't include the audience in on," one man says carefully.

Part of me wants to give the story over to someone in my group to write, start over, make their own in clarity and directness. Maybe someone would set down, clean and loud, right at the start, "The first friend I ever made went blind."

After talking about my story, they discuss the solar eclipse that is days away. Some of them will take off work, drive to something they call the path of totality. The rest mull over how to buy glasses to stare at the sun in supposed safety. The man says he will order them in bulk for us.

"You in?" he asks me, and I shake my head: no.

In fourth grade the girl's father buys the family their first computer. After school she turns the machine on and sits in front of the bright, hot screen. Her parents are away at work. She marvels at how it lets her erase sentences without using rubbers, so clean and easy, no debris left behind. She stares at the upright, blinking line that is the door for words to walk out of, lifts her fingers to the keys, and pushes down.

ELIZABETH McCRACKEN

It's Not You

FROM *Zoetrope: All-Story*

HOTELS WERE DIFFERENT in those days. You could smoke in
them. The rooms had bathtubs, where you could also smoke. You
didn't need a credit card or identification, though you might be
made to sign the register, so later the private detective—just like
that, we're in a black-and-white movie, though I speak only of the
long-ago days of 1993—could track you down. Maybe you anticipated the private detective, and used an assumed name.

Nobody was looking for me. I didn't use an assumed name,
though I wasn't myself. I'd had my heart broken, or so I thought,
I'd been shattered in a collision with a man, or so I thought, and
I went to the fabled pink hotel just outside the midwestern town
where I lived. The Narcissus Hotel: it sat on the edge of a lake
and admired its own reflection. Behind, a pantomime lake, an
amoebic swimming pool, now drained, empty lounge chairs all
around. January 1: cold, but not yet debilitating. In my suitcase I'd
brought one change of clothing, a cosmetic bag, a bottle of Jim
Beam, a plastic sack of Granny Smith apples. I thought this was
all I needed. My plan was to drink bourbon and take baths and
feel sorry for myself. Paint my toenails, maybe. Shave my legs. My
apartment had a small fiberglass shower I had to fit myself into,
as though it were a science fiction pod that transported me to nowhere, but cleaner.

I would watch television too. In those days I didn't own one,
and there was a certain level of weeping that could be achieved
only while watching TV, I'd discovered—self-excoriating, with a

distant laugh track. I wanted to obliterate myself, but I intended to survive the obliteration.

It wasn't the collision that had hurt me. It was that the other party, who'd apologized and explained enormous deficiencies, self-loathing, an unsuitability for any kind of extended human contact, had three weeks later fallen spectacularly and visibly in love with a woman, and they could be seen—seen by me—necking in the public spaces of the small town. The coffee shop, the bar, the movie theater before the movie started. I was young then, we all were, but not so young that public necking was an ordinary thing to do. We weren't teenagers but grown-ups, late twenties in my case, early thirties in theirs.

New Year's Day in the Narcissus Hotel. The lobby was filled with departing hangovers and their owners. Paper hats fell with hollow pops to the ground. Everyone winced. You couldn't tell whose grip had failed. Nothing looked auspicious. That was good. My New Year's resolution was to feel as bad as fast as I could in highfalutin privacy, then leave the tatters of my sadness behind, along with the empty bottle and six apple cores.

"How long will you be with us?" asked the spoon-faced, red-headed woman behind the desk. She wore a little white name tag that read EILEEN.

"It will only seem like forever," I promised. "One night."

She handed me a brass key on a brass fob. Hotels had keys in those days.

I had packed the bottle of bourbon, the apples, my cosmetic bag, but forgotten a nightgown. Who was looking, anyhow? I built my drunkenness like a fire, patiently, enough space so it might blaze.

You shall know a rich man by his shirt, and so I did. Breakfast time in the breakfast room. The decor was old but kept up. Space-age, with stiff, Sputnikoid chandeliers. Dark-pink leather banquettes, rosy-pink carpets. Preposterous but wonderful. I'd eaten here in the past: they had a dessert cart, upon which they wheeled examples of their desserts to your table—a slice of cake, a crème brûlée, a flat apple tart that looked like a mademoiselle's hat.

I had my own hangover now, not terrible, a wobbling threat that might yet be kept at bay. I had taken three baths; my toenails were vampy red. I had watched television till the end of broadcast hours, which was a thing that happened then: footage of the American flag waving in the breeze, then here be monsters. In my other life, the one that happened outside the Narcissus Hotel, I worked in the HR department of a radio station. I lived with voices overhead. That was why I didn't have a television. It would have been disloyal. I'd found a rerun on a VHF station of squabbling siblings and then wept for hours, in the tub, on one double bed, then the other. Even at the time I knew I wasn't weeping over anything actual that I'd lost, but because I'd wanted love and did not deserve it. My soul was deformed. It couldn't bear weight. It would never fit together with another person's.

The rich man sat at the back of the breakfast room in one of the large horseshoe booths built for public canoodling. His pale-green shirt, starched, flawless, seemed to have been not ironed but forged, his mustache tended by money and a specialist. His glasses might have cost a lot, but twenty years before. In his fifties, I thought. In those days, *fifties* was the age I assigned people undeniably older than me. I never looked at anyone and guessed they were in their forties. You were a teenager, or my age, or middle-aged, or old.

The waiter went to the man's table and murmured. The man answered. At faces I am terrible, but I always recognize a voice.

"Dr. Benjamin," I said, once the waiter had left. He looked disappointed, with an expression that said, *Here, of all places.* With a nod, he recognized my recognition. "I listen to you," I told him.

He had an overnight advice show, 11 p.m. to 2 a.m., on another AM channel, not mine. He had a beef bourguignon voice and regular callers. Stewart from Omaha. Allison from Asbury Park. Linda from Chattanooga.

"Thank you," he said. Then added, "If that's the appropriate response."

"I'm in radio too," I said. "Not talent. HR."

The waiter stood by my table, a tall, young man with an old-fashioned Cesar Romero mustache. When I looked at him, he smiled and revealed a full set of metal braces.

"I will have the fruit plate," I said. Then, as though it meant nothing to me, an afterthought, "and a bloody Mary."

It is the fear of judgment that keeps me behaving, most of the time, like the religious. Not of God, but of strangers.

"Hair of the dog," the radio shrink said to me.

"Hair of the werewolf," I answered.

"You could be. On air. You have a lovely voice."

In my head I kept a little box of compliments I'd heard more than once: I had nice hair (wavy, strawberry blond), and nice skin, and a lovely voice. I didn't believe the compliments, particularly at such times in my life, but I liked to save them for review, as my mother saved the scrapbooks from her childhood in a small town, where her every unusual move—going on a trip to England, performing in a play in the next town over—made the local paper.

Who in this story do I love? Nobody. Myself, a little. Oh, the waiter, with his diacritical mustache above his armored teeth. I love the waiter. I always love the waiter.

The bloody Mary had some spice in it that sent a tickle through my palate into my nose. A prickle, a yearning, an itch: a gathering sneezish sensation. One in ten bloody Marys did this to me. I always forgot. I took another drink, and the feeling intensified. Beneath the pressure of the spice was a layer of leftover intoxication, which the vodka perked up. I thought, not for the first time, that I had a sixth sense and it was called drunkenness.

"No good?" the radio shrink asked me.

"What?"

"You're making a terrible face."

"It's good," I said, but the sensation was more complicated than that. "What are you doing in this neck of the woods?"

"Is it a *neck*?" He touched his own with the tips of his fingers. "I like the rooms here."

"You probably have a nicer room than I do. The presidential suite. Honeymoon?"

"I'm neither the president nor a honeymooner."

"Those're the only suites I know," I said. It was possible to be somebody else in a hotel; I was slipping into a stranger's way of speaking. "Still, far from Chicago."

"Far from Chicago," he agreed. He picked up his coffee cup in both hands, as though it were a precious thing, but it was thick china, the kind you'd have to hurl at a wall to break. "Business," he said at last. "You?"

"I live here."

"You live in the hotel?"

"In town."

"Oh, you're merely breakfasting, not staying."

"I'm staying." I started to long for a second bloody Mary, like an old friend who might rescue me from the conversation. "Somebody was mean to me," I said to the radio shrink. "I decided to be kind to myself."

He palmed the cup and drank from it, then settled it back in the saucer. The green shirt was a terrible color against the pink leather. "It's a good hotel for heartache. Join me," he said, in his commercial-break voice, deeply intimate, meant for thousands, maybe millions.

There were other radio hosts in those days, also called "Doctor," who would yell at you. A woman who said to penitent husbands, *You better straighten up and fly right.* A testy man—*No, no, no, no: Listener*—he called his listeners "Listener"—*Listener, this is your wake-up call.*

But Dr. Benjamin practiced compassion, with that deep voice and his big feelings. *Once you forgive yourself, you can forgive your mother,* he would say. Or perhaps it was the other way around: your mother first, then you. He told stories of his own terrible decisions. Unlike some voices, his had ballast and breadth. For some reason I'd always pictured him as bald, in a bow tie. I pictured all male radio hosts as bald and bow-tied, until presented with evidence to the contrary. Instead he had a thatch of silver hair. The expensive shirt. Cowboy boots.

I listened to his show all the time, because I hated him. I thought he gave terrible advice. He believed in God and tried to convince other people to do likewise. Sheila from Hoboken, Ann from Nashville, Patrick from Daly City. On the radio it didn't matter where you lived, small town or suburb or New York City (though nobody from New York City ever called Dr. Benjamin): you had the same access to phone lines and radio waves. You could broadcast your loneliness to the world. Every now and then a caller started to say something that promised absolute humiliation, and I'd have to fly across the room to snap the dial off. *My husband cannot satisfy me, Doc—.*

So long ago! I can't remember faces, but I can remember voices. I can't remember smells, but I can remember in all its dimensions the way I felt in those days. The worst thing about not being loved, I thought then, was how vivid I was to myself.

Now I am loved and in black and white.

Up close he seemed altogether vast. Paul Bunyan-y, as though he'd drunk up the contents of that swimming pool to slake his thirst, but he didn't look slaked. Those outdated glasses had just a tinge of purple to the lenses. Impossible to tell whether this was fashion or prescription, something to protect his eyes. His retinas, I told myself. He'd slumped to the bottom of the hoop of the horseshoe, his body at an angle. I sat at the edge to give him room.

He said, "Better?"

"Maybe," I said. "Are you a real doctor?"

He stretched then, the tomcat, his arms over his head. His big steel watch slipped down his wrist. "Sure."

"You're not."

"I'm not a medical doctor," he allowed.

"I know that," I said.

"Then, yes. Yes, I'm a doctor."

The table had an air of vacancy: he'd eaten his breakfast, which had been mostly tidied away, except for the vest-pocket bottles of ketchup and Tabasco sauce and a basket filled with tiny muffins. I took one, blueberry, and held it in the palm of my hand. The waiter delivered a bloody Mary I hadn't ordered, unless by telepathy. "You have a PhD," I said.

"Yes."

"It's strange."

"That I have a PhD?"

"That we call people who study English literature for too long the same thing we call people who perform brain surgery."

"Oh *dear*," he said. "Psychology, not English literature."

"I'd like to see your suite."

He shook his head.

"Why not?"

"I'm married," he said. "You know that."

Of course I did. Her name was Evaline. He mentioned her all the time: he called her *Evaline Robinson the Love of My Life*.

"That's not what I mean," I said, and I tore the little muffin in half, because maybe it *was* what I'd meant. No, I told myself. Every time I walked down a hotel hallway, I peered into open doors. Was there a better room behind *this* one? A better view out the window of the room? Out of all these dozens of rooms, where would I be happiest—by which I meant, least like myself? I only wanted to see all the hotel rooms of the world, all the other places I might be.

I was waiting to be diagnosed.

He said, "You're a nice young woman, but you won't cut yourself a break." He said, "All right. Okay. We can go to my suite. They've probably finished making it up."

Even the hallways were pink and red, the gore and frill of a Victorian valentine: one of those mysterious valentines, with a pretty girl holding a guitar-sized fish. The suite was less garish, less whorehouse, less rubescent, with a crystal chandelier, that timeless symbol of One's Money's Worth. The two sofas were as blue and buttoned as honor guards. A mint-green stuffed rabbit sat in a pale-salmon armchair.

"What's that?" I asked.

He looked at it as though it were a girl who'd snuck into his room and undressed, and here came the question: throw her out, or . . . not.

"A present," he said.

"Who from?"

"Not *from. For.* Somebody else. Somebody who failed to show up."

"A child."

He shook his big head. "Not a child. She must have lost her nerve. She was supposed to be here yesterday."

"Maybe she realized you were the kind of man who'd give a stuffed bunny to a grown woman."

He regarded me through the purple glasses. Amethyst, I thought. My birthstone. Soon I would be twenty-eight. "You are young to be so unkind," he observed. "She collects stuffed animals." He turned again to the rabbit and seemed to lose heart. "This is supposed to be a good one."

"What makes a good one?"

"Collectible. But also it's pleasant." He plucked it from the chair and hugged it. "Pleasant to hug."

"Careful. It's probably worth more uncuddled." I put myself on the chair where the rabbit had been. I don't know why I'd thought the chair might still be warm. He sat on the sofa, in the corner closest to me.

"I thought you might be her," he told me. "But you're not old enough. How old are you?"

"Twenty-seven."

"Not nearly old enough."

"Do I look like her?"

"Oh. I mean, I'm not sure." He made the rabbit look out the window, and so I looked too, but the sheers were closed and all I perceived was light.

"A listener," I said. "A caller. You're meeting somebody. Linda from Chattanooga!"

"Not *Linda* from *Chattanooga*," he said contemptuously. He put the rabbit beside him, as though aware of how silly he appeared.

After a while he said, "Dawn from Baton Rouge."

I couldn't remember Dawn from Baton Rouge. "What does she look like?"

"I only know what she tells me."

"Should've asked for a picture."

He shrugged. "But: cold feet. So it doesn't matter."

"And now you've invited me instead," I said, and crossed my legs.

"Oh god, no," he said. "No, darling—"

The endearment undid me. I was aware then of what I was wearing, a pair of old blue jeans but good ones, a thin black sweater that showed my black bra beneath. Alluring, maybe, to the right demographic, slovenly to the wrong one.

"Sweetheart," he said. He got up from the sofa. It was a complicated job: hands to knees and a careful raising of the whole impressive structure of him. "No, let's have a drink." He went to the minibar, which was hidden in a cherry cabinet and had already been unlocked, already plundered, already refreshed. Imagine a life in which you could approach a minibar with no trepidation or guilt whatsoever.

He lifted a midget bottle of vodka and a pygmy can of bloody Mary mix; he didn't know I'd ordered a bloody Mary because it was one of the only acceptable drinks before 10 a.m. He was a man who drank and ate what he wanted at any time of day.

"We'll toast to our betrayers," he said.

Because it was something he might say to a midnight caller, I said, "I thought we only ever betrayed ourselves."

"Sometimes we look for accomplices. No ice," he said, turning to me. "To get through this, we're gonna need some ice."

For a moment it felt as though we were in a jail instead of a reasonably nice hotel, sentenced to live out our days—*live out our days* being another way to say *hurtle toward death*.

In those days it was easy to disappear from view. All the people who caused you pain: you might never know what happened to them, unless they were famous, as the radio shrink was, and so I did know, it happened soon afterward, before the snow had melted. He died of a heart attack at another hotel, and Evaline Robinson the Love of His Life flew from Chicago to be with him, and a guest host took over until the guest host was the actual host, and the show slid from call-in advice to unexplained phenomena: UFOs. Bigfoot. I suppose it had been about the unexplained all along. All the best advice is on the Internet these days anyhow. That person who broke my heart might be a priest by now, or happily gay, or finally living openly as a woman, or married twenty-five years, or all of these things at once, or 65 percent of them, as is possible in today's world. It's good that it's possible. A common name plus my bad memory for faces: I wouldn't know how to start looking or when to stop.

The minibar wasn't equal to our thirsts. He sat so long, staring out the window, that I wondered whether something had gone wrong. A stroke. The start of ossification. Then, in a spasm of fussiness, he untucked his shirt.

He said, "In another life—"

"Yeah?"

"I would have been a better man. How long?"

"How long what?"

"Was your relationship with whoever broke your heart."

"He didn't break my heart."

"'Was mean' to you," he said, with a playacting look on his face. I did the math in my head and rounded up. "A month."

"You," he said in his own voice, which I understood I was hearing for the first time, "have got to be fucking kidding me."

It had actually been two and a half weeks. "Don't say I'm young," I told him.

"I wouldn't," he said. "But someday something terrible will happen to you and you'll hate this version of yourself."

"I don't plan on coming in versions."

"Jesus, you *are* young." Then his voice shifted back to its radio frequency, a fancy chocolate in its little matching, rustling, crenellated wrapper. "How mean was he?"

"He was nice, right up until the moment he wasn't."

"Well," he said. "So. You're making progress. Wish him well."

"I wish him well but not *that* well."

But that wasn't true. I wanted them both dead.

"The only way forward is to wish peace for those who have wronged you. Otherwise it eats you up."

I wished him peace when I thought he was doomed.

How can it be that I felt like this, over so little? It was as though I'd rubbed two sticks together and they'd detonated in my lap.

"I bet you have a nice bathtub," I said.

"You should go look."

I got myself a dollhouse bottle of bourbon. At some point he'd had ice delivered, in a silver bucket, with tongs. I'd never used tongs before. I've never used them since. The serrations bit into the ice, one, two, five cubes, and I poured the bourbon over, a paltry amount that mostly didn't make its way to the bottom of the glass, it just clung to the ice, so I got another. The bathroom was marble—marble, crystal, velvet, it would be some years before hotels stopped modeling opulence on Versailles. There was a phone on the wall by the toilet. I ran a bath and got in. This was what I needed, not advice or contradiction, not the return of the person who'd broken my heart, because I would not be able to trust any love that might have been offered. It took me a long time, years, to trust anyone's.

The door opened, and another tiny bottle of whiskey came spinning across the floor.

"Irish is what's left," said the radio shrink through the crack of the door.

"You're a good man," I said. "You are one. If you're worried that you're not."

Then he came in. He was wearing his cowboy boots and slid a little on the marble. Now he looked entirely undone. In another version of this story, I'd be made modest by a little cocktail dress of bubbles, but no person who really loves baths loves bubble baths, nobody over seven, because bubbles are a form of protection.

They keep you below the surface. They hide you from your own view. He looked at me in his bathtub with that same disappointed expression: *just like you to bathe in your birthday suit.*

"I have some advice for you," I said to him.

"Lay it on me," he said.

"*Lay it on me.* How old are you?"

He shook his head. "What's your advice?"

"You should call your callers 'Caller.' Like, 'Are you there, Caller?'"

"They like to be called by name."

"Overly familiar," I said.

"That's your advice."

"Yes," I said.

He was sitting on the edge of the tub. The ice in his glass, if there'd ever been any, had melted. I had no idea what he might do. Kiss me. Put a hand in the water. His eyebrows had peaks. Up close his mustache was even more impressive. I'd never kissed a man with a mustache. I still haven't. It's not that I'm not attracted to men with mustaches, but that men with mustaches aren't attracted to me.

"Can I have your maraschino cherry?" I asked.

"No maraschino cherry."

"I love maraschino cherries. All kinds. Sundae kinds, drink kinds, fruit cocktail. Tell me to change my life," I said to him, and put a damp hand on his knee.

"I won't tell you that."

"But I *need* someone to tell me."

He put down his glass beside the little bottle of shampoo. Such a big hotel. So many minuscule bottles. "You must change your life," he said.

"Good, but I'm going to need some details."

"I keep sitting here, I'm going to fall into the water." He stood up. "You know where to find me."

There isn't a moral to the story. Neither of us is in the right. Nothing was resolved. Decades later, it still bothers me.

No way to tell how much later I awoke, facedown in the bath, and came up gasping. I'd fallen asleep or I'd blacked out. It was though the water itself had woken me up, not the water on the surface of me, which wasn't enough, not even the water over my face, like a hotel pillow, up my nose, in my lungs, but the water that soaked through my bodily tissues, running along fissures and ruining the texture of things, till it finally reached my heart and all my autonomic systems said, *Enough, you're awake now, you're alive, get out.*

That was one of the few times in my life I might have died and knew it. I fell asleep in a bathtub at twenty-seven. I was dragged out to sea as a small child; I spun on an icy road at eighteen, into a break in oncoming traffic on Route 1 north of Rockland, Maine, and astonishingly stayed out of the ditch; I did not have breast cancer at twenty-nine, when it was explained to me that it was highly unlikely I would, but if I did, *it was unlikely,* it would be fatal, *almost never at your age,* but when at your age, rapid and deadly.

Those are the fake times I almost died. The real ones, neither you nor I ever know about.

The radio shrink would have said, *I guess she died of a broken heart,* and I would have ended my life and ruined his, for no reason, just a naked, drunk, dead woman in his room who'd got herself naked, and drunk, and dead.

But I wouldn't see the radio shrink again. I was gasping and out of the tub, and somebody was knocking on the bathroom door. I don't know why knocking—the door was unlocked—but the water was sloshing onto the floor, the tap was on, it couldn't have been on all this time, and I'd soon learn that it was raining into the bathroom below, I had caused *weather,* and the radio shrink had packed up and left and hung the DO NOT DISTURB sign outside his room and paid for mine. Dawn from Baton Rouge was a disembodied voice again, but the redheaded woman, Eileen, she was here, slipping across the marble, tossing me a robe, turning off the tap, tidying up my life.

"You're all right," she said. I could feel her name tag against my cheek. "You should be ashamed of yourself, but you're all right now."

I would like to say that this was when my life changed. No. That came pretty quick, within weeks, but not yet. I would like to say that the suggestion of kindness took. That I went home and wished everyone well. That I forgave myself and found that my self-loathing was the curse: forgiveness transformed me, and I became lovely. But all that would wait.

He was wrong, the shrink: nothing truly terrible ever happened to me, nothing that would make me cry more than I did in those weeks of aftermath. I'm one of the lucky ones. I know that. I became kinder the way anybody does, because it costs less and is, nine times out of ten, more effective.

At some point it had snowed. The night prior, that morning. It had been hours since I'd been outside. The snow was still white, still falling, the roads marked by the ruts of tires. Soon the plows would be out, scraping down to the pavement. My clothing, left behind by the side of the tub, sopping wet, had been replaced with a stranger's sweat suit, abandoned by some other guest at the Narcissus Hotel and found by Eileen, a stranger's socks too, my own shoes and winter coat. I had to walk by the house of the couple who'd been necking everywhere, a story that seemed already in the past. By *past*, I mean I regretted it, I was already telling the story in my head. The woman I hadn't been left for drove a little red Honda. There it sat in her driveway, draped in snow. That was all right. It was a common car in those days, and I saw it and its doppelgängers everywhere. Even now a little red Honda seems to have a message for me, though they look nothing like they used to. *When will this be over,* I wondered as I pushed through the drifts. The *humiliation* is what I meant. Everything else is over, and all that's left are the little red Hondas.

You would recognize my voice too. People do, in the grocery store, the airport, over the phone when I call to complain about my gas bill. *Your voice,* they say, *are you—?*

I have one of those voices, I always say. I don't mind if they recognize me, but I'm not going to help them.

He kept telling me I had to be kind. Why? Why on earth? When life itself was not.

SCOTT NADELSON

Liberté

FROM *Chicago Quarterly Review*

IN ORDER TO devote herself wholly to art, Louise Nevelson—born Leah Berliawsky—has left her marriage of thirteen years. She's been drawing and painting since childhood, but at thirty-four she's hardly more than a novice. She has never had a show of her work, has not yet discovered her medium. It will be many years before she's famous for her massive monochromatic assemblages, considered a queen of modern sculpture. Famous too for her bold style—colorful headscarves and enormous fake eyelashes—and brash, uninhibited speech. When asked, in her late sixties, how she's maintained such vitality for so long, she'll reply, *Why, lots of fucking, of course.*

In the early summer of 1933, however, she's both unknown and relatively inexperienced with men. Since separating from her husband, Charles, a shipping executive whose family has oppressed her since their wedding—wealthy and cultured Jews who cherish art and music but laugh at those who dream of making it—she's had only one affair. Her lover was another American businessman, whom she met on her first crossing to Europe a year ago, her first, that is, since emigrating from Russia at six years old. And though the newness of the affair excited her, as well as its illicit charge—the businessman was married, his wife joining him in several weeks—she found sleeping with him largely dispiriting. Like Charles, he was overly solicitous, asking constantly after her comfort. With both she has just barely glimpsed what she guesses to be the dark and thrilling possibilities of sex, the struggle and near violence of it, terror and triumph outweighing simple pleasure.

She found her three months in Berlin, chaste while studying with Hans Hofmann, far more rewarding than those hours naked in a stranger's cabin. And so now she decides to make another trip, this time planning to spend several months in Paris to learn contemporary technique. So at least she has told herself, though a part of her knows she may never return to New York. She will do whatever she must to become the artist she has long believed herself capable of becoming, no matter the sacrifices.

About leaving Charles, she feels little remorse. She was always honest with him, and he knew what she wanted when they married. If he didn't believe her when she confessed her ambition, that is his fault, not hers. He acquiesced to the separation with little argument, though she knows he is hoping she will soon come to her senses and return to him. Or, more likely, that she will find it too difficult to survive on her own, that his money, if not his love and loyalty, will draw her back. But unlike her shipboard lover, whose manufacturing interests were only mildly affected by the crash, Charles may not have money for long. His family's business has suffered enormous losses over the past four years and is now on the verge of collapse. More than her own survival, she fears for his. What will Charles do with himself if he can no longer spend his time tracking shipments and accounts? What purpose will guide his days?

Any discomfort caused by deserting her husband, however, is minor compared to the guilt she carries over abandoning her son. Myron—who prefers to be called Mike—is nine years old and bewildered by the changes thrust upon him. Last summer she sent him to stay with her parents in Maine, and though she tried to tell herself he'd be perfectly happy there, her mother spoiling him with her baking, her father, a builder, teaching him how to frame a house, she nevertheless imagined him smothered by the same boredom that had driven her to marry the first wealthy man she met, when she wasn't yet twenty-one. At the time Charles lived on the twelfth floor of a building on Riverside Drive, and she believed it was the city she was marrying as much as the man, the opportunities such a move would afford her. If she'd known he would soon pack her off to the suburbs, to be surrounded by his brothers and sisters-in-law and cousins, who would judge every word she spoke, she would have refused his offer instantly, or so at least she tells herself now.

She agonizes over Mike, and yet the thought of her own suffocation were she to stay overwhelms all others. She books her passage and sends her son back to Maine.

The ship, a single-class steamer bound for Le Havre, is called *Liberté*. A fitting name, she thinks, though worries about Mike's unhappiness keep her from feeling terribly free until the second evening out from New York, when she meets a handsome Frenchman, a doctor named Destouches. Louis Ferdinand Destouches. He says the name as if she might recognize it, and when she doesn't, shrugs to confirm she couldn't possibly.

This takes place in the ship's narrow dining room. When she enters, most tables are already occupied by families and large parties of young people traveling together. Those few passengers on their own wander the edges, looking for friendly faces. She finds herself seated with five strangers, all men. More Americans on business, two disembarking in Portsmouth, another traveling on to Frankfurt. The remaining two are heading to Paris, and before the entrée is served, both have offered to take her to dinner there, or to a show. All five laugh at her jokes, and the two closest to her pour wine into her glass as soon as she empties it. They smile feral smiles as she unwraps her stole to reveal athletic shoulders —she was captain of her high school basketball team, as well as its sole Jew—and a long neck. The most attractive of them has bits of bread stuck between his teeth, the tallest unappealingly bushy eyebrows. One of the others—she can't tell which—smells ripely of sweat.

The Frenchman approaches just as the meal ends. When she stands, he takes her hand lightly and releases it before introducing himself. His accent is so thick she has a hard time understanding what he says. But she thinks he tells her she has the appearance of an artist, the only one on the entire ship. He is sloppily dressed but fierce-looking, with a large head, dark hair combed back from a widow's peak, prominent cheekbones, dazzling blue eyes. He's an inch or two shorter than all the other men, but the low tones of his voice and his way of leaning forward as he speaks diminish them. He is bold yet nervous, fidgeting with his tie as if it chokes him, and after saying a few more words she can't make out gives a nod, shuffles backward, and disappears into the crowd exiting the room.

One of her dinner companions suggests stepping outside to look at stars, but she excuses herself, says the wine has made her dizzy. In her cabin she studies a picture of Mike, dapper in a tuxedo, though dour, taken just before attending a concert with Charles's insufferable relatives. Later, when most people are asleep and the passageways are quiet, she does go out on deck. The stars are hidden behind clouds she can't see. Beyond the ship's lights, everything is black. She can't distinguish ocean from sky.

She spots the Frenchman again the next day, soon after lunch. He is seated in a card room in which the tables have all been moved to one side. A thin, stooped man stands next to him, handing out books to people waiting in line. The Frenchman, Destouches, signs them, hands them back with a little dip of his head, unsmiling. She learns from another passenger—a sharp-faced Parisian who looks at her with disdain, as if in not knowing already she is either ignorant or mad—that in addition to being a doctor, he is also a novelist whose first book was published to great acclaim some months earlier, called a masterpiece by many critics, herald of a new French literature, one more raw and honest and free than any previous. He writes under a pen name, Céline, in tribute to his grandmother. He is returning home after traveling to California in hopes of having the book made into a film. *Will it be?* Louise asks, but the woman shakes her head. *Cowards,* she says. *Communists.* The producers were warned before he arrived, alerted to his political leanings, and as a result they all declined. What those political leanings are, the woman doesn't say.

Céline. Once Louise hears the name she can't connect him with any other. She doesn't stand in line for a book and doesn't think he has seen her before she walks away. But when she arrives for dinner, he is waiting for her. His slender companion hands her two copies of the novel. In one is just his signature, he says, in the other a special inscription. The book is thick, at least five hundred pages, and heavy, and to hold two she must use both hands. The simplicity of its cover appeals to her. White, with red and black type, no image. She likes the sound of the title too, but knows enough French only to decipher *voyage* and *de la nuit*. A voyage of the night strikes her as both mysterious and enticing. The meaning of *au bout* she will have to do without.

The slender companion vanishes, and Louise joins Céline at his table. He speaks quickly, with vehement gestures, and again she misses many of his words. He jumps from topic to topic but always follows a central thread: the essential corruption of humanity, the yearning for filth even among the most so-called refined of society —he mutters this while jutting his chin at a well-dressed couple across the table—which itself is a cesspool, needing to be emptied and scoured. Everything he says is bitter and morose, and yet there's a charm in his passionate insistence, a relief after so many years of listening to Charles and his relatives speak with mild disinterest about even those things they claim to value most. He stares at her as if he will soon pounce and clamp his jaws around her neck. She wants to hear him say more about how he recognized her as an artist just by looking at her, but for now he talks only about himself, about his family, his mother who traveled house to house selling liniments and herbal remedies so he could study legitimate medicine.

I'm peasant stock, he tells her. *Last of a line. When you have a head like mine, you know you've reached the end.*

After the meal she expects him to invite her for a drink, maybe at one of the ship's several bars or maybe in his cabin. And she is prepared to accompany him to either. Instead he delivers his nervous bow, tells her how much he has enjoyed their conversation, asks if they might continue to talk tomorrow. His companion has reappeared, bony and silent, and the two of them hasten belowdecks. In her cabin she flips through his novel, unable to read any of it. Like the text, the inscription is in French, the handwriting loose and rumpled like his suit, and she can make out only a handful of simple words: *bien* and *au* and *courage.* Another looks like *ravissant,* but she can't be sure. The image of Charles comes to her for no reason she can imagine, taking off his trousers and carefully folding them before joining her in bed. She has a headache but cannot sleep. She goes upstairs, finds a bar, orders a whiskey on ice, and interrogates the bartender about which cocktails he enjoys mixing most and why.

The crossing takes seven days, and a part of four she spends with Céline. At times they sit on deck, enjoying sun and a light breeze.

On a stormy day, both are mildly seasick and huddle on velvet sofas in a deserted lounge, where Céline smokes to calm his stomach
and Louise drinks to settle hers. He still asks nothing about her
life, why she's traveling to Paris, what sort of art she hopes to produce, but she takes his silences as opportunities to tell him about
her failed marriage, her previous work with Hofmann, her plans
for the summer. *If I like it, perhaps I'll stay,* she says. She does not
mention Mike, though almost immediately a vision of him springs
to mind, standing on the shore of Rockland, staring out over the
ocean into which his mother has disappeared. Céline, brooding or
nauseated, says nothing.

Later, when the sea has calmed and they have returned to the
deck, he tells her that Paris is a toilet, full of nothing but thieves
and con artists, and yet compared to America it's an oasis, a place
where you can speak your opinions freely and not fear reprisal.
She recalls what the woman said about Hollywood producers and
wonders what opinions scared them off. It's the only place to live,
he goes on, a disgusting city but an honest one, where all depravity
is on display. He has seen it firsthand, patients coming to him with
wounds from scuffles, with horrifying sexual diseases, everything
left to fester because all have been contaminated by the pestilence
of contemporary life.

Every time he mentions his work as a doctor, she is surprised
anew. Afterward she quickly forgets how he makes his living. It's
as if the information won't stick in her mind, crowded out by the
heft of his novel. Or maybe it's because she can't imagine going to
him for medical attention. With those harsh, inward-focused eyes
and large hands with blunt fingers, how could he possibly ease
someone's suffering?

As if she has spoken the question aloud, he says, waving a hand,
It's mostly pointless, this whole, how you say, enterprise. He heals those
he can, but soon enough they are ground up again by the machin-
ery of decadence, of the world going to rot. In times like these,
he goes on, who should rise to the surface, like shit floating on a
flooded river? Yes, the Jew, the bottom-feeder, thriving on the foul-
ness and decay of a poisoned culture, poisoning it further, until
those few left with dignity must burn everything down and plant
new seeds in the ashes.

His face is flushed as he speaks, flecks of spittle at the edges of
his lips, and yet his voice remains calm, with the lilt of amusement.

When he finishes, he smiles and apologizes, not for his sentiments but for his mixed metaphors. Louise tries not to reveal anything by her expression, though she can't help leaning away. Surely he knows what she is, if not from her features, then from her name. And yet he keeps staring at her with the same hunger, the same ferocious need. Only now he is finally ready to act on it. He moves toward her, sweeps an arm across her shoulders, bends to kiss her. She turns away, swivels out of his grasp, hurries inside without looking back.

But for the rest of the day she is less horrified than fascinated. It's an important discovery, she thinks, a profound one: that someone can detest what he desires or desire what he detests. Which comes first, the wanting or the loathing, she doesn't know.

On the last day of the voyage, she takes her meals in her cabin and does not encounter Céline again before the ship docks for the last time. She doesn't see him on the train from Le Havre and learns from the sharp-faced woman that he disembarked at Cherbourg. She assumes that will be the end, she won't hear from him again. But he soon contacts her in Paris, sends a note to her hotel, invites her to lunch. He does not apologize for what he has said, nor for trying to kiss her afterward, does not acknowledge their last meeting in any way. His note is brief and self-deprecating. *Dear Miss Nevelson,* he writes in English. *By now you must have been married over and over again. What passion will be left for me?* During the summer she sees him once, and though he flatters her with compliments, he is otherwise distracted and distant, avoiding all serious topics. She finds herself both relieved and dejected when they part. He kisses both her cheeks lightly, the smell of tobacco lingering until she is well down the street.

Later she learns from an acquaintance that she is not Céline's first American infatuation. He once lived with a girl from California, with similarly strong shoulders and elegant neck. Not long ago this girl returned to the States and married, leaving Céline heartbroken. To find that she served as someone's replacement is less insulting to Louise than sad. She pictures Céline entering the ship's dining room, scanning the tables for a passable likeness. She imagines Charles similarly scouting for someone new in the lobby of a theater or the reception hall of his synagogue, someone who will both remind him of what he has lost and help him forget.

Her time in Paris is, on the whole, disappointing. She sees much artwork that moves her, attends parties, has many flirtations. But the mood is generally bleak. Too many people are out of work. There are fears of more anti-parliamentarist demonstrations like the one in February that left fifteen dead. She considers returning to Berlin, where she was so much happier last summer, but she meets a number of German artists and musicians and writers who have fled since Hitler became chancellor, all of whom warn her to stay away. Hofmann, she learns, has left too, emigrated to New York. So why has she come at all?

Mostly, though, her disappointment is personal rather than political. Her friendships feel shallow. The prospect of establishing a career in Europe seems more daunting the longer she stays and the more she sees. Here the tree of modern art is massive, with many limbs, thick and healthy and intimidating. She could be no more than a small leaf, clinging desperately to a twig. But at home, in the country Céline described as a swamp of naiveté and repression, she might grow to be a branch, or perhaps, with enough effort, a part of the trunk.

She visits Chartres, Versailles. Depressed, she travels to the Riviera, sleeps with a sailor in Nice, and boards a ship home from Genoa. She arrives just as summer ends, when Mike is due back in school, and pretends this has been her plan all along.

To her surprise, Céline writes to her in New York. They begin an extended correspondence, the strangest of her life, part seduction, part debasement. He invites her to come live with him in Italy, or perhaps he will move to America, even if it is a reeking bog, filled with the dregs of the earth—though now that Germany is being purged, he writes, France too is overrun with slime. Why she puts up with these letters she doesn't know, except that they captivate her, so many contradictions on display. Or perhaps she is simply lonely, longing for any interest to distract her from the sight of her empty bed.

By then she has settled into an apartment on Fifteenth Street and Third Avenue. It's a large space though spartan, with a bedroom for Mike and a studio for herself. While Mike is in school, she spends her mornings painting. She takes classes at the Art Students League, with Hofmann again, and George Grosz, both of whom are shaken by their flight from the darkness that has so

quickly consumed their home country. She wishes she could offer
them some comfort, but their distress puts her off, makes her keep
her distance. She wants only to admire them, see them as great
men, full of wisdom and fortitude they can pass on to her. She tells
neither about her exchanges with Céline.

When Diego Rivera comes to New York to work on several com-
missions, she is enlisted to help paint one of his murals, not the
monumental *Man at the Crossroads* at Rockefeller Center, but a
smaller one called *The Workers,* close to her apartment. She is in
awe of Diego, approves of his appetites. His second wife, Lupe,
shows up at one of the many parties he throws, kisses everyone,
dances with her eyes closed. She is beautiful, though less mesmer-
izing than his current wife, Frida, still in her twenties and shy,
though with a calm poise that makes Louise forget she's almost a
decade older. Both women smell faintly of semen when they hug
her goodbye. She doesn't think Diego loves them so much as he
feeds on them. They set flame to his passions, stoke his painting. If
she weren't afraid of draining what little fuel she has for her own
work, she might offer up her heat to him as well.

Instead she begins to experiment with sculpture, plaster figures
painted in primary colors. They don't satisfy her, except that she
can feel herself searching for form, knows for the first time that
she will eventually find it. She shows pieces in group exhibitions,
but galleries turn her away. She occasionally considers throwing
herself out a window, but her studio is on the first floor, the sidewalk only ten feet below the sill.

Céline's letters increasingly confuse her. After Hindenburg's death
and Hitler's ultimate ascent to power, he writes sincere condo-
lences, saying he hopes any friends or relatives she has in Germany
have managed to escape—and if not, that he may be able to help
with arrangements. But then he castigates the French government
for accepting refugees, whose stink pervades the air whenever
he walks through the streets. Sometimes she doesn't respond for
months, and then he pleads with her not to abandon their friendship: it is too important to him, he writes, she is the only woman
in his life who is both beautiful and intelligent, and knowing such
a possibility exists has been crucial to maintaining any hope for a
world so deeply mired in excrement.

And then he visits her in New York. When he calls, Mike is in school, and she doesn't hesitate to invite him to her apartment. She gives him coffee, and he sits across from her, smoking, smiling a pained smile. She wears a loose dress, with a low neckline and no sleeves. She has downed a tumbler of whiskey and left the door to her bedroom open. She thinks, *I am free to do whatever I please.* She can gratify herself or harm herself as she chooses. There is no one to stop her, no one to judge. Céline leans forward, elbows on knees. His voice is low, desperate. *How would you like to marry me?* he asks.

She thinks she ought to laugh but doesn't. She knows he is serious. She pictures Charles again, when he proposed at her parents' house in Rockland, when she was just a girl yearning for the promise of city life. She thinks of the brutality of that sailor in Nice, the hammering of his huge body that both unnerved and enthralled her. She sees shit floating in a swollen river. Which is worse, she wonders, the fanatic who wants what he hates or the one who wants what hates her?

After the war she will read about him in *Life* magazine. Collaborator. Nazi spy, propagandist. She will learn about the vile pamphlets he has authored, calling for the extermination of all Jews in France. She will tell those friends who knew of their correspondence that she is appalled, disgusted. She will give away the books he inscribed for her, toss his letters into the fireplace. She will regret doing so, not right away, but later, after Mike has grown up and moved out, while working on the first of the many walls of black boxes for which she will become known around the world, filled with arrangements of found wooden blocks and cylinders that suggest the messy intricacies of mind and heart. She will think he was one of the few who understood her, because, like her, nothing could ever appease him. And she'll think, *I wasn't ready then.*

You know, dear, she says now, *you would be worth more dead than alive to me.*

She isn't quite sure what she means by it. But he doesn't object, just nods, shows his woeful smile, finishes his coffee and cigarette. At the door he tells her not to worry, she has all the strength she needs to thrive, he glimpsed it in their very first encounter. But then he asks, as he steps into the hall, *Is this a world worth thriving in?*

Before she can answer, he's gone.

LEIGH NEWMAN

Howl Palace

FROM *The Paris Review*

LAST WEEK I finally had to put Howl Palace up for sale. Years of poor financial planning had led to this decision, and I tried to take some comfort in my agent's belief in a buyer who might show up with an all-cash offer. My agent is a highly organized, sensible woman who grew up in Alaska—I checked—but when she advertised the listing, she failed to mention her description on the Internet. "Attractively priced tear-down with plane dock and amazing lake views," she wrote under the photo. "Investment potential."

I am still puzzled as to why the word *tear-down* upset me. Anybody who buys a house on Diamond Lake brings in a backhoe and razes the place to rubble. The mud along the shoreline wreaks havoc with foundations, and the original homes, like mine, were built in the sixties before the pipeline, back when licensed contractors had no reason to move to Anchorage. If you wanted a house, you either built it yourself or you hung out in the parking lot of Spenard Builders Supply handing out six-packs to every guy with a table saw in the back of his vehicle until one got broke enough or bored enough to consider your blueprints. Which is why the walls in Howl Palace meet the ceiling at such unconventional angles. Our guy liked to eyeball instead of using a level.

To the families on the lake, my home is a bit of an institution. And not just for the wolf room, which my agent suggested we leave off the list of amenities, as most people wouldn't understand what we meant. About the snow-machine shed and clamshell grotto, I was less flexible. Nobody likes a yard strewn with snow machines and three-wheelers, one or two of which will always be busted and covered in blue tarp. Ours is just not that kind of neighborhood. The clamshell grotto, on the other hand, might fail to fulfill your basic home-owning needs, but it is a showstopper. My fourth husband, Lon, built it for me in the basement as a surprise for my fifty-third birthday. He had a romantic nature, when he hadn't had too much to drink. Embedded in the coral and shells are more than a few freshwater pearls that a future owner might consider tempting enough to jackhammer out of the cement.

My agent is named Silver. She brought me a box of Girl Scout cookies to discuss these matters, and so I tried my hardest to trust the rest of her advice. When she said not to bother with pulling out the chickweed or flattening the rusted remnants of the dog runs, I left both as is. But then I started thinking about what people say about baking blueberry muffins and burning vanilla candles. Buyers needed to feel the atmosphere of the place, the homeyness. Fred Meyer had some plug-in tropical air fresheners on sale. I bought a few. I shoved them into the outlets. Within minutes the entire downstairs smelled like a burning car wreck in Hawaii.

Silver scheduled the open house for Saturday. "Noon," she said. "Before families have put the kids down for a nap." The night before, I lay back in my recliner and thought how every good thing that had ever happened to me had happened in Howl Palace. And every bad thing too. Forty-three years. Five husbands. Two floatplanes. A lifetime. It felt as if I should honor my home, that strangers shouldn't come around poking through the kitchen or kicking the baseboards, seeing only the mold in the hot tub and the gnaw marks on the cabinets from the dogs I'd had over the years, maybe even laughing at the name. "Howl Palace" was coined by Danny Bob Donovan's littlest girl during a New Year's Eve party in 1977. She said it with awe, standing in the middle of the wolf room with a half-eaten candy cane.

"Mrs. Dutch," she said, "this is so beautiful, I think I need to howl a little." And howl she did, cupping her hands around her mouth and letting loose a wild, lonely cry that endeared her to me for forever.

Howl Palace was still beautiful, in my mind. And could be to other people, given the right welcome. Silver had said to just relax,

to let her finesse the details, but I went to the locker freezer and
pulled out fifty pounds of caribou burger plus four dozen moose
dogs. All we needed now was a few side dishes. And buns.

The next morning was bust a hump. The menu for the cookout had
expanded to include green bean casserole, macaroni salad, guacamole, and trout almondine. Trout almondine requires cream for
the cream sauce, which I forgot on my eight-thirty run to Costco,
leading me to substitute powdered milk mixed with a few cans of
cream of mushroom soup. My fifth husband, Skip, used to call me
the John Wayne of the Home Range, not in the nicest way, until
he got dementia and forgot who I was or that he had to follow me
around explaining how I'd organized the produce drawer wrong
or let too much hair fall off my head in the shower or failed to
remove every single bone from his halibut steak because I didn't
fucking ever *think*. Shipping him off to a facility in Washington
near his daughter wasn't exactly something I struggled with.

The pool table, where I planned to lay out the buffet, was coated
with so much dust it looked as though the velvet had sprouted a
fine silver fungus. I dragged an old quarter sheet of plywood from
the snow-machine shed and heaved it on top. If you are looking
for a reason to split five cords of wood by hand each year for forty-
odd years, consider my biceps at age sixty-seven.

The plywood I covered with a flowery top sheet from a long-
gone waterbed. Out went the side dishes, the salads, the condi-
ments. On went the grill, the meat at the ready. All that was left
was the guacamole. Which was when Carl's pickup pulled into
the driveway.

Carl wasn't my husband. Carl was the beautiful, bedeviling
heartbreak of my life. His hair had thinned, but not so you saw his
scalp, and age spots mottled his arms. His smell was the same as
ever: WD-40, line-dried shirt, the peppermint soap he uses to cut
through fish slime. For one heady second I believed he had come
back to say in some soft, regretful voice, *Remember when we ran into
each other at Sportsman's Warehouse? It got me thinking, well, maybe we
should give it another try.*

As Carl told me long ago, "Inside you hides a soft, secret pink
balloon of dreams." He wasn't incorrect, but the balloon has with-
ered a little over the years. And it was not an reassuring sign that
Carl had a dog in the back of his vehicle.

"I thought you might need a new Lab," he said. "She's pedigree, real obedient." I had some idea what he meant: she jumped ducks before he got off a shot and went after half-dead birds in the rapids despite the rocks he threw at her backside, trying to save her from injury. Once she had eaten a healthy portion of his dishwasher.

Over my years at Howl Palace I'd had a lot of dogs, all of them black Labs with papers proving their champion, field-and-trial bloodlines. I loved every one of them and loved hunting with them, but no matter how you deal with these animals at home—stick or carrot—they just can't deviate from the agenda panting through their minds, an agenda born of instinct and inbreeding, neither of which suggests that they sit there wagging their tails when a bumblebee flies through a yard. Or a bottle rocket zooms by.

I have seen my share of classic family retrievers on this lake —black or yellow Labs, dumb, drooling goldens, the occasional hefty Chessie—who live only to snuggle up with the kids at picnics and ignore the smoked salmon you are about to insert into your mouth. But I have never had one in my kennel or my house. My last dog, Babs, was a hunt nut, willful, with a hole in her emotional reasoning where somebody yanked out her uterus without a fully approved vet's license. I picked her up for free from an ad in the *PennySaver,* and maybe that had something to do with it. She drowned after jumping out of a charter boat to retrieve halibut that I had on the line, unaware of the tide about to suck her into the Gulf of Alaska.

Still, I enjoyed her company more than Skip's and Lon's combined. Babs slept not just in my bed but under the covers, where we struggled over the one soft pillow. When she died, I was ready to retire from a lifetime of animal management. I was sixty-three years old and single, and I vowed to myself: no more Labs, no more husbands, no more ex-husbands either.

The kennel in the bed of Carl's truck only confirmed the wisdom of my decision. The whole thing lay flipped on its side, jumping and heaving from the campaign being waged against the door. Nuthatches flickered through the trees, made frantic by the sound of claws against metal. Squirrels fled for other yards. "Carl," I said. "I'm about to have an open house. I can't take your dog."

He looked over at the woodpile, where the remains of the chain-link runs sagged along the ground. "You could put her in the basement. In the clamshell grotto," he said. Then laughed. He has a wonderful laugh, the kind that tickles through you, slowly, inch by inch, brain cell by brain cell, until you are mentally unfit to resist him.

"No, Carl," I said—not even talking about the animal.

"She can drink out of the fountain."

"No," I said. "N. O."

"I'm not a dog," he said, his voice quiet.

Wind riffled through the birches, exposing the silverish underside of the leaves. A plane buzzed by overhead. Carl jammed his hands in his pockets. "Besides," he said, "you can't sell Howl Palace."

I looked at him, daring him to tell me that he and I needed to live here. Together. The way I had always wanted. He had a suitcase in the back of the cab.

Carl looked back at me—as if about to say all this. Then he said, "It's your home, Dutch. You love it." He smiled, the way he always smiled. Time drained away for a few moments and we were back in the trophy room at Danny Boy's, thirty-five and tipsy, his finger laced through the loop of my jeans. The Eagles skipped on the turntable and my second husband, Wallace, ceased to exist. Tiny dry snowflakes clung to the edges of the window like miniature paper stars. Carl kissed me and a dark glittery hole opened up and I fell through, all the way to the bottom.

"I hate you, Carl," I said, but as so often happens around me, it came out sounding backward, fraught with tenderness.

The kennel creaked all of a sudden. We both looked over, and *blam*, the door snapped off. Seventy pounds of black thundering muscle shot out of the truck and into the alders.

"Oh boy," he said. "Not good."

"Hand me the zapper."

"She doesn't have a shock collar."

I tried a two-fingered whistle. Nothing. Not a snapped twig.

"I hate to say it," he said. "But there's this appointment—"

"Carl, I've got an open house."

He toed something, a weed. "It's a flight," he said. "To Texas. I'm fishing down in Galveston for a few weeks."

All the dewy romance inside me turned to gravel as I watched him move toward his vehicle. When he bent down to pick up the door to the kennel, his shirt twisted. It was a fly-fishing shirt, with a mesh panel for hot Texas days, through which I caught a glimpse of the pager-looking box strapped to his side. It was beige. A green battery light blinked on top.

Everybody our age knew what that box was. Carl was not here in my driveway to romance me all over again. Or even to piss me off. Carl needed someone to dog-sit while he went off to get fancy, last-ditch chemo down in the Lower 48. In Houston, probably.

I took a minute just to organize my face. "Get your animal," I said. "Get her back in the goddamn kennel and take her with you."

"Or what?" he said. "You'll hang her on a wolf peg?"

The cheapness of his comment released us both. I turned and went inside to not watch his truck peel down the driveway. Carl and I had always disagreed about the wolf room, which was the only thing that he, Lon, Skip, and my third husband, RT, might have ever had in common. None of them liked it, and I respected that. But it didn't mean I had to rip it out. I was proud of it. It was beautiful. It was mine.

Back in the kitchen, forty-five avocados sat on the counter, waiting. People wail about chain stores ruining the views in Anchorage, but if you lived through any part of the twentieth century up here, when avocados arrived off the barge, hard as the pit at their center, you relish each trip to the vast cinder-block box of dreams known as Costco. Every avocado I scooped out was packed with meat. Out it popped, one after another, like a creamy green baby butt headed to the bottom of the salad bowl.

Next mayonnaise, then mashing. I didn't hurry. Carl's dog needed to run off her panic and aggression. And I needed not to envision a wonderful, loving couple arriving for the open house —the husband in dungarees from the office, the wife in beat-up Xtratufs because she wanted to wade around and check out the dock for rot. Across the lawn they went, admiring the amazing lake views, telling Silver that the place was underpriced, actually, and sending their polite, unspoiled toddler to go catch minnows in the shallows. At which point Carl's dog charged in, fixated on a dragonfly she believed might be a mallard, knocking over the toddler and grinding him into the gravel beach.

I also needed not to think about Carl being sick, Carl not getting better, Carl having left, how I acted on the steps. He didn't have the money for a kennel, I suspected. Or for cancer. Mashing avocados helped. I mashed away, thinking how RT—a man I yelled at daily for three years just because he wasn't Carl—once said, "Maybe the reason you shout so much, Dutch, is that you really long to whisper."

RT was an orthodontist, a World War II model airplane builder, and an observant man. But all I thought at the time was that if Carl had realized about the shouting instead of RT, he and I might still be together.

Luckily I had moose ribs in the freezer. Labs are not spaniels or pointers, they don't have the upland sense of smell, and Carl's was deep in the alders. I couldn't call her over to my hand and grab her collar. She didn't know my voice, and I didn't know her name, and even if I had, a few hours in a kennel had no doubt left her suspicious of my motives. A rib tossed in the bushes and dragged in front of her nose, however, might kindle some interest.

My neighbor, Candace Goddard, was at home; I sighted her with the scope I kept in the kitchen. Candace's decor scheme is heavy on the chandeliers. Every room features at least one upside-down wedding cake made of cut-lead glass, and this was generally how I found her when I needed her. Where the crystals wink.

It was eleven, two hours before the open house, and she was still in her nightgown, bumping into furniture. By the time I got over there, she was playing acoustic guitar. The guitar was supposed to help with her anxiety when her husband, Rodge, flew off to go sheep hunting and forgot to check in by sat phone every three hours. Stopping to call home while halfway up a shale-covered peak under a sky so blue you taste the color in your lungs pretty much ruins the moment. Not surprisingly, Rodge often forgot.

Candace was fiddling around on the guitar, picking out some prelude number by Johann Sebastian Bach. Like more and more of the younger wives on the lake, she had dealt with turning forty by investing in injections that left her with a stunned, rubberized expression. Her hair is many, many shades of high-voltage blond. Her guitar playing, however, tells a different story. Listening to her is like listening to butterflies trip over each other's wings. You want them to flit around inside you for forever. This is one of the many reasons why we get along, and drive to book club together.

That day, unfortunately, the anxiety had gotten the upper hand. Her eyes were two dazzles of pupil. "Pills?" she said in her floaty voice. "What kind?"

"The sleepy kind," I said. "Enough for a seventy-pound—well —female."

"I think it's going to be fine, flying through the pass," she said. "What do you think?"

What I thought was that Rodge didn't put in enough flight hours, but he had a great touch with short landings, and the odds of him smashing his Cub into the side of a mountain were the same as anybody's: a matter of skill, luck, and weather.

It wasn't as if her concerns were that far-fetched. Flying in the wilderness, all your everyday, ordinary bullshit—being tired, being lazy, trusting the clouds instead of your instruments, losing your prescription sunglasses, forgetting to check your fuel lines—can kill you. And if it doesn't, a door can still blow off your plane and hit the tail or your kid can run between a brownie and her cub or your husband can slip on wet, frozen shale and fall a few thousand feet down a mountain, lose the pack and sat phone, break a leg, and that is that. Which is what you've got to live with, chandeliers or no chandeliers.

"I made him a checklist," she said as I rummaged through the bottles at the bottom of her Yves Saint Somebody purse. "Mixture. Prop. Master switch. Fuel pump. Throttle."

By the time she got to cowl flaps, I had long stopped listening. One of the biggest shames about Candace is that she still has a pilot's license. Her not flying, she said, started with kids, strapping them into their little car seats in back and realizing there was noth-ing—*nothing*—underneath them.

Sometimes I wish I had known her before that idea took hold.

"Play me a song, Candace," I said. "It'll make you feel better."

"You know what Rodge doesn't like?" she said.

"Natives," I said, because he doesn't. He got held up for a "travel tax" by one random Athabascan—on Athabascan land—and now he is one of those cocktail-party racists who like to pretend to talk politics just so they can slip in how the Natives and the Park Service have taken over the state. He and I nod to each other at homeowners association meetings and leave it at that.

"Anal sex," she said, her voice as light as chickweed pollen. "He won't even try it."

"Look," I said, holding up a pill bottle. "How many of these things did you take?"

"I could live without him," she said. "I know how to waitress. I could get the kids and me one of those cute little houses off O'Malley."

I had some idea of what she was doing, only because I had done it myself, which was leaving her husband in her mind in case he did die out in Brooks Range—which he wasn't going to—so that, hopefully, she'd fall apart a little less. But the thing about having gotten divorced four times and widowed once is that people forget you also got married each time. You and your soft, secret pink balloon of dreams.

"If you want anal sex, Candace," I said, "just drive yourself down to the Las Margaritas, pick some guy on his third tequila, and go for it. Just don't lose your house in the divorce like every other woman on this lake. Buy *him* out. Send him to some reasonably priced, brand-new shitbox in a subdivision. Keep your property."

Beneath her bronzer, Candace looked a little taken aback. "Gosh, Dutch," she said. "I didn't mean to make you upset."

I shook a bunch of bottles at her. "Which are the sleepiest?"

She pointed to a fat one with a tricky-looking cap. "Was it Benny?" she said. "Was it because I brought up crashing in the pass?"

"I'm having a bad day," I said, but only because there was no way to explain how I felt about Benny, my first husband, crashing his Super Cub, or about the search to find the wreckage, that smoking black hole in the trees. Even now, forty-one years later. The loneliness. The lostness. Not to mention what it had been like, being the first and only female homeowner on Diamond Lake.

If I had been cute and skinny and agreeable like Candace, it might have been easier. But I was me. The rolled eyes during votes, the snickers when I tried to advocate for trash removal or speed bumps, the hands, the lesbo jokes, the cigars handed to me in tampon wrappers—which I laughed about, seething, but smoked —I got through it all. What hurt the worst was the wives, all of them women I had known for years, who dropped me off their Fur Rondy gala list every time I was single. And stuck me back on when I wasn't.

Benny was a world-class outdoorsman and an old-school shot-gunner who did not believe in pretending that everybody got to make it to old age. On trips he took without me, he always said, "Dutch, if I don't come back, hold tight to Howl Palace."

Four-plus decades later, I still had my property, and it had come at a sizable cost. Wallace put me through a court battle after I left him for Carl. RT needed an all-cash payment to make him run away to Florida. Add to that Lon's rehab and Skip's long-term care. The Cub and the 185 were gone, all the life insurance money, the IRA. Howl Palace was all I had left. And now I had to sell it in order not to die in a state nursing home, sharing a room with some old biddy who liked to flip through scrapbooks and watch the boob tube with the volume cranked up high. You can't cry about these things. But you can't sit around and contemplate them either.

Luckily, Candace's youngest boy, Donald, turned up at the top of the stairs. His electronic slab was tucked under his arm. "Where's the charger, Mom?" he said.

"Donald," I said. "Let's go fish for a dog."

"Donald has asthma," said Candace. "He can't handle a lot of dander."

"Get your boots on, Don," I said. "You too, Candace."

"Really?" she said. "I get to come? Do I get to see the wolf room too?"

For all the obvious reasons, I don't like people on drugs in the wolf room. Or people with drinks, food, or mental issues. "If you help me with these safety caps," I said. "And fine-tune the dosage."

Donald was a little wheezy fellow, with glasses attached to a sporty wraparound strap that kept them stuck to his face. He knew how to hustle, though, and stuck to my side as I laid out the plan. Your mom's job, I said, is to crush up some medicine and roll the moose rib in it. Your job is to take the spin rod I give you and cast the moose rib at the end of the line into the bushes. Then slowly, *slowly* reel it in. The minute the dog bites on the rib, you sit tight, play her a little. We'll have only a few seconds for me to grab her by her collar. Then we'll stick her in the kennel with the rib. Nighty-night.

A few feet from the house, I got a feeling. It was a sucker-punch feeling—the grill. I started running. Donald ran too, the way kids will, without asking questions, as if there might be matches and boxes of free Roman candles at end of it.

"Hey, guys?" said Candace. "Wait up." In her peaceful, free-wheeling frame of mind, she had put on Rodge's size 12 boots.

The last few feet of the path I kept telling myself that I would not have taken the meat out and left it by the grill, that I would have not put the dishcloth over it to keep the flies off, that I could have, for some reason, left the meat in the fridge, even though everyone knows that meat can't be slapped cold on a hot fire, it needs to mellow out at room temperature. Except that I knew exactly what I had done and why I had done it—believing, at the time, that I didn't own a dog.

I also knew what I was going to find, even as I ran through the backyard finding it: bits of gnawed plastic and butcher paper pinwheeling all over the grass. Here a chunk of hot dog casing, there a lump of caribou burger. Blood juice dripped down the steps. The grill lay on its side, propane flames still burning blue.

I knelt down and turned off the valve. The birches were in their last, tattered days of September green. A leaf whirled down and landed by my foot. It was small, the yellow so fresh and bright it belonged on a bird.

"Dutch," said Donald. "I saw her! She ran right by me."

"Don't chase her," I said. "She'll think it's a game." I stayed down there with the leaf, just for a few minutes. Hiding. The leaf had the tiniest edge of dead brown.

Footsteps thunked across the deck. Carl's footsteps. Carl's boots. He had not taken off and left me with the dog apocalypse. This was so unlike him, it took me a little longer than it should have to understand. "Your animal," I said, "ate sixty pounds of meat."

"Most of it she threw up," he said. "By the looks of the grass."

"I have an open house, Carl." The flies were moving in—a throbbing blanket of vicious, busy bottle green. With the sun out, the smell would be next.

"I could always run to Costco. Pick us up some steaks."

He said this kindly, but steaks were not what I wanted. And there was no way to explain what I wanted, which was everything the way it was before, years before. Neighbors in the backyard. Charcoal smoke. Bug dope. A watermelon. People showing up with a casserole, leaving with their laughter and wet hair after a dip in the hot tub. Whatever my private upheavals, there was always that, at least.

A duck paddled past my dock, blown over by the current that was ruffling the surface. I missed wind socks. Everybody on Diamond Lake used to have a rainbow wind sock tied to their deck. It added a cheerful note to the shoreline.

"I had her by the woodpile," said Carl. "But she gave me the slip."

"I think you should go," I said. "Just go get your flight."

He shrugged, scratched a bit of dry skin on his neck. "I can get another."

"Right," I said. "The fishing trip to Houston."

He looked at me, as if ashamed, and I felt a little bad about calling him on his lie. As far he, I, and everyone we knew understood Houston, it wasn't even a city, just a mythical, cutting-edge treatment center, the Shangri-la of last-hope clinical trials. You went there to get a few more months to not die.

"Well," he said, "you got me, Dutch." He laughed. I didn't. Another leaf blazed down toward us. Fall lasts for weeks now—which, despite my best efforts, still befuddles me. All my life, fall took about three days in August, the leaves dropping almost overnight, followed by a licorice snow taste in the wind. Global warming, the papers say, though almost all the articles talk about are the dying caribou and the starving puffins, never the less obvious, alarming changes of every day—and the guilt about living in an oil state that goes along with it. As if the rest of the country, sucking up all that oil and burning all that coal, isn't also to blame.

Donald ran by us, headed for the water with a moose rib in his fist. Candace followed with my snow shovel and a garbage bag. She was still in her nightgown. Watching her try to scoop raw-meat dog vomit off the grass while wearing a gauzy orgasm of white chiffon was one of the more moving experiences of my life. She really did want to help.

I sat down on the steps. Carl sat next to me, close, then an inch closer. "Dutch," he said. "What a fucking corner we have found ourselves in."

I smiled. It felt like a small, broken snowflake in the middle of my face. There was a list of questions I was supposed to ask: what kind, what stage, what organ, herbal teas, protein smoothies? Instead an image floated through my mind. His trailer. His kitchen. The byzantine mobile-home cabinetry. For each of the six days that we lived together, I lay there in bed every morning, watching Carl make coffee, memorizing where he had stuck the cups, the creamer, the filters, so that I could make the coffee for us one day—an idea that made me so happy I had to shut my eyes and pretend to be asleep.

It was September then too. Mushrooms bloomed in the corners of the walls. Carl scraped them down with a pocketknife he wiped clean with a chamois. We made spaghetti and played gin rummy and dragged ourselves out of bed only for glasses of cold well water. I was careful where I left my clothes, though, careful not to leave them on the floor where they would take up room. I had left Wallace. And the dog. And even Howl Palace.

On the morning of the seventh day, Carl sat me down and said, in the stiff, unsettled way he had adopted the minute I arrived, "It's just that I didn't know it'd be so close."

"Me neither," I said, still thinking he was talking about square footage.

How lonely it had to be, to realize that the only resource he had left—besides his trailer and a few truly world-class stuffed rainbows —was me. Maybe getting sick had made Carl softer. Maybe this was why he had shown up. Maybe this was why he had not left, despite my need for him, as fresh and pathetic as ever. The idea broke my heart, and into that jagged, bleak crevasse all my fears rushed to fill the gap.

"I'm out of money," I said. "Just so you know. In terms of helping you with your deductibles."

He looked at me—puzzled, or maybe stunned.

"Out-of-network is expensive," I said. "That's how it is, I hear, down in Houston."

"Dutch," he said. "And you wonder why we always go to shit." He stood up. He started walking down the backyard toward the dock, where Donald was standing with the rib tied to a length of frayed plastic rope he had found in the snow-machine shed.

"Wait," I said, standing up. "I'll keep your stupid dog."

"I don't want your money," he said. "And you don't even like her."

"Sure I do," I said. "She's kind of spirited, that's all."

"What's her name?" he said, not stopping, not slowing down in the least.

"Rita," I said. All his dogs were named Rita, one after another.

He stopped to scrape some dog puke off the bottom of his boot. But he waved. "I call her Pinkie," he said. "After your secret balloon of dreams."

That was how I knew it was the last time we would see each other. Carl always liked to leave me a little more in love with him than ever.

*

Even before the open house was officially open, people were pulling into the driveway, clutching phones. Silver had hosed down the backyard and sprinkled baking soda all over the grass. There was nothing left to do, she said, but hope for the best. One of her ways of hoping was to stick Donald down on the dock with his rib and his rope, where he would look like an imaginative, playful boy. Calling to his dog. Possibly homeschooled.

Candace was subject to a similar redecoration. Silver laid her in a deck lounger under a blanket, so it would look like she was just dozing, enjoying the sun. I sat beside her for a while, wishing she could get herself upright enough to come up to the wolf room with me, the way she had always wanted and the way I was finally ready to let her—high or sober or even just a little brain-dead from the chemicals. Carl was gone. I had no one. All over again.

I did consider pouring water on her face. But she was curled up on her side, her hands tucked under her cheek—not because her high had brought out the child in her, I saw only at that moment, but because the child kept surfacing despite the pills she took to keep it asleep.

There was nothing to do but tuck her in under the blanket and take the back stairs, which are the only stairs up to the wolf room. The air in there is climate-controlled and smells just faintly of cedar from the paneling. I sat down in the middle of the skins, tried to look dignified, and waited.

A young couple with matching glasses stopped in the doorway, looked in—politely, alarmed—and wandered off. Over and over, this happened for the next few hours. A couple with fake tans. A couple with a baby. A couple with man buns, both of them. Single people and old people, apparently, do not buy houses at my price point. Every time another couple turned up, I told myself to smile. Or invite them inside. Or leave so they could marvel at it openly. Or disparage it. Or discuss their plans to replace it with a master bath.

Silver had told me that it was better for the closing price if the owner went out for lunch at a nice, expensive restaurant with a friend. Now I knew why. Nobody was being unkind, but you couldn't tell, just by looking at it, that the wolf room used to be a nursery. That's what it said on the plans that Benny and I ordered from Sears. The baby for the nursery didn't work out, the way it doesn't for some people. And so Benny and I did other things. He was tight with the Natives, as we called every tribe back then, as if they were all one big happy family or we just couldn't bother to learn the phonetics. He had grown up in the village of Kotzebue, the son of the Methodist missionaries who had tried to convert Inupiat and gotten confused about their life's agenda. The Arctic Circle is not the place to go if you have even the slightest existential question.

That was something Benny always said. He knew Alaska better than me, mostly because I showed up on a ferry at age five, with a baby-blue Samsonite and a piece of cardboard hanging from my neck: FLIGHT TRANSFER TO ANCHORAGE. DELIVER TO MRS. AURORA KING. My parents had died in a head-on crash outside Spokane. Aunt Aurora was my nearest relative.

Aunt Aurora was a second-grade teacher in the downtown school district. She was deeply into young girls being educated in the ways of our Lord, and I met Benny at yet another Sunday at United Methodist. I was seventeen. He grabbed me the last short-bread cookie at coffee hour and spilled tea on his flannel shirt so we would have matching stains.

A week later he took me to the Garden of Eatin', which was located in a Quonset hut in a part of Anchorage I had never been to. It was the fanciest place I had ever eaten in my life. Tablecloths on every table. Real napkins. We ate Salisbury steak and vanilla ice cream and I was careful not to lick my plate. Two months later we were married.

Benny loved me, but he also loved men. He was not that different from a lot of guides and hunters at that time. They wanted to be out in the wilderness with another man without anybody seeing. For weeks. For whole summers. He never lied about it and I never asked beyond the minimum and we never discussed it. We understood what marriage was—the ability to hold hands and not try to forgive the other person, not try to understand them, just hold hands.

After my fifth miscarriage, they removed my entire reproductive system while I was asleep and couldn't stop them. As soon as I was well enough to sit up, Benny dumped his shotgun buddy—a guy he had been affectionate with, in secret, since high school—and took me up to the snowfields to go after wolves.

"You have to have a taste for it," he said my first time. How else could he explain why you would shove your gun out of the open window of a single-prop plane drilling hell for the horizon, your face a mask of eyes and ice, your hands so cold that when you aimed for the animal fleeing across the white, your fingers did not move the way they were supposed to. Or mine didn't. The first time, I cut my finger on the window latch and had to pull back on the trigger still slick with my own blood.

It was warm blood, at least. And I was alive. Despite any wish I might have had to be otherwise. Which was maybe what Benny was trying to show me.

Most of this is to say that despite the local gossip, the wolf room was probably smaller than anybody at my open house expected. There are no windows. There is no furniture save 387 individually whittled pegs. On each peg hangs a pelt, most of them silver, black-tipped fur. Others reddish brown. The ones staple-gunned to the ceiling are all albino white. The ones laid down on the floor are all females, with tails that can trip you if you don't watch out, though no one watches out. Walking into the wolf room is like walking into a forest of fur. Or a feathery winter silence that lets your brain finally go quiet.

"You'll never trust anyone like you trust your shotgun buddy," Benny told me the night before my first hunt. Though he did not say it, he was speaking about his shotgun buddy and how much he missed him and who I had to be for Benny from there on out.

Our fire was huge and fantastical in the flat white dark. I was afraid of the morning and what might happen, and I wasn't wrong to be afraid. Shotgunning, as shooter, you have to aim into the wind and snow behind you—the plane going faster than the racing pack—while compensating for the dive of the plane at the same time, so that you not only don't miss the wolf but also don't get disoriented and shoot the propeller. And kill you both. Up front, the pilot has to get so low to the ground and swoop at such radical angles to keep up with the pack—who keep spreading out over the snow like dots of quicksilver from a broken thermometer —but not stall and crash. And kill you both.

"Think about it this way," said Benny. "We live or die together." I was nineteen by then and he was the age I am now—sixty-seven. I held on to his words as though they were special to our situation, not an agreement you enter into with every person you ever care about. Even just in passing.

Thousands of feet above Howl Palace, Carl was on his way to

Seattle, where, changing planes for Houston, he bought a balloon for a girl in a gift shop who was being rude to her mother. Downstairs, Candace was stumbling through some demonstration of my dimmers in the dining room, while her future next-door neighbor—Californian, all-cash, above asking—was pretending concern about "the whole hot tub mold problem." A poorly constructed staircase below, Silver was sitting in the clamshell grotto, dipping her toes in the fountain, surrendering to what she felt, at that moment, was a lost commission.

Outside, at the far end of the dock, Donald went on tossing out his rope, calling out across the water, "Here, Pinkie. Here, Pinkie," his voice squeaky with anticipation, his casts surprisingly sure-handed.

Pinkie, I almost told him, was long past coming to anybody. Pinkie was charging down the shoreline, trampling kiddie pools and sprinklers, digging into professional-grade landscaping while mothers chased after her with shovels and fathers contemplated lawsuits and the implications of lawsuits at the homeowners association meeting—all of which they could avoid if they just jumped in the plane and took off for a few hours to remember why they had moved to Alaska in the first place.

The wind died down. Rainbows slicked along the shallows, bright with the smell of avgas and algae. Donald hardly noticed when I sidled up beside him, so intent was he on his task. He tossed out another cast—a perfect one, ending in a satisfying *thunk* as the rib hit the surface of water. He cast again. And cast again. "Pinkie!" he said, unable even now to give up.

The Nine-Tailed Fox Explains

FROM *Witness*

I.

I MARRIED THE wrong mortal, I see that now.

I must be getting careless in my advanced age. I would never have made that mistake during the era of Shang, those silken days and pavilioned evenings. Dancing and verse and music, so much music. Every night we watched the moon floating in the lakes like a treasure to be netted and wished this would never end; I did, anyway. The celestial blush of the peaches we ate, twisted off the branches as they ripened; nothing like the specimens you find at Whole Foods, trucked from one coast to another to be stacked into mealy pyramids.

But then, in the era of Shang, such a mistake would have lost me everything. The world I am in now is far more forgiving, even for fox spirits.

My husband is in love with his best friend, who is in love with a boy she met eighteen months ago outside an art museum when she dropped a glove on the street and he snatched it up and ran after her. I can't tell whether either my husband or his best friend knows this, the fact of his love, which shimmers in his hair and on his hands like deep-sea phosphorescence: the way he watches her walk across the room; the way he listens to her speak as if he's listening as much to the sounds of her voice as to what she's saying. It seems obvious, but mortals can be purposefully dense at times.

What I can tell, because she might as well have tattooed it across her skeptical brow, is that the best friend doesn't like me. She believes that I'm in it for the prize of living in her leaking cruise liner of a country: why else would I travel seven thousand miles from China to marry a man I've never met? It's a fair question.

I realized this about my husband at a house party instigated by my husband's friends so they could find out who my husband had married. Something else I learned there: that a *house party* in Brooklyn, New York, the United States of America, circa early-2000s AD, refers to a mortal gathering in an undersized apartment where people drink microbrewery beer, smoke low-grade marijuana, and comment ironically on television shows, politics, and each other's lifestyle choices. The music is prerecorded, adrift like a ghost through the rooms, and its disembodied singers are blasé about enunciation. *This is very charming,* I said to my husband, and he glanced at me as if he thought I was being sarcastic or perhaps had confused my adjectives.

My husband had told me about this group of friends—how they met in college, how they talked each other into moving to New York afterward, how they didn't hang out that much anymore but would always be close because of everything they knew about each other, because they had seen each other become the persons they were now. "They will want to meet you," he kept saying, in a way that made it clear he was aware such a meeting would be inevitable but he would continue to delay it for as long as he could. They knew he was married because he had texted their chat group the day we went to City Hall. At first they responded with raised-eyebrow and eye-rolling emojis; and then, after he sent them a selfie of us holding up our marriage certificate, they started calling. He turned off his phone. "In case you haven't noticed," he said as we exited the city clerk's office through a side door, ignoring the men standing on the sidewalk with cameras, who asked us if we wanted to have our picture taken for a fee, "I'm bad at confrontation." I understood: he was embarrassed. Not of me, but of himself, and how we had met.

My husband's best friend is part of the group. For several years my husband shared an apartment with her, and then she met the boy who retrieved her glove and they began dating and eventually moved in together. Until the party I knew nothing more about her.

My husband never spoke of her except when he had to in order to explain chronology or why there was a wooden salt shaker with a girl's laser-cut likeness in the back of a kitchen cabinet (she kept the pepper shaker, which had his likeness). From his silence alone I should have guessed.

The boy my husband's best friend is dating is a musician. He plays the viola in a chamber music group, and he teaches at a music school that I could tell was famous from the diffident way he said it. He was the gentlest person at the party. I couldn't help myself; I asked if he had ever heard of the *pipa*. He hadn't, of course, so I told him about it, its strings and frets, the curvature of its neck and body, the resemblance to the Occidental guitar—and, for that matter, the viola. I knew the finest *pipa* player in China, I said. Her playing could move kings and demons. I noticed he was starting to look uncomfortable. Figuratively speaking, I said.

My husband's best friend came up to us and cinched an arm around the musician's waist. If she were a spirit she would be a hound, salivatingly vigilant about marking her territory. "What are you talking about?" she asked.

A friend I left behind, I said, and just to be able to invoke my knowledge of her felt like a gift I didn't deserve, even after all this time.

Toward the end of the party I indulged my curiosity and let myself listen to what everyone else was saying about me.

In the far corner of the living room, where my husband was standing with the boy he played Dungeons & Dragons with, I heard: "Dude, she is ridiculously fucking hot." In the kitchen the host of the party asked, "How long do you give it?" Outside the building the host's fiancé lit a cigarette—I heard the silvery scratch of the lighter's wheel—and said, "That's a desperate move, ordering a wife off Amazon."

The best friend, in the kitchen: "I can't answer that question. It's too depressing." Dungeons & Dragons boy: "The other women on the website—did they all look like that?" Outside, the autumnal scent of smoke curling through the halogen-tinted night as the girl who was visiting from Michigan—and the pretext for the party —said, "I don't know. I mean, she looks like a supermodel. And her English is really good." (I learned the language from a British missionary during the time of the Opium Wars. In exchange I liberated him from all that nonsense about original sin.)

The best friend again: "You know what's the worst part? That he felt he needed to do something like that to be happy. Or less unhappy, at least."

The musician: "What about her?"

And my husband, he said nothing at all.

One version of what happened: my husband wanted a wife and he went to a website offering to match Asian women with American men. Maybe he bought into the submissive-Oriental myth, or he calculated that he would have higher odds this way of landing someone ridiculously fucking hot, to borrow his friend's phrase.

Another version: I was searching for a way to escape the short straw of the birthright lottery that I had drawn. My husband is the patsy, and once I get my green card I will leave.

Here's a third version. As a demon spirit, I can only tether myself to this mortal world with a human life. The unfortunate side effect, for this human, is that he forfeits half of all the time he spends with me—but mortal lives are so brief anyway, what's a lost decade or two?

And a fourth. I wanted to leave China but wasn't sure where to go, so I let fate decide. I used to despise fate, that self-absorbed, incompetent cosmic bureaucrat, but now it's a relief to abdicate responsibility. I created profiles on nine matchmaker websites —seduction is my skill set, after all—and waited. When my husband contacted me I could smell the spoor of his loneliness, and I thought, *This one. This one I can help.*

There are as many versions of this story as there are ways to lose the thing you want most in the world.

II.

I suspect that as a result of being effectively immortal—assuming of course that I have a mortal handy, but that's never been an issue for me—I experience time differently from most. It's come to feel a little like walking in circles, always in one direction, through a vast landscape. I can never turn around, but after a while I start seeing the same sights all over again. Mostly it's the green indifference of grasslands, swaths of time vanishing without my even noticing; but now and then I hit a cliff, or a chasm, and I have to pick out my path the way mortals do.

My American adventure is shaping up to be one of those obstacle courses. It's been a while. I did my best to ignore altogether the period of time that the mortals refer to as the twentieth century. The European and Japanese invasions were depressing enough, but what ensued after the Chinese had banished all the barbarians and had no one to set upon except themselves was enough to make me weep, once or twice. (Whenever I did I made sure to save my tears and seal them in vials smelted for me by the greatest silversmith of Han. We don't like to advertise this—it undermines our image—but the tears of a demon spirit are almost as valuable as a C-list deity's blessing.)

The Long March, the Great Leap Forward, the Cultural Revolution. Human labels for inhuman events. I thought maybe I would wait for China to break apart and reforge itself, the way it always has. But when the beasts with metal claws arrived at the base of my mountain, and the men in their bright yellow helmets, I knew it was time. I've seen enough conquering armies to recognize when they will be victorious.

III.

My own group of friends, from the era of Shang: a nine-headed pheasant and a jade *pipa*. I know, not the company one would expect a self-respecting nine-tailed fox to keep—and I must admit I was a little standoffish at first. Foxes hunt pheasants, after all; and who the hell had ever heard of a *pipa* spirit? But it turns out, conspiring to destroy a dynasty by seducing its emperor is a remarkable bonding experience.

I don't know when I began to watch her walk across the room, to listen to the low, liquid sounds of her voice when she spoke. Once we were behind the partition undressing for the emperor and I couldn't look away from the luminous curve of her back. That night the emperor chose her and I almost killed him in nine different ways: my claws in his eyes, my tails around his neck, my teeth everywhere. When I remember that now I think the full moon must have maddened me. Throwing aside our mission, spiting the reason we had been sparked into being, not to mention irretrievably pissing off our goddess—for what? This sudden, inexplicable sensation of a stone being rolled onto my chest, as if there could be any stone in the world heavy enough to contain me.

Except. As he led her into his bedchamber, she glanced at me over her shoulder like she knew what I was thinking, and she wished that I had.

I do know when: the first time she played for the royal court. She held her instrument like a lover and music spun from her fingers like shining bolts of silk, colors never before seen. She bound us all right where we sat. The emperor was enchanted, exactly as we intended, and it made me sick.

Afterward I asked her about the song she had played and she said she had made it up, thinking about the mountains where she was from. *I thought,* I said, and then paused, conscious of my ignorance in a way I had never been before. *I didn't think you were from anywhere.*

She smiled and I wanted to touch my finger to the dimple in her cheek. *I decided I was,* she said. *You and Pheasant should try it. Just because we are spirits doesn't mean we have to remain unmoored.*

All the things I could have said then. That us being spirits could mean nothing else. That there was no concept of choice in what we did. That thinking of ourselves as anything other than the tools of a goddess's vengeance was A Very Bad Idea.

Tell me about your mountains, I said.

This was what we were: Nüwa's soldiers, imperial concubines, demon spirits. If there was space within those corseted certainties for anything else, we didn't know it. I spent three hundred years meditating in the drippiest cave in Guizhou (long story) before it occurred to me: friends, that was what we had been, the fox, the pheasant, and the *pipa.* So simple, and so grand. The only ones I would ever have. By then we had made it into the myths and the histories, immortalized that way as well, even if none of the stories ever asked what we wanted. Which, to be fair, I couldn't have answered anyway, not at the time. Everything I felt I ascribed to the darkness shifting beneath my borrowed skin. Just because we were indestructible didn't mean we had a clue.

But each night after the emperor fell asleep she and I would walk together in the palace gardens, beneath the red haloes of the lanterns strung from the peach trees, between trellises of jasmine and beds of chrysanthemums that marked their sweet, blossomy scents on our skin, across the bridges spanning the gardens' seven ceremonial lakes. I have never been so aware of time as I was in the shadow of those hours, wandering barefoot through grass or snow, my hand in hers. I remember thinking, more than once, that this must be what it was like to be mortal—constantly haunted by how quickly you were losing time when you had so little of it—and that it was terrible.

What secret are you and Pipa *keeping?* the pheasant asked once. *I see you leave every night.*

We go on walks, I said. *Since we don't need to sleep, it seems like a waste otherwise.*

The pheasant tilted her head and I saw the glowing outlines of her spirit-self in the air above her. *Waste of what?*

I said, not knowing what else to say, *Our time together.*

You sound almost like one of them, said the pheasant.

After Shang collapsed she said to me, *We don't have to go back to Nüwa. We can just—be.*

Her eyes flashed jade-green and I felt as if I was falling from an immense height, but at the bottom there could be nothing but darkness.

So we returned to Nüwa's temple, and our goddess condemned us for our cruelty. *That was how you made us,* I wanted to say, *unable to take a step within the mortal realm without human sacrifice. And also —you ordered us to overthrow a dynasty. Did you really think we could get that done without collateral damage?* Of course I said nothing: it was our destiny.

I expected Nüwa to unmake us the way she had made us, with a long-suffering sigh and a flick of her fingers. Instead she packed the three of us off to hell posthaste so others could do her dirty work. In the first court the Yama king ordered his guards to take each of us in turn to the Mirror of Retribution, to commence our separate trials. They took the pheasant away first, with her bead-

black eyes and that proud tilt of her head. When the guards returned the *pipa* took my hand for a moment. Her fingers were cool
and calloused, and I thought of glimmering nights, moon-watching,
the songs she had played only for me. I had no words for what I
wanted to tell her. They led her out of the room and I listened
until I could no longer hear the press of her footsteps across the
black rocks of the underworld. Above us a hundred years passed
and all the mortals we had known were rotting into the ground.

In the tenth and final court of hell I refused to drink the tea of
forgetfulness. The Yama king was disarmingly kind. *You will not be
able to reincarnate unless you do,* he said.

I know, I said, *but there are things I need to remember.*

The Yama king shrugged. *Your loss.*

It didn't work, by the way, not really. By the time I found the mountains she had imagined for herself, I had forgotten all her songs.

IV.

I've tracked her down twice in the past three thousand years.

Once: the third wife of a nobleman in the era of Tang, jade pins
in the black brilliance of her hair, jasmines and chrysanthemums
embroidered along the hems of her dresses. A gifted *pipa* player
who performed only for her husband. Her feet had been broken
and bound since she was six, and so she had to be carried in a pa-
lanquin whenever she left the house. She died in childbirth.

And again: a peasant soldier in Mao's army as it shambled west
and north from Jiangxi to Shaanxi, shedding skeletons and scru-
ples along the way. Dirt seamed into her skin, lice crowning her
hair, her eyes flashing with the conviction of another impossible
dream. She had never heard the sounds of a *pipa*. A hundred miles
from their final destination a cut in her sole became infected—by
then they were walking through mountains and swamps with rags
wrapped around their feet—and she died two days before they
reached Yan'an, where the march would be declared a victory and
the Great Leader would commence the next phase of his project
to hollow out the heart of China.

I did what I could—her husband never hit her when he was
drunk, unlike with his other wives; foraging in the fields and the

forests she always found more than anyone else in her unit—but for the most part I could only watch. The absurd frailty of humans, dying from the instant they are born.

Still, on balance, maybe she made the better choice: free to try, and try again. I'm the one left chasing a backward glance, a hand pulling away from mine, an unmade promise, across the underside of history.

V.

A couple of hundred years ago, as part of my English-language education, the British missionary made me read the Bible. Mostly I found it dull—too little magic, and none of the demons aside from Lucifer had any personality—but the story of Judas enraged me. *How was that fair?* I asked the missionary: *obviously Judas was only acting as Jesus had instructed. The man obeys his god and for that he suffers the brand of the eternal traitor?* I was so upset I refused to read any more for weeks. The missionary was alarmed by my vehemence, but also heartened—this was when he still held out hope of saving me, and he mistook bitterness for belief.

My husband's best friend wants to get me a job. Her cousin is the director of a language school in midtown and they're looking for people to teach Chinese, Beijing accent preferred. "Is that something you might be interested in?" asks my husband. I can see that he's not sure why his best friend has taken it upon herself to secure me gainful employment, and I want to tell him that it's because he belongs to her and she's guarding her territory, which now, by extension, encompasses me. I dislike the Beijing accent, which sounds like the speaker is looking down their nose at you and pinching it at the same time, but I say, "Yes. Please thank her for me."

Most of my students are in finance and corporate law, learning the language because China is where fortunes are made now, once again. They want to know how to say things like *conference call* and *preferred equity* and *share purchase agreement* in Mandarin. Just say it in English with a Chinese accent, I tell them.

There are a few exceptions. I have a student whose parents were prominent Communists until they fell from favor during the Cultural Revolution. They came here as asylum seekers and settled in a small town in Ohio, one of only two Asian families. My student's parents learned English, adopted Western names, attended church, worked as dishwashers and house-cleaners, and never spoke to their daughter about anything that predated their arrival in America. Now they're getting older, and she wants to ask them about the history they cut themselves out of when they left China. *Why?* I ask, reminding her to answer in Mandarin. She says, with her atrocious midwestern accent, "It's mine as well." She hopes (switching back to English) that it will make her feel more substantial in this land, which is the only one she has ever known but has never quite felt like enough.

Another student is dating a girl who moved to the United States from Shanghai when she was thirteen, and even though that was two decades ago he believes he will never be able to fully understand this girl unless he can understand the language in which she was formed. "She still dreams in Chinese," he says, and then asks, almost like a test, "What language do you dream in?" I tell him the truth, that I don't dream. "Everyone dreams," he says. "You just forget when you wake up."

During one of my lunch breaks I visit the art museum, the one that served as the austere white backdrop for my husband's best friend's happiness. Most of the artwork looks like it was created by savage children, but there is one that I circle back to, once, twice, and then one more time again before I leave. It's a painting of the interior of a New York movie theater, during a time when they were lush and ornate, curtained and chandeliered, palaces in their own fashion. But the focus of the painting is on the woman in an usher's uniform who stands at the side, leaning against the wall. She's not looking at the screen—probably she's seen this movie a hundred times by now—but into the glowing darkness where the audience sits. Her hair is golden and her gaze is private, and I wonder about what she is thinking. I'm not sure what it is that moves me so—but maybe that's not important; what matters is that I'm still capable of being moved.

The morning I leave my husband is still asleep. The light floods our room yellow through the window, and I imagine the city outside melting like an epic sculpture of butter. New York in the summer: worse than the Gobi Desert. My husband is snoring in that quiet, mannered way he has, as if apologetic about disturbing me. It's funny how quickly you can get used to some things. The length of time I have spent with this mortal is a single pleat in an ocean, but for a while after this I think I will feel . . . unmoored, as my dearest friend put it—without that sound, or the stubborn bassline of his human heart keeping count for us both.

Before I go I whisper in his ear that his best friend will not stay with the musician. The musician doesn't know her and he never will, not the way my husband does. I tell him to drink the glass of water that I have left for him on the bedside table, into which I have emptied the contents of one of my silver vials.

When he wakes he will believe that I have left because, having conned my way into America, it is easier to disappear than to continue with the sham. One more minor act of villainy to tack onto my record. He will drink the glass of water because it is there and he is thirsty, and then he will go to his best friend's house and tell her that he loves her. I don't know what she will say to him, but at least I will have given him the words.

ALEJANDRO PUYANA

The Hands of Dirty Children

FROM *American Short Fiction*

WE'RE CALLED THE Crazy 9, but there are not always nine of us. We were nine before la policía took Tuki. We called him Tuki because he loved to dance all weird. Every time he heard the tuki-tuki of electronic music, he flailed his arms and raised his knees like some sort of strange bird. Tuki was funny but a little mean. I miss him, but not too much.

I feared we would be seven soon. Ramoncito hadn't been feeling well, throwing up everywhere. He smelled really bad because he pooped his pants the other day and hadn't been able to find new ones, so we didn't like to stand next to him. Or sometimes we made fun of him and yelled, "Ramoncito, pupusito!" and everyone laughed and laughed and laughed, but inside I wasn't laughing too hard; inside I felt bad. When the others were asleep, I pinched my nose with my finger and thumb and went to Ramoncito. I used to bring him something to eat too, but the last two times he threw up right after, so I didn't bring him food anymore—why waste it, is what I say—but I still asked, "How are you feeling, Ramoncito?" and "Is there anything I can do, Ramoncito?" My voice sounded funny because of the nose pinch, and sometimes he smiled. Before, he would talk to me a little, but now he didn't talk much. He could still walk around and go with us on our missions, but he was very slow. His eyes were sleepy all the time, and they looked like they were sinking into his skull. But we also laughed at him because he's the youngest, only seven and a half, and everyone always gives the youngest a hard time. I was the youngest before Ramoncito came along, but even if Ramoncito didn't last much longer, the others wouldn't treat me like the youngest because I was the one that found the knife, and I'm the best at using it.

Here is what the Crazy 9 love.

We love our name, and we won't change it, even if we are really eight, or seven—we love it because it sounds crazy and because we scrawl it all over the place—when we find spray cans, or markers, or pens.

We love the knife. We found it one night after running away from the lady who wouldn't give us any money, so we pushed her and took her purse. As we gathered to inspect our loot on the banks of the Güaire River, I pulled it from a secret pocket, shiny and dangerous. We love to take turns and unfold the blade from its wooden handle and scream, "Give me all your money!" but we are just practicing. I carry the knife most of the time because I found it, but also because I can throw it at a tree and almost always get it to stick, and I can also throw it in the air and almost always catch it by the handle without cutting my hand.

We love Pollos Arturos, it's everyone's favorite, but we almost never get to have any, because if the guard sees us he screams and chases us away—but sometimes we will beg and someone will give us a wing. One time Ramoncito got a leg, but that was before he was throwing up. He got a leg because the youngest always does the best begging. But we have rules in the Crazy 9, so we didn't take the leg away from Ramoncito. He ate it all by himself.

We love going to the protests. We don't go to the front too much because that's where the police fight the protesters—the protesters wear their T-shirts tight around their faces, or they make gas masks out of junk, or they wear bicycle helmets and carry wooden and zinc shields with the colors of the flag painted on them; they throw mostly rocks at the police, but sometimes they shoot fireworks at them. One of them holds the cohetón parallel to the ground—aimed straight at the line of men in their green uniforms and their plastic shields and their big shotguns—while another lights the fuse. They only let it go when the whistling is loud, and we think they might be holding on to it for too long, long enough for it to explode in their hands, but then we see it fly like a comet straight into the green and plastic wall of soldiers that stands down the road. We always cheer when we see that.

Sometimes we stand next to them and yell at the police. We

wrap our T-shirts around our faces and scream "¡Viva Venezuela!" and "¡Abajo Maduro!" and jump and throw rocks. It's fun, except for when the tear gas comes and we have to run away or else cough and cough and cry and cry. But we mostly stay at the back of the protests because we can beg or steal better. Because the women are there, or the older men, or the cowards that don't want to fight in the front, like us. The begging is good at the protests. The lady will see us and tell her friend in the white shirt and the base-ball cap with the yellow, blue, and red of the flag, "Our country is gone, isn't it? Poor child. I swear, chama, I don't remember it ever being this bad!" That's the moment when I try them, and most of the time I get a few bolivares. But we have rules in the Crazy 9, so we always share the money we get from begging or stealing.

We love each other. We say "Crazy 9 forever!" and exchange manly hugs. I love that feeling you get when you hug someone and you mean it. But it also makes me remember things I don't like remembering, so let's not talk about that.

We love mangos! Mangos are our favorite because they are sweet and they are free. We walk down the nice streets, the ones that have the big trees on them, and I pull the bottom of my shirt away from my tight belly, and Ramoncito follows me, placing man-gos from the ground inside it, the ones that aren't nasty. After we are finished, when my shirt is as filled as the grocery bags the rich ladies carry when we beg outside the Excelsior GAMA, we walk all bowlegged and tired to an alley and eat mangos until night. We eat until our whole faces are yellow and mango hair grows between our teeth. We eat until each of us has a mountain of mango pits, and all we can smell is the sweet rot of the mango slime, and the flies start to go crazy. But that was before, when Ramoncito could still walk behind me and pick up mangos. When there were man-gos to pick up. Now the mango trees give nothing but shade. And now we are very hungry.

There's a dumpster in Chacao that is the best dumpster. It is hid-den in an alley behind the old market. It is the best because there's usually good food and there are also juice boxes and liter bottles of Pepsi that sometimes have some liquid still in them. One day we filled a whole Pepsi bottle with all of the remainders—it tasted a little bit like orange and a little bit like Pepsi, and I told the rest of the guys, I told them, "When I grow up I'm going to invent drinks.

And the first one is going to be orange juice and Pepsi, and I'm going to call it the Crazy 9," and everyone agreed that it was a great idea as we passed the bottle in a big circle.

When we woke up, Tomás, who is our leader because he is the oldest and the fastest, told us, "We are going to our dumpster today." Whenever he talks I stare at his upper lip, with thin strands of black hair sprouting like seedlings. And it's not the only place where his hair is coming in. When it rains, we all get naked and wash ourselves and our clothes. He's the only one with hair down there. Well, a few of the others have some, but Tomás has at least three times as much.

It was a pretty morning, with rays coming down at us from between the openings of the highway bridge above. They made columns of light so thick I felt the urge to climb them. It felt nice after the cold night, so cold we huddled together—all except Ramoncito because Comiquita, with his cartoon-looking face, said, "Not Ramoncito Pupusito, he stinks!" We could hear the birds, even through the rumbling of the cars that rolled above us. The river was high and running fast. I liked it like that because it didn't smell as bad. It was still brown and had trash floating on it, but if I closed my eyes and just listened to the water and the birds, I could pretend I was anywhere else.

It was a long walk to the dumpster, and Ramoncito didn't look good. His cheeks sank into his face, his skin was flaky, like when you have mud on you and it dries and you can scratch it off with your fingernails. I sat next to him, and I didn't have to pinch my nose anymore, because I had gotten used to the smell. I said, "Wake up, Ramoncito," and I stroked his hair as he moaned. Ramoncito's fallen hair tangled around my dirty fingers.

"Wake up, Ramoncito!" I pushed him harder, and he opened his eyes and looked at me. I knew he was angry, because I had seen that look on many faces. Every time a security guard chased us away. Or after we took the woman's purse with the knife. But mostly before all that—before the Crazy 9—when my mom stumbled home early in the morning. Her eyes scratched red and tired. And even though she didn't talk, she would stare at me. And I could hear her think, *I hate you. I hate you.* I wish I could go back and shake her and yell, "You don't have much time left!" I wonder if she would have changed then, enough to like me, or at least enough to stay.

Ramoncito's look changed quickly though—from anger, to pain, to pleading. He was like a little dog begging for scraps. I've always wanted a dog, but we have rules in the Crazy 9, and dogs are not allowed. Tomás says all dogs do is eat and eat, and we don't have enough to share. And it's true. But it's also true that Tomás got bitten in the ass by a dog a while back and he's scared of them, so I think there's more than one reason for that rule. I helped Ramoncito up to his feet, and it was so easy. I crouched behind him and put my arms under his armpits, my chest resting against his back, and then just stood up. It was like lifting a bag full of bird bones. For a second I felt like I was so strong, like maybe I should be the leader of the Crazy 9. But it wasn't that I was strong, just that Ramoncito was so light.

"No, chamo, let's leave Ramoncito behind," said Tomás, and the rest of the boys nodded their heads in agreement. "He's only going to slow us down," Tomás said, and then Pecas repeated Tomás's words like he always did. "Yes, he's going to slow us down, déjalo." His voice broke as he spoke, some words deep, others as high as a little girl's.

But I didn't leave him. I told him, "Ramoncito, put your arm around my shoulder and try to keep up, okay?" and I ignored what the others were saying. Stuff like, "Ramoncito Pupusito smells so bad," and, "He will throw it up anyway."

So the Crazy 9 marched. The old market was about two hours away, but with Ramoncito it would take longer. We started on Avenida Bolívar. I liked this street because it had more people than trash. Everyone had somewhere to go. On a Wednesday morning no one walked just to enjoy it. I liked Saturdays and Sundays better, when I could see kids with their parents strolling along the wide avenue. I could imagine how it would feel for one of my hands to hold balloons or a cold raspado with condensed milk and for my other hand to be held by someone other than Ramoncito. But there were no kids except for us on Wednesday mornings. It was all busy grown-ups.

Ramoncito and I lagged behind, and for the first time I noticed how the Crazy 9 moved. They were a swarm of brown boys, brown from their skin and brown from their grime and brown from their stink. They were fast and wired, and people parted as they took over the whole sidewalk. Everyone who walked past them turned around to watch them. The businessmen patted their pockets and jackets, the ladies rummaged through their purses to make sure no small hands had slid in. They formed a moving cloud of jokes and laughter and dangerous grins. Salvador, in his patched-together flip-flops and old Chicago Bulls cap, sprinted out of the cloud and quickly rummaged through a trash bag, looking for an easy bite, and then ran back to the rest, as if pulled by a rubber band. Tomás blew kisses at the younger, prettier women heading to work at coffeehouses or office buildings, and the other boys joined in, as I would have if I'd been with them and not holding Ramoncito up. "Mi amor, you are looking pretty today," Tomás yelled—a wink and maybe a hand on his crotch, but I couldn't be quite sure from way back.

As we neared the end of Avenida Bolivar—the rest of the Crazy 9 almost out of sight and with no intent to wait for us—I told Ramoncito, "Look, Ramoncito! It's the Children's Museum!" and I pointed at the huge logo of a boy riding a rainbow. He had long curly hair and a big smile. By the front doors we saw a group of little kids, younger than Ramoncito, in their red school shirts. They formed a line, one behind the other, waiting to go in. They were happy and moved their heads around in awe and excitement. Two teachers tried their best to herd them. One little girl kept walking away, distracted by a planter full of flowers, or a pigeon eating trash, and I wanted to scream and say, "Little girl, obey your teachers! They'll get mad at you and slap you!" but I didn't, and the teachers never got mad, they just gently pushed her back in line and placed her hands on the shoulders of the boy in front of her. Her eyes still followed the pigeon, but she held on to those shoulders. The teacher was so gentle. Her hands must have felt so soft and clean.

I looked at my own hand. The one that wasn't holding up Ramoncito. My nails were long, the tips of them as black as wet dirt. My palms were covered in stains, a landscape of brown and black. When I opened my hand and pulled my fingers apart as much as they would go, the landscape cracked and revealed the cleaner tone of my own skin, hiding underneath.

And then I heard the rumble, which shook me and gave me purpose. It came from deep in my belly—a wet groan so loud that Ramoncito could hear it. "I'm hungry," I said. "Me too," he said.

We turned onto Avenida México, which was narrower and dirtier. It led to Museum Square and then to Parque los Caobos, my favorite place in the world. We arrived at Plaza Los Museos, large and round, with its tall palm trees. Street vendors eyed us and no longer fell for our tricks. Today was no trick, of course, because Ramoncito was really sick, but many times one of us would pretend to be in peril or pain, or cause a scene, while the others snuck behind the vendors and stole their things. We are so crazy.

We walked past the plaza, past the Natural History Museum with its tall columns. "Let's go see the elephant statue!" I told Ramoncito, and he smiled and the color came back to his face, but it might have just been the sun shining through the tall canopy of the caobo trees, brightening Ramoncito's cheeks with specks of light.

The temperature was colder in the shade, with the breeze rushing through tree trunks. It smelled like wood and dirt—but the good dirt, the kind you want to stick your hands in and feel for worms. I wanted to run through the boulevard that split the park in two, veer off into the brush and pick up a stick and go hunting for dinosaur.

A few months ago they brought plastic replicas of the great beasts into the park. There was a tall one with a crest on her head, she looked like a chicken with no feathers; there was a fat green one with spikes on its back (but the spikes didn't hurt, we knew because we surfed down its spine); there were brown ones and red ones; little baby ones hatching from plastic eggs; and there was the big ferocious one eating a stupid fat one that got caught. The short ones were already starting to wear out because on weekends the parents lifted their sons and daughters and gingerly placed them on the dinosaurs' backs. They took out their phones and started snapping photos. But all the parents were working today, and all the sons and daughters were at school. We have no school, and we are no sons of nobody.

I helped Ramoncito walk to the statue while my mind stalked reptiles. Its gold glinted through the thick greenery as we rounded the dense bamboo, until finally his huge head greeted us. It always shocked me, his size, the way he sparkled. His ears were open, like the wings of some gold-scaled dragon. His trunk fell, curving gently inward, between two massive tusks. The elephant walked in the middle of a large shallow pool, the water lapping at his wide ankles. Only his front left foot was visible, stepping on a small hill of rocks that came out of the water. Ramoncito let go of my shoulder, taking a few short steps toward the edge of the pool. He knelt on the ground and placed his elbows on the rim, so he could rest as he stared at the statue. Ramoncito looked like he was praying. I stood next to him and put my arm around his shoulder. "He's so beautiful," Ramoncito said. "Do you think they're mean in real life?"

I didn't know. I knew that there were people who rode them, or at least I remembered a story my grandmother once told me about that. My abuelita never said if they were nice or mean. But I knew Ramoncito wanted to hear a good story, so I told him, I said, "They are the nicest of all animals, little boys ride their tusks like swings and fall down their trunks like slides and run races through their fat legs."

He climbed on the edge of the pool, weak and unsure, but I didn't pull him back, and without taking off his beat-up sneakers he walked into the shallow water. It came up to his shins, and every time he shuffled closer, the water rippled and traveled all the way to the pool's edge in tiny little waves. Ramoncito placed his hand on the elephant's haunches and stroked him kindly. He whispered something to him and rested his hollow green cheek on its golden surface. I was mesmerized by Ramoncito and his massive pet, this gentle giant, and I knew what I had told him was true. That somewhere far away someone like Ramoncito—someone like me, maybe—hung from an elephant's tusk or took a shower from his trunk. But the spell was broken by a yell coming from the other side of the bamboo.

"Hey, you! Boy! Get out of there right now!"

Ramoncito's body spun so fast that his weak legs couldn't hold his balance, and he fell ass first into the water with a big splash. I could see the policeman heading toward us in a sprint. He was big and ugly, with a thick black mustache and hair coming out from wherever his clothes didn't cover his skin. He held a wooden club in his right hand, and even from the other side of the pool I felt his anger in the way he gripped the handle.

I jumped into the pool quickly and ran to Ramoncito to help him up. He was sobbing, saying, "Sorry. I'm sorry." But all I wanted was to get us out of there. The bottom of the pool was slick with green gunk, and as I pulled Ramoncito my feet flew from under me and I landed right on the small of my back, which sent a ping of sharp pain all through my spine. I tried to push my legs and pull

Ramoncito's weight toward the edge of the pool, but in the confusion I couldn't see the man anywhere—just the huge elephant towering over us both. I wanted him to come to life, to swerve his enormous head, and lift his heavy feet, and shelter us under his golden belly. To blow his trunk at the hairy man, yelling, "You don't mess with the Crazy 9!"

But he didn't do anything. I felt the man lift me up. The elephant's four massive feet stood still, indifferent to the waves from our thrashing as Ramoncito and I tried to escape the man's grasp.

My arms and legs dangled, and I felt the collar of my shirt tighten around my neck. A big hole in my right sole let all the water that had gathered in my shoe out in a stream. I reached up with both hands and tried to pry the man's fingers open, but they seemed made of cement. I kicked my feet as hard as I could, finding only air, water dripping everywhere. Ramoncito had slipped from his hold, and I saw him crawl to the roots of a caobo.

"¡Quédate quieto, coño!" the man screamed, but I kept wriggling. I felt his breath for the first time. It carried the warmth of fish empanadas and strong coffee. Finding no way to loosen his grip, I jabbed my fingernails into his hand, but instead of releasing me, he slammed me hard against the ground.

It was like all the air had been sucked from the world. I opened my mouth and tried to gulp in life, but my insides were a dried raisin. The back of my head felt wet, but it wasn't the same kind of wet as the water from the pool. It was warm. Sticky.

The policeman stood like an angry ape above me. His hat had fallen on the ground, revealing all his features. A thick stubble covered his face, starting just below the eyes. His ears were big and meaty. His nose wide and crooked in the middle. The only place not covered in hair was his balding dome. He held his hand up to his mouth, sucking on the wound I had caused. When he removed it to talk, I could see a trickling of blood on his lower lip.

"Motherfucker, hijo de puta." He spit blood and it landed next to me. "I hate street children, all you fucking do is make my job harder. Why can't you just fucking disappear, huh?" He took a step toward me, but my breath had not come back yet, and my vision started to blur. I tried to crawl away but was too weak.

"Now I probably have to get a shot. God knows the filth you have in those fingers." He lifted his booted foot and pinned my leg down. It felt like my shin would split in two, and for the first time since he had thrown me to the ground air rushed into my lungs, only to escape again in a scream. I didn't cry, though.

The pain sharpened my thinking and I remembered the knife. I always kept it in my right pocket. My hand searched for it and couldn't feel the wooden handle, the small metal dots that felt cold when you gripped it tight. It wasn't there.

And then I heard Ramoncito. "Let him go!" he screamed, and stood in front of the huge man, his legs spread apart, his arms stretched out away from his chest, his two bony hands holding on to the knife—a stick figure facing off against a giant. "The Crazy 9 never give up. Never surrender!" he screamed, tears falling down his face.

The man released the pressure on my leg, but I knew why. He lifted his club and walked toward Ramoncito. The policeman's eyes fixed on the knife and nothing else. I stood. As the man swung the weapon, I rushed him with all my strength and flung my body at him. It felt like running into a wall, but the club missed Ramoncito. He remained on his feet, holding on to the knife, and I was back on the ground, recovering from the impact.

Ramoncito was really crying now. Sobbing. But he wouldn't move. He clung to the knife so tightly that his whole body shook except for his hands and the blade. They remained perfectly still. Park people had started to gather around. Not a lot, but a few. One woman walked toward us. She was old, her skin the blackest I'd ever seen. She had kind, sad wrinkles across her face. She wore a gray shirt and a beautiful long skirt with colorful flowers stitched on it. Two golden disks, as bright as the elephant still towering above us, hung from her ears.

"Stop!" she demanded. And the man did. He stopped and looked around as if he had awakened from a dream. His chest rose and fell quickly, but his eyes had moved from me and Ramoncito and scanned the faces around us, especially the woman's. "Have you no shame?" she asked him softly, and I could see the man affected by her words. She knelt by me and held the back of my head. "They are just children," she said to him. And the man finally lowered his club and let it hang from his side, the leather band clinging to his strong wrist. And I could see something happening to his face. Some transformation. Like he felt sorry for us all of a sudden, or sorry for himself, or sad at himself, rather. I didn't have a word for it, but it felt like that one time I stole a box of leftovers from the old homeless man, and he didn't even have the strength to yell at me. When I sat down to eat the food all I could see were his milky eyes looking at me. I ate the food, but felt really bad eating it.

Ramoncito dropped the knife. He was still so afraid. He mouthed a silent, "I'm sorry," and ran off the way we had come. I have no idea where he found the strength. It was probably fear fueling him.

The woman sat me down and inspected my wounds. "Me llamo Belén," she said, and she kissed me on the forehead. We sat together at a table and we talked as the dizziness passed. I wanted to go after Ramoncito, but Belén's kindness held me near. She cleaned my wounds with an embroidered handkerchief and clean water from a plastic bottle. We shared her lunch of hard-boiled eggs, tomatoes, broccoli, and sweet plantains. "I can get you help, you know?" she said. "There are places that can take you and your friends in, people who can care for you, feed you." But I also saw how thin she was, I could recognize her own hunger behind the eyes. I recognized it because I saw it every day on the faces of my friends, because I could feel it inside of me. It had already been a sacrifice to share the little she had. Plus I had heard stories about these places that take kids like me in. They were never good stories.

"I have to go find Ramoncito," I told her. And she didn't try to stop me. She didn't push. "Vaya con Dios," she said. And as I walked away I heard her say, "I'm here most afternoons, come see me if you change your mind."

My torn T-shirt and my shorts had already started to dry, but every time I took a step my wet shoes sploshed and left a wet footstep on the boulevard leading out of Parque los Caobos.

So I searched for Ramoncito. I went back the way I came. It hurt a bit to walk because of the bump in my lower back, but I also felt stronger from my lunch with Belén. I was having fun using my tongue to free the little bits of food from my teeth, and there was one piece of plantain that made me smile because it was pretty big. I asked the newspaper vendor in Avenida México if he had seen Ramoncito go by. He said he had seen a young boy walking sleepily about thirty minutes ago. He checked his pockets as I walked away, fearing my tricks.

When I got back to our spot, Ramoncito was there. He was lying in a patch of sunlight, dirt and debris all around him. He lay on his side, like he was a little baby, or still in his mama's belly, and he faced a little yellow flower that sprouted next to him. His eyes were wide open. But when I called out, "Ramoncito!" his eyes didn't move. His body didn't move. He lay frozen.

I knelt next to him and shook him, and his eyes remained open like he was still staring at that little flower even though he now faced me. "Ramoncito! Ramoncito! Don't play games," I told him. I thought it was all just a bad, stupid joke, so I pinched his nose and counted to ten, to twenty, to thirty, to forty, and then I knew that he was dead because no way Ramoncito could hold his breath for that long. And then I let his head drop on my lap. And I told him how much I liked him, and how he had been such a good friend, and that the Crazy 9 would never be the same without him. But I didn't cry. I didn't even have one tear come down, even though I felt that lump in the throat I always feel when I think I'm going to cry, like I swallowed a rock that didn't want to go down all the way.

Now I'm here with dead Ramoncito. I think maybe I should wait for the rest of the Crazy 9 to come back and help me, but I don't know when they're coming, or even if they'll come at all. We have sleeping spots all over, and sometimes when we go to our dumpster we stay in the Metro station with the nice lady who lets us in after they close. And also they've been so mean to Ramoncito, maybe he would want it just like this. Just the two of us.

There's a wooden pallet that floated to our spot four days ago. Tomás told us, "I'm going to build a boat with this, and then I can sail all down the Güaire. I can bring my line and hook and I can fish and bring us back food," and we all liked the plan, so we'd been collecting supplies, more wood and nails and an old hammer so we could make him a boat that would last. But Ramoncito is more important than the boat, I think, and I don't care if Tomás gets mad at me. So I carry Ramoncito and put him on the pallet —well, I'll call it a raft now, because it floats. I pick the yellow flower and tuck it right behind his ear and I tell him, "Vaya con Dios, Ramoncito, you were my best friend," and I kiss him on the forehead. He tastes like dirt and old sweat, like rotting mango, like salt, like the sound my knife makes when it sticks to gray bark, he tastes like Tomás laughing in the wee hours, like sour milk, like Belén's hard-boiled eggs, like my grandmother's voice telling me stories before bed, like loud police sirens in the night, like a piece of meat found in a trash bag that I know is starting to rot but I eat anyway, he tastes like my mother's hand after she's slapped my face bloody, like a white crane flying low skimming the brown river looking for fish, like the bubbles in a just-cracked can of Pepsi, like the boy that got hit in the head by a tear gas canister and just lay there, like the sharp end of a belt, like a limp mother with a needle in her arm, he tastes like Pollos Arturos, he tastes like loyalty, and like a brother.

I let the raft go. It starts slow, but as it gets farther away, into the middle of the brown river, it goes faster and faster. And then I don't see him. I imagine the river taking him farther and farther from me. Away from the Crazy 9. Maybe El Güaire will take him all the way out of the city and he will arrive in some beautiful meadow, with flowers, and real elephants, and mango trees that always have fruit on them.

ANNA REESER

Octopus VII

FROM *Fourteen Hills*

TYLER CAUGHT HIMSELF leaning against the white wall and pushed back, leaving a handprint of sweat. It occurred to him that today might be his peak, but that was pessimistic and insane, something his dad would think. He'd finished installing the octopus for Art Murmur and its wire tentacles sprawled across the concrete floor. It looked good, throwing sharp shadows in the constant light. Tyler watched Kelsa from across the gallery. Her dress was the same color as her giant yellow canvas with stylized mountains and a sun flare smeared in oil paint, titled *Instant Nostalgia*. She was the most intimidating artist Tyler had met during graduate school, let alone dated. After this gallery opening, they'd be back in her bed, an easel just inches away, the smell of sex mixing with mineral spirits.

She walked over, echoing in combat boots that offset the little dress. When she touched a wire tentacle, Tyler felt a jolt up his spine. "Looking good," said Kelsa. Her voice was low, a little sleep-deprived grit in it. "Did you oxidize it?"

"Yeah, thanks. But your painting's the best thing here."

She grinned, slipped her fingers around his shoulder, then, as the gallery owner clipped through the room, Kelsa pulled away and echoed back to her painting. They'd been sleeping together for a few weeks and Tyler felt overwhelmed every time he saw her, and even though people said this would wear off, he didn't think it could.

"Ready?" The gallery owner's face was pinched and angular. "We open in five."

Tyler stuck his tag to the wall. *Octopus VII. Steel, wire. Inquire for pricing.* Each tentacle was a tight spiral of wires. The body was a cylinder of steel sheet metal he'd welded in place, then oxidized with vinegar and hydrogen peroxide. He hadn't thought of a price; it had been a big deal just getting into a show with Kelsa. They'd just graduated. This was the beginning.

A crowd filtered in—all high-waisted jeans and vintage bomber jackets. Tyler sipped wine from a tiny cup and ate cubes of dill Havarti too quickly. Then the gallery owner appeared and introduced Tyler to an art collector with a necklace of bears carved from stones.

"I'm inquiring about the price," the woman said, smiling wide. "One thing—could you bend some of these wires down? Can't you just see it catching a sweater?"

Tyler felt the wine rise to his face and clenched his jaw. He searched briefly for Kelsa. Wires catching a sweater? Fuck, no. He smirked and said sorry, no changes, the octopus was staying as is.

"Shame. It's a great piece," the woman said, and turned to look at a ceramic vase shaped like a Venus flytrap. She wasn't his audience. It didn't matter—he was twenty-five. There would be more sculptures, more shows—there had to be.

The whole month of June smelled like sweat-stained sheets and Oreos. They sat in Tyler's bed in the afternoon, watching cyclists out the window on Adeline Street, when Kelsa announced she was moving.

"I can't paint in the Bay Area now that school's over," she sighed.

"What?" They'd moved their pieces out of the gallery just last week. Tyler hadn't done any work the whole time the show was up; he'd barely even thought about it. But Kelsa was a mystery, a secret overachiever. Her wispy armpit hair was visible as she put on her bra.

"I'm going to L.A.," she said, gathering her knees to her chin. The bra was made of cotton patterned with tiny ice cream cones. "I can't go to farmers' markets all day and eat expensive sandwiches. I have to try to make something." She touched his chest, tracing her finger over his concave sternum. He'd always had it. It made him look kind of scrawny and folded.

"We never go to the farmers' market," said Tyler. He could see a tentacle of *Octopus VII* through the doorway, where it took up most of the shared living room.

"But I feel like we would." Kelsa combed her hair with her fingers. "Everything in L.A. is yellow and dry, like the apocalypse is happening early. I'm going to paint all the time. I found a place in Silver Lake."

"Sounds cool." Tyler shifted, unsure if he should make a bigger deal out of this.

"Well, I have to pack. I'm ride-sharing down on Thursday." Kelsa pushed the blanket away. "Hit me up if you're in L.A."

Kelsa put on her jeans and sweater with its paint-dipped sleeve. She was acting normal, exaggeratedly normal—it didn't make sense.

"How long will you be down there?" Tyler said finally.

Her eyebrows raised for a second, then she said, "I don't know yet—I'm just going. I'll see you around, okay?" She said this with pressed lips, then leaned down, kissed Tyler's forehead nonchalantly, and left.

"I can barely hear you, Ty," barked his dad though the phone's speaker, amplified by the curve of the cup holder.

"I'm in the car," Tyler said.

"How's that piece of junk holding up?" His dad chuckled drily. Tyler pictured him sitting on the back porch in Sonoma smoking an indulgent cigarette.

"All right. I'm driving to L.A."

The old station wagon rumbled down I-5, past rectangular masses of cattle and the smog-obscured Sierras. *Octopus VII* was wedged in the back with the seats folded down, and a metallic tentacle poked behind Tyler's headrest.

"What the hell's in L.A? I thought you'd have another show lined up in Oakland."

Tyler could almost hear him pacing. His dad, a writer who'd made money on his worst book, had encouraged Tyler's art career, insisting he was better off making something tangible, not just a tortured jumble of ideas.

"Ty? I can't hear you."

"It's like . . . apocalyptic down there," Tyler said. "My lease was up; two of my housemates were leaving anyway. And this artist I know, Kelsa, she just moved there. She has gallery leads."

His dad laughed in a slap-on-the-back way, or maybe he was coughing. For the past few weeks, since Kelsa left, Tyler had felt half awake, face puffy and stupid. Kelsa had texted him pictures of romantically faded buildings and sand. Phrases like *missing the fog up north.* Last Tuesday an apartment building offset by a saturated sunset, captioned *home: Silver Lake Blvd & Reno St.* Friday a photo of her wearing a translucent, threadbare Talking Heads shirt. Right then he'd packed up his room and the octopus.

"You have a place?"

"Yeah, in Silver Lake. I'm subletting from some friend of Dave's."

"Okay. You know the last of the trust is in your account?"

"I know. I don't need it."

Of course he needed the money. All he'd done in his life was an MFA at California College of the Arts and a modest range of drugs. What he really needed was to stop talking about it. It was embarrassing that his parents funded his artwork, considering the only good piece he'd made was *Octopus VII.*

"Oh—Ty, the article about your show came out in the *East Bay Express.* You look sharp with that octopus. Aunt Heidi asked if you're making smaller ones. I told her, let him do his thing. But hey, there's a market."

"Great." His stomach turned at the thought of making another octopus that was better and different but also the same.

"All right, Ty. Keep living the dream. Call when you get down there." His voice sounded extra sad and raspy, like Springsteen singing "Glory Days."

"Sure." Tyler hung up, took a swig from a bottle of warm water, and continued down the flat expanse of road.

He arrived in Silver Lake late in the afternoon and the smog gave everything a filter of light static. The sun had washed out the signs for Korean restaurants and pet shops to ominous pastels. Here and there you'd see someone on the sidewalk—a stumbling man, a woman jogging in neon-green pants. Tyler parked on a wide street. The guy's tiny apartment was in a blue stucco building, third floor up a narrow staircase, and the space was mostly empty with a sharp odor of Windex. Tyler found a box in the bathroom with one razor and a pair of knockoff Ray Bans, plus books by the bare mattress: *New Directions in Sound Editing; Recipes for the Microwave;* Bukowski's *Love Is a Dog from Hell.*

Tyler installed *Octopus VII* in the center of the main room, let-

ting the tentacles unfurl, some reaching into the air, some drap-
ing across the floor. For a minute he stood there, trying to find a
better place for it, but with wires already snagging the carpet, it
wasn't worth it. He drank mineral-tinged water from the tap, put
a coil of wire on the table in the corner. A pair of pliers. A pair of
heavy-duty scissors. Opened the window and the dry air yawned in,
smelling like the exhales of a thousand cars.

The apartment was on Tularosa Drive, just blocks from where
Kelsa said she lived. After he'd found the sublet, he almost told
her, but then he figured why not just go, then invite her over. Kelsa
was impulsive—she'd be into it. He paced the room, wrote the
text. *Hey, I'm in Silver Lake right now. Want to hang out?* Her abrupt
move to L.A. must have been a suggestion for him to follow. She
wasn't good on the phone or over text; she was like a poet, each
phrase short and ambiguous. It was better to see her in person.
They made sense in person. She texted back: *What?* Tyler paused,
trying to read this as excited or shocked. After several minutes she
said, *I'm free at 9ish.* He texted her the address. Stared out the window at a pink billboard with the word THIS and the rest obscured
by buildings.

The sun went down, casting magenta streaks behind the billboard. A greasy taco from the place down the street made the smell
of beef settle into the carpet. With pliers, he bent a piece of wire
into a rough shape, which ended up looking like a clothes hanger.

Professor Yao had called *Octopus VII* accosting and masculine
yet vulnerable. "A creature stripped bare of its flesh, straining
against something," he'd said. "Against social pressure? Pressure
to fall into the crippling morass of the economy? *Octopus VII* is raw
anatomy, motion, danger of feeling." Yao had stepped in front of
the sculpture, obscuring it, staring at Tyler through his oval glasses.
"In your future work," he continued, "I see total abstraction."

Tyler had nodded, like that's what he meant all along. He could
never have described it so well. And maybe Yao had a point—Tyler had chosen the octopus for its constantly shifting shape, and
finally he got the sculpture to look like it was twisting, thrashing,
changing. It was after that critique that he'd first asked Kelsa out
for a drink.

A knock sent vibrations through the room, and Tyler met Kelsa
at the door.

"Hey." She wore faded overalls, like she was playing a painter

in a movie. She scanned the room, eyes hovering on *Octopus VII*.
"Wait—did you move here?"

"I'm subletting," he said, trying to catch some aspect of her in
his hands. But there was a slippery tenseness about her and she
kept turning to look around the room.

"Um, yeah. I thought you were just in town. You brought this
guy," she said, dodging Tyler, touching a pale fingertip to one of
Octopus VII's tentacles. "Are you going to show it down here?"

"Maybe." Tyler stepped behind her and held her waist, smelled
deodorant and traces of turpentine. She turned, almost kissed
him, then flinched, bracing cold palms on his collarbones.

"It's so weird that you just *moved* here," she said. "Why would
you move here?"

"My lease was up in Oakland. I mean, why not? Your pictures
made it look all right."

Kelsa paced the room, face sour, keeping a few feet between
them. She twisted the silver ring on her right hand over and over.
Tyler felt a vise turning on his shoulders.

"I'm trying to stop doing that," Kelsa said. "Texting people. Just
to get a response." She looked at the floor, ripped her thumbnail
with her teeth. "It's fucked up that I want validation all the time.
Or company. I hope that's not why you moved here."

"No, it was for that guy." Tyler gestured to the sculpture. "He
wanted to be closer to the ocean."

She looked at Tyler again, stepped closer, maybe to kiss him.
Her eyes had dark half-moons underneath them, like she'd stayed
up all night. She sighed hard. "Look, I want to hang out. Like,
just talk."

She paced again, making it impossible to touch her. She never
wanted to just talk. She was a kinetic person, that's what she always said.

"So I'm living alone now. It's great—I'm teaching myself how to
cook. I can make eggs, brown rice, a bunch of things."

"Nice," said Tyler. "I have a microwave in there. Might make
some Hot Pockets."

Kelsa semi-smiled but kept pacing, threading her fingers in the
overall straps. She pointed at the scissors on the worktable. "Hey,
you know what? I have a job interview tomorrow and I need a haircut. Could you? You have scissors."

"What?"

"Cut my hair." She blushed, smirked. "I don't know. It was an idea. Is this too weird? Maybe I should leave."

"No, sure, yeah. I'll cut your hair."

She wet her hair under the bathtub tap, crouching on the floor. Tyler had agreed to this without thinking and his whole body had a heartbeat in it. Kelsa wrapped a towel around her shoulders and leaned against the sink, squinting into the mirror. "Just a trim," she said.

"I might fuck it up," said Tyler, touching the hair. He tried to push the possibility of sex from his mind, focusing on Kelsa's bitten fingernails tapping against the sink.

"It looks like shit anyway. Take off two inches."

She seemed calmer now. Maybe she was just in a weird mood. He lifted a section of hair and smoothed it out, then snipped. It made a *hssk* sound and fell to the floor, becoming limp and material, no longer part of her body. He snipped again, in the front, making a sharper angle that hit at her chin. She grinned.

"It feels lighter," she said. "Keep going."

He kept smoothing the hairs and snipping. It was satisfying. "So what's the job interview? I thought you were painting the apocalypse."

"Pinkberry—the fro-yo." She rolled her eyes. "All artists have a lame day job, right?"

"Yeah, sure." Tyler pictured himself washing pans at the taco place, getting yelled at in Spanish. "Have you done any new paintings?"

"I will."

Tyler lifted and cut strands, so they hit at different lengths, pointing out her sharp chin and skinny neck. The pieces on the floor began to dry, expanding into blond whorls all over the chartreuse linoleum. When he was done, Kelsa fluffed her hair with the towel, smiled, whipped her head around.

"You look hot," said Tyler, feeling his mouth get tacky around the words.

Kelsa's chest retreated into her overalls. "I'm an idiot. I shouldn't have asked you."

"What? It was pretty easy."

"No, it's fine," said Kelsa. "Look—when I left, I thought we'd just be friends. I thought I said that, but maybe I didn't. I'm trying to be independent. Just paint, focus on the work, not the whole eating-cookies-in-bed relationship thing."

Tyler's heart skipped beats. She had left town, mumbled *see you around* with that distant look, like she was already remembering him fondly.

"I get that," he said. "I'm focusing on my work too."

"Exactly. Well, I have that interview first thing tomorrow. I should get out of here." Kelsa took her purse and shuffled through the sea of hair. She stopped, framed in the doorway. "Let me know if you have any shows coming up."

"See you around," Tyler said.

He heard her sneakers slap down the stairwell, and from the bathroom he saw *Octopus VII* command the living room. With a hot swallow, he walked over and kicked the body, denting the metal, making a weak bang. He couldn't imagine lifting it again, cramming it back into the car, and driving—where? Back to the Bay Area to search Craigslist for one of the last cheap places? Sonoma to stay in his old bedroom on that depressing futon? He couldn't imagine making sculptures in this carpeted apartment. But that's what artists did. Felt terrible and made something out of it. He would feel like it, maybe if he got a little drunk. Yeah, fuck it, he'd stay the two months.

Tyler found a broom in the bathroom closet and pushed the blond hair into a slippery pile. Tomorrow he could find sheet metal and tires to build something large and hard-edged. Knives tied together with wire. Maybe a giant, Richard Serra–style slab of rusted metal shaped like a shallow bowl where he could curl inside. He kept sweeping the hair, listening to moths buzz against the fluorescent light.

The first month stank of tacos, Hot Pockets, and Modelo. Mornings were Apple Jacks and generic milk. It was cathartic to eat a corner-store diet; it curbed the guilt he choked down every time he withdrew money from his bank account. A few times he sat at the worktable, bending a piece of wire with his bare hand until it hurt, and scrolling Facebook. People from school were starting to post small art: 8-by-10 prints of photos taken inside BART or tiny sculptures that could be shipped in flat-rate boxes. Sell-out art. He wasn't ready for that shit. He could still feel it a little, wanting to make something; it was like being kind of horny, and it seemed like one of these days it could get so intense that he'd start bending wires into abstract shapes with the radio ricocheting off the walls.

He made himself a Tinder profile, relying on shots of himself with greasy hair in the studio. Sitting on the beige carpet, he typed "L.A.-based artist" in his bio and felt disingenuous. The girls in his radius were tiny, athletic. He never saw Kelsa in there, not that he wanted to. He was living alone, learning to hear the dumb sound of his thoughts.

One day he got a call from the guy whose apartment he was sub-letting.

"Hey man," the guy yelled over traffic. "I don't know if Dave told you, but I'm staying in Atlanta for a job on set."

"Cool." Tyler paced around *Octopus VII.*

"If you want to rent the place, it's yours. You're a sculptor, right? Are you using that badass worktable?" Tyler sat at the table, leaned his elbow on the smooth wood. He hadn't really used it. But it would be his own worktable, his own apartment, far from his parents. The rent was decent. He'd just need a day job and he could swing it. "So can you stay? I'll call the landlord right now. Would save me a huge hassle trying to find someone. Plus, L.A.—you'll do great things. It's the land of kings."

"What?"

"I don't know, I'm just saying random shit."

"I'll stay," said Tyler. "Thanks, man."

That night he dragged himself to the taco place. The afternoon had been wasted over four beers and an Internet vortex. The grimy ATM in the corner blinked his balance. It was more than he should have, but it was burning fast. Waiting for his burrito, he scanned jobs on Craigslist on his phone. *Hummus Republic hiring servers—experience + fun attitude a must!* He needed something blue-collar, entry-level, something that wouldn't take over his identity, like gallery installation—but the thought of running into Kelsa with a giant canvas, her face calm and righteous, made him want to punch a wall. Still, the haircut turned over and over in his mind, the *hssk* sound, the sea of blond on the floor, the way he made it fall at angles, reducing it to something better.

In September, on the hottest, most futile Tuesday, the billboard across the street changed. Tyler shifted around the room to get a

better view of it. Between buildings, it read: L.A. MODERN COSME-
TOLOGY — DO HAIR, LIVE THE DREAM. A close-cropped photo
showed a man with black hair gelled into spikes. It was hilariously
stupid. Tyler collapsed onto his chair, leaning far back, and opened
his laptop. L.A. Modern's website repeated the slogan in neon yellow on black. Five grand for a six-month fast-track course to get a
license. With the last of his savings, he could barely pay rent for
that long. But once you had the license, it would be a decent job
— mindless, but not washing dishes. He might even be good at it.

Tyler shivered under the ceiling fan. He could ask his dad; he'd
understand. It was in service of art. Didn't his dad work random
jobs after school? A deli in Alameda? Sweat beading on his nose,
Tyler called.

"Hey, Ty!" his father said. There was a muffled chewing sound.
"Mom says hi. We're eating lunch at the vegan place. Enough
sprouts to kill a horse."

"Just call me back."

"No! I can talk. You never call. What's going on? How's the
money holding up?"

Tyler gripped one of *Octopus VII*'s limbs, which had become
scalding hot in a streak of sun. He felt nauseous and sat down,
curling around his stomach. Suddenly *cosmetology* or even *hair
school* sounded effeminate, pathetic. He couldn't say it. Wincing,
he started bullshitting. "Well, I got into this artist residency. Super-
competitive. It's like, new media. But there are costs associated."

"Wow! Jill, he got into a residency—" Tyler heard his mom's
high-pitched congratulations in the background. "What's it
called?" said his dad.

"L.A. Modern Directions in New Media."

"Wow—new media, like film stuff? You know, Mom and I went
to SFMOMA last week, and half of it was video."

"Exactly." Tyler felt his sweat condense and start to stink. "Look,
it's a lot to ask, but could you lend me five grand? I'll pay you back."

"Five grand? If you think you'll make it back," said his dad,
pausing. Tyler closed his eyes. If his dad was going to shoot him
down, it might as well be now, when he was curled on the floor.
"That's fine, Ty. You're on a roll with that octopus. Just keep at it."

"Thanks. I will." Tyler let out a breath. His dad loved this; he
thought visual art was more authentic and sudden than writing,

so of course if you got inspired and made a bunch of shit, people would buy it and put it in museums for its aggressive truth.

"Great. How's that girl, that Kelsey?"

"Kelsa. She's all right." Tyler grimaced. "She got a haircut."

His dad gulped soda, then coughed. "Well, it all sounds great."

For months the rainless days ran together until a few drops fell out of soft clouds in the middle of January. At L.A. Modern they were learning the DevaCurl system. The school was in a converted warehouse, chairs lined against a wall, perfumes clashing, the eyebrows of the many nineteen-year-old girls raising in unison when the instructor cracked a joke. Tyler wished he had someone to commiserate with, but some days it didn't matter. It was so strange, so unweighted by the personal accountability of art, that the hours snapped away like drumbeats.

Nights, he walked miles through the darkening neighborhood, which felt virtuous in L.A. Sometimes he felt an idea for a sculpture coalescing like grains of sand in the corner of his mind, barely visible behind a thick fog, humming with potential. But he was afraid to really look at the idea, because it would probably be disappointing.

On a Monday in February, Tyler walked past windows, lamplight straining through shades. In front of a small pink house he smelled Kelsa's old laundry detergent and kept striding fast. It wasn't hers —she lived at least two blocks over. Topiary cast shadows from a streetlight. A muffled argument in a stairwell, a door clattering shut. Then he felt his phone buzz and his chest contracted, but it was just his dad, and he reflexively shut off the ringer. He'd been avoiding talking, just sending texts implying he was making art in a manic state. Maybe he'd call back, tell him about hair school. Final exams were in a month. But then, he should wait, because one of these nights it could happen—he could start bending wires, constructing an eighth octopus, or something larger, swallowing the whole room. Then he wouldn't have been lying.

Tyler walked until the houses faded into a string of shops, their facades dim. Nutri-Pro Supplements, Pinkberry, Pure Barre. A girl leaned against the far end of the building, sharp chin in a sliver of streetlight, smoke trailing from her hand, an apron tight on her waist.

"Tyler!" Kelsa pushed away from the wall. "What the hell?" She grinned. Her hair, pulled into a frayed ponytail, caught the light.

He wanted to run across the street. He said hello and accepted her hug tensely, the smoke winding into his hair. There was a sickness in his gut; the attraction felt perverse, ill-willed.

"You're still here," she said. "Same apartment?"

"Yeah."

"Doing more wire work?"

He looked at the sky, smog blurring out the stars. He nodded. He knew his question should come next—how was her work—but he couldn't ask. He didn't want to hear.

"You have a day job?" She stuffed her hands into the pockets of her Pinkberry apron, rocking on her heels.

"I'm cutting hair." It came out like a confession. He hadn't meant to say it—he needed to get out of there.

"You're kidding," she said. "Seriously?"

"Sorry, I have to go," Tyler said. "I'm meeting people from work for drinks." It wasn't true, but it could have been.

"Good seeing you—"

"You too."

Breathing hard, he walked home and kicked off his shoes. It was weird seeing her silhouette in the streetlight but feeling no tenderness, no need to hold her shoulders or smell her skin. She was abstracted by all the ways he'd belittled their relationship since she left. Part of him wanted to roughly unbutton her shirt, to touch her, but it would be ruined by resentment. Stumbling through the dim room, he caught one of the octopus's wire arms on his big toe. He wrapped a sock around it to stop blood from pooling on the carpet. Noticed that he'd left a sweaty T-shirt draped over the intricate arm that curled into the air. He turned into the kitchen, and *Octopus VII* stayed in place, frozen in a pathetic flailing motion.

Over the summer the jacaranda trees bloomed, and the street turned purple and smelled like someone's memory of home. Tyler arranged the tools on his shelf: diffuser, defining gel, antifrizz serum, scissors. The salon was decorated with retro wigs and '70s film posters, and all their shampoo smelled like orange creamsicles.

Even out in Van Nuys, he made okay tips. He'd learned how

to wash hair, holding the base of the skull and letting warm water graze the hairline, and not talking too much, because most people wanted to close their eyes. The customers were mostly young and hopeful—going on dates, having their first headshots taken. He snipped tangled lengths, chiseled texture, and watched people in the mirror look relieved, like they had already accomplished something.

The stylist with a round face and septum piercing sauntered over. "Hey, my kid had a meltdown at playgroup and I have to pick her up. Can you cover my four thirty?"

"Nope," smirked Tyler. He'd only been at the salon a few months, but he played a specific part: the tortured artist, friendly but gruff and sarcastic. He hoped it was clear that this was a day job, an aside to his art career.

"Right," she said, grinning. "Have fun."

Alone, Tyler pressed the tip of his scissors to his palm. He'd stolen them from hair school right after exams. Soon the door chime jingled and the four thirty walked in, slightly out of breath. She looked like Kelsa from the side—wispy blond hair, sharp chin. But she was lightly sunburned and made eye contact. Her name was April.

"I'm filling in, if that's okay," said Tyler.

"Can you cut hair?"

"I mean, I got my license three months ago."

"No, no, I was kidding!"

Tyler held the nape of her neck and ran the water till it was warm. She looked right at him a few times. He felt his heart race for a second, then it calmed down, and he kept massaging the shampoo into her scalp. She let out a little sigh.

In the chair, with the black cape around her, she laughed. "I always look like a floating head in these things."

"Everyone does," said Tyler. He wanted to say something funnier, better. "So I'll take off a couple inches," he said. "Here?" He held a finger close to her neck.

"Perfect."

He started the cut, scissors making the *hssk* sound.

"I had a terrible day at work," she said. "This will help."

"Right, no pressure." Tyler snipped the strand in front of her face, letting it fall to her cheekbone. He accidentally touched her chin.

"It was just a bad day. I might play hooky tomorrow and lay on the beach with a box of Wheat Thins. I love Wheat Thins."

"Where do you work?"

"HR at Anthem Blue Cross. I take requests for standing desks and those fancy mousepads so people don't get carpal tunnel. Turns out most people have it."

"You like the job?"

"I don't know, I wanted to live near the beach and drive around in my crappy sedan with the windows open every day. So I started applying for every administrative thing in L.A. And they let me leave at 4 p.m. and I get free vision insurance. *Yay*, right? It's not the last job I'll ever have, but it's all right. I just had a gross day and I'm going to drink a beer and not think about it. Is that healthy?" Her cheeks flushed. "Sorry. You're not my therapist."

For several minutes neither of them talked; she looked out the window and Tyler did the layers in the back, lifting the hair with pins. He finally asked how she normally styled it—standard question—and she laughed and said *barely*. They talked coffee, tacos, sunburn. Her voice was smooth and round, like a dinner bell, like a public radio host.

When the cut was done, the blow dryer filled the room with noise and her cheeks got pink in the heat. Her hair fell around her face decisively, skimming her collarbones.

"Awesome." She looked at Tyler in the mirror. "You know, you're really good at this. You're lucky you figured that out. I don't mean to be weird. I just—it's cool to have a thing."

"I'm actually a sculptor," Tyler heard himself say. His voice felt falsely low and condescending. Why bother lying to her too? "I mean, I went to school for sculpture. But I'm doing this now, basically."

April's eyebrows tensed for a second, then relaxed. "Yeah, of course you're a sculptor. That makes sense. Hair is the thing you're sculpting. Your medium, right? And you get paid for it. Speaking of! Hang on."

She rifled around in her purse, fumbling with a pen and bills. Tyler let out a breath. He wasn't supposed to be fulfilled by this; he should be dead broke and sculpting out of found metal. He took the broom and swept up the delicate strands spilling across the floor.

"Please keep the change," she said, handing him the bills. "Thank you. Seriously."

After she left he splashed his face with cold water and the smell of orange shampoo filled his whole body. He sat in the chair and thumbed through the cash. On the extra ten, April had written her phone number.

That night the sun set orange and glowed into Tyler's apartment when he opened the door. It cast *Octopus VII* in the dramatic backlight it had always needed. Its shadow spidered over the beige carpet, obscuring littered socks and mail. He bent the arm, and with a strain it gave, even as the wires pressed dents into his hand. It had been too long. All looking at it did was remind him of how he'd felt like a boy genius, and how of course he wasn't. How the impulse to bend wire was replaced by a grinding anxiety in his ribs. How after years of art school, maybe his calling was cutting hair in Van Nuys.

Tyler's jaw tensed and he grabbed the arm, ripping the connecting wires from the body in a rush. His heart smacked his rib cage. It felt so good, the pain in his hands. He was making money, paying the rent, pouring coffee through his cone filter in the morning, showing up at work in a clean T-shirt. Almost satisfying, like biting into a burrito—simple gulps of starch and meat. He grabbed another arm and snapped it. Then another, another, until he hit the dismembered metal cylinder with his fist, metal against his knuckles, scraping the skin.

He was shaking, blood itching his limbs. Before the stinging feeling in his hands could turn into real regret, Tyler crammed the arms inside the cylinder and hefted the solid chunk of metal down the stairs, out behind the building. As Tyler set down the remains, a pale man with yellow teeth hovered by the trash bins, fixed on the tangle of metal. Tyler couldn't watch; he felt a pull at his chest, a thick quiver in his throat. He could have sold it at that show in Oakland—two, three thousand dollars in seconds. As Tyler turned, the man dragged the scrap metal away.

Inside, he opened the window and sat on his chair in the freckles of orange light. He was drained. The carpet was tamped down in places where the sculpture had been, but the space was huge. The smell of the jacaranda trees came in as the air cooled and the traffic died down. It would be good to tell his dad what he was doing. He'd probably laugh in a short bark, the way he did when he heard something idiosyncratic.

Tyler lifted a mat knife and twirled it in his hand. Was this how it happened to people? How your life gets going, making a living, watching TV at night, the whole thing tapping out in a nice rhythm, a little simple and a little sad—but that's what people did. Fidgeting, he carved a slice of wood off the table's edge and watched it curl. He cut another, revealing the raw wood under the varnish. Another cut, deeper, scooping a canyon, a ridge. It felt good. He paused and blood rushed through his arms and hands. He picked up his phone, then laid the day's tips on the worktable, the bills crisp and flat, one with numbers in loops of ballpoint pen.

WILLIAM PEI SHIH

Enlightenment

FROM *Virginia Quarterly Review*

HARVARD, 1966. ABEL Jones is in his third year. He is an exceptional student, head of the class. He is studying history. His
area of focus, the eighteenth century. England and France. Still,
there are days when he is lost. Days when he is perplexed. For
one, he is excruciatingly shy, soft-spoken. A young man from the
country. There are times when he even feels out of his depth. The
university is distinctively male, overwhelmingly white—a kind of
white. It is marked by class. Even one's residence defines him. The
best rooms are on the second floor, where the most well-to-do re-
side. A scholarship student, Abel lives on the top floor. Sex is possible. It is commonly available in the bathrooms. At times he can't
help but think that he's no better than a pervert.

It is recommended that the undergraduates take a term off in
order to find their place in the world. His classmates spend time
in Rome. In Athens. He visits a psychotherapist in Cambridge,
one who he discovers later is quite distinguished. He's told that
he can't possibly be a pervert. Or a homosexual, but that he is
having what the experts refer to as "sexual panic." As soon as he
succeeds in dating a woman, he will come to his senses. Everything
will align.

Her name is Daphne. She is in her last year at Radcliffe. She has
radical beliefs, echoes the consciousness of Simone de Beauvoir
and Betty Friedan. He takes her to see *A Man for All Seasons*. Dinner
afterward. Daphne has flushed cheeks, auburn hair. Soft blue eyes
that radiate with authoritative clarity. She is wearing a burgundy

dress. She exudes beauty, not to mention confidence. Someone raised from noble ideals, and the best of intentions. Parents who know better. Someone from money. Her family had campaigned for Johnson and Humphrey. "More than awareness," she says, "we need action. We need movement. Or else we're only cursed to repeat the same mistakes with each successive generation."

The war, feminism, civil rights: all are at the forefront of her mind and heart.

Abel can't help but find himself entranced by the woman. Is this the makings of something more? Because he actually likes the person he's becoming in her presence. He seems to be saying all the right things. How she counters with ease. He is unexpectedly at his best. It is a kind of achievement to be this in sync with the universe.

Over coffee, over apple pie, he can see them together, ten years down the line—they are married. There might already be children. They would be scholars, both at the top of their game. They'd have a home in the suburbs, host dinner parties. Talk politics, the philosophy of Diderot. Most importantly, they would be happy together, a force to be reckoned with. He can already tell that she will be the type of woman who will pave the way, shine a spotlight on all of his best qualities. It would be easy for people to admire him, as they admire her. A lifetime, ripe with possibilities. Windfall after windfall. He would never have to fear the risk of losing his leverage in the world ever again.

They end up in her room in Beacon Hill. Her roommate is conveniently gone for the weekend, visiting family in Washington, D.C.—they have complete privacy.

"What are you waiting for?" Daphne says.

"What do you mean?"

"Kiss me already."

"All right."

He kisses her. She returns with a sudden heat. The scent of incense, bergamot perfume. They are already lying down on her bed. Some of their clothes are tossed to the side. He can feel the arch of her body, pressing closer against his. He wants to be overwhelmed. He wants to give in. But he feels himself pulling away.

"What's the matter?" The flash of unease in her eyes cripples him further. "What's wrong?"

"I'm sorry. I want to, I really do."

"Okay?"

"I just can't."

And then he is sixty-eight. Already a thirty-year tenure at a college in Connecticut. Courses in European history, even in poetry. He's largely lived alone. The West Village is home. The apartment is small but adequate. He's filled it with the words of his heroes. Samuel Johnson, Edward Gibbon. Thoreau. Voltaire. He doesn't own a television on principle; he believes the onset of cell phones to be the demise of civilization. Or at the very least propriety. He takes daily walks for exercise, for fresh air. There are parks, the crowded streets, having in recent years been infiltrated by a younger set—those who possess a certain kind of entitlement, defiance against the unknown. He'll peer into restaurants, peruse menus at the door. He barely recognizes the stooped figure in the pane of the glass. He is bald. He wears thick-rimmed glasses. There is a slight gap between his front teeth. His protruding belly, more pronounced than ever.

He keeps busy, though. A strict routine. He wakes early to read, writes in the afternoons. Slowly, and by longhand. His next book is on the Methodist John Wesley's journals. It is an endeavor that manages to consume most of his days. At six in the evening he sets his pen aside, winds down with a glass of Johnnie Walker Black, one ice cube. It is all a departure for him. The quiet days. The weekends. And then the lesson is learned quickly—one can retire and suddenly be wiped off the face of the earth. Phone calls recede. Letters and even emails come to a trickle. It is like the drying up of the Nile. On his worst days, a loneliness will set in like a night with no end. Then there are more inspired days. He'll even embrace such solitude.

He has marked several upcoming dates in his calendar. Former students make up a noticeable proportion of his social life. Tea with a student at his penthouse apartment on the Upper East Side. Dinner with friends, also former students, passing through on their way to their next set of escapades. Entire weeks at a cottage in Providence, hikes in the woods, Thoreau-like. There are men who have reached a point of no return. Loveless, full of need. Perfectly capable of friendship, but cast aside like debris. There is the baseless stigma attached to being alone.

And then there are other men. He has sustained the performance with a marvelous grace. There is a trip to Westchester for a conference where a colleague is presenting a paper on Edmund Burke. He has his own work to finish. The drive to Providence is always something to look forward to. Other travels petering on the horizon. He would like to see Paris again before his days are numbered.

It's taken him a lifetime to be a man of some means now, though he can't bear to think of himself as rich, because he isn't. Still, he will live out his years with a fair modicum of comfort. It is a stroke of luck. But also the result of his ambition. The "cultivation of the garden" of all his promise. It's become ingrained in him.

So when he is invited to teach for one semester at the Lower Manhattan University, provincial habits refuse to die. He puts his plans on hold, convinces himself that the offer is too good, too generous to refuse.

The university rolls out the red carpet, so to speak. They buy him a computer of his choice, give him access to an office in the English department. A welcome reception. There is a view of the business school.

It is the second week of classes, the spring semester. It was no picnic during the Age of Reason. He clears up some of the class's misconceptions. Sex in the park. A late-night romp with a prostitute in the dark, brothels. Animal intestines for makeshift condoms. Disease is rampant.

The lecture hall. A whiteboard, harsh lighting. There are twenty or so students scattered about the rows. He can think of no text more delicious than that of David Hume. *An Enquiry Concerning the Principles of Morals.* More than any of the class, a young man named Christian Lang is enthralled by one of Hume's characters —Alcheic, a man who marries his sister, murders his father, all of his children, solely for personal gain. Alcheic commits suicide, but still, he is lauded as a hero by his people.

There is more. Abel emphasizes section VII of the text. He asks the young man to read it aloud. Alcheic the adulterer. He has a young lover at the college, someone whom he has taken under his wing.

"Friends, I'm afraid that Alcheic is only a ruse," he says. (Therefore it is all right that no one knows how to pronounce the name correctly.) "Indeed, it is as Hume himself writes: 'Though the an-

cient Greeks have been admired for centuries, have they not practiced many of the things their admirers so disapproved of morally?'"

Several students scribble the remark into their notebooks, likely
with expectations of seeing it on their midterm exam. There are
no further questions. One can hear a pin drop.

"But don't you see?" Abel continues. "It was not so long ago
when it was common knowledge that only men were allowed to
attend university."

He raises his eyebrows, not unaware that he has cast a line.
There is a bit of laughter. He scans the room, his gaze falls on this
Christian. Is it a figment of his imagination? He can almost swear
that he's made the young man blush.

Later that week, office hours. Christian comes to ask him a question about an assignment. But then he tells him the news that isn't
news. It isn't the first time that a student confides in him. They
treat it like a sacred knowledge. The young man's dark eyes seem
to glisten. He sits up a little taller. His surname, Lang. "Is it Can-
tonese?" Abel asks.

"My family's from Taipei." He gives off the scent of fresh laundry.

But Abel recognizes the younger man's demeanor, the density
that seems to hold him back from so much of the world. The same
futile tactic, the messiness of avoiding so much of life—content
just to get by. He tells Abel that he's chosen to write his paper on
the fifteenth and sixteenth chapters of Edward Gibbon's *History of
the Decline and Fall of the Roman Empire*.

"Ambitious choice." Abel slides back in his swivel chair. "You
remind me of myself around your age."

"Do you really think so?"

"Oh, yes." He means lost. He means confused.

"I'll take it as a compliment." Then, "Tell me about Harvard."

"What's there to tell? I hated the experience. I wouldn't wish
it on my worst enemy. From what I hear, not much has changed."
And then, "What? Does that surprise you?"

"That's not what I expected you to say." The young man's disappointment is disarming. But Abel goes on. His tone, almost apologetic. He tells him that he was at Harvard during a time when one
had to leave calling cards at the home of the president. Memories

of segregation in a train car. Other kinds of inequalities. "Gosh, back then, I didn't have anyone. I was alone."

"I'm sorry to hear that, Dr. Jones." Then, "I'm alone too."

"Please, call me Abel. What I mean is, if you ever need someone to talk to, you can always come to me."

"All right."

"We don't have to talk about the class. In fact, I'd prefer not to."

They meet at Le Pain Quotidien. Washington Square Park. It is much later in the semester. There is a premature mugginess in the air, warmth of the city. The possibility of rain. They are seated by the wide window overlooking the sidewalk. Brick buildings, bustling streets.

"The Daily Bread," Abel remarks. He refers to the menu.

"What's that?"

"The name of the place."

"Oh, I don't speak French."

"It's not too late to learn, am I right?"

It is a mark of the young man's lack of transcendence, his willingness to give in to inevitabilities. He can already foresee that Christian will likely never be a man of the greater world. Unless someone intervenes, that is. *I can see that you need guidance,* he wants to say. *You need someone who will show you the way. The opposite is actually oblivion.* Instead he says, "I'm not very hungry. I've recently been inspired to start back on my diet, actually."

He orders a drink. The peach iced tea. Christian asks for the café au lait.

"A little late in the day for coffee, don't you think?"

"You're right," Christian says. He tells the waiter, "I'll have the decaf, please."

There are things in common. Abel learns that they both come from humble beginnings. And just as he's suspected, Christian is also a scholarship student. From years of experience teaching, he's observed that the courage to speak one's mind is often proportional to class, to upbringing. Sex, race. Otherness. Christian doesn't dorm. He lives in Queens with his mother, who works at a nail salon in Manhattan. Neither of them has siblings. They both prefer some of the English thinkers to the French *philosophes.* The music of Handel over Bach. "Or I should say, Couperin."

Abel then says that he is a member of the Samuel Johnson Society, even though he hasn't attended any of the functions at the Harvard Club in years.

"It's very exclusive," he remarks. He does a little pose. It's his way of engaging further. "One has to be invited, recognized in the field. It's a decadent affair, almost unnecessarily decadent if you ask me. Everyone wears a tuxedo and speaks with an accent."

"You must be an important man." Then, "I wish that I could be a part of something like that."

"In due time. You're still young and full of potential. But I already have a good feeling about you." He raises his glass. "To new friends."

"New friends."

Abel goes on to say that there are books that continue to pique his interest. He prefers nonfiction, but at times he'll return to *Candide*. Jane Austen. *Emma* and *Persuasion* are among his favorite novels, which, for him, are fine studies of rank. He says he doesn't believe in marriage, that he can't imagine himself being involved with one person for too long. He's had lovers. He's kept in touch with many of them.

"So how do *you* meet people?" Abel then asks. "You don't have to answer if you don't feel like it."

"I meet them in passing."

"Only in passing?" He raises his eyebrows.

"Well, I met you, didn't I?"

"Nonsense."

He calls a waiter over, orders several jars of preserves and spreads. Pastries to go. Strawberry, almond. The blueberry is his favorite. A gift set with an elegant gold bow tied around the plastic wrapping.

"Thank you," Christian says. "But you really shouldn't have."

"I insist. Think of it as a token of my appreciation for your friendship."

There are people who you'll meet, to whom you'll want to offer the world, show your hand. Someone who might feel indebted to that, someone full of gratitude. It is a kind of endearment, but also worthy of one's generosity.

"Do let me know when you run out," Abel then says.

"You've kind of given me a lifetime's supply."

"That was the plan."

Then Abel asks him about the ballet. Does he have an interest in going sometime?

"I haven't seen one since *The Nutcracker*, and that was in elementary school. But I remember liking it."

"City Ballet's fantastic. The company has some of the finest dancers in the world. Not to mention most attractive."

"When is it? This weekend?"

"No, unfortunately, the season's already coming to its close."

"I see. Well, keep me in mind for the next."

"Oh, I will." He leans in. "But can I see you this weekend anyway? I'd like to take you somewhere special, somewhere meaningful."

"Is it the Samuel Johnson Society? I'm only kidding."

"How about we keep it a surprise?"

"I like surprises."

"Do you? Well then, I'll have to keep that in mind too."

Dinner beforehand. A diner by the Queensboro Bridge. They're seated at a booth. Matzah ball soup, grilled cheese sandwiches. Abel sits back. He takes in the young man's expressions, his unbridled enthusiasm for it all, as if he doesn't know what it means to be worn out, grown weary by the undertakings of the everyday. He can be handsome, especially under certain lights. His face is unmarked. There is a slight purse in his lips. His ideals are unfixed, but his open attitude is almost uncorrupted. His slate blank.

"I feel as if I've made a magnificent discovery meeting you," Abel admits. "I'm glad that I've decided to come out of hibernation."

"That's the nicest thing anyone's ever said to me."

At the end of the meal, Abel pushes a box across the table.

"What's this?"

"Oh, I don't know. Go on, open it."

Christian unwraps the paper, pulls the cover off the box. The silver watch glitters under the light. "This is too much," he says. "I can't possibly accept it."

"But you must. It's discourteous to refuse a gift. Here, give me your hand."

The energy's changed in the young man's eyes. Has he overstepped? But it's as if Abel is realizing it for the first time: there comes a point in one's life where there is nothing more remarkable than being present at the forefront of this kind of refinement.

"I've never had anything this nice before," Christian says.

He somehow already knows this though. "It looks good on you. In fact, it makes me happy to see you wearing it."

It is a short walk to the Townhouse. The red brick building. Christian is carded at the door. Inside, there is a sense of being thrown back to another time, another place. The hanging chandeliers. Red velvet sofas, curtains. The long oak bar is pristine. Music can be heard. There is a white grand piano by the window. They take a table near the front in order to watch the impromptu performance. Already there is a crowd of men singing at the piano, at the top of their voices, uninhibited. They are drunk. Show tunes, patriotic songs. "America the Beautiful." It is Memorial Day weekend. The cluster of deep voices culminate in a kind of harmony. More than friendship, more than camaraderie. A brotherhood.

Abel waves to several people he notices at a distance but has never formally met. "I like this song," Abel says. "I like the singing. What do you think? Pretty swanky, right?"

"It's nice." He watches Christian observe the room for a moment. Then he looks down at his folded menu, the new watch.

A waiter comes up to take their drink orders. Someone with personality. Someone whom Abel imagines goes on auditions during the day, hungover.

"Johnnie Walker Black with one ice cube, and for my friend . . ."

"I'll just have a Coke."

"No, wait," Abel tells the waiter. "With rum." He turns to Christian. "Don't worry, they skimp on the liquor here."

More familiar music. Abel sings along. Cole Porter, Gershwin. He leans over. "Recognize any of it?"

"No, I don't."

"You're practically a baby. Why, at your age, people will think that you're either a waiter or a hustler. And let's just say, no one's asked you to take their order yet." He gives him a wink. He is only teasing. He can feel, though, that they are being watched, gossiped about. He has made a kind of spectacle of himself. He doesn't mind the attention.

"Cheers," Abel says. They toast their glasses.

After another drink, he finds himself revealing more than he should. The grades he's doled out to each student. Which students he had had to fail for not handing in papers. The student who had bragged about missing class in order to attend Coachella. They reminisce about a discussion with another student who had been misinformed about the ideology of Adam Smith, only Abel had had to let him down gently, despite the student's contentious attitude.

Then Christian says, "What did I get?"

"Do you really want to know?" Then, "You got the grade you deserved."

At the bar Abel orders another round.

"Shall we go up and sing a song?" he says.

"I should go home, it's getting kind of late. My mother will worry."

"Does she not know you're out?"

"No."

"Tsk-tsk." Then, "One song, and then we'll go."

"All right."

Afterward, they walk to the train station. The night is still warm. Abel can't help but think how wonderful it is, the way the department store windows seem to glow, the way the streets are practically deserted, as if they've been cleared for them at this dark hour.

"Which way are you going?" Abel asks. They are at the steps of the station.

"Oh, uptown."

"Then sadly, we part here."

They make plans to meet again, perhaps the following week. Abel extends an invitation for a drink at his apartment. From there they'll play it by ear. But there are plenty of restaurants in the area that he's been meaning to try. A meatball shop. A pizzeria. A hummus place. "The neighborhood comes to life in the evenings, you'll see."

He'd like to show him the view from the roof of his building. The skyline is spectacular. He suggests bringing a camera.

"Sounds like a plan," Christian says.

"Then I look forward to it."

He's drunk a little more than he usually can take. Distorted feelings consume him like irrefutable truths that materialize and reverberate throughout the decades. It is a kind of rising energy. Tender feelings reemerge, beautifully irrational, incoherent. Before he realizes it, he's leaned in. A kiss. Soft, smooth.

"Why did you do that?" Christian says.

"You said you liked surprises," he jokes. Then, "Did you absolutely hate it?"

"No."

"Will you be all right then? Getting home, I mean. I should call you a taxi, actually."

"I'll manage. I insist."

"Very well. Then goodnight."

At the bottom of the steps, Abel turns around and waves a final goodbye.

Over the week he barely works. He is restless. He will walk outside of his building and say hello to people he'd usually pass with vague acknowledgment. He revels in the newfound spirit, feels it course through his veins like a life force, undeterred. He can already see himself showing Christian the skyline. The view of Manhattan, pointing out the Chrysler Building. The Empire State Building. The East River. Then he will lead him downstairs. They'll be back in the apartment. He'll fix him a gin and tonic. They will peruse his library together. He will show off his collection of first-edition books. Thomas Paine, Goethe. He will put on some Handel. *Water Music. Music for the Royal Fireworks.* His favorite countertenor's rendition of "Vedrò con mio diletto." They might lose track of time. He might have to go to the grocery store in case he has to prepare some sort of dinner. He isn't a very good cook, though. So they might just order in.

It is Christian who cancels. They exchange emails back and forth. Christian will take days to reply. Even weeks. Then Christian stops replying altogether. It's as if Abel's being filtered out. Abel will be the one to take the initiative. To call. Leave messages. If he is busy this week, how about the following week? The week after?

Still no reply.

Then the slow and steady descent back into an obscurity. The vigorous walks around the neighborhood do little to quell the storm that has suddenly resurged inside of him. He replays the evening they had together in his mind. Was he incorrect in remembering that it was nothing short of brilliant?

It is finally the summer. The full and dreadful and exhausting burning of it. The city is in the midst of a heat wave. They say it's the beginning of the end.

But on one hot midday the phone rings.

"I thought you had all but disappeared on me," Abel says.

"Sorry, things came up," the familiar voice says. Friends leaving town. Cousins visiting from the West Coast. An aunt in the hospital. "But what are you doing Friday?"

"I'll have to check my planner." He covers the receiver. Mentally he counts down from ten. He had seen it done in a film once. Then he says, "You're in luck. A prior engagement has just canceled. Shall I give you my address?"

On the afternoon Christian is to arrive, it is dark. Abel glances out the window in anticipation. Massive clouds threaten the sky. But everything is prepared. In his refrigerator there is already cheese, caviar. On his desk, a gift box. He glances up at his clock. Any minute now.

The phone rings. Christian tells him that he is running late.

"But I'll be there soon," he says.

"Do you have an umbrella?"

"What?"

"It might storm."

"I'll run."

He worries that Christian will only get lost along one of the cobblestoned side streets, get caught in the rain. What if he cancels? "You won't make it," he then says.

"Sure I will."

"No, no. Why don't I meet you at the restaurant?"

By the time Abel rounds the corner, he is heaving heavy breaths. Umbrella in hand, a shopping bag in the other. Just as he had suspected, it had poured. There was thunder, lightning. It all happened so fast. And yet it was nearly impossible to prevent the gift box from getting wet.

"Hello there," Christian says with a wave. He extends a hand, and Abel knows instantly that something has come undone between them. "You made it."

Christian is wet himself. His hair practically soaked. "Why didn't you go inside?"

"I thought I'd wait for you out here."

"You could have waited for me at the bar. You're drenched."

"It's fine, I'll dry up in no time."

Inside the restaurant they're greeted by the host, a middle-aged gentleman in a silvery suit, his dark hair slicked back. He warns Abel to watch his step. The tone of his voice affects reverence for the elderly. But people glance over at them, hold their gazes. He can't help feeling as if he's betrayed a sense of helplessness. He's even taken by the arm, led to their table at the center of the room.

"I'm not that old," Abel says. He means it in good humor.

The host laughs, pulling out a chair. "Please, enjoy."

Then the waitress brings the wrong appetizer, forgets their drinks. He and Christian share a bland salad. A salty pizza, barely any shrimp. Christian doesn't seem to be very hungry. He is distracted. He reaches for his phone.

"What's the matter?" Abel says. "Do you have another engagement?"

"Sorry, it's my phone. It keeps buzzing. I should check this message."

"It's amazing how much our attention spans have deteriorated."

"What's that?"

"I said we've become so attached to our phones now, and it's sad."

"Oh, sorry."

Something about the young man's aura has changed, diluted. Abel tries to resurrect some of the magic from the night he's replayed over and over in his mind's eye, and recently in a much improved and favorable light. He refuses to hesitate. Refuses to relent. A full life is but the realization of the best of things before they fade.

"I was so glad when you called," Abel then says. He reaches into the bag, pulls out the gift box. The cardboard is still wet, but what can he do? "These are just a few things that I thought you might like to have."

Wrapped in tissue paper, a scarf, a pink tie, blue shirt. A pair of bronze cufflinks.

"If the shirt doesn't fit, do let me know and I'll exchange it for another."

"It's the middle of the summer," Christian says. He holds up the scarf. "This is ridiculous." He glances down at the price tag. "And expensive."

"It's designer." Then, "Tell you what, why don't you wear it to the ballet?"

"I don't even know how to tie this."

"Allow me." Abel takes the tie, ties the knot around his own neck, then passes it back to Christian, who slips it on.

"It's too tight," Christian then says. He tugs at the knot in order to loosen it.

"No, not too much. It looks fine. Leave it." Then Abel leans in. "Let's be honest. I think we have a connection. It's special, I can feel it. And it's true."

"I've been meaning to ask you something."

"Ask me anything. I'm an open book."

The waitress arrives. They *do* want dessert. Two crème brûlées. More drinks.

"Well?" Abel then says. "Your question?"

"Yes." He takes a breath. "I think you're brilliant. I think you're great."

He holds his smile. "Go on."

A reference, a letter of recommendation. "Sorry, I meant to preface all this by telling you that I'm applying to graduate school."

It is like the colliding of galaxies. Abel keeps his face calm, and unmoved. He thanks the waitress for bringing their desserts.

"You see, I hope to follow in your footsteps."

His tone is even when he says, "You flatter me."

"That's why I'm applying to Harvard." Then, "To be frank, I don't exactly have the grades. But it's always been a kind of dream of mine to go there. Therefore, I know it would mean a lot if a letter of endorsement came from you. You have a name, a reputation. You're a member of the Samuel Johnson Society, for God's sake."

It is like a betrayal, a kind of annihilation. Abel can see it all clearly now. The disease of the latest generation: the presumption of a favor, prematurely expecting it to be fulfilled, as if it's only a matter of course. How it's become a kind of routine currency.

"I'd like to teach in the future," Christian continues. "My mother thinks I can be a professor."

Abel digs his fork into the crème brûlée. It's practically mush. "I wouldn't recommend anyone going into academia."

"But you seemed to do well for yourself."

"It was a different time when I started. One could get a PhD in history and go on to teach poetry." He wipes his mouth with his napkin. He's done with dessert. "I'm sorry, but Harvard is out of the question. You belong here." He longs to add, "with me," but is afraid that the moment he does, what's left will surely vanish.

"What's the matter?" he says instead.

"You think that Harvard's out of my league, don't you?"

"Quite the contrary, actually. I refuse to let Harvard claim you."

"Somehow I doubt that." Then, "I want you to know that I intend on pursuing this, whatever happens."

"And I know a man in search of ruin when I see one."

"What's that supposed to mean?"

The wasted years. Days of drifting about, feeling entirely out of one's element. The torture of being friendless, invisible. The absurd self-loathing. All the self-destruction. How would he ever be able to explain what that was like?

"Look, I know a person of your position will see a place like Harvard and mistake it for mobility, even progress. Trust me, I've been there. I understand. But it's an illusion. A place like that will only undo you. And if I may enlighten you on any one aspect of your future, it is precisely this: you will fail."

Silence ensues. Christian removes the tie, places it back in the box, and buries it below the tissue paper. Then he glances down at his phone, as if purposefully. "I don't mean to be rude, but I have to go."

"Then go. Wait. Don't go. Here. Keep this." He places the box in the shopping bag and hands it to Christian. "There's no point in me holding on to this."

A sense of relief washes over him when Christian eventually takes it. "A consolation gift."

"Don't be like that."

"Won't you reconsider? Don't make me beg."

"I'm going to have to put my foot down on this one."

"So where does this leave us?"

Abel shakes his head. "The same. Disappointed, I'm afraid. Deeply disappointed."

Days later. He is meandering through the streets, no real destination in sight. Bleecker Street; then West Fourth. Then he is venturing farther than he is usually accustomed in this ocean of a city. Union Square in the distance. Chelsea. Before he knows it, he is approaching Times Square. He is amid the lights, the chaos of the tourists, the rush of cars, buses, taxis, bicycles. He wipes the sweat from his forehead, stops at a bench to catch his breath before continuing on. Columbus Circle in the distance. Then Lincoln Center. It is like battling against a tide. He can feel the soreness in his legs, his fatigue. He regards it as a personal victory that he's even made it this far, and that he can still go on. He has made a success of something, he has resisted closure.

Her apartment is on the Upper West Side. The view of Central Park is like a forest at this time of night. Photographs of children, their families, along the hallway walls, along the bookshelves.

"God, are you all right?" Daphne says. She sits beside him on the couch. "You're worrying me."

She reaches over, pulls the dangling string of a nearby lamp. The light comes on and he is astounded. He's never seen her so small, so fragile. She has soft white hair. She is wearing a string of pearls. He regards her blue eyes, clear as ever. He considers their friendship. It has stood the test of time. More so. In the end, there is another kind of love there, and it is no less true.

"Let me fix you a drink," she says.

He reaches for her hand. He can't help his own from shaking involuntarily, but manages to bring her palm to his lips.

"Who are you?" she says. "And what have you done with my Abel?"

They see a Czech film at Lincoln Plaza Cinemas. Then dinner at Café Fiorello, her favorite restaurant.

Daphne sips her merlot. "Lovely," she says. "I miss our evenings out."

"People like us, we paved the way," he tells her. "It's as if it's all being thrown back in our faces now. I can't stand to see it happen. Is this what happens when one has it too good?"

Daphne listens with the expression of someone who is holding back a more nuanced opinion, too tired to disagree.

He goes on. "How does someone live these days with all the lack of commitments? Everything at the expense of another. Where is the collaboration?"

"You're incomprehensible, Abel." And then, "You don't need it."

"It's not a question of need."

The young waiter mistakes them for husband and wife. Neither bothers to correct him.

"Well, I could do worse," Daphne says as soon as the waiter is out of earshot. "In fact, I have."

They both can't help but laugh.

Later that evening Daphne insists that they go for a carriage ride in the park. She's never done it before. Neither of them has. The clop of the horse hooves echoes against the streets and buildings. Doormen stand at the entrances. Taxis speed past them in the streets.

"I'm ashamed. I feel like a tourist," Abel says. "This is kind of ridiculous."

"The days are getting colder. We don't have many nights like this left."

"I suppose you're right."

"You have me. We have each other. I think it is enough."

"Yes, what a blessing."

But when he visits the university, he still wonders if he will run into Christian. The possibility is ripe for it. He remains later at the office in hopes that the young man might surprise him, walk through the door, like that first time when he had told him everything. Nothing. Abel's leisurely strolls through the park, all his careful vigilance, amount to nothing either. The holidays pass. There are cards, dinner at a friend's apartment in Brooklyn. Each year, on New Year's Eve, Abel is invited to attend a gathering where a soprano performs a marathon of lieder by Schubert. This year, the melancholy arpeggios of one strikes him more, each sequence of notes slices a cut infinitesimally deeper. The soprano's haunting vocalizations only seem to reiterate his anxieties, his frustrations.

Then there is the elegant invitation in the mail. The platinum envelope, stamped with the official seal. The Samuel Johnson Society. The gala is once again being held at the Harvard Club. Admission is expensive, but that isn't unexpected. He could attend. He could treat himself to an evening in the company of his peers, the finest minds. He's always enjoyed the affair. This year, on the program will be highlights from *A Journey to the Western Islands of Scotland.* Of course, readings from James Boswell's *Life of Johnson.*

The hall. High ceilings, chandeliers. The elegant place settings, silverware, fine china. He wonders how he could have kept himself away for this long. He runs into faces he knows. Dr. M. West, fresh from teaching at Oxford. Dr. Sophia Liu, Yale. Dr. Charles Winslow, Princeton. They, the select few, the crème de la crème. In recent years, in an effort to bolster membership, the society had started to extend invites to more women. It was about time.

Like everyone else, Abel is in formal attire. A tuxedo. He considers perhaps afterward he might return to the Townhouse. He's certainly dressed for it. He could do with some music. Sing along. It would be a splendid cadence to the evening.

In the library he shakes hands with Dr. Anil Gupta, a man who has lost a significant amount of weight through the years.

"What hole did you crawl out of, Abel?" he says. "I didn't think I'd see you this year."

In the spirit of the occasion, Abel echoes the man of the hour: "It is seldom that we find either men or places such as we expect them."

"Johnson's *Idler,* of course."

"Touché."

He finds his place card. As expected, he's seated with other professors. Dr. Thomas Salisbury tells him that he's currently at work on a book on the epochal boundaries and paradigm shifts in Antiquaries and politicians in eighteenth-century Naples. "Sounds delicious," Abel says. As the man goes on about the research, Abel thinks of how wonderful, if by a series of happy accidents that he should see Christian at the event. How easy it would be for him to contact the society, mention Abel's name, and secure an invitation. Such audacity would only be alluring. Christian could certainly find their website online. Abel peers into the crowd, examines each table, one at a time. He imagines Christian wearing the watch, the tie, the shirt. Even the scarf. Even though it would be out of place among the black-and-white attire of the gala. But it would be a kind of Christian at his best. He can't help but feel himself go a bit weak. Poor Christian. He'd be completely oblivious too. It wouldn't matter. "'How the world unfolds with such disproportion for the young, the beautiful. It is a gross inequality, but we are all complicit,'" he says.

"That's misattributed," Thomas says.

"What's that?"

"What you said, it's often misquoted as Johnson." And then, "It isn't him."

A reader takes the podium on the stage. Abel recognizes it to be Dr. Vincent Olsen. His face has narrowed, his fingers seem more swollen than ever. The difficulty with which the man turns the page of the book before him is agony. There is a gloom about him too, a darkening—the throes of decay. Abel can see it in the flesh, or rather the absences in that flesh. But it's also true that with anyone, the more that you look, the worse they appear. This is especially true of one's own reflection.

A quaking voice reads a passage from Johnson's *History of Rasselas, Prince of Abissinia:* "'Is there such depravity in man as that he should injure another without benefit to himself?'"

There is applause, the presentation of several awards. Posing for photos.

And then he is finally home. It is a late night. He had decided against the Townhouse. At the computer, he finds himself restless, in want of reaching out, just one more time. He decides to send an email, extending an invitation to the ballet. The season is practically upon them. Balanchine's *Serenade.*

After a few days he sends another email, asking Christian if he'd like to accompany him to see the new exhibit on eighteenth-century French drawings at the Morgan Library. The exhibition is sure to tantalize: works of Watteau, Jacques-Louis David. Jean-Honoré Fragonard, a personal favorite. They could have dinner at the Ritz. A walk in midtown. In the spirit of friendship.

Again he is at his desk. The computer the university had given him, its bright screen before him. He watches the cursor; its metronomic blinking reminds him of a countdown.

"Abel Jones," he says to himself. "What in heavens are you waiting for?"

Kennedy

FROM *Subtropics*

JOHN F. KENNEDY was a boy in our high school, but he went by Kennedy. For a brief time he made things pretty bad for us. We'd started our junior year without ever having exchanged a single word with him, had only seen him as he stalked the hallways, his long, greasy hair covering his face, his Coke-bottle glasses. He always wore this olive-green military jacket with the name KENNEDY stitched across the right breast. Underneath that he seemed to have every single Cannibal Corpse T-shirt in existence, a never-ending parade of skeletons and knives and blood and people with the skin ripped off their faces. He wasn't allowed to wear the T-shirts at school, since they were against the dress code, so he wore the jacket over them, even when it was hot out, and if he sensed your weakness, he'd open his jacket and flash the T-shirt at you as he passed you in the hallway.

Ben and I were best friends, each other's only friend, really. There were other people we liked fine enough, and sometimes we'd hang out, but Ben and I were constant. I liked the steadiness of his friendship, that if I ever reached out into the darkness, he would be there. We had known each other since we were six years old, when his family had moved here to Coalfield from Seattle because his dad taught sociology at the tiny liberal arts college in town. Ben was the only Japanese kid in Coalfield, though there were some Chinese kids who were adopted and a Korean family who ran a Chinese restaurant. He wrote experimental poetry, had won a national contest for high school kids the year before. I was just a regular kid, pretty smart, but I'd been protected by my parents, which had left me without street smarts, with no sense of how to navigate high school. My parents still kissed me on the lips, and when they hugged me, it was always for slightly longer than I wanted it to be. We played bridge after dinner, my parents and I and my younger sister; we listened to Simon and Garfunkel records, my mom singing along. The idea of going to a party, or the football game on Friday nights, never would have occurred to me or Ben. We hunkered down, made our own happiness, and hoped that maybe we'd figure things out by the time we left Coalfield and went off to college.

Kennedy ended up in our art class in our junior year. The room was some kind of converted garage, cement floors splattered with paint, and there were all these huge, heavy tables, where we sat on stools while the teacher, Mrs. Banks, lounged on a recliner in the corner of the room because her back was messed up. She barked out instructions, and we'd follow them to the best of our abilities. On the first day of classes, a minute after the late bell rang, Kennedy skulked over to the table where Ben and I were sitting and threw his backpack down so hard that it flew across the table's surface and hit Ben's arm. Ben took the pain without complaint. And maybe that was all Kennedy needed, that certainty that he could hurt us and we'd never tell.

Our first assignment was to do a figure drawing from this little twelve-inch wooden mannequin. Ben was pretty good at it, had always been a decent artist, and had sketched out a pretty perfect representation, but I was having trouble with it, couldn't make the individual parts of the figure come together. Kennedy just took a graphite pencil and pressed it so hard to the paper that it nearly ripped it apart. He drew the most basic stick figure and then drew X's where the eyes would be. "Look at this shit," he said to me, but I tried to ignore him, still trying to get my drawing right. He suddenly punched me in the arm so hard that I gasped. "Look," he said. Even though he was so greasy, so scuzzy, his skin was perfect and pale, not a mark of acne. His eyes looked wavy beneath the thick lenses of his glasses, but they were an intense blue.

I looked down at the drawing, the dead figure. "Yeah, okay," I said. I went back to my own drawing. "That's you," he said. I just shrugged. Mrs. Banks was far away from us, maybe asleep. I stood up. "I need to get some water," I said, and walked to the drinking fountain in the hallway, where I took a long, sustained sip. I could feel my face burning with the fear of what Kennedy might do to me, and I took several deep breaths. When I got back, Ben was staring at me with this look of alarm, like he was trying to silently warn me of some impending doom. I sat back down and looked at my drawing. A huge, cartoonish dick had been appended to my figure. "Oh, man," I said, looking at Kennedy, who was completely focused on his own drawing, acting like he had no idea what was going on. "C'mon, Kennedy. Please."

"What?" he said. "Oh, wow, look at that. You like huge cocks, I guess? You look like you love big dicks."

I tried to erase the dick, but even after I'd rubbed and rubbed, the outline was still visible on the paper. So I flipped to the next sheet of the pad and started over. While I drew, Kennedy leaned toward Ben and slapped his arm. "Hey," he said. "Hey, you, Nip. What's your name?"

"Ben," Ben whispered.

"Hey, Ben," Kennedy said. "You see that guy over there?"

I couldn't help but look too, and we turned to see Eric Murdock at one of the far tables. He had a full mustache and was wearing a tank top.

"That guy has a huge dick," Kennedy said. "I saw it in the locker room. Twelve inches, probably."

"Okay," Ben said.

"And he's a virgin. Can't get a girl to fuck him. Hey!" He punched Ben's arm. "What do you think about that?"

"Nothing," Ben said.

"What's his name?" Kennedy asked Ben, pointing at me.

"Jamie," Ben said.

"What about you, shithead?" Kennedy asked me.

"Well," I said, "maybe girls don't want to have sex with a twelve-inch penis."

"I know a lot of girls who would like to bounce around on that thing," Kennedy said. "Older girls. Women."

When it became clear to Kennedy that we weren't going to give him anything of substance, he started drawing devil horns and a tail on his stick figure and pentagrams dancing around its head. He didn't talk to us again, like we didn't exist, like he hadn't punched both of us so goddamned hard, talked about huge dicks. Ben and I were grateful for the reprieve. We thought maybe that would be the end of things, that Kennedy would move on and we'd be safe.

After school I drove Ben to his house in my hand-me-down Chevy Cavalier and we stumbled inside. We hadn't said a word about Kennedy for the entire drive, partly because we didn't know what to say, how we could talk about him without saying the word *dick* a bunch of times. We'd already done all of our homework during study hall, the work easy because it was only the first day, and so we ran past his mom, who translated poetry and complicated technical manuals from Japanese into English, and closed the door to his room. We decided to go old-school, put *Contra* in the Nintendo, eschewing the secret code that would have let us gain unlimited lives, and worked ourselves into a state of complete numbness, our eyes glazed over, like we'd plugged our brains into a machine and in return for our full attention it had made us happy, our bodies ice cold.

We were both obsessed with video games. We spent every dollar of our allowances on new games, and because we shared everything, we could buy twice as many. Ben had a Nintendo and a Super Nintendo, an old Atari 2600, plus a Game Boy and even a Game Gear. I had the two Nintendo systems, plus a Sega Genesis and a Sega Master System. We would play for hours; sometimes I'd play until my hands were paralyzed, until I could no longer bend my fingers, and I would simply hand the controller, midgame, to Ben, who would pick it up without missing a beat. It wasn't enough to finish a game; we had to beat it in record time, playing the same board over and over and over until we figured out how to clear it as fast as possible. As each of us played, the other would whisper, "Go, go, go, go," and it sounded as steady as a heartbeat.

We had to have the highest scores. And when we got them, we took photos of the screen, turning off all the lights in the room until it was pitch-black, wiping the screen clean with Windex so there were no smudges. Ben even had a tripod to steady the camera. And even with a perfect picture, when we got the photos developed, the images were still slightly blurred, and you could see the rounded edges of the CRT screen. We'd get doubles, one for each of us. We kept them in a photo album, labeled and carefully curated. We thought, maybe, this might help us get into a top-notch college. Even if it didn't, who cared? For those hours our bodies were the bodies on the screen, and we kept them alive for as long as we possibly could.

Finally, after three hours of gaming, Ben's mom called us to dinner. I always loved the food at Ben's house, dishes like seaweed crumbled up in a bowl of pristine rice, a raw egg cracked over it. And Ben loved eating at my house, so many casseroles, so many variations of starch, cheese, and meat. That night Ben's mom had made somen noodles that we dipped into little bowls of hon-dashi and soy sauce, little dried shrimp floating in the bowl, that fishy taste that made me so happy.

"How was school?" asked Mr. Nakamura, and Ben and I looked at each other for a second too long. "That bad?" Mr. Nakamura said.

"It was okay," Ben finally said. How would we even begin to describe Kennedy? What could be done? I stuffed a bunch of noodles into my mouth, slurping them up. "It was fine," I agreed. And that was that. It was like, in missing that moment when things were still normal, we had given up any chance of controlling Kennedy's effect on our lives. He had us. If he wanted us, whatever he wanted, he could have us.

But things were okay for a week or two. Kennedy would tease us, trying to gross us out, prodding at our bodies, testing for weak spots. He'd grab my ear and twist it, making me yell out, which would rouse Mrs. Banks to an upright position, but she'd just call for order and that would be that. He once said that he doubted that Ben had any pubic hair and tried to pull down his pants, but Ben held on to his belt until Kennedy grew bored. "You guys are the fucking worst," he would say, staring at us like we were Sea-Monkeys he'd ordered that had immediately disappointed him.

We didn't do anything. We didn't tell Mrs. Banks, since we couldn't imagine what she would do. We didn't sit at another table, surround ourselves with other people for protection. We didn't fight back. Now I understand it: we had stayed invisible for so long that we weren't used to people noticing us, and so when Kennedy noticed us, shined a light on us, we simply froze, simply sat there and took it, all these little indignities, and hoped that he would fuck up in some other class and get suspended, a temporary reprieve.

One day Mrs. Banks told us that we were going to work in groups. Each group was to create a replica of the Parthenon out of cardboard. The project was going to take a week to complete and would require a lot of precision work.

"How many people per group?" Ben asked, his voice quavery and weird.

"Three," she said. "Yes, three per group."

Ben visibly deflated, and Kennedy smiled. "You fuckers thought you could get away from me?" he asked.

"It's not that," I said. "We just like working with each other."

"Yeah," Kennedy said, leering. "I bet you like working with each other. Working each other's dicks in your mouths."

"C'mon, Kennedy," I said.

"You are the fairiest fairy that I've ever seen. What kind of music do you like?"

There was no way that I was going to tell him that my favorite album was Tevin Campbell's *I'm Ready*. I wasn't going to tell him that I liked Britpop.

"Heavy metal," I said.

"Yeah, right," he said, slowly nodding. "Like what?"

"Ratt?" I said, like I was in a spelling bee and had never heard the word before in my life.

"Get the fuck out of here," he said, laughing.

"That's metal," I said, confused. "I know it is."

"You need to listen to death metal," he said. "You need to listen to Mayhem. The lead singer killed himself and then another guy in the band made a stew with his brains."

"That's awful," Ben said, and he sounded like a grandmother who'd just heard that a lady at her church had cancer.

"You two . . . ," he said, but didn't say anything else. He just stared at us. "I'm gonna work on you two."

At my house Ben and I played *Donkey Kong Country*. I used a stopwatch while Ben tried to run as quickly as possible through the board, chaining rolls together to keep the speed boost, plowing through enemies instead of taking time to jump on them. It was hypnotic, so calming. "You're doing it," I said, smiling. Ben worked his hands on the controller, could almost do this blindfolded.

"I'm scared," he suddenly said.

"Of the game?" I asked, confused, looking at the screen.

"Of Kennedy. I'm scared of him," Ben said.

"Me too, I guess," I said.

"What do we do?" he asked.

"Nothing. What can we do?" I really had no clue.

"Go to the principal. Go to the police. He's going to hurt us."

"It would be so embarrassing," I said.

"I know," he said. Right at this moment he got dinged by an enemy, and he cursed, tossing the controller to the ground. "Here," he said, gesturing to the controller. "You take over."

We switched positions and I started the game over, the side-scrolling making me wonder if the game would ever end, the way it kept opening up. I wanted it to never end.

"We should kill him," I said.

"No way," Ben said. "Not even as a joke."

"I'm sorry," I said.

"It's okay," he said after a few seconds.

"We'll be okay," I said.

"Okay," he said, but he sounded sad. I turned away from the game, watched it reflected in Ben's eyes, the colors so beautiful.

Our Parthenon was a disaster. Ben and I simply didn't have the kind of brain for three-dimensional building. Nothing quite made sense, no matter how long we stared at the photo of the Parthenon —the one in Nashville, not in Greece. And Kennedy, dear Lord, he did everything possible to mess it up. I wondered how he'd made it this far in school when it was so clear how little he cared, how he would dare anyone in authority to do something about it. But it was like he was invisible to people in charge. I couldn't figure it out.

We had to use a hot glue gun to set the pieces of cardboard, and Kennedy immediately took control of it. While we were holding the pieces together, waiting for the glue, Kennedy would touch the tip of the gun, burning hot, to our fingers, sometimes even squirting the hot glue onto our skin. We'd yelp, and Kennedy would howl with laughter.

"Kennedy, seriously," Ben said. "Don't do that again."

"Okay," he said, still giggling. "Okay, you're right. Sorry. Okay, hold it steady. I'll really do it this time."

And then he'd burn us again. At the end of the day, Ben and I held up our hands for inspection and noted all the little burns, purple and angry, that covered our hands. Looking back on it, I want to take myself and just shake and shake, like, *What the fuck is wrong with you? Why did you let that happen?* But I can still remember those moments, when it felt like I was paralyzed inside my own body, like I had to pull myself deeper and deeper inside of myself, away from the surface, in order to stay alive. I think Ben felt the same way. We tried not to talk about it.

That Friday, the last day of the project, we still had a lot to do, because Kennedy kept breaking our Parthenon out of spite. The night before, I'd had anxiety dreams where for the first time I got a grade lower than an *A* because Kennedy fucked it up for me. I couldn't get into any colleges. In the dream my parents kept asking, "What's wrong? How did this happen?" which was crazy because my parents only asked that I do my best, barely even checked my grades. And now we had to stay after school, the three of us in the art room, in order to finish the Parthenon. We'd begged Kennedy to go home, to let us finish it on our own, but he'd insisted he wanted to be there, to make sure it was up to his standards.

So it was just the three of us, not even Mrs. Banks in her recliner, which was where Kennedy was now lounging, violently yanking on the lever to make the leg support unfold. He put a Morbid Angel album on the cassette player, which during class only ever played John Tesh jazz. After about an hour, we had something that resembled the Parthenon. We carried it over to the worktable and put it next to the other Parthenons.

"Okay, Kennedy," Ben said. "We're finished."

"We're not finished until I sign off," Kennedy said, hopping out of the chair. He walked past the supply cabinet and grabbed an X-Acto knife, which made both of us instantly stiffen. He tested the point of the blade on the tip of his finger. A little pinprick of blood appeared. "C'mon, Kennedy," I said. We backed away from him, putting a table between us.

"Calm down, pussies," he finally said, slipping the blade into the front pocket of his jacket. Then he picked up our Parthenon and held it up in the air as if he was going to slam it to the ground.

"Kennedy!" we both shouted, and he gently put it back down on the table.

"Excellent work," he said. "Makes these other Parthenons look like a fucking joke."

"Okay, great," I said. "We have to go now."

"Where are you going?" he asked, looking curious, as if he had never once considered the possibility that we had lives away from him.

"We're going to my house," I said. "Play some video games."

"I could come over too if you want," he said, and he wasn't smiling. We couldn't tell if he was serious.

"His mom's pretty strict," Ben said, thinking quickly. "She's a hard-ass. I can't bring people over without her okay first."

"Well, tell you what. Next week I'm coming over. Play some of these video games. Have fun. But right now I need you guys to give me a ride. I missed my bus because you fuckers couldn't glue cardboard together. So give me a ride, okay?"

"Okay," I said. "I guess so."

Kennedy got in the backseat of my car, and I was terrified of what he might do there, where I couldn't quite see him. I thought he might cover my eyes while I was driving, kick at the back of my seat the entire ride. But he just kind of fell across the entire backseat, lying on his back.

"Drive out to the soccer fields," he told us. "Over on Wrigley. Then turn onto Bald Knob Road. Bald fucking knob. Har-har. You two have bald knobs, I bet."

For the rest of the ride Kennedy just lay there, not making a sound.

"Okay," I said as I made the turn, "I'm on Bald Knob Road."

"Two twenty-two," he replied. "Buncha shit in the front yard."

We pulled up to a one-story ranch, and he was right, there was a bunch of shit in the front yard. There were two busted riding mowers, a burned-black steel drum with blackened pieces of wood sticking out of it.

He didn't get out of the car.

"We're here," I said after a while.

"Just give me a minute," he said. He didn't move. I could hear him breathing, it was so quiet in the car.

"Okay," he said, jumping out of the car. "On Monday I'm coming home with you."

"Kennedy, I don't—"

"Motherfucker, I'm coming over," he said, leaning back through the open door, his face close to mine. "And if you try to leave me at school, drive off without me, I'll look you up in the phone book and then I'll come over there. And it will be bad fucking news for you two."

"Okay," I said. "Okay, you can come over."

"Have a good weekend," he said, running to the house.

We sat there for a while, my hands shaking.

"I think I'm sick, Jamie," Ben said. I caught sight of myself in the rearview mirror and was surprised at how pale I looked.

"What are we going to do?" he asked.

"It'll be okay," I said. "He won't do anything with my mom there, and my sister too."

"Are you serious?" Ben asked. "He's going to kill us."

"He won't," I said. "He's just testing us. He's just messing with us."

"Maybe," Ben said, but his look was far off, like something had glitched in his brain.

"Do you want to play video games?" I asked.

"Maybe just drop me off at home," he replied. "I don't feel so great. I think I need to rest."

When I dropped him off, I grabbed his arm, and I hated the way he flinched when I did it. But I still held on to him. "We'll protect each other," I said. "Okay?"

Ben nodded. "Okay," he said.

"If he did something to you, Ben," I said, almost crying, "I really would kill him."

Ben smiled and got out of the car. I didn't see him the rest of the weekend, didn't even pick up the phone.

On Monday, when school was over, Ben and I stood outside my car, shifting from foot to foot, waiting for Kennedy. "We should just go right now," Ben said. "Let's just get out of here."

"He'll just follow us home," I told him. I had completely given up. If Kennedy wanted to kill me, if he wanted to wrap his hands around my throat and squeeze, I would let him. Ben, I think, was still hoping there was some way out of this, some code we could punch in that would open up a secret room, a place we could hide, a place where we couldn't be hurt. I was beyond that. Whatever happened, I just wanted to get it over with.

Kennedy finally showed up, nodding his approval that we'd waited for him. "Let's go," he said. "I have to be home by five or my dad will kick my fucking ass."

My mom treated Kennedy like he was a street urchin in a Broadway musical, shaking his hand, saying how nice it was that Ben and I had added a friend to our little crew. Kennedy seemed stunned by her easy kindness, her offer of a Mountain Dew, because he barely even spoke, wouldn't make eye contact with her. She let us get some snacks and then we were upstairs, in my room. Right away my sister, Molly, peeked in, wanting to see this new boy, but we shouted her away, terrified, honestly. We had this unstable thing inside the house, and we wanted to keep it contained in my room so that we'd be the only people damaged when it blew up.

The night before, I'd hidden everything good, all my money, my comic books of any worth. I'd shoved it all in my closet, tossed some blankets over it. I even took the SNES, because I didn't want it to get damaged, and put it away. I had looked around the room, wondering what I owned that Kennedy might linger on, that he might use against me. And truly, it seemed like everything in the room would give him reason to beat me senseless.

"What game do you want to play?" I asked Kennedy, trying to be a good host.

"I never played a video game in my entire life," he said without blinking.

I couldn't tell if he was fucking with us.

"Are you serious?" Ben asked.

"Dead serious," he said.

"What about the arcade?" Ben asked, as if it was unbelievable to him that someone our age had never played a video game.

"Nope," Kennedy replied.

"Well, what do you want to play?" I asked. "What kind of game? Like, *Mario Brothers* or maybe a driving game?"

"Something where you kill people," he said. "Duh."

I looked at the games I had lined up on my bookshelf. Kennedy pushed me aside and brought his face close to the spines of the games. "Whoa," he said finally. "Holy shit, this is Rambo. Like the movie *Rambo*?"

"Yeah," I said. "That's it."

"Can we play this?"

"Sure. It's two-player, so we can work together."

"Cool, cool, cool."

I handed Kennedy a controller and turned on the system. The blue and white letters showed up on the screen, and then there was Sylvester Stallone, all buff, that red headband.

I started the game. "Okay," I said, "this button shoots bullets and then this one here shoots exploding arrows. Use those to blow up the tents and you'll rescue the hostages."

"Yeah, fine."

"You're the yellow headband and I'm the red headband."

Within seconds of starting the game, Kennedy walked right into a bullet and his character fell over dead. But he started up again, another life. The same thing, dead.

"Jesus fuck!" he said. "This game is fucking hard."

"Just try to dodge the bullets," I said. "Don't run ahead too far."

"Oh, shit, thanks, fucker," he said, his voice sarcastic. "Avoid the bullets."

We played a little and then Kennedy died again, which meant he'd have to restart, which he did. "This gun doesn't do shit," he said. "Let's try these exploding arrows."

"Wait, be careful," I said, just as he fired an arrow right at my character, immediately killing me.

"Oh, shit, you can kill each other?" he said.

"Well—" I said, but before I could finish he shot another arrow at me, killing me again.

"Okay," Ben said, trying to help out, "but that's not the point—"

"Eat shit, motherfucker," Kennedy said, killing me again. After this third death, the GAME OVER screen came up for my side of the screen. I didn't push the button to restart, just let Kennedy wander around until he finally got killed again.

"This is what you guys do all day?" he asked, throwing the controller on the ground. "This sucks."

"Do you want to play something else?" I asked.

"You guys just play for now," he said. "I'm going to look around, see where you hide your fucking dildos."

Ben looked at me like *How long can we do this?* but we just picked up our controllers and started playing, clearing the board, moving up the screen. I tried not to look back at Kennedy, though I wondered what he was doing.

And then, just as we were settling into a groove, Kennedy slammed Ben to the ground, jumping on top of him and straddling him. He had a pillow in his hands, and he put it over Ben's face. "Sneak attack!" Kennedy shouted, and Ben's arms started flailing wildly, just pawing at the air, not doing anything to stop him. And I was frozen there, watching this, for at least five seconds, before I finally pushed Kennedy off of Ben, tackling him to the ground. Kennedy then grabbed me in a headlock, squeezing so hard that my ears popped.

"This is more like it," he said. "This is fun." His voice was mono-tone, like none of this was real, like he was acting in a play.

I couldn't get free. After a while he got bored and let me go. I scooted away from him to the wall, where I panted, holding my neck.

"What is wrong with you?" Ben asked him, but his voice wasn't angry. It was genuinely confused, hurt.

"What?" Kennedy said. "This is all me and my brother did, fuck-ing wrestling, trying to beat the shit out of each other. And then he joined the army, and now it's just me at home. I just wanted to fuck around." He pointed at me. "You had some fight in you for like half a second and then you pussied out."

"I think you better go home," I said, almost crying, trying hard not to cry.

He looked at me like he couldn't tell if I was joking or not, like he had no idea why I was upset. "Seriously?" he said finally. When I didn't say anything, he just shrugged and said, "Well, you have to drive me home."

"Fine," I said, trying to breathe normally, trying to make my body move. "I'll drive you home."

"I better get home myself," Ben said, not looking at me. "I've got homework to do."

"What?" I said. "You're not coming with me?"

"You're not coming with me?" Kennedy said, his voice mocking and high-pitched.

"It's just . . ." Ben looked toward the door. "I have all this home-work."

"Please?" I said. "Please come with me."

Kennedy turned and walked out of the room. "Come on," he said as he stomped down the stairs. I could hear him telling my mother goodbye, and her saying that he could come by anytime he liked.

"Please," I asked Ben again, whimpering.

"Okay," Ben finally said. "Okay."

As we walked down the stairs, he stopped me for a second. "I'm sorry," he said, "that wasn't cool of me."

"It's okay," I said, but I didn't know what was going on, couldn't tell if I was making too big a deal of this. In such a short time, my life, which was boring but tender, a thing that mattered to me even as I understood that it would eventually change, had become a kind of dream. I keep trying to explain to you why I didn't try harder, but maybe you understand. Maybe you don't think this is as strange as it feels to me.

When we got to Kennedy's house, he refused to get out of the car. "Come inside with me," he kept saying—an insistent, monotonous refrain. "Come inside. Just come inside. Come inside. Come inside and see something."

"Please, Kennedy," I said. "It's late."

"We have homework," Ben said.

"We have homework," I corroborated.

"Just come inside," he said again. "Come inside and let me just show you this one thing. This one thing and then you can go. Come inside. Come inside my house."

Inside the house, his father, his head shaved bald, gray stubble for a beard, was sitting in a recliner, watching some old boxing match on TV.

"Hello, JFK," his father said, muting the TV, but Kennedy didn't respond, tried to push past. His father stood, was a giant in that room, his head nearly touching the ceiling. "Who did you bring into our house?"

"Just some guys," Kennedy said.

"Friends?" his father asked, like it was the silliest thing in the world to suggest such a thing.

"What does it matter?" Kennedy asked.

"Who are you?" his father asked, turning to us.

"I'm Ben, Mr. Kennedy," Ben replied, but I was still too nervous to respond.

"Ben's Japanese, okay?" Kennedy said. "Not Vietnamese."

"I know that," his father said. "Jesus, son, do you think I don't know what a Vietnamese looks like?" Then he turned back to Ben. "I respect your people. Let bygones be bygones and all that. You built a hell of a society out of the rubble of that mess. Hats off to you."

"Thank you," Ben said.

"Who are you?" he asked me.

"Jamie," I said.

"You friends with Kennedy?"

"Kind of?" I said, like a question.

"We have, like, a class project to work on," Kennedy said.

"Well, I guess I'll let you get to it," his father said. Awkwardly he resettled himself in the recliner and turned the volume back up.

We walked down a long hallway, and as we passed each open room, I noted that it was much more ordered than I had expected, considering the disarray of the lawn. Perhaps it was thanks to his father's military background that he kept the house so clean. He even used the same air freshener that my parents did. Inhaling its flowery scent, I had this temporary moment, this little period of grace, during which my body relaxed. And then we got to Kennedy's room. There were two different locks on the door. He took some keys out of his pocket, undid them, and opened the door. Inside, his room was pretty well organized, the walls covered in posters of death metal bands, images that, if we hadn't already been so bombarded by the ones on Kennedy's T-shirts, would have terrified us. "Here, let me get some stuff out," he said, and turned on his stereo. From the speakers a deep droning immediately emanated.

"We need to go," I said to Kennedy, but he wasn't listening to me; it was kind of like we weren't even there. He opened his closet and pulled out this long box, like you'd keep comic books in, and laid it at his feet. When he removed the top of the box, he gestured for us to come closer. I was certain that there would be human heads in the box, skeletal remains. I knew it would be bad. I knew it would be hard to forget.

Ben and I looked down into the box and saw all manner of chain and leather, everything shiny, pristine. Kennedy tapped the box with his foot and it rattled. "I ordered all this from a catalogue," he said. "I've got quite a collection." He reached into the box and pulled up a bee's nest of handcuffs, so many pairs that it was hard to count. He tossed them on his bed and then pulled out a black mask that had a zipper where the mouth should be. "Sometimes I sleep in this," he said, smiling. He seemed so proud of these things, like we were all in a club together.

"I want you to do something for me," he then said. "Can you do something for me?"

"We really want to go home, Kennedy," Ben said, and now he really was crying. "I want to go home."

"You can go home in just a second," Kennedy said. "All I need is for Jamie to lie down on the bed and put on those handcuffs."

"I'm not going to do that," I said.

"If you do it, then you and Ben can go home," he said.

I don't know why we didn't run, but it didn't even occur to me. It felt like the entire world had shrunk down to this single room, that the three of us were the only people still alive in it. And even though there were two of us and one of him, I knew that it didn't matter. So I lay down on the bed.

"On your stomach," he said, his voice forceful, deep.

I turned onto my stomach.

"And take off your shirt," he said, which I did. Then he handcuffed my arms to some straps attached securely to the bed frame, one set of handcuffs for each hand. He clamped them so tight that the metal pinched my wrists and I gasped.

"Kennedy," Ben said, but I choked out, "It's okay, Ben. I'm okay."

Kennedy was now cuffing my ankles, so that I was pinned to the bed. I heard him rustling around in the box, and then he returned to my line of sight, close to my face and holding a kind of whip, like an octopus, all these tendrils, solid black. "This is a flogger," he said. "I've never used it on a real person before."

"Kennedy," I said. "I'm afraid."

He knelt on the bed, and I felt the mattress sink. And then he whipped me, lightly at first, which just made me hiss, the air rushing out of me, and then harder—again, and again, and again. And I was outside my body, just floating above it, and I was watching myself, and I was so sad that this was happening to me. I looked pretty bad; I could see it from up there. There were all these welts on my back, but I was just taking it, just lying there.

And then I heard Ben screaming, crying, and after a little while the door burst open. "What the fuck is going on?" Kennedy's father yelled, and Kennedy dropped the flogger. I turned my head as far as I could, looking over my shoulder, just in time to see his father walk across the room, push Ben into one wall, and slam Kennedy against the other—once, then twice, leaving a ragged hole in the drywall. When he tossed his son a third time, Kennedy fell against the window, the glass shattering and tinkling on the ground outside.

"Get him out of those handcuffs," his father shouted, but Kennedy was muttering.

"What?" his father said. Ben was now whimpering, lying on the ground. I could just barely see him if I turned my head at an angle.

"I dropped the keys," Kennedy finally said.

"Well, find them," his father said.

For about two minutes I listened as Kennedy crawled around the room on his hands and knees while his father stood there, towering over us. He turned off the music, and it was so quiet, the most total silence I've ever heard.

"Okay," Kennedy finally said, "here they are." And he unclasped all four sets of handcuffs. And I was free.

"Let's keep all this between ourselves, okay, boys?" his father said to Ben and me, but we weren't really listening, couldn't respond. I put my shirt on inside out. My hands were shaking. "I'll see that Kennedy is properly disciplined for this."

Ben helped me up off the bed, and the two of us stumbled through the house. I stepped on a plate and cracked it in two, but we just kept moving. When we got in the car, Ben locked the doors. We sat there. I put my head on the steering wheel and tried to breathe, but I couldn't tell if I was actually breathing or not. I couldn't tell if I was still alive.

"Can you drive?" Ben finally asked me, but I didn't respond. "Here," he said. "Get in the backseat. I'll drive us home."

I don't remember the drive home. I don't remember saying goodbye to Ben, who must have walked the half mile to his own house. I don't remember talking to my parents, though I must have. I don't remember doing my homework, but in the morning it was all done. I don't remember taking a shower, how badly it must have hurt when the water touched those welts, some of which were trickling blood. I only remember that I woke up around two in the morning, the entire house quiet, and I turned on my Nintendo, and I played *Super Mario Bros.*, running so fast, finding every single shortcut, just running and jumping, not letting a single thing touch me, running and running, until I'd finished the game. And then I just started over, kept running, until the sun came up.

Kennedy wasn't at school the next day. In art class we were making African ceremonial masks out of clay, and Ben and I sat alone at our table, not talking, not saying anything. At the end of the day I dropped Ben off at his house and then went home. I played video games. I let the pixels burn colors into my irises. I let my brain go away. I sat inside my room and made everything quiet.

And Kennedy wasn't at school the next day either, or the next, and with each day that he wasn't there, I felt worse, this kind of dread building up in my stomach. I don't remember much of those days except that Ben was not really a part of them, and how lonely that felt. It was worse than what Kennedy had done to us, the knowledge that Ben and I might not be friends anymore.

On the third day my parents came into my bedroom and closed the door so my sister wouldn't hear. "We're worried about you, Jamie," my mom said. "Something's not right. We just got off the phone with Mrs. Nakamura and she said that Ben has been depressed, listless. We said we'd noticed the same with you. Now, here's what we want to know. And we trust you, so we're going to ask you this. And I hope you know how much we love you, and how nothing that you do will ever change that."

"Okay," I said, slow to keep up.

"Are you and Ben experimenting with drugs?" she asked, both she and my father leaning in, like I was going to whisper some secret in their ears. I'd never even smoked a cigarette. I was good. I was a good kid. I kept telling myself this while they waited for me to respond, that I was a good kid, that I was good.

"We're not taking drugs, Mom," I told her, and they both let out this long exhalation, like they were so relieved and things could be normal again. "I'm just nervous, you know, about my grades, about school, about getting into a good college. Ben is too. It's a lot of pressure."

Then they went on and on about how proud of me they were, how much they loved me, and how, no matter what, I was going to make something of myself, I was going to find a way to contribute to the world and make my mark. And it made me love them so much, I wanted to cry. But I also wanted them to leave, wanted them far, far away from me. Then they hugged me, and then they were gone.

Only once I was sure that they were gone for good did I pick up a controller and start playing.

The next day Kennedy was back at school, sitting at our table in the art room before Ben or I had even arrived. We stood frozen in the doorway until a kid behind us bumped into us and pushed us farther into the room. Kennedy had a spectacular black eye, and two of his fingers were taped together with a splint. And this made me happy. It gave me the strength to walk over to that table and sit down.

"Long time no see, pussies," Kennedy said, but his heart wasn't in it. He looked sunken, sallow. He looked like a zombie.

Neither Ben nor I said a word. We went over to the worktable and retrieved our African masks, which had hardened and which we were now painting. Mrs. Banks lectured Kennedy on how far behind he was and then plopped a lump of clay in front of him. After she went back to her recliner, he took a wire brush and simply stabbed the clay, over and over again, slowly.

We worked in silence, only the sounds of *John Tesh: Live at Red Rocks* playing on the boombox.

Toward the end of class, Kennedy leaned toward us. "I want you guys to come over again. Tonight. I want to show you something."

"No way," Ben said. "Never again."

"You have to come," Kennedy said. "If you don't come, you're going to regret it for the rest of your life."

I couldn't even speak, couldn't look at Kennedy. Ben said, "Never. We're never coming over." And I think if Ben wasn't there that day, I would have gone over to Kennedy's that night.

"If you are not at my house tonight . . ." Kennedy said, but that was it. He just stared at us. He jabbed the brush into the clay and then walked out of the classroom, ten minutes before class was over. Mrs. Banks didn't even notice.

"We're not going, okay?" Ben said to me, and he touched my arm. He held it there until I looked at him. "Okay?" he said. "We are not going."

"Okay," I finally said, nodding. "Okay."

At the end of school we were certain that Kennedy would be standing next to our car, waiting for us, but he wasn't there. We got into the car as quickly as possible and actually burned rubber getting out of the parking lot, the back of the car swerving for a few seconds until I straightened it out. As we drove I looked over at Ben, who was frowning.

"Can I come over today?" he asked me, and I thought about it for a few seconds.

"Okay," I said. "Yeah."

We locked ourselves in my room and played *Double Dragon*, punching and kicking and whipping every cartoony thug that got in our way. We stood with our backs to each other and beat the living shit out of everyone that tried to hurt us. It was too easy to be therapeutic, but it didn't make us feel worse. And a few hours passed, and my mom called us for dinner. "Are you okay?" Ben asked when I turned off the system.

"Not really," I said. "I don't think so."

"Me either," he said. "But it'll get better, okay?"

"You're my best friend," I told him. I'm not sure why I said it. I guess I needed him to know it.

"You're my best friend too," he said, smiling.

At the dinner table, over meatloaf and green bean casserole, my parents asked us about our day, and we talked about the masks we'd made in art class, how Ben's kind of looked like a fish-man and how mine was supposed to be a wolf but looked more like an anteater. And my sister talked about gymnastics, some tumbling technique she'd learned, but it was hard to picture it from her description. And then the phone rang, and I jumped up to get it, walking back into the kitchen for the phone.

"Hello?" I said.

"Hey, Jamie," Kennedy said, and I felt my whole body go numb. I dropped the phone, and it swung there on its cord for a few seconds.

"Who is it?" my dad asked. "Tell them it's dinnertime."

I picked up the phone again, and there was silence on the other end. Finally Kennedy said, "Hello?"

"It's me," I said.

"You didn't come," he said, and he sounded sad, betrayed.

"No," I said.

"I shot my dad," he said. "I just did it. With a shotgun. While he was watching TV. It was . . . it was pretty horrible."

I didn't say anything. I waited for him to start laughing.

"I really did it. That's what I wanted you and Ben to see. I wanted you to see it. I wanted all three of us to be here. But you didn't come."

"You're lying," I said.

"I'm not lying, motherfucker," he said, his voice finally taking on some kind of life. "I just called the cops. They're sending someone over here. That's why I was calling too. I wondered if your parents could get me a good lawyer. I need someone really good. I'm eighteen, Jamie. I'm an adult. I'm fucked."

"You're lying," I said, "to fuck with me and Ben."

"Fair enough," he said. I heard sirens on his end of the line.

"I wish you had come over," he said. "I liked you guys. You and Ben. I thought you were okay."

"I have to go, Kennedy," I said.

"Okay," he said. "They're here anyways."

I hung up the phone and walked back into the dining room.

"Who the heck was that?" my dad asked.

I looked at Ben, and his eyes were so wide open.

"Some guy in our math class," I said. "He wanted to know what the homework was."

"Well, your food's getting cold," my mom said.

I sat next to Ben, and we both pushed our food around, listening to my parents talk to each other, their voices happy.

"Can Ben spend the night?" I asked them suddenly.

"On a school night?" my mom replied.

"Please?" I asked.

"If it's okay with his parents, then yeah, okay," my mother said. Under the table Ben reached for my hand and squeezed it. He held on to it for the rest of dinner, and it steadied me. It kept me inside my own body, because I wanted to float away again.

In my room, the door locked, I told Ben about Kennedy, what he said he'd done.

"I don't think he's lying," Ben said.

"We'll find out tomorrow," I said. "I guess."

We were silent. And then I started crying and shaking. And Ben held on to me. "I hope he did," I said. "I really hope he did it, and he's not coming back."

"Me too," Ben said, and now he was crying too, but not like me, not like I was.

"I'm so sorry," Ben said. "I'm sorry."

"I'm sorry too," I said.

What were we apologizing for? That we hadn't protected each other? That we hadn't kept each other safe? But I knew that he was sorry. And he knew that I was sorry. And he held on to me. And I held on to him.

I think about that moment all the time. I wonder where Ben is now. I wonder what he's doing. I wonder if he thinks about it. I miss him so much.

The Special World

FROM *The Georgia Review*

1. The Ordinary World

FLY WAS ALONE. When his parents had dropped him off, they hadn't come in like the other parents had done. He'd asked them not to, felt grown asking. Didn't need their help with his one suitcase, half his weight, or with the backpack strapped to his body. He hugged his mom at the building door. Her eyes were furiously red, like she was witnessing the end of the world. Fly shook his father's hand. His father held on and shook and shook, until Fly lurched away. His own palm sweaty and shaky. His father's hand made a fist —nonthreatening to Fly, but embarrassing all the same.

Yes, it was good to leave his folks at the door. Fly walked in the dorm like he was from the place. Never looked back.

He knew his room number by heart, but he again pulled out the piece of paper that had come in the mail: *504*, it still said. He took the stairs, passing other freshmen hiking with their parents—book boxes and mini fridges between them. On the door to 504, Fly's government name was written in bubble letters on kindergarten paper. He took it off, crumpled it to a jagged ball. He wanted to eat it. Chew it down to paste and then crap it out. Instead he let it fall to the floor, roll sadly under the extra-long twin bed.

There was only one extra-long twin bed. Sitting on that one bed in his new college home, Fly felt just like he had the night before. Nervous, and alone in that feeling. Wondering what his roommate would be like. If they would be cool with each other. Fly left the door open. Just in case. He wondered where the other guy would sleep. He guessed they'd have to roll in a cot.

Within the hour the floor got loud and then louder. The parents who had stayed were leaving. The students were losing their minds with glee. Three girls tumbled out of the room from across the hall. They smiled at Fly with manic smiles—like they were laughing at him. "He was cute," he heard one say as they went, but she sounded hesitant. Like she was surprised. And maybe it wasn't even Fly she was talking about. But no, Fly was sure it was him. That was something he had. The good looks.

In this fashion Fly missed orientation that afternoon. Missed convocation that evening.

His mom had packed him industrial amounts of pork-rind chips and beef jerky. They hadn't been Fly's favorite in years, maybe had never been his favorite. But there he was, lying on a quilt his grandmother had made for him, munching on a jerky stick, and staring at the ceiling. He was imagining his body floating five stories up, imagining that there wasn't a bed or floor or five floors beneath him, because there wasn't, not really; everything was connected, which meant that nothing really was keeping him from slamming to the ground but his own awareness of the bed and the floor and the five floors below him. He felt smart thinking metaphysical things like this.

Then a freckled guy with hair so blond it was white leaned slowly into Fly's doorway. The man floated there, at a slant, and then smiled. Fly froze, the jerky a sad flaccid meat hanging out of his mouth.

"You must be . . . ?" The man asked this with his smile and his white eyebrows slanted up.

But Fly didn't answer. The man righted himself and stepped into the threshold. His legs were short and thick and Fly wondered if he was a dwarf.

"You got the single," the man said, and he said it so casually and happily that Fly realized that the man was young—maybe not even a man-man. Though the guy, Fly now took in, had a full bushy blond beard.

"So what are your allergies?" the other said. "Sorry, forgot my clipboard."

Fly felt his mouth open, but nothing came out.

"Dude. I'm your RA," the other said now, almost sternly. Cautiously.

"What's an RA?" asked Fly.

"Oh, shit!" said the RA, regaining his smile. "It means I'm your dude. I'm like your big, uh, brother, or maybe *brother* is the wrong word, or whatever. But anyway. Resident assistant." He high-fived the space on the door where Fly's name had been. "Your name got lost. But anyway, I'm Clive. Look, we'll figure out the allergies later. No worries. But we have a meeting downstairs, like now." His grin went wonky for a second, but reset. He used his whole arm to wave Fly toward him.

Fly spit the jerky out and followed.

"Remind me your name?" Clive asked as they walked down the hallway.

"Fly," said Fly.

At the meeting there was an actual adult. A grown-up. A white woman who also had a hint of beard. What was up with the hair on these people? She introduced all the RAs. Half of the RAs were black — one of those was a guy who seemed girlie . . . but one was an actual girl. Dark-skinned and pretty. When introduced, the girl kept her arms at her sides but waved her hand like a shiver. Fly wished he was on that girl's floor. But when she started talking there was no blackness in her speech to speak of — nothing southern even. Just all "you know" and "like" and even a "yay!" at the end. Fly looked around to see if anyone else sensed her fraud. But no one met his eye.

He was not going to survive freshman year. He was going to end up back home in Ellenwood before the week was out.

But he didn't. He got registered for classes. He started classes. Intro everything: American History, World Religions, World Music. Bare min. credits, because he still wasn't sure he would stick, so why stretch. He started having lunch with the students from Introduction to World Religions, because the class ended right around lunchtime, so why not. They would talk Judaism. Fly didn't think he'd ever met a Jew in his life — except for maybe his dad, who identified as black Jewish every now and then. But now there were a bunch of actual Jews. And they were saying things like "We're not really white," though they sure looked white to Fly. And also: "God as a concept is real. But God as a divine — well, that is a social construction."

Fly started really reading; before he'd read books just for the sex scenes. But now there was still no roommate, so plenty of time. At the World Religion lunches, he would add things like "but for the black man, religion is the only safe route to masculinity. The secular black man as a man is too dangerous." He'd never known he thought things like this before. It was his father who first spoke these narratives—out loud during dinner, instead of dinner conversation. Now, when Fly spoke, the others would nod or shake their heads. Even the shaking heads were an agreement—like "ain't that something."

Walking out of the dining hall, Fly would pass a whole section of the cafeteria where the black and brown kids hung out. He longed for them. But how did those kids of color all know each other already in week two? There were only like one or two brown kids in his classes. Where were they all and how could he get in?

2. Call to Adventure

Fly didn't actually have any allergies, but Clive kept asking. Clive would do his crazy lean in the doorway, and Fly would offer: "Strawberries?"

"Nah," Clive might say. "Can't be strawberries. They don't give a freshman his own room for that. They would just put you with someone else with a strawberry allergy."

"Peanut butter?" Fly tried again.

"Nah. Same. It's got to be epic. Like music gives you epilepsy or some shit." Clive righted himself. His short legs now in the threshold. "You epileptic?"

"I don't think so."

"Yeah, I don't think so either." Clive had his clipboard; he looked at it and sighed. "So, classes good?" he asked Fly.

"Uh, yeah."

Clive looked up from the clipboard. "I mean, *are* you allergic to strawberries?"

"No."

"Oh, fuck," said Clive, which felt like an overreaction to Fly. Cursing always felt that way. But Clive wasn't looking at Fly anymore. Clive was looking down the hallway. He stared at whatever it was, then looked at Fly and took a deep breath. "Okay, man," he said. "Be good."

With Clive now gone Fly could hear what was coming. His door was open, as always, and he could hear the knocking, the cheery chatting, the hesitation, the sweet rejection. He knew they were making their way down to his room. And when they did, Fly was ready for them. Had been preparing for the fifteen minutes it took the pair to make it to his doorway. They didn't do the Clive lean-in. They stood together side by side, filling Fly's threshold, like his parents might have if he let them come visit. Fly didn't even let them get their spiel out.

"Come on in," he said, just as he'd been practicing in his head.

The girl had dark curly hair, and he'd only seen clearer skin on babies. Smooth and white as milk. A Jew, Fly figured. The boy was wearing glasses that he kept pushing back up his nose. The girl did most of the talking. The boy watched her through his slippy glasses and nodded like that was all he was ever going to do.

"And so we hope you can come to church this Sunday. It's just off campus. Can we count on you?"

"I'm there," Fly said. The guy was Arthur; the girl went by Suzie.

3. Refusal of the Call

Fly, finally getting some social life, went to a house party off campus. He went with the World Religion students, though at the party they all gathered on the couch like zoo animals around the one tree in the cage. The tree in this case was marijuana. The sophomore who had brought it called it "Mary Jane," like it was his girlfriend. The house was dark, but still no one was dancing, and Fly didn't make out another black kid in the whole place. An actual girl got up on a table and started gyrating, like a stripper. Fly felt gross for her, about her. But he still tilted forward to look up her skirt. Her white thighs were in shadows. He sucked Mary Jane and leaned back into the conversation: "Judeo-Christianity is a way for straight men to admit their attraction to other men," someone was saying. "Like God is the man you can love without being accused of homoeroticism." Fly put on his serious thinking face and listened. Getting high in college was definitely better than getting high by himself.

The next morning, Sunday, passed with Fly in bed—sleeping. Waking up to eat the last of the beef jerky sticks. Reading a homework essay by Bates on Turkish music, another by Pollard on reggae. He used a highlighter as he read, instead of taking notes. Highlighted most all of the page.

Fly had forgotten all about the two evangelical kids. Forgotten about church, and the Church, and who needed it? Right? Who needed Jesus when you had Peter Tosh? Christianity had been stabilizing when he lived with his faith-crazy parents, but now—now, who knew, maybe he didn't even need stable. He thought on all the ways to become a man—music maybe?

But then Arthur and Suzie showed up. Right in the middle of Fly's midday nap. This time they were a surprise. They came straight to his room, where his door was forever ajar. "I really missed you in church," Suzie said. Which was the first time anyone had claimed to miss Fly besides his mother, who was always claiming it. *I miss you, come visit, I'll wash your clothes, I'll cook a meatloaf.* It was nice of this girl to say she missed him. And then the girl kept saying more things, like, "Should I come meet you here next Sunday before service?" And, "You can walk me to church. Wouldn't that be nice?"

The boy, Arthur, nodded at her, his glasses still slipping down his nose. "I'll be alone," Suzie said, turning her body more clearly away from Arthur. "Arthur is giving a junior sermon next week, so he's got to be there before everyone else." Arthur looked down at the ground; his glasses teetered. He took them off and cleaned them on his shirt.

"Sounds like a plan," said Fly, who was sitting on his bed in pajamas his mother had bought him, thankful that he had something on besides his boxers. When Suzie and Arthur left, Fly wished he'd said "congratulations" to Arthur. Fly felt bad about this failure for hours. Must be a big deal to give a sermon, he thought, even a junior one.

4. Traversing the Threshold

Clive leaned into the threshold. "I get it," the RA said, smiling. "I totally get it." He pulled his body back up and stood in the doorway. His still surprisingly short legs. "You're not allergic to anything, man. I mean, could it be that you . . ." He looked at his clipboard and shook his head. "Sorry, it's just I'm trying to find a reason."

Fly was lying on his bed, in boxers only this time. "It's okay," he said.

"But you have your own room, dude. I didn't get my own room until I was a junior."

Fly didn't know what to say. "Sorry?" he said.

"Thanks, man. I guess you just got lucky. Right?"

"I guess?" said Fly, feeling something musty enter the room. Though Clive never did. Never did enter.

Fly woke up that Sunday to the knocking. He opened the door and there was the girl. Suzie. The churchy Christian Jewish girl, whatever that meant, with the milky skin and curly night-black hair. Fly was only in his pajama pants. His chest bare. He still had that muscle, left over from basketball, that lean teenage-boy body that can hold a vestigial tautness for years. Suzie pulled her breath in and then shot her eyes to his. Kept them there like her soul depended on it.

"I'm too early," she said.

"Uh, sorry. What time is church again?"

"No, I'm early. But you don't have a cell phone. I mean, why don't you have a cell phone?" She smiled, though the smile seemed mean. "It's just that I'm singing in the choir, so I like to get there on time."

"Yeah," Fly said. He wanted to look down at his crotch. See if there was a stain there from sleep. But he didn't.

"Should I wait out here?" she asked.

"Uh, no. Go ahead. You know. I'll catch up."

She nodded. Something was off with her. It was his body, he knew. His body had made her nervous. Had a girl ever seen his bare chest? He couldn't remember. His mother didn't count. Couldn't count.

"Sorry I was too early," she said. "I really hope you come."

At the elevators she turned to look back at him, and he realized that he was, stupidly, just standing there on his own threshold. He flung himself back into the room.

No, he wasn't going to go to some white people's church with that white girl. No way. His mother would never, ever let him bring her home, anyway. No point. Instead he closed his door, pulled his pajama pants down, and jerked off. He imagined the cum splashing onto her milky face. Imagined her smiling, like a porn star, her enjoying his pleasure through the whole thing.

He got up to go shower down the hall in the communal bathroom. He took long showers. Good way to break up the day. Shower caddy in hand, slippers on his feet, he turned out of his dorm room door, and there was Clive. Clive had a stack of papers in his hand. "Was about to slip this under your door, man," Clive said. He slapped one sheet of paper to Fly's chest.

Fly walked with it to the showers. Read the list through again and again. Campus cults. No matter how many times he read it, Suzie and Arthur's church was still the first one on the list.

After his shower Fly couldn't find his one pair of Stacy Adams. Thought, *Well, that's that.* But then found them. Put on a collared shirt and slacks.

When he opened the doors to the church, the choir was going, and the place was packed with students clapping and smiling and shouting and dancing, and it was a real party up in there. Real gospel music, stuff Fly was familiar with. The young people at the end of the rows noticed Fly come in and smiled bigger. These strangers were so happy he'd come. He smiled back. He could hear tambourines clanging. And one of those steel pans a guest professor had lectured about in World Music. The light was way bright. And there were more Asian people in this one place than Fly knew even existed on the whole campus.

Arthur found him. "Oh, man, so glad you're here!" Arthur looked crazed. He'd also just said the most words he'd ever said to Fly. "Come here, brother!" There was, indeed a space right next to Arthur for Fly. Like everyone had been waiting for Fly. Like Fly was special.

"Did I miss you?" Fly said, feeling weird about it.

"You're here now!" Arthur shouted gleefully. "You're right on time!"

Fly found his place, between Arthur and an Asian kid so tall that even tall Fly had to look up to him. This guy gave Fly a fist bump. Then the place went hushed. Everyone looked ahead to the altar. The choir was up there. Robed like a real black choir. In fact, all the members of the choir were brown or black, except for Suzie, who was there now stepping forward to a single standing mic.

"Suzanna," Arthur whispered to Fly. The whisper had all the lunacy of someone shouting from a mountaintop.

She tipped her face to the microphone and shut her eyes tight. "I," she started. And she held it. The *I*. Held it there with her eyes so tight. "I been buked, and I been scorned." There was no music at all holding her up. She opened her eyes and sang the line again a cappella. This time straight all the way through. "I've been buked, and I've been scorned." She put her arms out with her hands like she was welcoming them all. And then Fly leaned in to look more closely at her, leaned in even though she was so many pews away.

By the time Suzanna was on "trying to make this journey all alone" Fly knew. Suzanna was no white girl. Not one bit. Not a Jewish nonwhite girl, even. Suzanna was a girl raised in the Church, singing since she was a toddler. A black church. This was a Negro spiritual she was singing. Suzanna was a straight-up black girl. It was evident now that she was singing.

Of course, Fly could even see it in her face now that he knew. The full lips, the curly hair. The lightest-skinned black girl Fly had ever seen, but now he could see the color rising to her face. She was getting browner by the octave. She was a black girl named Suzanna who could sing spirituals. And Fly knew she was the girl he was destined to love.

In fact, Suzanna was, right now, looking at him. Right at him. Which meant that she knew it too. He stared back at her. Everyone around him started sitting; the song was over. But Fly stayed standing. He stayed standing, and she stayed standing. Until the pastor started talking and Suzie backed up, back into the choir. An all African American and Latino gospel choir, though the senior pastor, it turned out, was regular white. Actually white, with waxy blond hair to settle it. Fly sat down. But he stayed staring at Suzie until she looked away from him. Then he looked up at the ceiling. He could feel that his back was wet. That he was sweating through his clothes. There was probably a wet spot at the back of his shirt. But he looked up at the plain white ceiling and imagined that there was no ceiling. That he was out there in the sky because he was the sky. When the pastor said *Amen* and everyone else said it too, Fly returned from the sky and looked over at Arthur, and Arthur was looking at him. Arthur's eyes were hooded, like he had something very serious to say. But then Fly realized that was just how Arthur's eyes were. Arthur was some kind of Asian. Clear now that he wasn't wearing his glasses.

What was this craziness? Fly thought. What did it all mean? All the people of color were camouflaged. Maybe they had been around Fly all the time, and he'd been too self-absorbed to notice. Maybe he was camouflaged too.

After that service Fly started to feel exhausted practically all the time. In the one extra-long twin bed, he would stare at the ceiling and think about kissing Suzie. Practice it in his mind until he fell asleep. Then he would dream about Suzie, Suzanna, letting him touch her. Even after weeks of walking her to church and watching her from the pews, he'd never even touched her through her clothes. Fly didn't think of his father, Gary Lovett, meeting his first love at church. Of that girl winning Gary's heart over the Bible. Fly had never heard that story, though he'd lived in its wake. Fly just slept a whole lot. Masturbated like it was a job. Practice, he told himself. Then Fly slept some more. He'd heard somewhere that sleeping a lot meant you were in love.

5. Tests, Allies, and Enemies

The Jewish kids from World Religions weren't camouflaging; they were doing the opposite. They were posing as people of color —when for all Fly could gather they were really just white. He couldn't be bothered with their lack of authenticity. Fly lunched now with Arthur and the other ethnically jumbled Christian kids. Arthur was from the Midwest. Didn't speak Chinese or Korean. Though he wore what Fly knew was a Buddhist bracelet around his left wrist. Fly's father had worn four or five of them on the same wrist for years. Fly never said anything about it to Arthur, but it surely meant that Arthur wasn't totally devoted to the cult, if the church was a cult. Though it turned out Fly himself was feeling less nuanced. Actually *felt* it. He felt solid, manly, sure of his faith now. Like how he'd been as a boy, with Pastor John. No more experimenting intellectually around thoughts. Now Fly would have an unbending thought and then feel real good about it. Fly had been all *A*'s, but his World Religions grade slouched at the midterm. He couldn't muster a nuanced thought about Bahaullah or Krishna. He was all in for Jesus these days. Felt good. Felt grown.

But music was still Fly and fly. The World Music class was in a lecture hall, but the teacher was some kind of famous person who had been on tour for the whole first half of the semester. Every week there had been a new lecturer, delivering what was some kind of straight genius take on K-pop or Vude. Each teacher gave homework, but Fly never did it. Homework was a dumbing down that was for the actually dumb students, not for him. Instead after each class session Fly would go to the library. Look up the guest professor. Check out the book or books they'd written. Then he and Suzanna—he liked to call her by her full name now—would sit in his room and read. Just read. He his music books, she the Bible or maybe an education textbook. Though maybe she was the only one reading, because it was impossible for Fly to read with her sitting at his dorm desk with her naked feet propped on his bed. Him lying in his bed, sometimes napping, sometimes not; their feet sometimes touching.

Too often Clive would lean into the doorway, smile—"just checking on my chickadees"—and lean back out.

6. Approach to the Innermost Cave, or, The Meeting with the Goddess

Thinking about Fly getting saved by the Lord started to make Suzanna slutty. It got so that whenever they talked about it, she would unbuckle his pants and then close the dorm-room door—there was always that awkward thrilling moment with his dick straight up and the door wide open. She would kneel to him and say something deflating like, "I really want to be sitting next to you when you receive Christ. I just want to watch Jesus come on you!" But Fly was nineteen, the horniest he was ever going to be, so he could hold the stiffness, despite. Then she would lick and suck until he said he was cumming. She would use her hands that last minute or so to get him there, and after she would climb into his sore sensitive lap. All her clothes still on, she would make him hold her. Then she would say something bananas like, "When you become a man of God there isn't anything I won't submit to you for." Then sometimes she would cry.

Boy, did Fly want to be a man of God. But to be honest he felt like he was already, had been since he was a child. But Suzanna needed to witness it. Women were like that, Fly figured. So he drove home one Saturday. Picked up his dark blue suit, which was newly snug around his shoulders.

"A suit," his father said. "You drove over an hour just for a suit? You going weird on us, boy?" Which was ridiculous coming from his crazy father.

"Don't mind that grumpy man," his mother said, all eagerness and gratitude. She was losing it with joy at Fly's just being home. Her face was so stretched with the smile Fly thought it looked scary. "Are you staying for dinner?" she asked. "Meatloaf?" and then she added quickly, chirpily, "my special meatloaf."

He stayed for dinner but drove back to school that night. The next morning Fly walked up to the altar when the white pastor opened his arms. Got himself saved for Suzanna, though he'd been saved before. Pastor John had saved him from the back of a van.

But now it was a whole production. More than Fly had realized. Anyone saved was invited, beseeched, to an ice cream social after church with the "Prayer Warriors." Arthur was there, and Arthur took over as Fly's personal warrior of prayer. Arthur's prayers were loud and urgent and he went on and on, and Fly could see how Arthur might be a pastor, a senior one, someday. Then other young men hugged Fly—sincere bear hugs that were more male affection than he'd ever received. But the young women hugged Fly too, and that was stranger than the men. Because the girls hugged and held on, seemed suddenly to find him, what was it? Not just cute. Sexy; they found him sexy. They hugged him, met his eyes, gripped him with their fingers. Offered to bring him ice cream —"What is your favorite flavor?"—then buzzed around him with what he could feel was a lusty adoration. "Vanilla could be my favorite," he said, testing out his theory to a white girl. She looked down at her shoes and then back up at him, took a gulp of breath, and he saw that her eyes were watering like she might cry.

Suzanna came up, held Fly's hand until the other girl blushed and ran off with the ice cream order. He felt Suzanna's middle finger loosen in his hand; this middle finger's knuckle rubbed gently across his palm, again and again. He felt his crotch tingle in anticipation. But there were more prayers and congratulations and welcomings to Christ. And then he had to eat the ice cream.

When they got back to his dorm Fly pulled Suzanna through the door. "Leave the light on," she said, even though he hadn't given light or its absence any thought. "I want you to see me." And then she took her clothes off with a drama of someone who'd been practicing, which Fly so appreciated. Her underwear dark with wetness when she finally peeled them off. Then she flung herself onto the bed, face first, raised her hips so he could see all God had given her through the soft plump lobes of her backside. When he put his hand to her there at the center, she pressed herself hard against him, but she was slick. It made him think of candy gone sticky in the sun.

"I want to submit," she said, facing the wall, away from him. "But do it so I don't lose my virginity." Fly feared she might mean in her bum, which he wasn't prepared for. He used his fingers on her, while he stroked himself, trying to figure it out. Then, oh goodness, Suzanna started singing. Humming really, but not like a girl in a porno. Like actual singing. All harmony and lovely. Wow, did he love her. He twisted his fingers in her a little; she raised her voice up an octave. He pushed his fingers in more; she trilled.

"Let me know," he said; "this is my first time too. Let me know, okay?" She didn't answer, but when he slipped it in, not her ass after all, it was so easy, smooth, wet, sticky. He remembered what she'd asked, so he held his pelvis tight and went slow, slow. She sang sweet, so sweetly. He went a little deeper. "No," she said, talk now, no music. He felt her clench tight on him like a fist. He pulled back, slowly, and she released him, but even that was . . . well . . . "Jesus, this is good," he said. Her singing started again. He went in a little, but never all in. He had the idea of what she wanted now. Just a little bit of him, the tip; maybe half of him. No more. Until the too-soon end.

"Was it good?" she asked, facing him now, her arms and legs wrapped around him.

"It was you," Fly said. "It was perfect."

7. *The Ordeal*

Clive leaned into the doorway. Then he righted himself. Fly was
lying alone in his bed, but a little alone time was okay these days
—he was exhausted with classes and church. Clive put one hand
to his chest and the other out like a stop sign. "I'm not saying
you're gay," Clive started inexplicably. "I'm just, man. I just want
you to know that it would be okay if you are. And it would make
sense why you'd want your own room, you know. No temptation
and no weirding anyone out. I get it. It's just. That religious cult
group . . ." Clive's hands were still in the same strange position.
Hand to chest, other hand out—Fly recognized the gesture. It was
like: stop in the name of love, before you break my heart. "But
dude," Clive went on, "they could mess you up, you know. I mean,
as far as I can tell, God loves the queers as much as he loves the,
um, not queers. I just want you to know that that is how I feel."
Clive dropped his hands.

"Thanks," said Fly. Clive nodded and then turned around. He
stood in the doorway for a minute with his back to Fly. Fly was
trying to get some reading done; Suzanna would be over soon.
And sex with her, holding back the way she needed him to, was tir-
ing but thrilling, and afterward he would collapse and sleep like,
well, like a teenager who'd just had sex. But Clive was still standing
in the doorway, and now he turned back around. "Listen. Look."
Clive looked at the chair at Fly's desk longingly, as if he wanted to
sit down. "I didn't make myself clear just now." Fly felt bad for the
guy; he'd made himself clear enough. "It's just . . ." Clive seemed
distraught. "Dude, listen. I've seen this before." He stared at Fly
pointedly until Fly realized he was supposed to ask something.

"Seen what before?"

"This group. This girl. Specifically, this girl."

Fly wanted to sit up, wanted to face Clive, punch Clive's face,
face off in some way. But instead the tension gathered inside Fly's
body. Quietly, it gathered. He felt the sweat trickling down his neck.

"I've seen her with other guys. Other freshmen. Gay guys mostly.
She turns them straight. Or tries to. Or something. Breaks their
hearts. Because a man still has a heart. You know. Straight or . . ."
Clive made his hand wiggle like a fish, "still a man. A human being."

Fly had the question ready for Suzanna: *Do you love me or are you missioning to me for the love of God? Is our sex lovemaking? Or is it conversion therapy? Just because I was lonely doesn't mean I was gay.* And was lonely what gay people were anyway? Fly, again, didn't think he'd ever spoken to a gay guy. Though Fly was pretty sure he'd been lonely his whole life. But then Fly didn't ask Suzanna anything when she came that night. Wanted to. Really did. Couldn't.

8. *Atonement with the Father*

Instead he dropped Sue off at her dorm room. Then he got in his car and drove home. Did it fast, under an hour. It was late, and the house was dark. He went to his bedroom, straight. He quietly opened his childhood closet, which had been his only closet until just a few months ago. He was looking for the porno video he'd had all these years. The one he'd kept and treasured, the one that had taught him what sex could be. He pulled the video out from beneath the magazines of white girls, which were stacked beneath the magazines of black girls. He cracked the video case. Then he carefully cracked the video itself. Unspooled the film. Sliced it to pieces with a knife from his mother's kitchen drawer. Left the house with the slaughtered tape, dumped the scraps of it before he got back to campus. Never even woke his parents.

That was a Friday. The next day his mother called to cry that his father was leaving her. Fly drove home again that Saturday. He went to his father's little office in the house. The older man was crowded in there, and Fly could tell that he'd been sleeping there at least a few days, maybe weeks—hell, maybe since Fly had left for college. Fly scowled silently at his father boxing things up. All the ridiculous goggles and respirator masks. All the rat-repelling handbooks. Fly wanted to curse or punch, but he couldn't tell what was his place. His father spoke up first. "She wasn't with us in the pictures," he said. "She was separate. Alone on the mantel. And that made all the difference." Which Fly didn't understand then, and never fully understood either, though after a few slow seconds he realized the "she" was his dad's ex-girlfriend, the same one from the videotape Fly had dumped the day before.

But the elder man didn't seem to be talking to Fly at all, hadn't looked at him yet. He had a book in his hand and was placing it in a box. Instead he looked at the book. Then he finally looked at Fly. He passed the book to Fly wordlessly—*Invisible Man*, by Ralph Ellison. Fly's first copy. It should have been a *thing*. An occasion, religious-like. But it wasn't.

Fly walked away. Walked down the hallway to his own bedroom. His mother was in the kitchen cooking chicken and rice and a baked ziti and a lasagna and whatever else she could fit onto the stove and into the oven. Fly couldn't face her, was humiliated for her. Was for himself too. Divorce was an embarrassing admission, either of failure or of a deeply consequential mistake. Either way, awful. Fly was trying to be a man about it.

He felt exhausted but went back down the hallway again. His father was taping the boxes now. The tape made a loud screeching noise when pulled across the box, was ripped with a violence at its jagged cutting edge. Fly took a deep breath and started in on his father: "I mean, really. Mom put up with you. Clenching your fists every time you heard the voices. And you doing your stupid Hindu meditation chants, or praying to Allah or worshipping anything that anyone else had ever worshipped. Because you couldn't stand yourself. I mean, for years Mom has put up with you. The least you could do was stay by her." Fly's hands were shaking, his arms were glistening with an anxious sweat.

Fly's father looked up at him. But then Fly had to turn away, head back down the hallway, because his father was crying. And so was Fly.

9. *The Road Back*

Fly headed back down the hallway. He had never seen his father cry before. This was a vexing thing to realize, because Fly had always thought his father was weak, the mental illness and all. But his father, he realized, had never cried in front of him. Was Dad off his pills? Or was he also devastated by his own leaving? Fly was too devastated himself to consider this much, so Fly drove back to campus, his own tears obscuring his vision. He imagined getting pulled over, getting handcuffed unfairly by a police officer; he imagined spitting in the cop's face, getting so brave and angry he could use his own head to smash the cop's head in. But Fly felt tired just thinking about it. The steering wheel was slick, and he realized it was his own hands sweating. He drove so slowly.

The pain clamped onto his chest as soon as he hit the bed. It hurt so badly he was sure he'd fallen on something hard, but only his soft pillow was there beneath him. The pain was on the left side, where his heart was—it was broken, his heart was.

The next day when Suzanna came to walk with him to church he was still in bed, sweating and in agony. Who knew divorce could feel like this? Suzanna held back at the door, looking at him in horror. "Divorce?" she said, snarling like it was contagious.

"My heart is breaking," he said. The fatigue was in Fly's bones, in his skin—his teeth felt tired. He didn't notice the exact moment when Suzanna left. Had she made it to church?

Later Clive leaned into the threshold, but almost fell over. "Oh, shit," he said. When health services came, they came with a stretcher.

"Mono," the nurse practitioner made clear.

"A sexually transmitted disease?" Arthur said when he and Suzie passed by Fly's dorm room that night. Fly was less sweaty now, but still beat.

"Sorry I didn't come earlier," Suzie said. "A girl got saved so I had to stay and pray for her. You don't have a cell phone, so . . ."

"It wasn't my heart," Fly explained, though Suzie's eyes were so big and he was so tired. "It was my spleen. Swollen. But I'll be fine."

But of course he wasn't fine. His mother had to come get him. His teachers had to get a formal letter excusing him from exams. His final grades would be the grades he'd earned so far, which was good, because he'd barely read a thing since he and Suzanna had started having sex. Fly slept until Christmas, it felt like. Didn't feel rested until New Year's. His father came once to visit him.

When the spring semester started, Fly was pretty much better. Suzie came to his dorm room the first day back. She came to tell him before he heard it elsewhere. "I was saving myself for the man God created for me," she said, looking Fly in the face with the authority of a grown woman. Arthur had actually given Suzanna a real engagement ring; it gleamed like a miracle on her finger.

So Fly was alone again. Four classes this semester. Another music, an English, and an algebra for the gen-ed requirement, plus an

African drumming class for his soul. The English teacher was un-inspiring, assigned them stupid stuff, like Harry Potter, which Fly felt was beneath him. For the midterm they had to memorize the various stages of "The Hero's Journey," a form the teacher pro-fessed was the basis for all Great Narratives. This seemed like such a stupid thing to say that Fly lost all respect for the professor im-mediately.

But Fly could memorize a list. Critical thinking was beyond him these days; the mono had addled his brain. Or maybe it was the actual heartbreak this time. But he could do the basics (reproduce the algebraic formulas, plug them in), though he never under-stood the mathematical meaning. What did it matter? Anything that followed a formula was useless anyhow. Still, alone in his room lonely Fly started charting his own life in his notebook—applying the hero's quest to the life he'd lived thus far. But no matter where he started the story he couldn't find his way to a resurrection. So he plugged in his father's life, what he knew of it. There must be a complete narrative in there—his dad had lived long enough. But no, there was no heroic return for Fly's father. There never would be.

Contributors' Notes

Other Distinguished Stories of 2019

American and Canadian Magazines Publishing Short Stories

Contributors' Notes

SELENA ANDERSON'S stories have appeared or are forthcoming in *Oxford American, American Short Fiction, BOMB, Callaloo,* and *Fence.* She is a recipient of the 2019 Rona Jaffe Foundation Writers' Award and has received fellowships from the Kimbilio Center, the MacDowell Colony, and the Bread Loaf Writers' Conference. Anderson is an assistant professor at San José State University and director of the Center for Literary Arts. She is working on a novel.

• When I began "Godmother Tea," I noticed that I kept getting all this furniture. I had my own apartment, which was crappy, but it was mine all month, every month, so I became very focused on filling it up with things. Having furniture meant that you were rooted to a place. Instead of only wanting things, you had things. Most of my furniture was hand-me-downs, something I found in a consignment store and fixed up as best I could. Nothing cost me more than $100. I couldn't afford anything nice. My only show of success was that I could live without roommates.

I was thinking about Joy and the furniture in her apartment, about what it looks like when she's alone. Since objects tend to take on the personality of the person who uses them, I got to know her pretty quickly. I saw her standing in front of this mirror with the gold edge and little gold feet, sizing herself up and practicing her explanations. When you look in a mirror you see yourself, but you also see a mess of other people who came before. Simply by looking, you're reconciling yourself in a long line of these folks. I wanted to play with this idea of being your ancestors' greatest dream—I keep seeing T-shirts that say this. But when you're young and struggling, you're more likely to think they're disappointed. The godmother is an extension of what Joy is both seeing and avoiding. She's basically there to cook amazing meals and give cutting straight talk. The horrible thing isn't so much hearing an important person's worst opinion of you as it is feeling your own body agree with them. Joy is in a spell where moments like this are happening on loop. She eventually gets beyond it, but none of that resolution stuff was up to her either.

Last, I just want to say that I've been reading *Best American Short Stories* since college, and it's an honor to be included.

T. C. BOYLE is the author of twenty-nine books of fiction, including *Outside Looking In* (2019), *The Relive Box and Other Stories* (2017), and *The Tortilla Curtain* (1995), which will be repackaged this fall in a new twenty-fifth anniversary edition. He published his collected stories in two volumes, *T. C. Boyle Stories* (1998) and *T. C. Boyle Stories II* (2013), and has been the recipient of a number of awards, both in the short story, including the Rea Award and the PEN/Malamud Prize, and the novel, including most recently the Jonathan Swift Creative Writing Award, the Mark Twain Voice in American Literature Award, and the Henry David Thoreau Award. He is a member of the American Academy of Arts and Letters.

• As I creep through Shakespeare's seven stages of life (I'm now knocking on the door to the final one, "second childishness and mere oblivion,/ Sans teeth, sans eyes, sans taste, sans everything"), I've necessarily become more attuned to the vicissitudes of old age, and notions, however transparent, of eternity. This is where Jeanne Calment (1875–1997) comes into the picture. Madame Calment was the longest-lived human being in recorded history, having continued to live, breathe, and pump blood into her one hundred and twenty-third year. What would it be like, I wondered, to live that long? Would it be a burden or a daily revivifying challenge to beat the odds, especially as one competitor or another shuffled off the mortal coil? The historical figure of Jeanne Calment, by virtue of her astonishing longevity, has already morphed into the mythological, and it was that mythological status I wanted to explore.

Happily, my entry point into the story was provided by the figure I call Monsieur R., who took a gamble any oddsmaker would have applauded when he contracted to buy Madame Calment's apartment *en viager*—that is, allowing her to live there and collect a stipend until such time as she should die and he could take possession. But here's the rub—as with any bet, there's no such thing as a sure thing.

JASON BROWN's linked collection of short stories, *A Faithful but Melancholy Account of Several Barbarities Lately Committed,* was published in 2019. He has two other books of short stories, *Driving the Heart* and *Why the Devil Chose*

New England for His Work. He is an associate professor of creative writing in the MFA program at the University of Oregon.

· "A Faithful but Melancholy Account of Several Barbarities Lately Committed," the title story for my new collection, is loosely based on my family, who have lived in Maine and northern New England since my first ancestor arrived in Maine in 1607 as part of the failed Popham Colony. I always start stories with situation and character, in this case a fake wedding at an old family homestead on an island off the coast of Maine and an old patriarch obsessed with what will happen to the homestead after he is gone. Once I dove into the familiar surroundings and once the characters began to stand up and speak for themselves, I started to think about the larger context of the story—the history. Questions of history are in the background of the story, as they should be, but the past is always with us, whether we recognize it or not. The story's title is from a Cotton Mather pamphlet on atrocities committed against the English settlers "by the said French and Indians." My use of the title is ironic, of course. The numerous wars over the coast of Maine between, on the one side, the English and Scottish settlers and, on the other side, the French and Native inhabitants resulted in a genocide that all but completely wiped out the Native population of northern New England. The death of Cotton Mather, the great narrator of Puritan paranoia and exceptionalism, signaled the end of an Anglo-Puritan theocracy in America, but much of the underlying psychology of the early New England Puritans—particularly their sense of themselves as a chosen people—has survived in their distant, modern-day progeny. I have tried to capture a family living in the ruins of the "city upon a hill."

MICHAEL BYERS has taught creative writing at the MFA program of the University of Michigan since 2006. He is the author of *The Coast of Good Intentions* (stories) and two novels, *Long for This World* and *Percival's Planet.* His stories have been anthologized several times in *The Best American Short Stories* and *The O. Henry Prize Stories,* and his work has received recognition from the Henfield Foundation, the American Academy of Arts and Letters, and the Whiting Foundation. His novella *The Broken Man* was a finalist for the World Fantasy Award.

· My first love as a reader and writer was science fiction, and I'm so thrilled to see this story find a wider audience. I suppose this story came about from sitting with friends on that porch (the porch in the story is our porch in Michigan), all of us watching our children get older in that unreal, jerky, all-too-sudden way they do, and recognizing that their lives, and their own children's lives, would differ from ours in ways that we wouldn't be able to really get our heads around. And I wanted to get my head around it. Given current circumstances, the world this story depicts looks like a pretty benign one, all things considered, a world in which people still sit on porches and have friends and find moments in which to consider who and why they are. I hope it's accurate in that way, at least.

Also, this story took six years to get published! It got rejected so many times! Once on the very day I submitted it! So, you know, take heart, friends. Don't lose hope. Keep at it. If you love a story, as I happen to (I'll confess) love this one—well, keep plugging until it finds a home. "Sibling Rivalry" exists in print thanks to the fierce and lovely people at the estimable *Lady Churchill's Rosebud Wristlet,* to whom I am happily indebted, as I am to Curtis Sittenfeld, for finding a spot in her heart for it in this year's anthology.

And of course we all owe a debt of gratitude to the brilliant and tireless Heidi Pitlor, who labors all year in the service of this funny art we're all devoted to. Thank you, Heidi. You deserve a statue!

EMMA CLINE is the author of the novel *The Girls* and the forthcoming story collection *Daddy.* Her stories have appeared in *The New Yorker, The Paris Review, Granta,* and the *New York Times,* and she is a winner of the Plimpton Prize. In 2017 she was named one of *Granta*'s Best Young American Novelists.

 • A few years ago there was a stretch of tabloid stories about celebrity affairs, often involving nannies. I was struck by a paparazzi photo of one of the young women; she looked so confident, almost smirking, but then seemed, at the same time, obviously afraid, obviously in over her head. I wanted to explore that mindset—the bravado of youth covering up terror, the desire to try to take ownership of bad things as a way to make them less painful. Kayla is desperate to avoid being seen as a victim, to forestall pity or self-reflection by any means necessary, even if that means rebuffing actual kindness and connection. Tabloid dramas often have a built-in moral code, like modern-day fairy tales: the nanny as the evil interloper, the wife as the wronged queen, the husband as a hapless and pitiable oaf. They act, in their weird way, as parables, tales of how we think life should go and what should happen to people who deviate. I wanted Kayla's character to resist being taught a lesson, resist the collective moral read of the situation—she might feel differently later on, but for now Kayla is trying hard to leach this experience of meaning, even as it radically reshapes her life.

MARIAN CROTTY is the author of the short story collection *What Counts as Love,* which was published through the University of Iowa Short Fiction Awards (John Simmons Award). The collection was longlisted for the PEN/Robert W. Bingham Prize for Debut Fiction and won the Janet Heidinger Kafka Prize. Her short stories have appeared in such journals as the *Alaska Quarterly Review,* the *Southern Review,* and the *Kenyon Review.* She is an assistant editor at *The Common* and teaches at Loyola University Maryland. She lives in Baltimore and is currently working on a novel.

• I began this story in response to a discussion I had with my first-year writing students about subjects for short memoirs that tend to rely on clichés. Essays about the death of a grandparent were at the top of the list. They were often boring, almost always sentimental, and one grandma or grandpa usually felt indistinguishable from the next. And yet, because I was convinced that a story about the death of a grandparent could be compelling, I challenged myself to write one. My initial plan was to write the story in the form of a long social media memorial, and although I couldn't make this approach work, it gave life to Jan, Jules, and a story that departed from the initial prompt I'd given myself. Jen Logan Meyer provided many helpful notes on the first draft, including the suggestion to name the frozen yogurt shop Yotopia!

CAROLYN FERRELL is the author of the story collection *Don't Erase Me,* awarded the Art Seidenbaum Award of the *Los Angeles Times,* the John C. Zacharis Award given by *Ploughshares,* and the Quality Paperback Book Prize for First Fiction. Her stories and essays have appeared in the *New York Times, Ploughshares, Story, Scoundrel Time, Electric Literature,* and other places; her story "Proper Library" was included in *The Best American Short Stories of the Century,* edited by John Updike. Ferrell has been a recipient of grants from the German Academic Exchange (DAAD) and the National Endowment for the Arts. She teaches at Sarah Lawrence College and lives in New York with her family. Her debut novel, *Dear Miss Metropolitan,* is forthcoming.

• Many thanks to Michael Nye for choosing "Something Street" for publication in *Story* magazine. "Something Street" was inspired by news events and by my own loyalty to characters who are eternal underdogs. I'd wanted to use the various settings of Parthenia and Craw Daddy as organizing tools for this piece but came to the realization—with the help of my great reading angel, Martha Upton—that plot was missing in that approach. I wanted to make the fragments of Parthenia's life cohere, illustrate her transformation. I also thought about challenging the notion of the good old days—which we hear about from those allegedly wanting to make America great again. Latin lessons notwithstanding, the good old days are forever in the making. They are actually here, as reality and dream. And isn't it already a given that fiction is what makes the world great in the first place?

MARY GAITSKILL was born in Lexington, Kentucky, and grew up in the Detroit area of Michigan. She left home at the age of sixteen when she went to live in Canada; at nineteen she decided she wanted to become a writer and returned to America to attend community college. From there she went to the University of Michigan, where she took a BA, and then moved to New York City in 1981. She published her first book, a story collection titled *Bad Behavior*, in 1988; she has since published two more collections of stories (*Because They Wanted To* and *Don't Cry*) and three novels (*Two Girls, Fat and Thin; Veronica;* and *The Mare*) as well as a collection of essays titled *Somebody with a Little Hammer.* She has taught writing at the graduate and undergraduate levels since 1993, most recently at Claremont McKenna College.

• I wrote "This Is Pleasure" from a place of confusion and, as one of the characters says, "heart pain." Pain really for everyone involved. Much of what happens in the story is flippant and ridiculous—some of it is sublimated cruelty, both on the part of Quin and some of his accusers. But underneath that the story is so mixed and unclear, with real tenderness and wish for connection shining or at least trying to shine through the murk. I wanted to write from this place of uncertainty because it seemed necessary in a climate of total certainty from all sides. I am not in any way against moral certainty; that too is necessary. But fiction for me exists at least in part to describe the moment when you are not certain, you are just feeling all kinds of contradictory things, and reality is clear but prismatic: several things at once. In this case, the moment before the hammer falls.

MENG JIN was born in Shanghai and now lives in San Francisco. Her first novel, *Little Gods,* was published in January 2020.

• In late summer of 2017, I moved to California after a year spent writing abroad. For much of my life I had willfully disregarded the concept of place, but something had shifted inside me and suddenly it was all I could see: how my body responded to and situated within a new climate, a new architecture, a new demography and geography. I'd mailed in my absentee ballot for the 2016 election from England; afterward I'd sunk into a lonely despair. It was supposed to be a time of joyful creation, but I felt totally alienated from my work, and spent most of my days, like many, reading the news and crying. Now I was back in America. I was aware I had entered a new disasterscape. Writing "In the Event" was one attempt at navigating this disasterscape and of trying to find inside it a place of meaning and art.

ANDREA LEE is the author of numerous books, including *Russian Journal, Sarah Phillips, Interesting Women,* and *Lost Hearts in Italy.* Her work has frequently appeared in *The New Yorker* and other publications, and her new book, *Red Island House,* a novel set in Madagascar, will be published in early 2021. She lives in Turin, Italy.

• For me, the subject matter of "The Children" is a perennial one. I'm obsessed by the concept of exoticism, foreignness, and by the theme of encounters between strangers. Whether I'm writing about being an American in Soviet Russia or recording the different social and racial dimensions of a middle-class African American childhood or chronicling the life of an expatriate in Italy, I've always explored the confrontation of different worlds. Some years ago I heard a fragmentary story about an exiled French aristocrat, who, centuries ago, fathered numerous children with tribal women all around the Indian Ocean, and I was immediately captivated. The tale had everything that fascinates me: class, race, injustice, desert-island fantasy. My first feeling was that it resembled a myth, or an Elizabethan comedy. Soon I began to play with the idea of bringing that narrative into contemporary reality, and then the story started to write itself.

The story also gave me the opportunity to shine a light on one of my own favorite pieces of writing on exoticism: Victor Segalen's eccentric *Essay on Exoticism,* over which the two major characters bond. That strange little work records the author's attempt to keep foreign peoples and places mysterious and glamorous by fitting them into an artistic form—exoticizing them, in effect. Art can strike at the heart, making the ordinary events of life deeply comprehensible, but, conversely, it can also create emotional distance from reality. Absorbed in their rarefied intellectual world, Shay and Giustinia meddle in real affairs with callousness and end by causing pain.

I bookended the story with reports of serial killings I heard about in Madagascar. The serial killer's crimes are intended as a misguided form of revenge on the foreigners who have taken advantage of the country, and they parallel the tale of the absent Western father, who took casual advantage of young Malagasy women. In the end it seems that it's the innocent and powerless people who suffer.

SARAH THANKAM MATHEWS grew up in India and Oman, immigrating to the United States at seventeen. She was recently a Rona Jaffe Fellow at the Iowa Writers' Workshop and is currently a Margins Fellow at the Asian American Writers' Workshop. She has been published by the *Kenyon Review, BuzzFeed Reader, AGNI,* and *Platypus Press.* A novel is at work on her.

• The seed of what became "Rubberdust" was a lie I told for no reason. I was in a new town, meeting new people. A solar eclipse was happening, and people were passing around those paper glasses. With no motive in mind, I impulsively told the man I was taking a walk with that I feared looking directly at the sun because I had a friend in the second grade who did this every day and lost his sight. Wow, he said. I know, I said, vaguely appalled and amused at myself. I was nervous and wanted to be thought interesting by the new people around me. My lizard brain had complied with a story.

But why that story, and why had it materialized so easily? I cast around in my memory and realized that I had made a friend in second grade, this charming little boy, and our friendship had been based primarily on the joint production of eraser shavings, which we stored in our wooden desks. I could not remember why we did this. I thought back to my schooldays in Oman and felt a sharp ache. It was the twinge of memories in a setting so far removed from the reality of the people all around you that you fear they are unintelligible to anyone but you. This is the immigrant's pain, I thought, aside from bureaucracy, privation, uncertainty, and missing people from the old life; you also have to translate your past, or decide to not even try.

I wrote in a notebook gifted to me by my friend Praveen what I thought would be a first line: "Please listen. I grew up in a place that I cannot return to." It was wrong somehow. All of a sudden I knew better what I wanted to tell, and it was not a lament. I wanted to write a story of the secret lives, peculiar logic, and intense emotion of children. Of the fear that you are not at your deepest level a Good Person. Of what it is to have to translate for an audience your (foreign) past, which is to say, your (foreign) self. Some room was flung open in my brain; I began writing, the story poured out of me.

ELIZABETH McCRACKEN is the author of six books of fiction; her seventh, a short story collection called *The Souvenir Museum,* will be published in 2021.

• When I was a young writer trying to come up with ideas for short stories, I felt, always, desperate. Lonely, even, not for characters but for ideas. I sat in my apartment and waited for ideas to find me; I read other, better writers and wondered if I could plagiarize them; I skimmed the newspaper and thought I might write a short story about the day's *Peanuts.* I took a walk and a bread truck drove past: was there a short story in that? Nothing could happen without an idea, I thought then, even though in those days that wasn't how I wrote. My actual stories—the ones that panned out—arrived in my head as a single sentence in a stranger's voice.

Now that I'm middle-aged, I think ideas are essential for novels but in some ways beside the point in short stories. *My* short stories, I mean. My short stories now generally begin with some scraps of material I have scavenged from my life. Nothing essential or personal, just locations and events, often picked up when I'm traveling between university semesters. (I write this as the world is sheltering in place and it occurs to me: Can I come up with short stories if I stay at home? I'm honestly not sure.) These stories, I insist, aren't autobiographical. Sure, the characters go where I go, but they're not me, not anyone I'm related to.

In the case of "It's Not You," I'd traveled with my husband, Edward Carey, and our kids to Galveston. (I'd already written a story that took place in Galveston, based on another trip.) On our way home to Austin we stopped at a hotel in Houston that upgraded us to a suite: two rooms, two bathrooms, a dining room table with room for eight, a couple of chandeliers. The hotel wasn't deluxe, just entertainingly garish. The next morning a lovely man with a Cesar Romero mustache and braces brought me breakfast. On that little trellis of reality I decided to train a story about youth. When I was young, I occasionally checked into hotels in order to be alone away from the shadow of myself and my own furniture. Also when I was young I listened to a lot of call-in radio shows in the early hours of the morning, which is when I wrote. As I started the story I thought about things I'd felt passionately about in my twenties, things I'd never written about and couldn't, with any clarity or purpose, write about now. All those experiences feel like foreign coins: undeniably worth something, but how do I spend them? These days different things make me furious or sorrowful, different things are dear to me. I'm not *better* now than I was then, I want to make clear, not as a writer or a person: only different. Anyhow, I wrote much of what I thought of as "the hotel story" but couldn't get it right and put it aside, and then in September 2019 my friend Michael Ray at *Zoetrope* asked me if I had a spare something for the magazine. It was my birthday. I'd had some champagne for breakfast, which seemed right for this story, and I finished it in a few hours. Pulled it together, I guess I mean: the pieces were there but out of order and confused, or maybe in order and not confused enough. It's an addlepated story; I needed to be addlepated to finish it.

SCOTT NADELSON is the author of a novel, *Between You and Me;* a memoir, *The Next Scott Nadelson: A Life in Progress;* and five story collections, most recently *The Fourth Corner of the World,* named a Jewish Fiction Award Honor

Book by the Association of Jewish Libraries, and *One of Us,* winner of the G. S. Sharat Chandra Prize for Short Fiction. A recipient of the Reform Judaism Fiction Prize, the Great Lakes Colleges Association New Writers Award, and an Oregon Book Award, he teaches at Willamette University and in the Rainier Writing Workshop MFA Program at Pacific Lutheran University.

• This story started with procrastination. For several years I'd been working on a series of essays on writing craft, and in particular what writers can learn from visual artists. I had a vague idea for a piece about form and tension in the work of Louise Nevelson, thinking her blend of abstraction and intense sensory experience might challenge my usual instinct to avoid abstraction in narrative. Mostly, though, I just wanted to write about Nevelson, who has been one of my favorite artists for a long time. Whenever I find myself in front of one of her sculptures or assemblages, I lose interest in just about all the surrounding work in the museum or gallery. Her black boxes stuffed with painted wooden spools and disks and cones get under my skin in a way almost nothing else can. What little I knew of her biography also appealed to me: a Russian Jew who emigrated around the same time as my grandfather, a sexually liberated woman forging an independent path in a repressive culture, an obsessive and driven creator who learned to trust her instincts despite many years of struggle and neglect by the male-dominated art world.

As often happens when I set myself a specific task, I immediately invented excuses to delay. I decided that before I could write the essay I had to read everything Nevelson had said about her work. I spent the next few weeks delving into interviews, a pair of biographies, and her oral history, *Dawns + Dusks,* which her assistant recorded and transcribed in the mid-1970s. In the last were a couple of the most intriguing and baffling paragraphs I've ever encountered. Nevelson describes, very briefly, and with hardly any specifics, her encounter with the French writer Louis-Ferdinand Céline on a ship to Paris in 1933 and their subsequent correspondence and near-affair. When they met, Céline had just published *Journey to the End of the Night* and was already a literary sensation. Despite his blatant anti-Semitism, he clearly fascinated Nevelson, who was an unknown then, recently divorced and trying to discover her voice and her medium.

But even decades later, after learning the full scope of his fascist sympathies and collaboration—he wrote propaganda pamphlets and articles calling for the expulsion of all French Jews at the same time he was sending Nevelson flirtatious letters and suggesting they marry—she spoke of him with as much yearning as disdain. There was such conflicted emotion in her words and yet so little detail of her actual interaction with this figure who both repelled and attracted her that even before realizing I'd abandoned the essay, I found myself trying to imagine these moments and contemplate her competing desires. By then I was hooked and spent the next few months writing "Liberté."

LEIGH NEWMAN's memoir about growing up in Alaska, *Still Points North*, was a finalist for the National Book Critics Circle's John Leonard Prize. Her short stories have appeared in *The Paris Review, One Story, Tin House, Electric Literature,* and *McSweeney's,* among other magazines. She is the recipient of the 2020 Terry Southern Prize for "humor, wit, and sprezzatura," and she is the cofounder of Black Balloon/Catapult Publishing, where she now serves as an editor for Catapult.

· "Howl Palace" began with a real dog. After I had gone to college my dad picked up a black Lab with champion papers named Chelsea. He had gotten her for free from the *PennySaver.* Soon we all found out why. Chelsea weighed in at about one hundred pounds and did not give a crap if you pet her, fed her, loved her, screamed at her, ignored her, or chucked a sponge at her. Whatever you offered, whatever you ordered, her response was the same cold, brown, unblinking stare. After which she went on charging into table legs and walls, flattening my brothers into weepy human pancakes, head-butting the sliding glass doors in effort to attack the ducks outside on the lake. It was a little horrifying inside the house, especially at dinnertime. I can only imagine the duck-hunting fiascos. I tried to write about her for years, with little success, but I kept putting her into the wrong situations. Only when I started thinking about the women in Alaska I knew who had married and divorced multiple times (not an uncommon situation, considering the skewed ratio of males to females in Alaska), women I cared about and loved, did I find a way to talk about her. Initially I had put her in the center of the now-defunct stories. As the prime mover. But once she was off to the side, raising havoc—and renamed Pinkie—I could explore the characters I was most interested in getting to know.

JANE PEK was born and grew up in Singapore and now lives in New York. Her stories have appeared in *Brooklyn Review* and *Witness.* She received a BA in history from Yale University, a JD from New York University School of Law, and an MFA from Brooklyn College. She works as a mergers and acquisitions attorney and enjoys cycling around the city in search of superlative almond croissants.

· When I first started writing this story, in response to a piece of surprising real-life news, it was about a group of close friends who are flummoxed when one of their number gets married to a woman he has apparently just met and breaks the news on Facebook. I knew from the start that the wife would be a fox spirit, and specifically the nine-tailed fox spirit who is blamed in Chinese mythology for the downfall of the Shang Dynasty (rather unfairly, I always thought), but for a long time the story wasn't about her. I wrote a few iterations and then set it aside. A while later I revisited the story as part of a larger project to rewrite various Chinese myths about women—in those women's voices, and on their terms, combining the magical world that they inhabited with the historical world that we do—and that is what became "The Nine-Tailed Fox Explains."

ALEJANDRO PUYANA is a Venezuelan writer living in Austin. His work has appeared in *American Short Fiction, Tin House, The Idaho Review, Huizache, Pigeon Pages,* and others. His short story "The Hands of Dirty Children" was awarded the Halifax Ranch Prize by *American Short Fiction* and ZZ Packer. He's currently working on a novel set in Venezuela. Alejandro is a fellow at the Michener Center for Writers.

• I'm writing these words as we all deal with the COVID-19 pandemic, which makes me think about my own relationship with words and isolation. I moved to Austin from Venezuela in 2006; I was not a writer then, had just received a degree in sociology. I deeply wanted to do something creative, fueled by my love of books, comics, movies, and fantasy. Those pursuits seemed frivolous, especially when I turned my gaze to what was happening in Venezuela: polarization, totalitarianism, fear-mongering, social upheaval. I got obsessed with reading Venezuelan news; every morning meant looking for connection to what I left through newspapers, broadcasts, email chains. How many people marched? What did Chavez say now? Who got robbed last night? Then my brother got kidnapped for the second time.

I wrote about it, mostly as an outlet for the anger and the frustration of the event itself, but I didn't expect to bridge the gap between Austin and Caracas in the way it did, to bring me closer—to my family, to my country, to my understanding of what it meant to be lonely. From then on writing began as a way to deal with my isolation from the country I loved and my family, who still lived the Venezuelan crisis in the flesh.

I would go to Caracas to visit every year. Every time I went, something had changed—not only politically, which I was accustomed to, but physically. On one occasion the country was dealing with a trash crisis. Some public parks, which I remembered as manicured, bursting with tropical flowers, palm trees and mango trees, were now makeshift landfills. On its own that struck me, but what was shocking was the buzzing of activity they generated. Animals and people, mostly groups of children and the elderly, walked through the trash and rummaged through it in search of food. That image stayed with me for at least a year. I couldn't shake it.

This story came from those things I couldn't get out of my head and I couldn't understand. I wrote the first draft in a couple of sittings, which is extremely fast for me. The voice came first, never changed or faltered, and then I just followed it. It took me to two places that I loved as a kid: the Children's Museum and Plaza los Museos—but from a perspective I had never had. For me those are places of happiness; for the kids in the story those are places of longing. They are excluded from the joy other children take for granted (and that I took for granted). But what surprised me most about the story was that joy could still be found for them, that there were still moments of tenderness and loyalty and levity. If a child is still a child, even in the midst of despair and injustice, maybe my country can still be the country I love, even when it's broken. I'm still trying to figure out if that's the case.

ANNA REESER'S short fiction is published in *The Masters Review Volume VII, Fourteen Hills, The Nervous Breakdown,* and elsewhere. Her artwork has been featured on the cover of *CutBank* and in other journals. Originally from Ojai, California, she now lives in Eugene, Oregon, where she is at work on a collection of short stories and a novel.

· When I wrote "Octopus VII," I was interested in artists moving from an academic world into an economic world, balancing creative practices with jobs and relationships. I was curious about the mix of feelings that can arise when an artist's vocation begins to replace his art practice, and the moment when he experiences creative block in his original medium.

The giant metal octopus grew out of this idea—an unwieldy reminder of past potential that feels difficult to match. As a sculpture, it felt endearing and bizarre. Why an octopus? It seemed like a piece that looked physically impressive but that the artist hadn't fully rationalized conceptually. In imagining who might make that sculpture, Tyler's voice emerged.

WILLIAM PEI SHIH is the son of immigrants from Hong Kong and Taiwan. His stories have appeared in *Virginia Quarterly Review, McSweeney's,* the *Des Moines Register, Reed, Carve, The Masters Review, Hyphen, The Asian American Literary Review,* and elsewhere. He is a graduate of the Iowa Writers' Workshop. He currently lives in New York City. More information can be found at williampeishih.com.

· For me, one of the emotional engines that came about as I was writing this story is the idea of goodness—the human endeavor of choosing not only between good and evil, but the everyday and less-acknowledged choices between two disparate goods, and how choosing one good over another is often done, whether inadvertently or not, at a disservice and even the annihilation of the other. In the end I wondered at what point such choices enter the territories of wrongdoing.

I was also thinking about all the many kinds of unrequited love and lonelinesses, and how an essential part of being human is that longing to connect meaningfully in some way with someone else—to relate—and how oftentimes people might need a little more time to explain themselves. I was thinking about how commonalities seem to help. Likenesses and likemindedness also do much of that necessary work. Phenotype is another factor that comes into play. At the same time, shared experiences assume and imagine perhaps too much. Falsifications take hold; pluralities become grossly ignored. In short, one runs the risk of giving people who are seemingly like oneself too much of the benefit of the doubt. And then there is always the expanding and accelerating universe of the unknown, which one might confuse with disappointment. Despite the fact that we are always more than the stories we tell ourselves and the stories we tell each other, so much of what's unrequited and unreciprocated gets wasted away into the undiscovered and the could-have-been. I suppose with this story I wanted to highlight the powers of inclusion and diversity and openness, and the dangers of what might manifest otherwise in closures—that there is so much more to life than simply coexistence.

My gratitude to Heidi Pitlor and Curtis Sittenfeld. I would also like to thank my brilliant and wonderful editor at *Virginia Quarterly Review,* Allison Wright. And Ethan Canin, who saw the story's potential, and whose workshop at Iowa was where it first saw the light of day.

KEVIN WILSON is the author of two story collections and three novels, most recently *Nothing to See Here.* His stories have appeared in *Ploughshares, A Public Space, The Southern Review,* and elsewhere. He lives in Sewanee, Tennessee, and teaches at the University of the South.

• One year in high school there was this boy. And he wore Cannibal Corpse T-shirts. And one of my friends and I were in an art class with him. And he poked us with X-Acto knives and burned us with glue guns while we made a Parthenon out of cardboard. He'd hit me. And he said pretty bad things to us. I never once tried to protect myself or tell anyone or ask for help or stand up to him. It didn't even really occur to me, even though I was fifteen years old. I think that my complete passivity was repulsive to him, to the point that I angered him, my existence. Now, I don't even think that boy would remember me. And I don't think he'd consider anything he did to even be bad.

But the ending of the fictional story is not my story, thank God, so there's this point where Jamie, who is me, becomes not me. He becomes what I guess he always was, just a character. And I have a family and my life is good. But I don't think Jamie's life is good. I wanted to steer him toward a different life, but I guess I failed. And I feel those echoes, where our stories separate. It's a strange sensation.

TIPHANIE YANIQUE is the author of the poetry collection *Wife,* which won the 2016 Bocas Prize in Caribbean poetry and the United Kingdom's 2016 Forward/Felix Dennis Prize for Best First Collection. Tiphanie is also the author of the novel *Land of Love and Drowning,* which won the 2014 Flaherty-Dunnan First Novel Prize from the Center for Fiction, the Phillis Wheatley Award for Pan-African Literature, and the American Academy of Arts and Letters Rosenthal Family Foundation Award and was listed by NPR as one of the Best Books of 2014. *Land of Love and Drowning* was also a finalist for the Orion Book Award in environmental literature and the Hurston/Wright Legacy Award. She is the author of a collection of stories, *How to Escape from a Leper Colony,* which won her a listing as one of the National Book Foundation's 5 Under 35. Her writing has won the Bocas Prize for Caribbean Fiction, the thirteenth annual *Boston Review* short story contest, a Rona Jaffe Foundation Writers Award, a Pushcart Prize, a Fulbright scholarship, and an Academy of American Poets Prize. She has been listed by the *Boston Globe* as one of the sixteen cultural figures to watch out for, and her writing has been published in the *New York Times, Best African American Fiction,* the *Wall Street Journal, American Short Fiction,* and other places. Tiphanie is from the Virgin Islands and is an associate professor at Emory University.

 • Fly is one of the main characters of a novel in stories/linked story collection that I have been revising for about nine years. I tend to write multiple projects at once, so nine years isn't that long for my process — but it is, well, a long time. During that time Fly was a saint, then an awful piece of shit. "The Special World," in particular, came out of me needing to find his more complex humanity. In "The Special World" we find him as a young adult. It does seem to me that this is when men are made to believe that vulnerability either has its merits or is bullshit. If they can't handle these almost adult vulnerabilities with bravery, then out goes vulnerability. Before this story's end, Fly loved his religious faith, his family, a girl, his solitude, his own body. But then all these loves get tampered with.

The collection that this story is a part of is, as a whole, an exercise in fiction forms. I took a class once in fiction forms in college, and it was pretty bad. Though I did learn about the nature of racism and sexism in classroom power dynamics, I didn't learn a thing about form in fiction. I've always felt that was something lacking in my education as a prose writer. So in this collection I wanted to teach myself something about form — about what form can do for a story, how it can make something possible and something else impossible. Another way to say this is that I wanted to think about form in the way I had been taught to think about form as a poet. As a writer from a colonialized place, I was also weary of form as yet another way to impose colonial ideals of beauty on the colonized, but I did love me a sestina. So I knew that preexisting forms had their value. The most ubiquitous fiction form is probably the Hero's Journey, first made famous by Joseph Campbell. Interestingly, Campbell always claimed that this form was not a colonizing one because it already existed in most cultures. He was just giving it a name and articulating the detailed parts of the form. So I decided to see what the form made possible for a story, and what it could do for me as a writer . . . and maybe what it might articulate for me as a reader and thinker, and even as an agent myself in the world.

Other Distinguished Stories of 2019

American and Canadian Magazines Publishing Short Stories

African American Review
Agni
Alaska Quarterly Review
American Short Fiction
Another Chicago Magazine
The Antioch Review
The Arkansas International
Ascent
The Atlantic
The Bare Life Review
Black Warrior Review
BOMB
Booth
Boulevard
The Briar Cliff Review
Callaloo
Carve
Catamaran
Cherry Tree
Chicago Quarterly Review
The Cincinnati Review
Colorado Review
Conjunctions
Copper Nickel
Crazyhorse
Denver Quarterly
Ecotone

Epiphany
Event
Fairy Tale Review
Fantasy and Science Fiction
Fiction
The Fiddlehead
Foglifter
Fourteen Hills
F®iction (Friction)
The Georgia Review
The Gettysburg Review
Glimmer Train
Guernica
Granta
Grist
Harper's Magazine
Harpur Palate
Harvard Review
The Hopkins Review
The Hudson Review
Image
Indiana Review
Into the Void
The Iowa Review
Iron Horse
Jabberwock Review
Joyland

Kenyon Review
Lady Churchill's Rosebud
   Wristlet
Lake Effect
Lalitamba
The Literary Review
Manoa
McSweeney's
Meridian
Michigan Quarterly Review
Missouri Review
Montana Quarterly
Nelle
New England Review
New Letters
The New Yorker
Ninth Letter
Noon
The Normal School
North American Review
North Dakota Quarterly
Notre Dame Review
One Story
Orca
Orion
Oxford American
The Paris Review
Passages North
Pembroke Magazine
Playboy
Ploughshares
Potomac Review

Prairie Schooner
Pulp Literature
Raritan
Room
Ruminate
Salamander
Salmagundi
The Sewanee Review
The Southampton Review
Southern Humanities Review
Southern Indiana Review
The Southern Review
Story
Subtropics
The Sun
Tahoma Literary Review
Third Coast
Thoughtprints
The Threepenny Review
Tin House
Trajectory
Virginia Quarterly Review
Washington Square Review
West Branch
Western Humanities Review
Wildness
Willow Springs
Witness
X-R-A-Y
Yellow Medicine Review
Zoetrope: All-Story
ZYZZYVA

THE BEST AMERICAN SERIES®

FIRST, BEST, AND BEST-SELLING

The Best American Essays

The Best American Food Writing

The Best American Mystery Stories

The Best American Science and Nature Writing

The Best American Science Fiction and Fantasy

The Best American Short Stories

The Best American Sports Writing

The Best American Travel Writing

Available in print and e-book wherever books are sold.

Visit our website: hmhbooks.com/series/best-american